Sacrilege

ALSO BY S. J. PARRIS

Heresy
Prophecy

Sacrilege

{ A Thriller }

S. J. Parris

DOUBLEDAY

New York   London   Toronto   Sydney   Auckland

Copyright © 2012 by Stephanie Merritt

All rights reserved. Published in the United States by Doubleday,
a division of Random House, Inc., New York.

www.doubleday.com

DOUBLEDAY and the portrayal of an anchor with a dolphin are
registered trademarks of Random House, Inc.

Book design by Maria Carella
Jacket design by Patti Ratchford
Jacket illustration © Steve Vidler/SuperStock

Library of Congress Cataloging-in-Publication Data
Parris, S. J., 1974–
Sacrilege : a novel / S. J. Parris— 1st ed.
p. cm.
1. Bruno, Giordano, 1548–1600—Fiction.
2. Christian heretics—Fiction.
3. Philosophers—Fiction.
4. London (England)—History—16th century—Fiction.
5. Canterbury (England)—History—16th century—Fiction.
I. Title.
PR6113.E77S23 2011
823'.92—dc23   2011047763

ISBN 978-0-385-53547-2

MANUFACTURED IN THE UNITED STATES OF AMERICA

1   3   5   7   9   10   8   6   4   2

First Edition

Sacrilege

Chapter 1

I knew that I was being followed long before I saw or heard my pursuer. I felt it by some instinct that by now had been sharpened by experience; a shifting of the air, a presence whose movements invisibly shadowed my own. Someone was watching me and had been for several days: from the mouths of alleyways, from behind pillars or walls, amid the crowds of people, carts, and animals that thronged the narrow streets of London or out among the river traffic. At times I even sensed eyes on me in the privacy of my room at Salisbury Court, though that was surely impossible and could only have been the tricks of imagination.

It was the twenty-third day of July 1584, and I was hurrying to deliver my new book to my printer before he left London for the rest of the summer. A merchant ship from Portugal had recently docked at Tilbury, at the mouth of the River Thames. Plague was raging in Lisbon and the crew had been forcibly quarantined; despite these measures, rumours that the infection had begun to claim English victims were spreading through the city quicker than the disease itself ever could. Outbreaks of plague were common enough during London summers, I had been told, and any Londoner with the means to move to healthier air was packing as fast as they could. At the French embassy, where I lived as the ambassador's houseguest, whispers of the black plague had sent the household into such a frenzy of imagined symptoms that the ambassador had dispatched his private secretary to enquire about country houses in the neighbourhood of the Palace of Nonsuch, Queen Elizabeth of England's summer residence.

Fear of the plague had only added to tensions at the embassy in the past few days. Our peace had been shattered the previous week by the arrival of the news from the Netherlands that William the Silent, Prince of Orange, had been assassinated, shot in the chest on the staircase of his own house in Delft by a man he knew and trusted. I imagined that in all the embassies of the Catholic and Protestant powers throughout the greatest cities of Europe, men and women would be standing much as we did when the messenger arrived, speechless in the face of an act whose repercussions would shake the world as we knew it. The shock and fear occasioned by the deed were still palpable in the streets of London; not that the English people gave two figs for William himself, but it was well known that the Catholic King Philip II of Spain had offered a reward of twenty-five thousand crowns for his murder. And if one Protestant ruler could be knocked down as easily as a skittle, there was no doubt that Queen Elizabeth of England would be next on Philip's list. The sense of foreboding was all the greater at Salisbury Court because William's assassin had been a Frenchman.

John Charlewood, my printer, had his lodgings at the Half-Eagle and Key in the street known as Barbican, just to the north of the city wall. He also had a press nearby at the Charterhouse, the old Carthusian monastery which had been converted into a grand private residence, but I refused to visit his business premises; the Charterhouse was now owned by Thomas Howard, half brother to the young Earl of Arundel. I had made enemies of the Howards—the most powerful Catholic family among the English nobility—the previous autumn and preferred to avoid the possibility of running into any one of them. This amused Charlewood, but he never asked questions; he was sufficiently eccentric himself to tolerate the apparent caprices of others, or else shrewd enough to realise that, in these days of tangled loyalties, it is often safer not to know another man's business.

The sun was already high when I set out from Salisbury Court with a leather satchel containing my manuscript pages slung around my back. Sharp diamonds of light glinted from the windows of the buildings on Fleet Street, mostly printers and taverns that served the nearby law courts. As I walked, my feet scuffed up clouds of dust from the cobbles; occasionally I had to step aside to avoid a heap of fresh horse dung, but elsewhere the heat had hardened older piles into dry, straw-scattered crusts. The smell of rotting refuse and the sewage stink of the Thames weighed down in the still air; I pressed the sleeve of my linen shirt over my nose and tried to breathe through my mouth. The sun beat hard on a street that was curiously quiet. The law terms had finished now, so Fleet Street was missing the bustle of the Inns of Court, yet one would have expected more traffic on the main thoroughfare from Westminster to the City of London. I glanced around. Perhaps people were staying indoors for fear of the plague; perhaps they had all left for the countryside already, and the few souls remaining at the embassy were unwittingly living in a ghost town. This thought made me impatient; life was so fraught with natural hazards and those we invite on our own heads that if you were to spend your life hiding from the prospect of trouble, you would never leave your chamber. I should know, having spent the past eight years on the run through Europe with danger's cold breath constantly at my neck, ever since the night I fled from my monastery in Naples to escape the attention of the Inquisition. Yet my life had been fuller, more vivid, and infinitely more precious to me during those eight years, when I had come close to losing it several times, than in the thirteen years I had lived safe inside the sacred walls of San Domenico Maggiore.

I had just crossed Fleet Street and turned into Shoe Lane when I saw it: a disturbance at the edge of vision, brief as a blink, and then it was gone. I whipped around, my hand flying to the hilt of the bone-handled dagger I had carried at my belt since the night I became a fugitive, but the lane was almost empty. Only an old woman in a thin smock walked towards me, her back bent under the weight of her basket. She chanced to glance up at that moment and, seeing me apparently reaching for my knife, dropped her goods and let out a scream that echoed across the river to Southwark and back.

"No, no—good madam, don't be alarmed." I held my hands out, palms upwards, to show my innocence, but hearing my accent only made things worse; she stood rooted to the spot, shrieking all the louder about murdering Spanish papists. I tried to make soothing noises to quieten her, but her cries grew more frenzied, until the door of a neighbouring house opened and two men emerged, blinking in the strong light.

"What gives here?" The taller glared at me from beneath one thick eyebrow. "Are you all right, goodwife?"

"He went for his knife, the filthy Spanish dog," she gasped, clutching at her chest for good measure. "He meant to cut out my heart and rob me blind, I swear it!"

"I am sorry to have caused you any alarm." I held up my empty hands for the men to examine. "I thought I heard someone following me, that is all." I glanced up and down the street but there was no sign of movement apart from the shimmering heat haze that hovered over the ground up ahead.

"Oh yeah?" He tilted his chin at me and gave a little swagger. "Likely story. What business have you here, you Spanish whoreson?"

"Stand back, Gil, he might be one of them with the plague," his companion said, half hovering behind the big man's shoulder.

"Have you come here bringing plague on us, you filth?" the man named Gil demanded, his voice harder, but he took a step back nonetheless.

I sighed. Most Englishmen, I have discovered, know of only two other nations, Spain and France, which their mothers used interchangeably to frighten them as children. This year it was the turn of the Spanish. With my dark hair and eyes and my strange accent, I found myself accused several times a week of wanting to murder honest English folk in their beds in the name of the pope, often while I was simply walking down the street. In some ways, London was the most tolerant city I had ever had the good fortune to visit, but when it came to foreigners, these islanders were the most suspicious people on earth.

"You are thinking of the Portuguese. I am neither Spanish nor Portuguese—I am Italian," I said, with as much dignity as I could muster. "Giordano Bruno of Nola, at your service."

"Then why don't you go back there!" said the rat-faced fellow, glancing up at his friend for approval.

"Aye. Why do you come to London—to murder us and make us bow down to the pope?"

"I could not very well do both, even if I wanted," I said, and quickly saw that humour was not the means to disarm him. "Listen, good sirs—I meant no offence to anyone. May we all now go on our way?"

They exchanged a glance.

"Aye, we may . . ." said the big man, and for a moment I breathed a sigh of relief. "When we have taught you a lesson."

He thumped one meaty fist into the palm of his other hand; his friend cackled nastily and cracked his knuckles. With a reflex quick as blinking, my knife was out again and pointed at them before either of them had even stepped forward. I did not spend three years on the road in Italy without learning how to defend myself.

"Gentlemen," I said, keeping my eyes fixed on them both as I shifted my weight onto my toes, primed to run if need be. "I am a resident of the embassy of France and as such a guest of Queen Elizabeth in your country and under her protection. If you lay a finger on me, you will answer directly to Her Majesty's ministers. And they will know where to find you." I nodded towards the house behind them.

They looked uneasily at each other. The smaller one appeared to be waiting for his companion's verdict. Finally the bigger man lowered his hands and took a pace back.

"Piss off then, you pope-loving shit. But stay away from this street in future, if you have a care for your pretty face."

Relieved, I sheathed my knife, nodded, straightened my shoulders, and walked on, bowing slightly to the old woman, who had stooped to gather up her fallen wares. I almost offered to help, but the force of her glare was enough to keep me moving on. I had barely walked ten paces when something whistled past my left ear and clattered onto the ground; I leapt aside; just ahead of me a stone the size of a man's fist was rolling to a standstill in the dust. Whipping around, I saw the two men cackling as they stood together, legs planted firmly astride, arms folded. With more bravado than I felt, I seized my knife again and made as if to come back for them; they faltered for a moment, then the smaller one tugged his friend by the sleeve and both retreated hastily into their house.

I put away the knife once more, wiping the sweat from my upper lip. My hands were shaking and I could feel my heart hammering under my ribs; those two louts had meant to frighten me, but they could not have known how well they had succeeded. Last autumn, I had almost been killed by just such an attack, a rock hurled at my head with no warning, out of the night. If I had become more skittish since then, it was not without reason. I looked around, still taut with fear, one hand laid protectively over my bag. The old woman had almost reached the far end of the street; otherwise there was no sign of life. But I thought I knew who was stalking me through the streets of London; I had been half expecting him since last year. And if I was right, he would not be satisfied until I was dead.

"Giordano Bruno! Come in, come in. What's happened, man? You look as if you've seen the Devil himself." Charlewood flung open the door of his lodgings, took in my appearance with one practised glance, and gestured for me to come inside. "Here—I will have the housekeeper bring us something to drink. Are you in trouble?"

I waved his question aside; he called down the corridor while I went through into his front parlour and began the task of unpacking my manuscript from its satchel and linen wrappings.

"Well?" He followed me in, rubbing his hands together in anticipation. "Is the masterpiece finally ready? We don't want to keep Her Majesty waiting, do we?" He grinned, stroking his pointed beard.

What I liked most about Charlewood was not his willingness to print and distribute books of radical and potentially inflammatory ideas, nor that he was well travelled, spoke several languages, and had a much broader mind than many of the Englishmen I had met; it was the fact that he was an unapologetic rogue. A slightly built man of about forty-five, with reddish hair and mischievous eyes, Charlewood so crackled with restless energy that he seemed barely able to stand still for five minutes together, and was constantly picking, fiddling, hopping from one foot to another, tugging at his sleeves or his beard or the little gold ring he wore in his right ear. He cared nothing for what was said about him and he was as unscrupulous as the business required; more than once he had been in trouble for printing illegal copies of books to which he had no licence, and he was happy to dress up any book with invented credentials if he thought it would help the sales. But to his authors he was always loyal, and he was fiercely opposed to any censorship of books; on that point, we agreed wholeheartedly. His latest innovation was to publish works by Italian authors for what was still a small but elite aristocratic readership in England. I had been introduced to him by my friend Sir Philip Sidney, the unofficial leader of the little group of liberal-minded intellectuals at Queen Elizabeth's court who gathered to read one another's poetry and discuss ideas that many would regard as unorthodox or even dangerous. It was Sidney who had told Charlewood that the queen was interested in reading my work in progress; naturally the printer saw an opportunity for his own advancement and had gone so far as to create a fictitious Venetian imprint to add authenticity. Queen Elizabeth was fluent in Italian, as she was in many of the languages of Europe, and was reported to possess a formidable intellect and an unusual appetite for new and experimental ideas in science and philosophy, but even her broad mind might balk at the audacity of my latest work. I looked at the carefully written pages in my hands and wondered if Charlewood really had any idea of what he was undertaking.

Laying aside the linen cloth that had wrapped the manuscript, I handed him the bundle, bound with a silk tie. He accepted it reverently, smoothing the topmost page with the palm of his hand.

"*La Cena de le Ceneri*. The Ash-Wednesday Supper." He looked up, his brow furrowed. "We might need to work on the title, Bruno. Make it a little more . . ." He waved his fingers vaguely in a circular motion.

"That is the work's title," I said firmly.

He grinned again, but did not concede anything.

"And will it be wildly controversial? Will it set the cat among the pigeons in the academies?"

"You are hoping the answer will be 'yes,' I can see," I said, smiling.

"Well, of course," he said, loosening the tie that held the pages. "People love the thought that they are reading something the authorities would rather they didn't see. On the other hand, a royal endorsement—"

"She has not said she will endorse it," I said, quickly. "She has only expressed an interest in reading it. And she doesn't yet know of its contents."

"But she must know of you by reputation, Bruno. The whispers that followed you from Paris . . ." His eyes glinted.

"And what whispers are those, John?" I asked, feigning innocence, though I knew perfectly well what he was talking about.

"That you dabble in magic. That you are neither Catholic nor Protestant, but have invented your own religion based on the ancient wisdom of the Egyptians."

"Well, I have been excommunicated by the Catholic Church and imprisoned by the Calvinists, so I suppose that much is true. But it would take a man of extraordinary arrogance to dream of creating his own religion, would it not?" I raised an eyebrow. One corner of his mouth curved into a smile.

"That is why I can believe it of you, Bruno," he said, giving me a long look from under his brows. He tapped the pages with the back of his hand. "I will take this with me to Suffolk to read over the next few weeks. There will be no business done in London anyway until this blasted heat abates and the plague threat is over. But come the autumn, we will produce a book that will cause the biggest stir in Europe since the Pole Copernicus dared to suggest the Earth is not the centre of God's creation. Let us hope no one else is assassinated in the meantime to steal its thunder. Agreed?"

He held out his hand and I shook it in the English fashion. The door creaked open and his housekeeper appeared, head lowered, carrying a tray with an earthenware pitcher and two wooden cups, which she placed on the oak dresser that stood against the back wall of the room. Charlewood laid my manuscript on a stool and crossed to the dresser.

"Here, Bruno." He poured a cup of small beer and passed it to me. "This weather, the dust sticks in your throat, does it not? It is a little early for good wine, but let us drink to a successful partnership. The manuscript is not your only copy, I trust?"

"No." I took a welcome sip of beer. Though warm, it was at least fresh-tasting. "I made another which I have locked up at home."

"Good. Keep it safe. I will guard this with my life, but with so many travelling out of London at this time, there are plenty of cutpurses and bandits on the roads. You do not mean to stay in London, do you?"

"The ambassador would like to move the household near to the court if he can find somewhere. I am in no hurry to leave." I shrugged. "I see no evidence of plague."

Charlewood shook his head.

"By the time you've seen the evidence, it's too late. Take my advice—get out of the city. We cannot have you struck down at—what age are you now?"

"Thirty-six."

"Well, then. You want to be alive to present this book to the queen in person, don't you? And the next one, and the next. A dead author is no use to me."

I laughed, but my mind flashed back to that stone rolling in the dust at my feet and the unseen presence that had been haunting my steps for the past days. If my pursuer had his way, I would be lucky to see the autumn, plague or no plague.

I LEFT CHARLEWOOD'S house with a lighter heart, encouraged by his enthusiasm. The streets around the Barbican were still unusually empty, the sun overhead bleaching colour from the red-brick houses that lined the roads. Behind the rows of chimney stacks, the sky was a deep cloudless cobalt, almost as blue as the skies I remembered from childhood over the village of Nola, at the foot of Monte Cicada. I had not known England was capable of such a sky. My shirt stuck to my back with sweat and I loosened the lacing of it at the collar as I walked, glad that I had always avoided the English fashion for wide starched neckruffs; the young dandies at court must be desperately uncomfortable in this heat.

As I crossed Aldersgate Street and was about to turn into Long Lane, I sensed it again: a flicker of a shadow, the merest hint of a sound. I spun around, hand to my knife, and for the first time I caught a glimpse of him, perhaps fifty yards away, just before he vanished between two houses. I had no time to make out more than a tall, thin figure, but my blood boiled and before I had given thought to my actions I was hurling myself after him, feet pounding through the dust; if I must fight, so be it, but I would not be made to live this way any longer, always looking over my shoulder, feeling vulnerable at every corner like a hunted creature.

Slipping into the alley where he had disappeared, I spotted the fellow running out of the far end, heading northwards up Aldersgate Street. I forced my legs to a faster pace; I may not be excessively tall like some of these Englishmen, but I am lean and wiry and can move at a clip when I choose. Emerging from between houses, I saw him clearly and realised with a sinking feeling that he was heading towards the Charterhouse. But I was too fired up and too determined to shake him out of this cowardly pursuit to worry about the Howards.

As I drew closer, he scuttled out of sight around the corner, keeping close to the boundary wall that enclosed the maze of old buildings. All I had seen of him was that he wore a brown jerkin and breeches and a cloth cap pulled down low over his ears, but even at a distance he didn't look like the man I had expected to see, the one I feared was after me—unless the man in question had lost a lot of weight since the previous autumn.

I had no time for such considerations, though; as I rounded the corner, my quarry was attempting to scale a low wall that separated the lane from Pardon Churchyard, the old plague burial ground that formed part of the Charterhouse lands. He threw himself over; I scrambled up in pursuit, landed on the other side, and then I had a clear view of him across the graveyard, with no more buildings to hide behind. He moved nimbly, dodging tussocks of grass and the crumbled remains of old headstones, aiming for the wall on the far side and the backs of the houses on Wilderness Row. With one determined burst of speed, I gained on him enough to grab at his jerkin before he reached the wall. He twisted away, the fabric slipped from between my fingers; my foot turned on a rabbit hole in the bank and I almost fell, but just as he jumped for the wall, I threw myself at him, caught his leg, and pulled him to the ground. He fought viciously, lashing out with his fists, but I was the stronger, and once I had him by the wrists it was no great effort to pin him facedown in the grass and keep him there by kneeling astride him until his struggle subsided and he lay still.

His cap had come off in the tussle but he pressed his face into the grass; I grasped him roughly by the hair and pulled his head up so that I could see his face. I was not sure which of us cried out the louder.

"*Gésu Cristo!* Sophia?" I looked down, incredulous, into the face of the girl I had known, and briefly fancied myself in love with, more than a year ago in Oxford. I barely recognised her, and not just because her hair was cut short like a boy's. She had grown so thin that all the bones of her face seemed sharper, and those wide tawny eyes that had been so bewitching were now ringed with dark circles. She muttered something I couldn't make out, and I leaned closer.

"What?"

"Get off my hair," she hissed through her teeth.

Startled, I realised I was still gripping her hair in my fist. I released her and her head sank back to the grass, as if it were too heavy to hold up.

"Sophia Underhill," I repeated in a whisper, hardly daring to speak her name aloud in case she should vanish. "What the Devil . . . ?"

She twisted her face to look up at me, blinked sadly, and looked away.

"No. Sophia Underhill is dead."

Chapter 2

We walked side by side down Long Lane towards Smithfield Market. She said nothing, her boy's cap pulled low over her eyes once more, and I did not press her. She seemed so dramatically altered since I had last seen her, waving goodbye to me from an upstairs window in her father's lodgings, that I could only guess at the circumstances that might have brought her to London in such a state. But I knew that bombarding her with questions would be the surest way to make her retreat from me. I stole a sideways glance as we walked in search of a tavern; her beauty seemed undiminished, even enhanced by her gauntness, because it lent her an air of fragility. I had to remind myself that in Oxford Sophia had not shared my feelings; her heart had been entangled elsewhere. Yet she had come to London to seek me out, or so it appeared. I could only be patient and wait to hear her story, if she was inclined to tell it.

As we neared the marketplace, the bleating and bellowing of livestock rose into the air with the sharp tang of animal dung, fermenting in the heat. Fear of plague had not stopped the business of commerce here, and we made our way around the edge of the pens where cattle and sheep jostled in their confinement and pressed up to the fences, snuffling frantically, while farmers and butchers bartered and haggled over prices. Sophia covered her mouth and nose with her sleeve as we passed the animals; I was more intent on watching where I was putting my feet. At the entrance to St. Sepulchre's Lane, which the market traders called Pie Corner, gaudy painted tavern signs hung from the houses and a couple of girls waited listlessly in the shade, trays of sweating pies slung around their necks. I indicated the tavern on the corner, under the sign of the Cross Keys. On the threshold, Sophia hesitated and laid a hand on my arm.

"My name is Kit," she whispered. "I am come to London to look for work, if anyone asks."

I stopped, my hand on the door, and stared at her, searching her face. These were the first words she had spoken since announcing her own death in the churchyard. She looked back at me with earnest eyes and in that moment I recognised her haunted, fugitive look and cursed myself for being so stupid. She was on the run from something, or someone; this was why she was disguised as a boy. I knew that look only too well; once I had spent three years travelling through Italy under a different name. I understood what it meant to be a fugitive: always moving on, never trusting a soul, never knowing if the next town where you stopped for food or shelter might be the place they finally caught up with you. I nodded briefly, and held the door open for her.

"Well, come on then, Kit. You look as if you need feeding up."

The tavern was a functional place, catering for the needs of the market traders; the taproom smelled as strongly of animals as the square outside, but I found the corner of a bench by a window and ordered some barley bread and a jug of ale. I leaned back against the wall and watched Sophia as she hunched into herself, tugging her dirty cap farther down and glancing around nervously. When the bread arrived, she tore into it as if she had not eaten in some time. I sipped my ale slowly and waited for her to speak.

"Forgive me," she said with her mouth full, wiping crumbs away with the back of her hand. "I have forgotten all my manners, as you see. Whatever would my father say?"

There was no mistaking the bitterness in her tone. Her father, the rector of Lincoln College, had disowned her when he discovered she was with child, and sent her to live with an aunt in Kent; this was the last I had heard of her. When I left Oxford she had given me the aunt's address and asked me to write, but I had never received any reply.

"I wrote to you," I said, eventually. She looked up and met my gaze.

"I wondered if you did. I had no letters. I expect she burned them all." Her voice was flat, as if this no longer mattered.

"Your aunt?"

She nodded.

"Do you hear from your parents?"

She stared at me for a moment, then gave a snort of laughter.

"You *are* joking, I suppose?"

I both wanted and did not want to ask her about the child. She would have expected it in November, so it must be eight months old by now. If it had lived.

"Why did you say you were dead?" I asked, when it became apparent that she was not going to elaborate. She gestured to her clothes.

"Look at me. This is who I am now. The girl you think of as Sophia Underhill no longer exists. She was a fool anyway," she added, with venom. "A naïve fool, who believed that books and love were all she needed in life. I am glad she is dead. Kit has no such illusions."

I was shocked by the force of grief and anger in her words, but on reflection I should not have been. She was only twenty and already life had dealt her some cruel blows: her beloved brother had died young, the father of her child was also dead, and her family had abandoned her. A sudden image flashed into my mind, of Sophia running towards me across a garden in Oxford, her long chestnut hair flying out behind her, laughing, eyes bright, hitching up the skirts of her blue dress as she ran. She had been well educated, beyond what was expected of a young woman of her status; her father had planned a respectable marriage for her. But her independent spirit and determination to shape her own life had brought her, in the end, to this.

"You didn't need to skulk around in the shadows after me, you know," I said gently, as she ripped into another hunk of bread. "You could have just knocked on my door."

"On the door of the French embassy? You think they would have received me? Invited me to dinner, perhaps?" She swallowed her mouthful and fixed her eyes on the table. "In any case, I didn't know if you would want to see me. After everything that happened." She did not look at me, and her words were barely audible, the scorn melted away. "I told you, I never had any letters from you. I wanted to find out about your situation before I made myself known. I—I was afraid you might not want to know me."

"Sophia—" It took a supreme effort of self-control not to reach across the table and take her hand in mine. The ferocity of her warning look confirmed that this would not have been welcome. I was finding it difficult to remember that she was supposed to be a boy. "Sorry—*Kit*. Of course I would not have turned you away. Whatever help you need—if it is in my power to give—"

"You might feel differently when you know the truth," she mumbled, picking at a splinter of wood on the tabletop.

I leaned closer.

"And what is the truth?"

She looked up and met my eye with a flash of her old defiance.

"I am wanted for murder."

A long silence followed, filled by the clatter and hubbub of the taproom and the farmyard noises and shouts from beyond the window. Motes of dust rose and fell in the sunlight that slanted across our end of the table. I continued to stare at Sophia and she did not look away; indeed, I could swear there was a hint of a smile playing at the corners of her mouth. She seemed pleased with the effect of her announcement.

"Whom did you murder?" I asked, when I could bear the silence no longer.

"My husband," she replied, quick as blinking.

"Your *husband*?" I stared at her in astonishment.

She smiled briefly. It did not touch her eyes.

"Yes. You did not know I'd got myself a husband, did you?"

I could only go on staring in amazement.

"You are thinking that I don't waste any time, eh? Barely finished pushing out one man's child before I've married another?"

"I thought no such thing," I said, uncomfortably, because the idea had fleetingly crossed my mind.

"My aunt sold me like a piece of livestock." She gestured towards the window. "Like one of those poor bleating beggars in the pens."

"So you *murdered* him?" In my efforts to keep my voice down, it came out as a strangled squeak.

Sophia rolled her eyes.

"*No*, Bruno. I did not. But someone did."

"Then who?"

This time she could not disguise the impatience in her voice.

"I don't know, do I? That's what I want to find out."

I shook my head, as if to clear it. "Perhaps you had better tell me this story from the beginning."

She nodded, then drained her tankard and pushed it towards me. The ale was not strong, but drinking it fast had brought a flush of colour to her hollow cheeks.

"I'll need another drink first."

"THERE IS NO use in dwelling on all that happened before you left Oxford," she began, when a fresh jug of ale had been brought and she had finished a second piece of bread. I mumbled agreement, avoiding her eye. I wondered if she remembered the night I had kissed her, or if that memory was buried in all that had happened after. I remembered it still, as sharply as if it had been a moment ago.

"My father sent me away to my aunt in Kent, as you know. My mother cried when I left and promised it was only for a season, until my *disgrace,* as she put it, was past, but I could see by my father's face that she was fooling herself. The stain to his reputation and his standing in the town was more than his pride could bear. I truly believe he would rather I had died than brought him a bastard grandchild."

"He as good as said so to me," I recalled.

"Well, then. I was under no illusion when I set out to Kent in the company of one of my father's servants. I had been cast off by my family for good and I had no idea what my future was to hold. It was several days hard riding and I was near four months with the child by then. I was ill the whole way and I feared . . ." She looked down at the table, suddenly bashful. "I knew so little of such matters, I feared the rough journey would dislodge it before its time. Stupid." She shook her head, embarrassed.

"Not at all," I said. "It would be an unnatural woman who did not worry about the safety of her unborn child."

"It turns out they are tougher than you think, these creatures," she said, allowing herself a soft smile. "In any event, I was safely delivered to my aunt—my father's elder sister, so you may imagine she took the insult to his honour very much to heart. She was widowed, with modestly comfortable means, and she made sure that I was adequately fed and housed for the duration of my confinement. But it came at a price. The state of my immortal soul was her real project." She grimaced, and paused to take another gulp of ale. "I was allowed no books except the Bible and a book of prayer. Naturally, I was not permitted to step outside the house—she had told her neighbours that I was sickly and likely to die and that she was nursing me through my last months. Whether they believed her, I have no idea, but I was shut in my room whenever she had visitors."

"You were not moved to any religious feeling, despite your aunt's efforts?"

She snorted and tossed her head in a way reminiscent of how she was before, when she still had long hair to toss.

"I told you, Bruno—I am done with religion, of any stripe. If there is a God, I am sure He must look with despair on His representatives, end-lessly bickering over trifles. For myself, I would rather live without it."

"That makes you a heretic," I said, suppressing a smile.

She shrugged.

"If you say so. It does not seem to have done you any harm."

"Oh, Sophia. Sorry—*Kit*. How can you say that? Do not take me as your model. I can never return to my home because I am called a heretic, you know this."

"Neither can I," she said, pointedly. "We are in the same boat, you and I, Bruno. We both live in exile now."

I was tempted to detail for her all the ways in which our situations could not be compared, but I wanted to hear the rest of her story.

"So your aunt was determined to make you repent . . . ?"

"I never knew how much my father had told her of the circumstances that brought me to her house. She was certainly of the belief that I had been wilful and disobedient and had made my long-suffering family pay the price for my dishonour. And she made it very clear that I would have no choice about the life I lived from then on, if I expected to be given food and shelter." She stopped abruptly, looked away to the window, and swallowed hard. I sensed we were nearing the heart of her story; she had kept up the careless bravado convincingly so far, but I noticed she had barely mentioned the child. Perhaps she found it too painful to talk about.

"Her plan was this," she continued, when she had taken another drink. "That I should wait out my confinement in her house, hidden away, stuffing my head with Bible verses day and night. Then, when the child was born, if it was healthy and a boy, it would be adopted by a couple of some standing in a neighbouring town, who could not have a child of their own. She had it all worked out, it seems, and I am certain that money changed hands, though I never saw a penny of it. But she was very insistent that a boy would be the best outcome for all concerned—as if I could influence what was in my belly."

"And if it was a girl?"

"I suppose they would have found a place for her, somewhere. There'd have been less reward, though."

"But it was a boy?"

Finally she looked up and met my eye.

"Yes. I had a son. And he was healthy—so I was told. I only held him for a few minutes. They didn't even let me nurse him. She said it was best that my body did not get used to him, nor him to me. Someone came at night to take him away, under cover of darkness. Those people—the people who *bought* him—they had a wet nurse ready, I'm told. So I'm sure he was well looked after."

Here her voice cracked a little; I wanted desperately to reach out for her hand, but she held herself proud and upright, and simply clenched her jaw together until the danger of showing emotion had passed.

"I don't remember much about those days, to tell you the truth, Bruno. I was in a lot of pain while my body recovered from the birth, but that was nothing compared to the blackness that descended on me after they took him away. I had always believed I was someone who could bear grief with fortitude—I had done so in the past—but this was different. I could not eat or sleep nor even cry. All I was good for was lying on my bed, staring at the ceiling, and wishing it would all come to an end somehow. At first my aunt was terrified I had taken an infection and would die—she had the physician out to me every day, at her own expense, and she had to pay extra for his discretion. I foolishly imagined she was doing this out of genuine concern and a sense of family duty."

"It must have been terrible."

She shrugged again.

"I suppose it was. But I had reached a point where I no longer cared what happened to me. I could feel nothing—not hope, nor fear, nor anger. Only blankness. I thought my life was over. I might as well have taken my chances being drowned on a boat to France."

She held my gaze steadily as she said this, and although she had spoken the words gently, they cut to my heart. The previous spring, Sophia had been all set to flee Oxford for the Continent; it was my actions that had prevented her. I had intervened because I believed—with good reason, I still felt—that by stopping her flight I was saving her life, and that of her child. Over the months since then I had thought of her often and wondered how her life had unfolded as a result of my interference; I remained sure that I had done the right thing, but there was always room for a sliver of doubt. I feared, however, that even now she clung to her romantic hopes, and blamed me for stealing from her the future she had planned.

"But then your child would not have lived," I said softly.

She lowered her eyes and picked another splinter from the tabletop.

"True enough. And he is alive and well, somewhere, I trust. I hope they are kind people," she added, with sudden force. "I wish I could have seen them, to know what they are like." Her voice shook again, and she wiped her eye brusquely with her sleeve.

"They must have wanted a child very badly, whoever they were. I'm sure they will treat him like a little prince."

She looked up, her lashes bright with tears, and forced a smile.

"Yes. I'm sure you are right. So I lay there in the dark, day after day, until eventually the bleeding stopped and the milk dried up, and my body was my own again. I'm sorry if this detail offends you, Bruno, but it is a messy and unpleasant business, being a woman."

I spread my hands out, palms upwards.

"It is difficult to offend me. But I am sorry to hear you suffered."

She watched me for a moment, her expression guarded. Did she blame me for her suffering?

"The physician came and bled me daily, which only made me weaker, but he could find nothing wrong. Of course, once my aunt was satisfied that I had no bodily affliction, she concluded it was just monstrous idleness and warned me repeatedly that as soon as I was able I would be expected to take on some of the household chores. Hard work was the best cure for melancholy, in her view." The note of bitterness had crept back. She took a deep breath, steadied herself, and continued. "One morning I woke—I think it was around the Feast of Saint Nicholas—

with the sun streaming in through the shutters, and for the first time in weeks I felt like getting up. It was still early and the household was asleep, so I put on some clothes, wrapped myself in a woollen cloak, and went outside. My aunt lived on the outskirts of a small town with rolling countryside all around, and in the early-morning sun, all laced with frost, the view was so beautiful it took my breath away. I walked for an hour, got myself lost a couple of times, but although I almost wore out my poor exhausted body, I felt I was coming back to life." She smiled briefly at the recollection. "My aunt was furious when I returned—I think she feared I'd run away. She railed at me: What if the neighbours had seen me in that state, looking like some wild woman of the woods? She had a point; I had not washed in weeks and I was thin as a wraith. In any case, she made me undress and looked me over thoroughly, as you would with a horse, then she heated water to bathe me and spent a long time untangling my hair and washing it with camomile. I was surprised, as you might imagine—she was not usually given to such extravagance. She fed me well that evening and told me I was welcome to walk in the countryside if I chose, so long as I stayed away from the town and one of her housemaids accompanied me. So over the next few weeks, this is what happened. I recovered my strength, and something of the balance of my mind, or at least I learned to lock away my pain where it could not be seen and appear human again on the surface. But I was suspicious of my aunt's changed attitude—she seemed almost indulgent towards me, and I knew enough of her to doubt that this was prompted by affection. She had also taken to locking me in my room at night."

"What happened to the household chores she had threatened?"

"Naturally, I wondered. Until the child was born, I was protected, because they needed me. I had tried not to think too much about what my life would be once I'd served my purpose—I supposed that at best she would use me as some kind of cheap servant in return for a roof over my head. I expected her to hand me a broom the moment I was on my feet again, but instead, she started coming to my room in the evenings to comb out my hair—it was still long then," she said, rubbing self-consciously at the back of her neck—"and smooth scented oil into my hands. Not what you'd usually do for someone you mean to do laundry or wash floors."

"She had something else in mind."

Sophia nodded, her mouth set in a grim line.

"I found out a few days before Christmas. She came into my room one morning with a blue gown. It was beautiful—the sort of thing I used to wear—" She broke off, turning away.

I remembered how she used to dress in Oxford; her clothes were not expensive or showy, but she wore them with a natural grace that cannot be purchased from a tailor, and always managed to look elegant. Very different from the dirty breeches, worn leather jerkin, and riding boots she was dressed in now.

"I hadn't thought I cared about such trifles anymore," she continued, "but when she laid it out on the bed, I couldn't conceal my pleasure. She told me it was an early Christmas present, and for a moment I really thought I had misjudged her, that there was a buried vein of human kindness under that crusty surface. I was soon disabused of that, of course."

I was about to reply when the serving girl appeared at our table to enquire whether we wanted any more of anything. I asked for cold meat, more bread, and another jug of ale; Sophia's tale clearly demanded some effort and I felt she should keep her strength up. When the food had been brought and she had helped herself to the cold beef, she wiped her mouth on her sleeve and resumed her story.

"She made me put the dress on and turn around for her. She seemed satisfied with the result. When she had pinched my cheeks hard to put colour in them, she stood back, looked me up and down, and said, 'You shall do very well, as long as you keep your mouth shut. Only speak if he asks you a question, and then make sure it's a "Yes, sir" or a "No, sir." Understood?' When I asked whom she meant, she merely tutted and shoved her sour old face right up to mine. 'Your husband,' she said."

"I imagine you took that well," I said, breaking off a piece of bread, a smile at the corner of my lips.

"I screamed blue murder," Sophia said, a grin unexpectedly lighting her face. "I'd have bolted if she hadn't locked the door. As it was, she had to slap me around the face twice before I would be quiet. Then she sat me down on the bed and made me listen. 'Do you know what you are?' she asked me. 'You're a filthy whore, that's what, with no respect for God nor your family. Plenty in your situation have no one to look out for them, and they end up making their living on the streets, which is no more than you deserve. But you can thank Providence that I have found a better arrangement for you. A decent man, respectable, with a good income, has agreed to take you to wife. You can change your name and leave your whole history behind you. You're still young and can be made to look pretty. All you have to do is be obedient and dutiful, as a wife should be. If you'd learned those qualities as a daughter, your life might have been very different now,' she added, just to twist the knife. 'What if I don't like him?' I asked. She slapped me again. 'It's not for you to like or dislike, hussy,' she said. 'You can marry Sir Edward Kingsley and live in comfort, with the good regard of society, or you can make your own way. Beg for bread or whore for it, I care not. Because if you mar this on purpose, girl, after everything I have done for you, don't expect me to feed and clothe you for one day more.' So saying, she locked me in the room and told me I had until the afternoon to make my choice."

"Sir Edward Kingsley?" I rubbed my chin. "A titled man. You'd think he'd have his pick of women—no offence, but why would he choose a wife whose history could bring him disgrace, if it were to become known? What did he get from the bargain?"

Sophia's face was set hard.

"Control, I suppose. He got a wife who was young and pretty enough—though that's all gone now," she added, passing a hand across her gaunt cheek.

"Not at all," I said, hoping it did not sound insincere. A flicker of a smile crossed her lips.

"The fact that I had a past to hide appealed to him," she continued. "He thought it would be a way of keeping me bound to his will. He imagined I would be so grateful to have been saved from a life on the streets that I would put up with anything, not daring to complain. Absolutely *anything*." She fairly spat these last words. "Of course, I didn't learn any of this until after we were married. He could be very charming in company."

"So you agreed to marry him?"

There was a long pause.

"Don't look at me like that, Bruno. What choice did I have? I had nothing left—nothing. You of all people should understand that. The hotheaded part of me thought of running away, of course. But perhaps having the child had changed me." Her voice grew quieter. "I knew it would be hopeless—I had seen beggar women and whores in the street, I knew I would not survive long like that. Besides, I had formed an idea—you will think it foolish . . ." She looked at me tentatively.

"Try me."

"I thought that one day, when he was older, he might somehow be able to find out my name and come looking for me."

"Who?"

"My son, of course. I had this idea that, when he grew, he would realise he did not look like the people he believed to be his parents, and then the truth would come out, and he might want to learn of his real mother. I didn't want him to find me dead or living in a bawdy house if that day came. And this Sir Edward seemed affable enough, when he came to visit. The way my aunt fawned on him, you'd have thought he was the Second Coming. So I made my choice. I would swallow my pride and marry a man I did not care for. I would not be the first woman to have done that, in exchange for security and a house to live in."

She fell silent then, and picked at her bread.

"Tell me about this Sir Edward Kingsley," I prompted, when it seemed she had become sunk in her own thoughts.

"He was twenty-seven years older than me, for a start." She curled her lip in distaste. I tried to look as sympathetic as I could, bearing in mind that I was a good sixteen years her senior and had once desired her myself. And did still, if I was honest, despite the alteration in her. I could not help wondering how she would feel about that; would the idea prompt the same disgust that she expressed at the thought of this aging husband?

"He was a magistrate in Canterbury," she continued. "Do you know the city?"

"I have never been, but of course I know it by reputation—it was one of the greatest centres of pilgrimage in Europe, until your King Henry VIII had the great shrine destroyed."

"The shrine of Saint Thomas Becket, yes. But the cathedral dominates the city even now—it is the oldest in England, you know. I suppose it would have been a pleasant enough place to live, in different circumstances."

"What was so wrong with your situation, then?"

She sighed, rearranging her long limbs on the bench in an effort to find a more comfortable position, and leaned forward with her elbows on the table.

"Sir Edward was a widower. He had a son of twenty-three from his first marriage, Nicholas, who still lived at home. They didn't get along, and he resented me from the outset, as you may imagine. But that was nothing compared to my husband. Sir Edward was of the view that behind closed doors a wife ought to combine the role of maid and whore, to save him paying for either, and do so meekly and gratefully. And if I was *stubborn*, which was his word for refusing his demands, he whipped me with a horsewhip. In his experience, he said, it worked just as well on women."

She kept her voice steady as she said this, but I noticed how her jaw clenched tight and she sucked in her cheeks to keep the emotion in check. I shook my head.

"*Dio mio*, Sophia—I can't imagine what you have been through. Was he a drinker, then?"

"Not at all. That made it worse, in a way. There are those who will lash out in a drunken rage—that is one kind of man, and they will often repent of it bitterly the next day. My husband was not like that—he always seemed master of his actions, and his violence was entirely calculated. He used it just as he said, in the same way that you would beat an animal to break it through fear."

"Did anyone know how he was treating you?"

"His son knew, I am certain, but we detested one another. And there was a housekeeper, Meg, she'd been with Sir Edward for years—I'm sure she must have known, though she never spoke of it. She was afraid of him too. But she showed me small acts of kindness. Other than that, I only had one friend I could confide in."

"And I suppose she could do little to help you."

"*He,*" she said, and took another long draught of her ale. Immediately something tensed inside me, a hard knot of jealousy I had no right to, and for which I despised myself. Of course it was absurd to think that Sophia could have lived for months in a new city without attracting the attention of some young man, but whoever this friend was, I resented his invisible presence, the fact that he had been there to comfort her. Had he been a lover? On the other hand, I tried to reason against that voice of jealousy, where was he now, this friend? Had she not found her way to London, in her hour of desperation, in search of me? I composed my face and attempted to look disinterested.

"*He,* then. He could not help?"

She shook her head. "What could anyone have done? Olivier listened to me, that was all."

Was it really, I thought, and bit the unspoken words down. I felt as if I had a piece of bread lodged in my throat.

"Your husband did not mind you having friends who were . . . ?" I left the sentence hanging.

"French?"

"I was going to say, men."

Sophia's teasing smile turned to scorn.

"Well, of course he would, if he'd known. He didn't even like me to leave the house, but fortunately he was out so often at his business that I sometimes had a chance to slip away on the pretext of some chores. Olivier was the son of French weavers—his family came as refugees to Canterbury twelve years ago, after the massacre of Saint Bartholomew's Day."

I shivered, despite the stuffy air; the mention of that terrible event in 1572, when the forces of the French Catholic League rampaged through the streets of Paris, slaughtering Protestant Huguenot families by the thousand until the gutters ran scarlet with their blood, never failed to chill me to the bones. The memory of it was kept fresh in England, as a warning of what could be expected here if a Catholic force were ever to invade.

"I had heard that many Huguenots came to England to escape the religious persecution," I said.

"Canterbury is one of their largest communities. They are really the best of people," she added warmly, and instantly I disliked this Olivier all the more.

"But tell me how your husband died, then," I said, wanting to change the subject.

Sophia passed a hand across her face and held it for a moment over her mouth, as if gathering up the strength for this part of the story. Eventually she laid her hands flat on the table and looked me directly in the eye.

"For six months, I endured this marriage, if that is what you want to call it. I was known as Kate Kingsley, and my official history was that my father, a distant cousin of Sir Edward's, had recently died, leaving me an orphan with a useful parcel of land in Rutland. I suppose he thought that was far enough away that no one would be likely to check. When I appeared with him in public, I was demure and well turned out, which was all anyone seemed to expect of me. And at home, I was regularly beaten and forced to endure what he called my wifely duty, which he liked to perform with violence, though he was always careful never to leave marks on my skin where it might show." She flexed her hands, trying to keep her expression under control.

"How did you bear it?"

She shrugged.

"It is surprising how much you can bear, when you are obliged to—as you must know, Bruno. My greatest fear was that I would get another child, he forced himself on me so often, and I knew I could never love any child of his. With every month that passed, I worried my luck would not hold. Lately I had started to think about running away. Olivier was going to help me."

I'm sure he was, I thought, uncharitably.

"Did your husband suspect?"

"I don't think so. He was always preoccupied with his own business. In fact, from the first days in that house, I'd begun to notice odd things about my husband's behaviour."

"Aside from his violent streak, you mean?"

"Odder than that, even. He was often out of the house at strange hours, leaving in the dead of night and returning towards dawn. Once I asked him where he'd been when he got into bed with the cold air of night still on him, and he fetched me such a slap to my jaw that I feared I would lose a tooth." She rubbed the side of her face now at the memory of it. "After that, I always pretended to be asleep when he came in."

"So he was a man with secrets. Women, do you suppose?"

She shot me a scornful look.

"When he had a whore ready at his disposal in the comfort of his own home, at no extra charge?" She shook her head. "I told you, my husband didn't like to part with money if it could be avoided. No, there was something else he was up to, but I never found out what. Underneath the house there was a cellar that he always kept locked, with the key on a chain at his belt. And sometimes his friends would come to the house late at night." Her face darkened. "By his friends, I mean some of the most eminent men of the city. My husband was a lay canon at the cathedral, as well as being magistrate, so he was a person of influence. They would shut themselves in his study and talk for hours. Once I tried to listen at the door, and it seemed they were arguing among themselves, but I could not stay long enough to hear anything useful—the old house-keeper found me there in the passageway and shooed me off to bed. She said Sir Edward would kill me if he caught me there, truly kill me, and she had such fear in her face that I believed it was a serious warning, honestly meant." She paused to take another bite of bread. "But two weeks ago he had been up to the cathedral, to a meeting of the chapter, as he often did, and afterwards he was to take his supper with the dean. He never came home."

"What happened?"

"One of the canons appeared at my door, about nine o'clock at night, with two constables. He had found Edward's body in the cathedral precincts. He must have been on his way home when he was attacked."

"How did he die?"

"Struck down with a heavy weapon from behind, they said, and beaten repeatedly while he lay there until his skull was smashed. They said his hands were all broken and bloodied, as if he'd been trying to cover his face." She pressed her lips together. "I wasn't sorry—the man was a brute. But it must have been a dreadful way to die. His brains were all spilled over the flagstones, they told me."

"His brains . . ." The detail sounded familiar, as if I had heard the description before, but I could not place it. "You did not have to see it, I hope?"

"No, they took the body away. It was a vicious act. The killer must have been someone who violently hated him."

"Were there people who hated him that much?"

"Apart from his wife, you mean?" She gave me a wry glance.

I acknowledged the truth of this with a dip of my head. "But you said no one knew how he treated you in private. So how did they come to suspect you?"

She poked at a piece of bread and leaned in.

"I had the wit to realise when the canon came that if I didn't give him a good show of shock and grief he would find that curious, to say the least. He handed me the sword that my husband had been wearing, still sheathed, and his gold signet ring, all daubed in blood. I played the distraught widow, thinking that would make them go away."

"I find it hard to imagine you in that role," I said, with a fond smile. She almost returned it.

"Oh, you would be surprised, Bruno, how convincing I can be. He said the body had been taken to the coroner and asked if I wanted someone to sit with me that night, to save me being alone. I thanked him and said I had old Meg, the housekeeper, for company—that was stupid of me, because it was Meg's day off and she had gone to visit a friend, but I just wanted him to go so I could stop pretending to cry and enjoy an untroubled night's sleep. I could hardly explain to him that I wanted more than anything to be left on my own, for once."

"Did he know you were lying?"

"Not at the time. He went away, and perhaps an hour later my husband's son, Nicholas, came home, with the smell of the alehouse on him. The constables had found him in there with his friends and given him the news. He was cursing and shouting at me in his drunken rage that it was all my doing. He said nothing had gone right in that house since the day his father brought me into it." She paused, and I saw the anger flash across her face before she mastered it. "Then—well, I'll spare you the details. Suffice to say, he thought he could take his father's place in the marriage bed."

"Holy Mother!" I drew a hand across my mouth and felt my other fist bunch under the table.

"Don't worry, I fought him off." She gave a brief, bitter laugh. "I was damned if I was taking that from the son as well. Fortunately, he was too drunk to put up much of a fight. But he was sober enough to be angered by the refusal. He told me I would get what was coming to me, gave me a slap for good measure, and stumbled and crashed his way to his own room."

"What did he mean by that threat?"

"I hardly dared sleep that night—I thought he might come in and attack me while I lay in my bed. But I heard him leave the house early, at first light. I fell asleep again and the next I knew, old Meg the house-keeper was shaking me awake, whispering frantically that I had to run."

"Run? Why?"

"She'd met the cathedral gatekeeper on her way back to the house. He'd come to find her, to say that the constables had discovered evidence at the scene to arrest me for the murder of my husband and were on their way round. I barely had time to get dressed. Fortunately I knew where my husband kept his strongbox."

"In his mysterious locked cellar?"

She shook her head.

"No. Whatever was in there, it was not money. He kept that in various chests in the room he called his library, and the keys were hidden in a recess in the chimney breast. I took two pursefuls of gold angels, which was all I could carry, and fled through the kitchen yard."

"So . . ." I sat back, feeling almost breathless at the pace of her tale. "Where did you go? What was this evidence—did you ever find out? Surely this Nicholas had something to do with it?"

"One question at a time, Bruno. I ran through the back streets to Olivier's house. His parents had already heard about Sir Edward's murder—news spreads quickly in a cathedral city, where everyone knows everyone. But they didn't know I was to be accused of it. They offered to hide me for a while, but I was afraid it would be too danger-ous for them—the Huguenots are already treated with suspicion in the city, just because they are foreigners who keep close within their own community and try to preserve their own customs. We English are not terribly accommodating in that regard, I'm afraid."

"I have noticed."

"Later that same day, old Meg came by to tell us she had been ques-tioned by the constables. They learned, of course, that I had lied about being at home with her the previous evening—poor thing, she had no idea I had told them that. But apparently early that morning someone had found a pair of women's gloves, stained with blood, thrown on the ground in the cathedral precincts. Put that together with my lying about my alibi, stealing my husband's money, and taking flight, they think they have all the answer they need."

She folded her arms and dropped her head to stare at the table, as if the account had exhausted her.

"Well, that is absurd," I said, indignant on her behalf. "Were they your gloves?"

She hesitated.

"I don't know—one pair of gloves looks much like any other, doesn't it? I certainly wasn't wearing them. But how am I to prove otherwise? When my husband was respected and influential, and I have no money of my own even to pay a lawyer? I'm sure it won't take long for someone to uncover Mistress Kate's real name and past, and that will be seen as proof of my degeneracy."

"Someone has tried to ensure you were blamed for this murder. Did this Nicholas, the son, know who you really were?"

She shook her head.

"No. But it was plain he hated me."

"Hated you and desired you."

"Isn't that often the case with men and women?" She lifted her chin and fixed me with a twisted smile.

I was on the point of arguing when I recalled a woman I had known last year, and this memory gave me pause. I did not answer one way or the other.

"What about the key?" I asked.

"What key?"

"The one to his secret cellar, that you said he wore at his belt. If this canon gave you the valuables he took from the body, was the key not among them?"

She stared at me, her lips parted.

"No! By God, with everything that happened after, I never once thought of that key. You mean the killer could have taken it?"

"I don't know. Only it seems that, if he was found with a gold ring and a sword still on him, the killer was not interested in robbery. Perhaps the key was not given to you because the person who found him didn't regard it as valuable, that is all."

"Or because they knew precisely what it was and kept it." She frowned. "You think someone wanted to find out what was in that cellar?"

"I don't know. But surely any sane person would force the lock rather than hack a man to death for the key? I was only thinking aloud. So— then you came to London?" I said.

"As you see," she replied. "It took over a week."

I shook my head, half in disbelief, half in admiration.

"You are fortunate you were not robbed or killed on the road, or both. Did you travel alone?"

She smiled, and there was a hint of pride in it.

"No. Some of the Huguenot weavers were coming to London, bringing samples of cloth to trade. It was safe enough to travel with them. Especially like this." She indicated her boy's clothes. "These are Olivier's. It was his idea to dress as a boy. Oh, I hated the thought of cutting off all my hair at first, but then his mother sensibly pointed out that they would cut it off for me on the gallows anyway." She gave a bitter laugh, but it didn't mask the fear in her eyes. Although I couldn't quite ignore my childish resentment of this Olivier for being the first man to her aid, I had to admit my admiration for this practical French family who had taken a considerable risk to help Sophia to safety. My eyes strayed inadvertently to her chest under the rough shirt as I wondered how she had managed to strap herself up. She noticed the direction of my gaze and smiled.

"To tell the truth, Bruno, there was not much left of them after I had the child and then grew so thin. I wear a linen binding, but I had hardly anything to bind in the first place."

I felt my face grow hot, which only seemed to amuse her further.

"You are too easy to embarrass, Bruno. I suppose that comes of being a monk for so long." Then her expression became serious. "I thought if I could just get to London and find you," she continued, turning those wide, golden-brown eyes on me once more, "then everything would be all right. All those miles with the weavers' cart, it was my only thought."

I wanted to speak, but the words wedged in my throat. Instead I reached out and laid my hand over hers. She did not snatch it away, and for a moment we stayed like that, in silence, looking at each other with everything still unspoken as the dust danced in the thick sunlight, until she nodded to her right with a mischievous grin, and I glanced across to see two men at the next table watching this display of affection with expressions of disgust.

"They will take me for your catamite," Sophia whispered, giggling.

I withdrew my hand quickly. "Careful, then. They hang you for that here as well."

WE LEFT THE tavern and walked back in the shimmering heat along Gifford Street and on down Old Bailey, Sophia contained in her silence, as if all her words were spent. I glanced sidelong at her as we walked, but she appeared deep in concentration, biting at the knuckle of her thumb, her dirty cap pulled down low over her brow, eyes fixed straight ahead. I decided it was best not to press her any further for now. At the bottom of the lane I paused; my way lay to the right, up Fleet Hill, but I had no more idea of where she intended to go in London than I did of where she had sprung from.

"I have taken a room at the sign of the Hanging Sword, off Fleet Street," she said, pointing ahead, as if she had read my thoughts. I laughed.

"But that is almost opposite Salisbury Court, where I have my lodgings."

She seemed pleased by my expression of incredulity and grinned from under the peak of her cap. The food and the ale had heartened her, or perhaps it was the relief of having unburdened herself, and not having been turned away.

"Of course. Why do you think I took the room?"

"So how long have you been spying on me?"

"It's five days since I arrived. But I lost my nerve a little once I saw what a grand house you lived in—I knew I couldn't just bang on the door. So I thought I would watch you, see if I could judge from your routine when might be the best time to approach you, if at all."

"My routine has little of interest to offer at the moment, I'm afraid," I said, spreading my arms apologetically, though the idea that I could have been watched for five days from the tavern across the street made me uneasy. Sophia wished me no harm, but there were those who did, and if she could follow me around London so easily, then so might they. I must not imagine for a moment that I was safe anywhere, I silently reprimanded myself, and resolved to keep my wits sharper in future. "As for the embassy, its grandeur is sadly faded, I think, but it is comfortable enough. I am fortunate to have such a residence."

We fell into step in the direction of the Fleet Bridge, silent again as I turned over in my mind what assistance I might be able to offer Sophia. Money I could just about manage, and perhaps in the longer term I might be able to use some of my contacts to help her into work, but for that she would have to remain in her boy's disguise, and it seemed impractical to think of keeping that up. It was easy enough to hide in London, with its rabbit warren of old streets and the thousands of people coming and going daily in search of work or trade, but the world was always a smaller place than you imagined, as I had learned to my cost when I was living as a fugitive in my own country. For as long as Kate Kingsley was wanted for the murder of her husband, Sophia Underhill, or whoever she chose to become next, would never be able to live freely in England.

"Listen, Sophia—*Kit,*" I corrected myself hastily before she could. "You know I will give you whatever help I can while you are in London, and if you need money, well, my stipend from King Henri of France is sufficiently generous to allow me to support you for a while." This was untrue; my living allowance from the French king, in recognition of the fact that I had been his personal philosophy tutor, was barely enough to live on, and unreliable in its arrival. Such income as I had to allow me a reasonable standard of living in London came not from King Henri but from my work for the English government, though naturally no one at the French embassy knew this.

"The Hanging Sword is expensive," I continued, "but I could help you look for cheaper lodgings elsewhere while you give some thought to what you are going to do. You might find it difficult to remain as a boy indefinitely, but perhaps . . ."

I stopped when I saw the look on her face. She had halted abruptly in the middle of the street and was staring at me, her brow knotted in confusion.

"Bruno—have you not understood any of my story? Why do you think I came all this way to seek you out?"

"Because . . ." I faltered. Had I misunderstood? She was looking at me as a governess might look at a child who has failed to absorb anything of his lesson, despite hours at the same exercise. "I presumed because you had few people left whose friendship you could rely on, in the circumstances," I said, a little stiffly.

"Well, that is true," she said, impatient. "But I remembered how you unravelled those murders in Oxford, when no one else seemed to have the slightest idea who was behind them. That's why I wanted your help. I need you to find out who murdered my husband and clear my name. I don't want to live the rest of my life looking over my shoulder, wondering when they will come for me."

"No, you don't," I said with feeling, though I could not believe she was seriously asking this of me. She clutched at my sleeve then, and made me look her in the eye, her face close to mine. I could hear the urgency in her voice.

"If you don't help me, Bruno, I shall live as a wanted murderess all my life, and if they find me I'll be straight for the pyre. You know that's the punishment for women who murder their husbands? Because the man is master of his wife, it's regarded as an act of treason. So instead of hanging, they burn you."

"Like a heretic," I said, softly.

"Like a heretic." She fixed me with a meaningful look.

I stepped back, rubbing my hand across the growth of stubble on my chin and shaking my head.

"You want me to go to *Canterbury* and find the killer?"

"If you could do it in Oxford, why not in Canterbury?" She sounded petulant, and I was reminded, despite her weight of experience, how young she still was.

"It's not quite as simple as that. I can't just take off across the country—I would need permission . . ." But as I considered the possibility, I felt my blood quicken with the prospect of it: a change of scene, a new challenge, and the ultimate prize of freeing Sophia from a sentence of death.

"Permission?" She looked scornful.

"From the ambassador. As a member of his household, out of courtesy I must consult with him before I go anywhere. And with the diplomatic situation so fraught at the moment, he may be reluctant to let me leave." But it was not the ambassador's permission I was concerned about. I sincerely doubted whether my real employer would want me away from the embassy at such a time.

"You are not the ambassador's ward, Bruno. You are a grown man, or so I thought. Well, it doesn't matter, then." She wrapped her arms tightly around her chest and started walking briskly away towards the narrow bridge; I watched her for a moment, before hurrying to catch her up.

"Wait!" I had to work hard to match her determined stride, but on the bridge I caught her by the sleeve. "I have said I will help you, and I meant it. I will see if this can be arranged. But it will be difficult—I would have no authority to undertake an investigation of any kind in Canterbury, and you said yourself how they are suspicious of foreigners there."

"You could pretend to be a visiting scholar," she said brightly. "They have a fine library in the cathedral precincts, I am told. *Please,* Bruno? You are all the hope I have now." Her eyes widened, and the pleading in them was in earnest. "If you don't help me, no one will."

She looked down at her boots, shamed by her own helplessness; Sophia, whose independent spirit chafed at being beholden to a man, any man. She kicked at a small stone, her arms wrapped again around her chest, as if to protect herself from further hurt. It was a gesture that clutched at my heart, and I knew that, whatever the obstacles, I must find a way to help her. If nothing else, it would assuage the lingering sense of guilt that still needled me over my actions in Oxford, and the fear that I had somehow been the indirect cause of everything that had happened to her since. I owed her a debt, I believed, and she had counted on my conscience.

"Very well then. *Santa Maria!*" I grabbed at my hair with both hands in a gesture of mock exasperation that made her laugh. "You would wear down a stone, Sophia. But what will you do, if I get myself to Canterbury?"

"I will come with you, of course." She looked nonplussed.

"*What?* And how are you going to do that? You are wanted for murder."

"I wouldn't venture into the city, obviously. I will stay as a boy, and you can say I am your apprentice."

"Travelling scholars don't have apprentices."

"Your scribe, then. Or servant, it doesn't matter. But you will need me there, Bruno, to point you in the right direction—I know the city and I can direct you to Sir Edward's associates. We could find lodgings somewhere on the edge of town. I could keep out of sight."

Her face was animated now, her eyes bright and eager. We could *find lodgings*? Was she proposing that we share rooms together? I looked at her doubtfully, but I could find no trace of teasing in her eyes, only earnest hope. Perhaps she believed her disguise was good enough to convince both of us that she really was a boy. Was that the kind of friendship she envisaged between us, despite the fact that in Oxford I had once been so bold as to kiss her, and she had responded? I wished I had a better sense of how she regarded me.

It would be an enormous risk for her, returning to the city where, even with her cropped hair and dirty clothes, there was every chance of being recognised as the murdered magistrate's wife. On the other hand, she was right: I would fare better with someone to guide me around the city of Canterbury, and what would she do otherwise in London, alone and friendless as her money rapidly ran out? At least if she came with me I could do my best to take care of her—and the thought of spending days in her company, reviving the conversations we had enjoyed in Oxford, was more than I had dared to hope for, even if, for now, she saw me only as a trusted friend. Until that morning, I had thought she was dead to me, and I knew that I could not abandon her to circumstance again.

"Let me see if I can make arrangements," I said.

"Good. But we must leave soon. Because of the assizes."

"The assizes?"

"Yes. Once a quarter a judge comes from London to try all the criminals taken since the last session, the cases too serious for the local justice. The next one is due in early August. If you were to find the real killer by then, he could be tried at the assizes and I would be free."

"You don't ask much, do you?"

Outside the Hanging Sword, we parted company, I assuring her that I would secure permission from the ambassador as soon as possible, and warning her in the meantime to keep her money close about her person and not to walk around the streets of London after dark.

"But I have this," she said, pulling aside the front of her jerkin to reveal a small knife buckled to her belt.

"That will come in very handy if you should need to peel an apple. But I don't suggest you try your hand at any tavern brawls with it," I said.

She smiled, and her face seemed more relaxed.

"I'd prefer not to."

We stood awkwardly for a moment, uncertain of how to say goodbye. Sophia seemed less stooped, less diminished, as if a weight had lifted from her. "Thank you, Bruno," she said, checking in both directions to see that the street was empty before leaning in and giving me an impulsive hug. "You are a true friend. One day I will find a way to repay you."

I could only blink and smile stupidly as she stepped back and turned away towards the tavern. I moved to cross the street towards Salisbury Court, wondering what on earth I had undertaken.

"*Ciao,* Kit," I called, glancing over my shoulder to see her pause at the tavern door. She lifted a hand in farewell, then executed a mock bow.

She moves too much like a woman, I thought, watching the way she snaked her narrow hips to one side to avoid a man coming out as she slipped through the doorway. This Kit will need some lessons on being a man, if we're not to be arrested. Before that, though, I needed to find a way to make this madcap plan palatable to the two men whose authority I must respect while I live in London: Michel de Castelnau, the French ambassador, and Sir Francis Walsingham, Queen Elizabeth's principal secretary. Both were certain to be opposed. I sighed. Sophia might imagine that a man enjoys the freedoms she lacks, but we are all beholden to somebody, in the great chain of patronage and favour that stretches all the way up to the queen herself; and even she is not truly free, as long as she lives in fear of the assassin on the stairs, like the poor Prince of Orange.

Chapter 3

*C*anterbury?" Sir Francis Walsingham fairly spat the word across the room. "What on earth for?"

"To travel," I said lamely. "I was thinking that I have been in England over a year now and I have seen so little of the country . . ." Walsingham gave me a long look and the words dried up. Since I had agreed to work secretly for Queen Elizabeth's master of intelligence the previous spring I had become skilled at dissembling to everyone around me, but there was no point in lying to Walsingham. Those calm, steady eyes gave you the impression they could penetrate lead. Many a suspected conspirator against the queen had cracked and confessed under that gaze before they were even shown the inside of the Tower of London, with its ingenious array of instruments to assist confession.

"Pilgrimage, is it? Following the example of your patron?" He raised a sardonic eyebrow and tapped the rolled-up letter I had brought from the French ambassador Castelnau on the edge of his desk for emphasis.

Leaning against the mantelpiece, I shifted my weight from one foot to the other and avoided his eye.

"It'll be a book," Sir Philip Sidney observed from his perch on the window seat, where he sat with one of his long legs bent up on the cushions, the other stretched out before him. He had barely aged since I first met him in Padua, I thought; especially when clean-shaven, as he was today, he could pass for nineteen, ten years younger than his true age, with his fair hair that always stuck up in a tuft at the front, no matter how he tried to tame it, and the bright blue eyes that lit up his handsome face whenever he sensed adventure. He was wearing only a lace-edged shirt with his breeches instead of the usual starched ruff that was the fashion among the young men at court, and without his stiff brocaded clothes he seemed less self-conscious. "Bruno wouldn't rouse himself unless it was in pursuit of a book." He waited until I glanced up and gave me a broad wink.

"Or a woman?" Walsingham looked back to me and I could almost fancy a hint of amusement in the twitch of his mouth.

"I understand the cathedral is very fine," I said.

"The oldest in England," Sidney said. "But I don't believe you've developed a sudden fascination for architecture, Bruno. Come on— what's really tempting you to Canterbury?"

I hesitated; Walsingham grew impatient.

"Never mind the cathedral—what are we going to do about *this*?" He brandished the letter again, a shadow of irritation flitting across his face.

We were gathered in the principal secretary's private office at his country home in Barn Elms, some miles along the Thames to the west of the City of London. Since Sidney had married Walsingham's daughter the previous autumn, the young couple had lived at Barn Elms, Sidney's finances being too precarious to support a household of his own at present. From my point of view, the situation was ideal—I could visit my friend and arrange meetings with Walsingham at the same time without arousing the French ambassador's suspicions unduly, though I know it chafed at Sidney to be living in such close quarters with his in-laws.

Behind the wide oak desk, Walsingham sat back and folded his hands together, his gaze focused on the empty fireplace as if deep in thought.

Despite the warmth of the day, he wore his customary suit of plain black wool and the small black skullcap that always made him look a little severe. His was a strong face, with wisdom and sadness written into its lines and the pouches beneath his eyes; there were moments when those eyes seemed to contain the weight of all the kingdom's strife. This was not far from the truth. Walsingham and the intelligence he gathered from his network of informers all over Europe were the queen's last defence against the myriad plots on her life and the security of England. At fifty-two, Walsingham's hair and beard were almost entirely grey now; only his black eyebrows served as a reminder of how he must have looked in his youth. Over the past year I had grown to respect this rational, sober man above any other, though I also feared him a little.

The letter that had so infuriated him contained a grovelling apology from Castelnau on behalf of King Henri of France, who said he could not receive Sidney as a guest in Paris as he was unfortunately about to go on a pilgrimage to Lyon.

"Her Majesty will be livid," Sidney remarked. "I'm quite piqued about it myself—I fancied a trip to Paris." He leaned back into the patch of sun that spilled through the diamond-paned glass and clasped his hands behind his head.

Walsingham frowned.

"Henri of France is weak, though this is not news to us. He knew Her Majesty was not sending Sidney on a social call, but to persuade him to commit French troops to a joint intervention in the Netherlands. I suppose Castelnau thought we would be less likely to shout at you, Bruno?"

"I believe that was his reasoning, Your Honour."

"Well, he can explain himself to the queen face-to-face in due course. France cannot dither on the fence for much longer." He shook his head. "This war against the Spanish in the Netherlands has been a bloody mess for the last twenty years, but the queen is now seriously considering an offer of troops to help the Protestant rebels. If Henri had any conscience he would do the same. Especially since it was his idiot brother who made the situation a hundred times worse," he added, regarding me darkly from under his brows as if I were somehow implicated.

"My uncle the Earl of Leicester has long argued for an English military intervention to aid the Dutch rebels," Sidney said, sitting forward with sudden vigour and clenching his fists. "And I would go with him in an instant. Teach those Spanish curs a lesson they won't forget."

Walsingham looked up sharply. "Don't be too hasty, Philip. That war could easily rumble on for another twenty years, with thousands more deaths on each side. In my opinion, it can't be won, except with a concerted effort by united Protestant forces from all across Europe, and I see little prospect of that."

Sidney sat back, chastened, and I wondered if Walsingham had interpreted his eagerness for a military adventure as a personal slight, a desire to escape his domestic life here at Barn Elms. Moments passed in silence, the only sound a persistent fly buzzing against the window. I watched the sunlight cast patterns on the wooden boards, broken by flickering shadows from the leaves of the trees outside, and waited for someone to speak.

"God's death!" Walsingham cried suddenly, slamming his fist down on the desk so that his tortoiseshell inkwell rattled and Sidney and I started out of our private thoughts. "The Prince of Orange has just been shot on his own stairs as he left his dinner table. Can you imagine how this news has shaken Her Majesty? You will not see her show it in public, but she no longer sleeps. She knows Philip of Spain means her to be next." He took a deep breath and passed a hand over his head as if smoothing his thoughts, looking from me to Sidney like a schoolmaster. "The Catholic forces in Europe are gaining strength. If Spain regains control of the Netherlands, the Protestants there will be massacred. And then Spain will turn his attention to England. Who will France support when that day comes? King Henri *must* talk to us, he cannot hide his head in his rosary beads forever." He pounded his fist on the table again and glared at me, as if he held me responsible for the French king's havering. "Sidney and I saw Saint Bartholomew's Day in Paris with our own eyes, you know," he added, more quietly. "Little children and their grandmothers cut down with swords in their own homes. A thousand lifetimes would not be enough to forget such sights." He closed his eyes, and his features seemed weighed down by sorrow.

Sidney and I glanced at each other; it was rare to see Walsingham ruffled by foreign affairs. Part of his incomparable value to Elizabeth was his faultless composure in any situation. Walsingham is frightened, I thought, and the realisation made me feel for a moment as if the ground had shifted beneath my feet, just as I felt as a child when I first saw my soldier father afraid. The murder of the Prince of Orange had struck at the English government in its tenderest spot. This thought brought me back to the other murder that had preoccupied my thoughts for most of the night.

"I could meet him in Lyon, when his pilgrimage is finished," Sidney offered, resting his feet on the window seat and pulling his knees to his chest, the way a child would sit. "It would be no great trouble to journey to Lyon instead."

Walsingham looked at him again with a sceptical frown. I was certain that he heard, as I did, the note of longing in Sidney's voice. My friend itched for the life of travel and adventure he had known in his youth; the longer he stayed cooped up at Barn Elms and the court, the quicker he would be to volunteer for any mission that offered different horizons, even if it meant going to war.

Walsingham stood, making a show of sorting the papers on his desk into two piles and arranging them neatly side by side.

"Well, we will put that to Castelnau when I summon him to an audience with the queen. Tell him to give it some thought, Bruno. Meanwhile, I am intrigued to hear about *your* pilgrimage. What attraction can Canterbury hold for you, hmm?"

I hesitated again. There was a risk in telling Walsingham the truth; he might forbid me outright, for any number of reasons, and to make the journey against his express wishes would result in my being dismissed from his service, which I could not afford either in terms of income or patronage. But there was a greater risk in not telling him, since he would discover the truth anyway; no one kept secrets from Walsingham, not even the king of Spain or the pope himself. So I stepped forward, as if taking my place on a stage, and gave them a brief précis of the story Sophia had told me, leaving out any details that I thought might compromise her. When I had finished, Sidney was leaning forward, elbows on his knees, staring at me with new admiration, while his father-in-law looked fiercer than ever.

"I remember the rector's daughter," Sidney said, with a lascivious grin. "You sly dog, Bruno."

Walsingham's face remained serious. "You have had your head turned by this woman before, I think, Bruno. What proof have you that she didn't murder her husband?"

I spread my hands wide. "No proof except her word, Your Honour. But I am willing to take the risk."

"So I see. But I'm not sure that I'm willing for you to put yourself in that position." He cupped his chin in his hand, his long fingers stretched across his mouth as he continued to regard me with a thoughtful expression. It was a familiar gesture of his, one he employed when he was weighing up a situation, as if his hand were a mask to hide any telltale emotion. "There was some doubt over her religion, as I recall?"

I paused briefly before looking up and meeting his eye.

"I assure you that she follows no unorthodox religion now, Your Honour." I refrained from adding that she followed no religion at all.

Walsingham scanned my face with his practised gaze, as if for any twitch of a nerve that might betray a lie. My throat felt dry, and I reminded myself that I was still on the same side as Walsingham, even if on this matter I needed to bend the truth a little. What must it be like to be interrogated by him, I wondered. That steely, unswerving stare could break a man's defences even without the threat of torture—a measure he did not shy from in the interest of defending the realm.

This scrutiny seemed to last several minutes until, with a flick of his hand, he dismissed the idea.

"Impossible, anyway. I need to know what is unfolding in France the minute King Henri writes to his ambassador. We can't afford to have you away from the embassy."

I bowed my head and said nothing; from the corner of my eye I noticed Sidney looking at me with concern.

"With respect, Sir Francis—Bruno is not our only source of intelligence from France," he said, his former languor all brushed away and his tone serious. "And he could be useful in Canterbury."

Walsingham looked taken aback at this unexpected mutiny and a small furrow appeared briefly in his brow, but when he realised Sidney was in earnest his expression changed to one of cautious curiosity.

"That is the first time I have heard you express any interest in your constituency." He turned to me. "You know Sidney was returned as Member of Parliament for Kent this year? Though I don't think the people of Kent could accuse him of being over-attentive to their needs."

"Never been," Sidney said, with cheerful insouciance. "Bruno can report back for me. That way I'll be fully briefed in time for the autumn session."

"Bruno would be too conspicuous," Walsingham said, after a moment's reflection.

"Not necessarily," Sidney countered. "No one knows him there. He might have an easier time of it than Harry. Besides, if men of standing in the city are being murdered—you never know . . ."

Walsingham frowned again and I swivelled my head between them, trying to follow this new direction. Sidney glanced across and gave me an almost imperceptible nod of encouragement while Walsingham was deep in thought.

"Canterbury is not an immediate priority," Walsingham said at length, with a tone of finality.

"We do not know how much of a priority it is, since Harry's letters are so patchy," Sidney said, without pausing for breath. "Remember how well Bruno served Her Majesty in Oxford?" he added, with a subtle smile.

"I have not forgotten, Philip. But neither have I forgotten that he helped save England from an invasion of Catholic forces last year, and he did that from within the French embassy."

"I still think Bruno has a talent for making friends and gaining confidences in places neither you nor I nor Harry can go. He may uncover more than a murderer in Canterbury, given the chance." Sidney folded his arms across his chest and sent Walsingham a meaningful look; I recognised the stubborn cast to his jaw and knew that he did not mean to back down in this argument. While I appreciated his willingness to square up to his father-in-law on my behalf, I was not entirely sure what he was petitioning for. Too conspicuous for what?

"Forgive me," I said, as they continued to glare at each other, "but who is Harry?"

Walsingham turned to me, sighed, and waved me towards a chair. Then he pushed his own chair back, stood up from behind his desk, and moved in front of the fireplace, diamonds of bright sunlight patterning his neat black doublet and breeches as he paced, rubbing his beard with his right hand.

"What do you know of Canterbury, Bruno?"

I shrugged. "Only that until the English church broke with Rome, it was one of the most important pilgrim shrines in Europe."

"And one of the most lucrative. The monks of the former priory raked in a fortune from pilgrims through their trade in relics and indulgences, and the rest of the city profited greatly from the vast numbers of the faithful—hostelries, cobblers, farriers, every industry that serves those who travel long distances." He set his mouth in a grim line. "There are a great many in that city who have seen their incomes dwindle and their family's fortunes fall since the shrine was destroyed."

"So there are plenty who hanker after the old faith, I imagine?"

"Exactly. Remember, the shrine was only destroyed in 1538. Forty-six years is not long for a city to forget or forgive such a loss of status. There are plenty still living who carry bitter memories of what the Royal Commissioners did to the abbey and the shrine, and they hand that resentment down to their children and grandchildren."

"Who watch and wait, clinging to the belief that one day soon England will have a Catholic sovereign again, and the shrine of Canterbury will be restored to its former glory," Sidney cut in.

"Except that lately we fear they have been doing more than merely watching and waiting," Walsingham added.

"But the Archbishop of Canterbury is the most senior prelate of the English church," I said. "Surely he is extra careful about religious obedience in his own See?"

"The archbishop is never there," Walsingham replied. "He is too busy politicking in London. The dean and the canons have de facto power in the city, and one never knows how many of them may hold secret loyalties in their hearts."

"One in particular," Sidney added darkly.

"Who has connections to some of those involved in the conspiracy against the queen last autumn." Walsingham looked at me. "Including your friend Lord Henry Howard."

I recalled Sophia saying that her late husband had been a lay canon at the cathedral. If there were plots brewing there, might he have known something of them, given his penchant for secrecy?

"Then there is the cult of the saint," Walsingham added, lowering his voice as if to begin a ghost tale. "Do you know the story of Thomas Becket, Bruno?"

"Of course—we had shrines to him even in Italy. The former archbishop who was murdered in the cathedral."

Walsingham nodded. "He was a great friend of the king—Henry II, this is—who thought he could use Becket to promote his own interests against the Church. But Becket refused the king's demands. In 1170 their quarrel came to a head."

"'Will no one rid me of this turbulent priest?'" Sidney declared, with relish. "So the king said, according to the legend, and four of his knights chose to take that as a direct command."

"They murdered him as he knelt at prayer, if I remember right," I said.

"Struck him down with their swords." Sidney's eyes gleamed; he had not lost his schoolboy fascination for the details of violent death. "Cut off the crown of his head, so his brains spilled all over the stone floor."

"The king was stricken with remorse, of course," Walsingham continued, but I was staring openmouthed at Sidney.

"What did you say?"

He looked surprised.

"They struck him down with a sword."

"After that. His brains."

He made a ghoulish face. "An eyewitness account said the knights trod the whites of his brains across the flagstones, all churned up with his blood. Sorry to upset you, Bruno—I forget you have never been to war." He meant it as a joke, but his smile faded when he saw that I was not laughing with him. Sophia's description of her husband's murder had echoed dimly in my memory, but now it was clear; I had been thinking of the death of Thomas Becket. To cut a man down in the precincts of Canterbury Cathedral in the same manner as its most famous murder victim seemed a grim coincidence. But did it signify any more than that?

"Are you all right, Bruno?" Walsingham asked, leaning closer, his sharp eyes missing nothing.

"Yes, Your Honour." I quickly composed my expression. "I was remembering the story."

He looked at me shrewdly for a moment, then continued.

"Becket's body was buried under the floor of the crypt, for fear it would be stolen. Before long, the tales of miracles began and grew in the telling, as martyrs' legends will, and the monks realised they were sitting on a pot of gold. If they could keep inventing stories of miraculous healing by the power of Saint Thomas's body, the penitent would keep bringing their offerings."

"Until the tomb was destroyed," I said, almost in a whisper.

"Well, that, of course, is the great question." Walsingham folded his arms and looked at me expectantly.

"It was not destroyed?" I turned to him, confused.

"The shrine was smashed, certainly, and all its gold plate and jewels taken for the royal treasury," he said.

"And the bones in the tomb were scattered on the ground with every last fragment crushed to dust," Sidney added.

"Then what is the question?" I asked, looking from one to the other.

"Whose bones were they?" Walsingham smiled as he watched my widening eyes.

"Ah. So the body in the tomb was a substitute?"

"No one knows for certain. But the legend persists that in 1538 some among the priory monks, knowing the sword was about to fall on the cathedral shrine, hid the real body of Becket to save it from destruction. Since then, custody of his bones has passed down to a small number of guardians, who are preserving it in secret until the great Catholic reconquest that many would like to believe is inevitable, when the shrine can be rebuilt. You understand?"

I nodded slowly.

"If people believe the holy relics of Becket are still safe, they have a focus for their resistance."

"Precisely. The bones of Saint Thomas are said to have miraculous powers. Some claim they have even raised the dead. For those who believe, they can certainly raise the city of Canterbury back to prosperity again."

"But you have no idea where the body might be hidden?"

"We have no idea if the story is even true," Walsingham replied, a little curtly, as if I had cast aspersions on his efficiency. "But the fact that it exists at all is a problem. Someone with enough cunning could wave around the thigh bone of an ox, claiming it was Becket's, and there are plenty who would flock to it if it promised them prosperity and salvation."

"And is there a suggestion that this could happen?"

"There are always rumours," he said, with a dismissive wave. "Most of my work is sifting through rumour and speculation, hoping to chance upon a grain of truth like a gem in a dung heap. You have seen for yourself how the English love their superstitions and prophecies." He gave a quiet snort and resumed his pacing. "And Canterbury is significant, in that it is close to the Kent coast. If the city was sympathetic, it could be of great assistance to a French invading force. I have a man there inside the cathedral chapter, Harry Robinson, who keeps an eye on those we suspect of disloyalty and reports back to me."

"But Harry grows old now, Sir Francis, and his eyes and ears are not what they were," Sidney persevered. "And there are many places he cannot tread, given his position." He made his voice persuasive, but Walsingham looked unmoved.

"This is not a good time to be a foreigner in England, Philip. The poor harvest, the threat of plague—and now there will be more refugees arriving from the Netherlands if the Spanish come down harder on them. Her Majesty would not countenance closing our ports to Protestants fleeing persecution, though there are those on the Privy Council who would argue for it. But the feeling among the common people is that there are just too many incomers now, taking bread and work from Englishmen. Resentment stews until it erupts in violence. Saving your presence, Bruno. But you would be a good deal safer if you stay at Salisbury Court."

"Not if the plague comes," Sidney argued, with a note of triumph. "Besides, you cannot rely on Harry to tell you the truth about the money."

"What money?" I looked at Walsingham.

He sighed. "Do you know how much the cathedral foundations of England are worth, Bruno?" I shook my head. "More than thirty-five thousand pounds, put together," he continued. "And what are they? For the most part, that money does nothing but support small communities of learned men to live in fine houses debating theology among themselves over a good dinner. While the poor parishes all around are served by barely literate priests, and superstition and popery are allowed to flourish. England's cathedrals have become no better than the monasteries they replaced. With sufficient evidence of misspending, it would be quite admissible to close some of them down."

"My father-in-law wants to do for the cathedrals what Lord Cromwell in the queen's father's time did for the religious houses," Sidney said, with a mischievous glance at Walsingham. "To pay for the Dutch war."

Walsingham looked exasperated, and seemed about to reprimand him when we heard a sharp knock at the door.

"Yes?" Walsingham snapped, and his steward put his head apologetically through the smallest possible gap.

"There is a gentleman at the door says he must see you, sir."

"What gentleman?"

"He will not give his name, but he says you will want to hear his message."

I was touched to see how Sidney rose instantly, his hand reaching instinctively to his left side, where he would carry his sword if he were more formally dressed.

"Should I come?"

"He has been searched, Sir Philip, and he is not armed," the steward assured him.

Walsingham laughed then, and I read affection in the way he looked at his son-in-law. "Peace, Philip. I have survived this long without you guarding my every step. Besides, there are armed men at the gate."

It was true; given the number of Catholics who would like to run the queen's principal secretary through with a dagger, Walsingham's house was as well guarded as if he were a royal heir.

"Don't go anywhere," he said, with a warning finger directed between us, "while I see whether this messenger brings a gem, or more dung."

As soon as the door had shut, Sidney turned to me and grinned broadly, stretching his legs out on the window seat and clasping his hands behind his head again. "He will let you go, fear not. He only objects to remind you who is in charge, and because he hates the idea of changing plans without due consideration."

"Well, I thank you for your efforts on my behalf," I said, loosening my collar and flapping the material of my shirt to create a semblance of a breeze. "Anyone would think you wanted rid of me," I added, returning his smile. I was curious as to why he would run the risk of displeasing Walsingham in order that I should have my own way.

"Listen, Bruno . . ." He yawned, stretched his long limbs, and fixed me with an earnest look. "It would do you good to get out of London. God knows, I feel the need for it myself. But you have been confined to the embassy for a year, spending all your time with that book of yours. I don't like to see you brooding so much."

"I prefer to call it 'thinking,'" I said. "I am a philosopher, after all."

"Call it what you will, I think you could do with a bit of adventure in every sense. You need to live a little." He gave a crude thrust of his hips and winked.

"I had my share of adventure during my first six months in England. I cheated death more than once. Besides," I added, "I am not the one idling around the house growing fat while my wife embroiders my shirts."

He jumped to his feet and I thought he would feign a punch in my direction, but instead he looked down at himself in alarm, both hands laid flat across his stomach.

"Oh, God, you speak the truth, Bruno. I am grown soft." He appeared so stricken that I had to smile.

"I was only baiting you. But you are happy?"

He glanced at the door, then gave a half shrug. "I have an eighteen-year-old wife and my debts are settled. What man would not be happy?" But there was an edge to his voice that I could not miss.

"And yet you want to go to war?"

"And yet, yes, it seems I have this inexplicable longing to torment the Spanish. I just want to be *doing* something, Bruno, you understand?" He clenched and unclenched his fists and after a moment's silence produced a tight laugh. "But I had better not go to war until I have got myself an heir, had I? Just in case. And there seems no sign of that, despite my best efforts. Anyway," he sat down again, patted his belly, and forced a lightness into his tone, "we were not talking about me. You should get yourself a woman, Bruno, you spend too much time alone. I see how your face changes when you talk about the rector's daughter—no, don't deny it. She matters to you. You've saved her life once already, at the risk of your own."

"Then I abandoned her to a fate she didn't deserve."

"Well then, don't make the same mistake twice," he said, matter-of-factly. "I will work on Walsingham. But be prepared to find yourself hunting for the corpse of a dead saint as well as a murderer."

"Since I seem to have a knack of stumbling over corpses wherever I turn, perhaps I am the man for the job," I said. But again the similarity between Sophia's words and Sidney's pricked at my thoughts, and I pictured the dead man's brains spilling out of his shattered skull across the worn flagstones.

I hoped Sidney's optimism was well founded. Their story about the secret cult of Saint Thomas had piqued my interest in the city of Canterbury yet further, but above all I wanted to visit Sophia at the tavern that evening with good news, to see the colour in her face and hope in her eyes. Two impossible tasks—to find a dead saint and a living murderer—but, as Sidney said, it was better than sitting idle, waiting for fate to unfold its design around you.

Canterbury

Chapter 4

The road out of London towards Kent, known as Watling Street, was still busy with traders and drovers, though the traffic of pilgrims had long since stopped. We set out early, but weeks without rain had baked the unpaved track hard as stone and before we had even reached Southwark my eyes and throat were stinging from the clouds of dust flung up by hooves and cartwheels. Every traveller we passed wore a cloth tied around his or her mouth and nose, and I resolved to buy something similar in whichever town we came to next.

Sophia rode beside me, the peak of her cap pulled low over her face. She had barely spoken since we set out and, though I could see little of her expression, the tense line of her jaw betrayed her anxiety at the journey we were now undertaking. Perhaps, after pinning so much hope on its outcome, she had finally begun to appreciate the grave danger she would face when she rode back through the gates of the city that wanted her arrested for murder. Now and again she would clear her throat and I would turn expectantly, waiting for her to speak, but she would only smile wearily and indicate the dust.

I had hired two strong horses at considerable expense, paid for partly out of the purse Walsingham had sent to cover my stay in Canterbury.

Eventually he had relented, according to the messenger who had been waiting for me in the street outside the embassy with an encrypted letter two days after my visit to Barn Elms. In it Walsingham had included a fully stamped travel licence, without which I would risk arrest for vagrancy, and instructions that I was not to travel under my own name, nor was I to reveal it under any circumstances to anyone in Canterbury except Harry Robinson.

My host, the French ambassador, had been reluctant to let me go, but he acknowledged that he had no power to forbid me from travelling, since I did so (he believed) at his sovereign's expense. He bade me farewell with genuine affection and regret in the midst of his own arrangements for moving the embassy household to the countryside, and I felt a pang of sadness at leaving, though it was outweighed by the delight on Sophia's face as she flung her arms around my neck when I told her the news.

Now she was riding at my side as the sun climbed higher into a sky of untouched blue and the road stretched out before us, and I could not suppress a swelling sense of anticipation. Sophia's future depended on the outcome of this journey; if I could clear her of the charges of murder, I could also clear my own conscience of the guilt that had hung heavy on any thought of her since the events in Oxford. Freed of these burdens, might we not begin again, as if on a fresh page?

There was also the prospect, after almost a year spent at a desk buried in books and astronomical charts, of proving my worth again to Walsingham and the queen. The goodwill of princes was fickle, as every courtier knew, and an ambassador could be recalled or expelled at a moment's notice. I was certain that my own best prospects, if I wanted to go on writing my books without fear of the Inquisition, lay at the court of England, not France, but to ensure myself a future there I needed Walsingham to value me for my own skills and not merely for my useful connection to the French embassy.

Sophia's horse gave an impatient little whinny and tossed its mane, making her start in the saddle. I turned, but she recovered her poise and purposefully ignored my expression of concern, her eyes fixed on the road. She rode competently enough, though she looked uncomfortable astride the horse, her long legs pressed tightly against its sides. I tried not to dwell on this thought. She was unused to riding like a man, I supposed, and the stiffness of her posture in the saddle could give her away. One more small trap to avoid, if her boy's disguise were to hold up. I concentrated my gaze again on the tips of my horse's ears. There would be danger in this for both of us; I was not so caught up in dreams of adventure as to pretend otherwise. If Sophia was recognised within the city walls of Canterbury, she would be arrested to await trial for her husband's murder, and if my search for the evidence to vindicate her did not succeed before the assizes, she would face certain execution. There were other dangers; if the real killer was still in the city and thought he had escaped blame, he would not thank a stranger for asking awkward questions. Anyone who could strike a man down with such force that his brains spilled over the ground would surely not hesitate to dispatch those who seemed overly curious. And as for the legend of Becket's corpse, I could not help but remember that my last attempt to infiltrate the underground Catholic resistance had very nearly ended fatally.

The one consolation was that no one knew me in Canterbury; I was free to present myself in any guise I chose. At my belt I wore a purse of money, with another inside my riding boots and another wrapped in linen shirts in the panniers slung over my saddle. Across my back I carried a leather satchel containing my travel licence and a letter sealed in thick crimson wax with Sidney's coat of arms, recommending me as a visiting scholar to his former tutor, the Reverend Doctor Harry Robinson, and requesting that he make me welcome during my stay in Canterbury. The letter was a cover, naturally, in case I needed to explain myself to any inquisitive authorities along the road. Robinson had never been Sidney's tutor, though he was apparently acquainted with the family of Sidney's mother, but the Sidney coat of arms ought to be sufficient protection against the bullying of petty officials. So that I might travel anonymously if I should be searched, Walsingham had sent a fast rider ahead to Harry Robinson two days earlier with an encrypted letter explaining who I was and the true nature of my business in Canterbury, and requesting Doctor Robinson to assist me for Walsingham's sake as best he could.

What I was to do with Sophia was another matter, I thought, glancing over at her as she rode, head bowed, teeth gritted. I had omitted to mention to either Walsingham or Sidney that I was planning to take her to Canterbury with me—I already knew all the arguments they would make against such folly. My belt held a sheath for the bone-handled knife that had saved my life more than once, and which a more superstitious man might have been tempted to regard as a good-luck charm.

The low, whitewashed taverns and brothels of Southwark, London's most lawless borough, ended abruptly and beyond them the horizon opened up into a wide vista of drained marshland converted to fields now parched yellow, the Kent road threading through the bleached landscape, lost in the shimmering distance. As soon as we left the narrow streets behind, the fetid smells of the city receded to be replaced by the ripe scents of baking earth and warm grass. Despite the dust, I inhaled deeply, tasting for the first time in weeks air that was not thick with the stench of rot and sewage. Swallows looped patterns in the empty sky. Out here, the birdsong was loud and insistent, with a joyful lilt in its cadences, so different from the shrilling of gulls that I had grown used to, living so near the river. Along the way we passed travellers heading in the same direction, many with mules or carts piled with what looked like domestic possessions, and children precariously balanced on top—families fleeing the threat of plague.

"Where will they go?" Sophia wondered, as we passed one straggling group with a small donkey cart and several barefoot children who stared up at us with watchful expressions. One of the older children held a baby in her lap, and I saw Sophia's eyes latch on to it. She spoke so quietly she might almost have been talking to herself.

"To relatives, I suppose."

"What if their relatives will not take them in? Coming from a plague city?"

I shrugged. "Then they will have no choice but to return to London, I imagine."

"To the plague," she whispered, barely audible. She appeared stricken; I watched her for a moment as she turned back to take a last look at the child and the baby. She has a new understanding of what it means to be a refugee, I thought, a raw sympathy with the desperate, those who must throw themselves on the mercy of others. I remembered my own early days as a fugitive on the road to Rome and then north through Italy; how quickly I was exposed to the best and worst of human nature at close quarters. I was taught to survive by bitter experience, but I learned more about compassion in those months than I ever did in thirteen years of prayer and study as a Dominican monk.

"No one has yet seen any sign of plague," I reminded her.

Sophia turned to me with a distant smile, as if seeing me properly for the first time since we had set out.

"So you would not believe there is plague in London until you see a man fall dead of it at your feet, is that it?"

"I would ask for some proof beyond marketplace rumour, if that's what you mean."

"And yet you will believe that the Earth goes around the Sun, and that the fixed stars are not fixed, and the universe is infinite, full of other worlds, all with their own suns? Where is your proof for that?"

"There are calculations based on measurements of the stars—" I began, until I noticed the smile of amusement playing at the corners of her lips. Her chin jutted defiantly. "Very well, you are right—I have no firm proof that there are other worlds. The question is, rather, why should we assume there are not? Is it not arrogance to think we are the only creatures in the cosmos who know how to look up at the night sky and consider our place in it?"

"The Holy Scriptures say nothing about any distant worlds."

"The Holy Scriptures were written by men. If there are people who inhabit other worlds out there"—I gestured with one hand—"it is reasonable to suppose they would have their own writings, no? Perhaps their books have no mention of us."

She smiled, shading her eyes with one hand as she turned to look at me.

"Have you put all this in your book for the queen?"

"Not all, no."

"Just as well."

She laughed briefly before retreating into her pensive silence again, but there had been warmth in that laughter. The brief exchange had offered a glimpse of the old Sophia, as if she had thrown me a scrap of what I had hoped for from this journey, the conversations we had known in Oxford, when I had sensed she wanted to sharpen her intellect against mine. Perhaps I had been a fool to imagine we would have the leisure for that kind of talk, with such a burden weighing on her shoulders. But to a hungry man, even a scrap is enough to quicken his appetite.

BY EVENING WE had reached the small market town of Dartford. As if sensing an end to the journey, the horses slowed their pace along the main street as I scanned the painted signs that hung immobile from the eaves of low timber-framed buildings in search of a suitable inn. The fierce heat of the day had begun to subside, but the air remained heavy and it was a welcome relief to ride into the shade of houses. At the end of the high street we found an inn that must have stood in that spot beside the river for more than a century; I pictured generations of long-dead pilgrims pressing through the wide gates into its yard, footsore and dry-throated, hoping desperately—as was I—that there would be a room.

I pulled my horse gently to a halt outside the gate and turned to Sophia. She had remained unusually quiet through the afternoon's long hours of riding as the sun hammered down, the road affording little respite except for the few brief stretches where we passed between copses of beech trees. Now she raised her head to reveal a face streaked with dirt and sweat, lips crusted with the dust of the road.

"Don't clean yourself up too much," I remarked, quietly. "You look more like a boy with all that filth on you."

She rubbed the back of one hand across her mouth. "I must smell appalling."

"No worse than any other traveller in here."

My body ached from the ride, my thighs, back, and behind sore and stiff from the hours in the saddle, but Sophia had not uttered a word of complaint, though I knew she was unused to riding and I had noticed in the last hour of our journey how she winced whenever she shifted position. My horse gave a little jog on the spot and whinnied with impatience; perhaps he could smell fresh hay from the inn yard. I looked down at my hands on the reins for a moment, then back at Sophia. There was one subject I had not dared to broach with her on the journey, but it could not be avoided any longer.

"I fear we will have to share a room tonight." I had not meant to state it so baldly, but there was no point in being coy. She appeared not the least surprised by this; her expression, beneath the dust, seemed unperturbed.

"I know."

"Because you are travelling as my servant, you see, and it would arouse suspicion if we did not," I continued, speaking too fast. "Besides"— I tapped the purse at my belt—"we must use our money wisely. We don't know how long we will need to make it last."

Sophia nodded, as if all this had been understood and agreed; her calm only made me more flustered. It also brought a sharp pang of rejection; I realised that, for her, the prospect of sharing a room carried none of the implications it held for me. I looked away, sizing up the inn, scratching the damp hair at the back of my neck until I was sure my eyes would not betray me.

"We must take great care from now on, especially in the company of strangers," I said, lowering my voice. "There may be people on the road looking for you, and we do not know if a reward has been offered in Canterbury for your capture. And your disguise is flimsy, to say the least." I looked her up and down. "The best thing you can do is to speak as little as possible. Your voice is more likely to give you away than anything. You can always pretend to be simple."

She smiled, and rolled her shoulders back to ease the stiffness.

"And you, Bruno, must remember to call me Kit. And don't keep looking at me the way a man looks at a woman. If anything is likely to give us away, it is you." She wagged a finger, pretending to chide, but I did not laugh. So she had noticed how I looked at her. Was she as indifferent to that as she sounded, or was she simply better at being practical than I in this situation, as women so often are? "Try to forget you ever knew me as Sophia," she whispered, glancing around to make sure no one could overhear. "You must think of me as a boy all the time now."

"I will do my best. Though you must understand, I don't find that easy."

She smiled again, and behind the exhaustion and the dirt I saw a gleam in those amber eyes that might have been an acknowledgement of my meaning.

"You had better call me by another name too," I added, shifting my weight in the saddle to ease my back. "I travel as Filippo Savolino, scholar of Padua."

"Why? Do you think your fame has reached as far as Canterbury?" The corners of her mouth twitched in amusement.

"Don't laugh—my last book was very popular in Paris. It's not impossible." I smiled. "It's just a precaution. There are people who would like to track me down too, don't forget." And not just the Inquisition, I added silently, thinking of the various enemies I had made in barely more than a year in England.

"Why that name? Is it someone you knew?"

"In a sense. It was the name I used in Italy after I fled the monastery.

Filippo is the name my parents baptised me—I took Giordano when I entered the Dominican order. Savolino was my mother's family name."

She nodded slowly, her eyes narrowed as if reappraising me.

"So all this time, I have never even known your real name. What other secrets do you hide, Filippo?"

"Oh, hundreds. But I do not give them up to just anyone."

I winked, and gently kicked my horse onwards towards the inn yard, pleased to think that I had in some small way intrigued her again.

THAT NIGHT, AFTER an uncomfortable supper in the inn's crowded taproom, eaten almost in silence to avoid any more attention from the travellers, traders, and itinerants who regarded us suspiciously from beneath their brows, Sophia and I faced each other by the light of a candle across the narrow bed of our small room. For the first time all day she took off her cap and scratched violently at her sweat-plastered hair until it stuck up in tufts. An earthenware jug and bowl stood on a washstand under the one grimy window; she poured out a little water and splashed it over her face and neck. I turned abruptly, aware that I had been watching her too intently.

"You take the bed," I said, sitting on it to ease off my boots. The money hidden there had rubbed my ankles raw and I hoped we would reach Canterbury undisturbed so that I could find a more secure hiding place at the house of Doctor Harry Robinson.

The inn was spartan, but by no means among the worst places I had endured as a traveller; it smelled strongly of the sweat of men and horses, but so did every place in this heat. I tugged my shirt out from my breeches and flapped it up and down. The room the innkeeper had given us was at the top of the house and the heat of the day was trapped under the eaves; even with the casement open, the air seemed to crush the breath from you. I glanced down at the small truckle bed that pulled out from under the main bed, meant for a servant to sleep alongside his master. I decided I would sleep in my underhose; even if Sophia had not been there, I had learned from experience that it was never wise to go to bed entirely naked in a roadside inn, however hot it might be. You never knew when you might need to leap to your feet at a moment's notice.

I unbuckled the belt holding my purse and the bone-handled knife and laid them carefully on the floor before turning back to look at her. Her hair was spiked at the front from the water and her efforts at washing had merely succeeded in spreading the dust over her face in different patterns, giving her an endearingly impish look. She met my eyes, then wrapped her arms around herself awkwardly before glancing across the room. Her gaze fell on a cracked piss-pot in the corner and immediately I understood.

"I think I will just go and check on the horses," I said quickly, pulling my boots back on. Poor Sophia—this was one of the hardest parts about her disguise, and the one most likely to betray her, I thought—that she could not piss like a man. Earlier in the day I had had to wait by the side of the road holding her horse's bridle while she looked for a spot in some trees, away from the eyes of passersby. More than her voice, we must take care that her refusal to relieve herself on any street corner alongside other boys did not attract undue attention. "Latch the door behind me and don't open it to anyone," I added, standing up. I tucked the knife into the waist of my breeches, just in case. We had drawn stares in the taproom, I supposed because between us we looked so exotic. One day's ride in the sun had tanned my Italian skin the colour of olivewood, making me look yet more foreign, and Sophia, for all her filthy clothes, was so striking as to make any man look twice. Even if no one suspected she was a woman, there were always plenty of men in any roadside tavern whose tastes were broad enough to include a pretty, soft-skinned boy.

Outside in the courtyard the day's heat had ebbed away, leaving cool shadows and a gentle night breeze. It would be more comfortable to sleep out here, I thought, picturing Sophia lying alongside me among the hay bales stacked against the wall of the stable, under the stars. I wandered across to the open door of the stable building, to give her time to finish her ablutions in private, exchanged a few words with the stable-boy, gave him a groat to make sure our horses were well brushed down and fed for the morning, and strolled back slowly towards the inn, glancing up at the windows, some still lit by the flickering amber glow of candles. Occasionally the shadow of a figure would cross in front of the casement, and I looked up at the row of gabled windows in the attic storey, trying to work out which was ours. In one of those upper rooms, Sophia was undressing, unbinding her breasts, stretching out her long, aching limbs on the coarse sheets. I shook my head and tried to discipline my wayward thoughts. This business in Canterbury would be difficult enough without deliberately tormenting myself over Sophia and fantasies of what I could not—yet—have. The surest way to secure her trust and affection was to perform the role she required of me, which for the moment was that of trusted friend.

Between the bullying husband and his drunken, lusty son, she had seen enough of men whose only interest was what they could take from her. She had come to me because she believed I was different, and I wished her to see that she was right. Though I was a man like any other, I had learned during the years I lived as a monk to master the urges of the body that prove such a powerful distraction to men, especially those trying to concentrate on the life of the mind or of the spirit. As a sixteen-year-old novice I had served for a little time in the infirmary as assistant to the physician, and there I saw some among my brother Dominicans writhing in pain, burning up from within, clawing at festering sores, screaming every time they passed blood-streaked water, or sinking towards death in the incoherent ravings of madmen, all because of an ill-judged tumble with a whore or a serving girl. I had asked the brother physician what had brought these men—some of them not much older than me—to such a pass. "*Sin,*" he had replied emphatically, through clenched teeth. No further explanation was needed. These early lessons in the price to be paid for the fierce cravings of desire had led me to value my health and my sanity above the insistent clamour of my body;

it was partly thanks to those poor tortured souls that I had chosen to devote myself to philosophy and worked hard to acquire the discipline needed to live the life of the mind. But Sophia was something different altogether; from the first moment I had seen her, across her father's dinner table in Oxford, I had found her impossible to forget. Her return to me had all the irresistible force of an event decreed by the stars—or so I could almost believe.

I laughed drily at myself as I stopped to piss against a wall of the courtyard.

"Be another hot one tomorrow."

I looked up; the speaker was a stocky man also relieving himself a few yards along from me. He nodded up at the cloudless sky.

"I think you are right," I said, finishing my business and retying my breeches.

"We'll have no harvest at all if we don't get some rain soon," he remarked, his stream still splashing vigorously against the stones. His words were slurred from drink and he swayed slightly as he continued to let loose the evening's beer. I could not see his face in the half-light. Across the yard a horse whinnied, making me start. "Then there'll be riots, you'll see. Where you from, then?"

"Naples." I took a step towards the inn, then added, "Italy," when I saw there was no response. I had no wish to engage in small talk with this fellow, particularly about myself, but neither did I wish to give offence. Sophia and I were vulnerable enough without deliberately putting ourselves on the wrong side of fellow travellers.

"And the boy? What is he, your servant?"

It was a casual question, thrown over his shoulder as he finished, shook off the last drops, and tied himself away, but immediately I felt myself tense and the skin on my neck prickled. Whoever he was, he must have been watching us earlier and was sober enough to have recognised me. More than that, he had taken notice of Sophia.

"My assistant." I answered him coolly enough, but my fists were clenched at my sides.

"Assistant, is it?" He laughed as he lurched towards me in the direction of the inn's rear door. To my ear it sounded lascivious, though I knew I may have been oversensitive. "What's he assist you with, then?"

"My business is books."

"Oh, aye? Do you get much trade?"

"I make a living."

Fortunately, it seemed he had little more to contribute on the subject of the book trade. He fell clumsily into step beside me as I made for the tavern door.

"Come and have a game of cards with us, my friend, you and your assistant. Too hot to sleep, night like this." He clapped me on the shoulder; instinctively I flinched, though he was too drunk to notice.

"I thank you," I said, moving a step away as we reached the threshold, "but we must make an early start tomorrow. Besides," I added, trying to keep my tone light, "I'm afraid I am a hopeless card player, no matter what the game."

"You'd be all the more welcome at our table, then," he said, with a wheezing laugh that showed a few remaining brown stumps of teeth. I smiled and bade him good night, only realising as I climbed the stairs how I had been holding my breath. The man's curiosity had seemed harmless enough, but it was further proof that Sophia and I made an odd sight travelling together, and one that attracted the eyes of strangers. We would need to be vigilant at every moment; one careless word or gesture, one instant of forgetting who we were supposed to be or failing to keep an eye over our shoulders, and our mission in Canterbury might be over before we even reached the city walls.

I gave a soft tap at the door. After a moment, I heard the lifting of the latch and slipped through into the warm darkness. The candles had been blown out; Sophia was standing behind the door, wrapped in a sheet from the bed. In the dim light from the open casement I saw that her shoulders were bare. Quickly I turned away. The room smelled faintly of sweat and something sharper, the private scent of a woman. I pulled my shirt over my head and lay down on the straw pallet, leaving my breeches on to hide my gently swelling erection, even though I knew she could see nothing in the soft blur of shadows.

"Tomorrow, as we ride," I murmured, partly to distract myself, and partly to confirm, for my own benefit, that she was still awake, still conscious of my presence as I was of hers, "we must set to work. I need you to tell me as much as you can remember about your husband, every detail of his work, his habits, his friends, his enemies, his religion. No matter how insignificant it may seem. If we are to clear your name, we must first learn who else could have gained from his death."

"His *religion?*" Through the dark, I could picture the quizzical expression that accompanied her tone; the slight wrinkling of the nose, the dip of the brows. "He was a lay canon of the cathedral, as I told you. Though his sense of Christian duty didn't go beyond securing a position of influence for himself, as you also know."

"But you and I know very well that a man's public face does not always reflect the faith of his heart," I whispered back. She remained silent. "Canterbury, like Oxford, is a place of tangled religious loyalties. The cult of the saint still holds many in thrall, I am told. And if your husband was a man with secrets, it's not impossible that they involved matters of faith. It is, after all, a city with religion soaked into its stones."

"My husband thought it all superstitious nonsense, the saint and the shrine," she said, dismissively. "He regarded himself as a man of reason. Religion for him was a question of civic duty and social advancement. Whatever his secrets, I doubt they were concerned with faith."

Since her voice implied that this was the last word on the subject, I turned over uncomfortably and closed my eyes. A timber creaked outside the room and I sat bolt upright, hand on my knife, muscles tensed. But whether it was a footfall or merely the old building shifting in its sleep, there was only silence. Sophia laughed softly.

"Sleep, Bruno. It's like having a watchdog in the room."

I lay back, staring at the ceiling, one hand still resting lightly on the knife. A watchdog. It was how I felt. The room settled into the muffled stillness of night. Beyond the casement, the lonely cry of an owl floated through the dark. Sophia's breathing grew deeper and more regular, almost lulling me out of my watchfulness until, long after I thought she was asleep, I heard her whisper, "Bruno?"

"Yes?"

"From now on," she said, "let us not speak about Oxford. The past is gone. I was someone else then. I want to forget everything that happened there. Those terrible murders," she added, after a while, barely audible. "And then my husband. Violent death seems to touch everyone who comes near me."

There was a slight break in her voice, a note of despair that restrained me from telling her not to exaggerate. Sophia had known more than her share of misfortune in her young life, but this century is indifferent in its cruelty, and we are taught to regard suffering as our due. Her father and her aunt would no doubt say that she had been the author of her own troubles, that they were a punishment from God because she would not be submissive as a woman should. Someone with less orthodox views—someone like me, for example—might more generously suggest that Sophia's only fault was to be born with intelligence, an enquiring mind, and a yearning for independence in a world where those qualities are seen as positively dangerous in anyone, let alone a girl. There was only one woman in England who had the freedom to indulge her intellect and her passion, and even her throne could not protect her from daily threats upon her life. I said none of this.

"But your past has shaped who you are." I turned onto my side so that I was facing her bed; despite the darkness, I knew she was looking at me. "You carry it with you, even if you would rather not."

"No." She spoke firmly. "I want only to begin again, once this is all over. I will be no one's daughter, no one's mother, no one's sister, no one's wife. Everyone has gone. I wish to live like you, Bruno, with no ties. It must be a wonderful thing, to have such freedom."

I said nothing. She was twenty years old; how could I make her understand that exile was not freedom, that solitude was not necessarily liberty? I was tired of travelling; the yearning to belong somewhere, to rest in the knowledge of a secure position, seemed to grow stronger with every year that passed. What she saw as my freedom had been forced on me by the Roman Inquisition.

I shifted again onto my back, the straw pricking at my skin through the thin sheet, and watched the frail moonlight slowly spread across the ceiling. Sophia's breathing slowed again; occasionally she gave a little moan in her sleep, a reminder of her warm presence, while I lay awake, tormented and watchful, my ears straining for any sound of a tread on the stairs.

Chapter 5

We reached Canterbury by noon on the fourth day. Alone, I could have made the journey in less time, but Sophia was increasingly suffering the pains of long hours on horseback, and though she never complained, I reasoned it was better to take the journey at a slower pace, for her sake and for the horses'. My anxiety only increased each time we rode into an inn yard at dusk. The second night we spent in Rochester, a small town straddling the river estuary, where I bought some cloth and had it cut into makeshift kerchiefs we could tie around our faces to keep from breathing the dust. The third night we stopped in a village by the name of Faversham, where the clamour of the gulls and cool salt breeze made me long for the nearby sea. That night, she stood by the open window for a long time after I had blown out the candle, looking into the blue-black distance without speaking; when I tentatively approached and she turned, I realised that she was crying. I didn't ask why, merely allowed her to rest her forehead against my shoulder until the moment passed. Before she got into bed, she touched my hand lightly, twining her fingers with mine for the space of a breath, as if to say thank you. Neither of us spoke, but I felt a surge of hope as I stretched out uncomfortably on my pallet, as if something essential had been communicated without the need for words.

We kept to ourselves, spoke as little as possible in the company of strangers, and survived the three nights and the hard ride with few unwelcome attentions. In every village where we broke our journey to water the horses and buy bread, rumours of the plague travelled before us, quick as flames through dry tinder; the old pilgrim road crawled with refugees with few belongings and less money, and the taverns were closing their doors to many. The townspeople wanted as little as possible to do with travellers from London; we were fortunate that money still spoke with a voice louder than fear.

A mile or so outside the walls of Canterbury we stopped in the village of Harbledown to let the horses drink. It was a pretty enough place, surrounded by orchards, no more than a few houses straggling along a single street which rose steeply towards the city in the distance. We led the horses off the road by an old almshouse and found a spot in the shade to sit down and prepare ourselves for the riskiest part of our journey. My head ached and my throat was gritty with dust, despite the kerchief.

"If the plague fears have reached Canterbury, we may find them more vigilant than usual at the gates," I said, passing Sophia a leather bottle of small beer, warm now from hanging by my side along the road, but better than nothing. "Though the fact that everyone has a cloth tied around their face ought to work to our advantage. If they stop us, just keep your eyes down, your cap low over your face, and your mouth shut. We can pretend you are a mute. You shouldn't find that too hard," I couldn't help adding, at the sight of her sullen expression.

She reached for the bottle, held my gaze for a long moment, enough to be sure that I knew she was still angry with me, then took a swig and looked pointedly away, squinting into the sun above the trees. For the best part of an hour she had refused to speak, ever since I had broken the news to her that morning that she would not be able to stay with me in Canterbury and would need to presume again on the hospitality of her Huguenot friends. I had expected her to be displeased by the idea, knowing she would fear for their safety, but I had not anticipated the flash of fury it provoked. She had railed at me, accusing me of reneging on my promise to help her, until I pointed out sharply that we were not the only travellers on the road and that shrieking like a girl-child was the best way to give herself up before we even reached the gates. She had fallen silent after that and remained so, with the occasional simmering glance from beneath her cap, until we stopped.

Now she propped herself up on one elbow and regarded me dispassionately before offering me the bottle. I took a brief sip and winced; my stomach had been feeling queasy since I first awoke and the heat of the day was not improving the symptoms.

"What if the French houses have been searched, looking for me?" Sophia said. "Someone will have told the constables that I was friends with Olivier, I am sure of it."

"Then you should be all the safer. You have been gone from Canterbury a fortnight; if the authorities have already searched the city, they will not expect you to return."

"I still don't see why I can't come with you, if I am supposed to be your servant." She tore up a clump of grass with some force, then flung it away as if she found it offensive.

"Because innkeepers, and especially their wives, are the most professionally inquisitive people in all creation," I said impatiently. "Their whole business is to observe and speculate on the travellers who come through their doors. We've been lucky so far, but any more than one night in the same hostel and someone will deduce right away that Kit is not what he claims to be. No." I shook my head. "Lie low with the Huguenots. I will be enough of a curiosity on my own." I rubbed a hand across my chin; four days' growth of dark beard only reinforced the foreignness of my appearance, especially now that the sun had tanned my face to a colour it had not been since I was a boy running free all day on the slopes of Monte Cicada. My hair, too, had been neglected over the past weeks when I was preoccupied with finishing my book; I could not remember the last time I paid a visit to the barber, and it had grown so that it fell across my eyes at the front and curled over my collar at the back. "One of my first tasks once we are inside the city gates must be to get a shave and a haircut," I complained, pushing my fringe back from my face.

"You look better with no beard," she remarked, her voice brighter. "Younger, I mean. It suits you."

I glanced up, surprised, but she remained preoccupied with plucking blades of grass and scattering them around her and did not look at me. I was reminded again of how little I understood a woman like Sophia. I hardly considered myself an expert on the ways of women, but it had been eight years since I cast off my Dominican habit and with it my vows, and at the court of Paris I was given ample opportunity to observe the flirting and simpering of fashionable ladies at close quarters. Sophia had learned none of these wiles, yet her artless frankness was far more disarming; she could offer a compliment as casually as remarking on the weather and every time, like a fool, I allowed it to quicken a little spark of hope.

"It's a pity we can't get you a beard somehow," I said, after a moment's silence, watching how the shadow of the leaves fell across her smooth cheek. "It would help your concealment no end."

"My aunt had the beginnings of one," she said, looking up with an unexpected grin. "She was forever trying to pluck hairs from her chin. I suppose we can't wait for me to reach her age."

"If we don't make your disguise convincing, you won't live to reach her age," I said, and immediately regretted it; her smile vanished on the instant and her eyes clouded again. She returned to pulling up the grass with renewed force.

"Are you afraid?" I said.

She looked directly at me then and held my gaze in those expression-less, honey-coloured eyes.

"Canterbury is a small city, as you'll see. Now that we are so close to its walls, I wonder what I was thinking, coming back." She passed a hand across her brow and sank onto her elbows. "But this place has never been anything other than a prison to me since I was first brought through its gates. I don't suppose a real prison would be all that different."

The careless note in her voice was betrayed by the tightness around her mouth, the way she pressed her lips into a white line. I remembered her silent tears in Faversham. She was afraid, but she was damned if she was going to let me see it. I glanced up at the sky, where a single skein of pale cloud interrupted the eggshell blue.

"Well, then," I said, levering myself to my feet. "Into the lion's den."

THE VAST CIRCULAR towers of the city's West Gate loomed up ahead of us on the road, solid and forbidding in dark, flint-studded stone, set in the thick walls like the entrance to a fortress and visible from some distance away. To either side the road was lined with modest buildings of wood and plaster. We crossed a little stone bridge over a rivulet just before the gate and as we followed the road into the cool shadow of its great central archway I felt my skin rise in gooseflesh and my bowels clench. Now that we were on the threshold, I acknowledged the truth in Sophia's words; if we should be stopped here, I had as good as led her to her death in my eagerness to save her. A foreigner and a fugitive; what chance did we have of passing unnoticed in a small English city with an entrenched suspicion of outsiders? I glanced across at Sophia, but could see little of her face between the peak of her cap and the cloth she pulled up tighter over her nose. I did likewise, and nudged the horse onward under the gate.

But the guard at the gate gave only a cursory glance to my travel licence before waving us through; his main concern seemed to be keeping the flow of traffic moving, though I felt every muscle tense with the expectation of a hand on the reins at any moment. The greatest impediment to our free movement came from the jostling vegetable carts and the press of people carrying baskets and bundles in both directions through the gate, most of whom, I noticed, also had cloths tied around their faces. Perhaps the citizens of Canterbury were less alarmist about the plague rumours, or perhaps the necessity of making a living prevented them from being too picky about incomers. A trickle of sweat ran down my open collar and I tugged it away from my skin with one finger, my eyes still roving the street for any sign of danger.

We found ourselves at the end of a thoroughfare that ran between lines of two- and three-storey houses in the English style, of white plaster and dark timber frames, each upper storey overhanging the one below, so that it seemed the buildings were leaning inwards in order to share some gossip with those opposite. On both sides the ground floors of these buildings had their shutters up and their windows employed as street counters from which to sell their wares; we passed chandlers, ironmongers, drapers, shoemakers, and apothecaries, each shop with its own distinctive smell, all clamouring for the attention of passersby. Barefoot children chased each other, laughing, through the crowds, dodging the mounds of horse dung and refuse and amusing themselves by throwing odd vegetables that had fallen from the carts at stray dogs. Washing had been hung to dry from the windows of the upper storeys, though the closeness of the buildings kept the street shaded. On every corner the painted signs of inns or taverns creaked above doorways, a reminder of the days when Canterbury had played host to travelling pilgrims in their thousands, though many of the hostelries appeared run-down and neglected now, their plaster cracked and paint forlornly blistered. Outside them, old men lolled on wooden benches, jugs of beer in their hands, fanning themselves and watching the life of the street. Passing too close to strangers, I caught the smell of sour sweat. I craned my head back; above the line of crooked rooftops to my left rose the bell tower of the famous cathedral, standing sentinel over the city.

"Turn left," a voice behind me growled. I turned sharply, and saw Sophia motioning to me with her eyes. "Left here," she said again, this gruffness apparently an attempt at sounding masculine.

I almost laughed, but did my best to swallow it and urged the horse to the side of the street down a narrow alleyway between houses. Towards the far end of this lane the dwellings grew smaller and poorer, but along the right-hand side where the lane bordered the river stood a row of compact three-storey houses joined together. Their frontage was neat and clean, the steps by the front doors swept free of refuse and to each side of the door earthenware pots brimmed with red flowers. I rode as far as I could go, until the lane petered out in a cluster of shabby cottages. Here I turned the horse in a tight circle and looked expectantly at Sophia.

"The white houses near the road—those are the weavers' houses," she hissed. "The middle door. Ask for Olivier Fleury."

I nodded briskly, dismounted, and handed her my horse's reins. The little street was empty, but I glanced around uneasily, imagining curious eyes behind the glass of every window. Surely it was not unusual for the French weavers to receive visitors, I told myself; I must shake off this conviction that everyone regarded us as suspicious or I would cause them to do so by my behaviour.

Stiffly I approached the low doorway of the middle house and knocked, pulling the cloth down from my face with the other hand as I did so. Through the open windows I could hear sounds of industry: the rhythmic clicking of wood against wood, a clanking of metal, the odd muted voice, sharp, as if giving instruction or calling out some demand. A hot, heavy smell drifted out; steam and wet wool and some other ingredient I could not identify. I knocked again and eventually the door was opened and I jumped back in surprise.

A tall, wiry youth, barely into his twenties, stood in the doorway, his shirtsleeves rolled to the elbow. He looked at me, suspicion in his eyes. There was a faint hint of arrogance in his expression that sowed a seed of dislike in me. Nonetheless, I smiled graciously.

"Olivier Fleury?"

"Who wants him?"

He spoke in French, so I replied in kind.

"An old friend."

He considered me for a moment.

"I have never seen you before, monsieur."

He possessed that combination of sullen carelessness and self-regard that I had observed often among the French courtiers, though it seemed misplaced in the son of émigré weavers. But if I was honest, I found myself disliking this Olivier because, despite his sulky expression, he was undeniably handsome. His dark brown hair was cropped short and his skin was tanned, making his blue eyes appear all the more vivid. He had a manner of looking at you from under hooded lids with his head tilted back that implied disdain, and his full lips were set in a permanent pout. I could see how a young woman of twenty, trapped in a cruel marriage, might choose to seek solace in the company of a sympathetic youth with a face like this. Though I was unsure of the details of their friendship, I wished I did not have to deliver Sophia directly into his home, and fleetingly considered the possibility of taking her to stay with me at the inn instead. Reluctantly, I was obliged to concede that her safety was more important than my jealousy.

"The friend I speak of is a young man of your acquaintance recently returned from London, on personal business." I gave him a meaningful look; his blue eyes registered first confusion, then slowly widened in disbelief as he leaned forward on the step, bunching his apron in his fist, his gaze anxiously searching the street to left and right. I nodded to my left; he pulled the door to behind him and followed me around the bend in the lane to where Sophia sat, still mounted, holding my horse by his reins.

If there had been some connection deeper than friendship between them, however, their initial response gave no indication of it. Olivier stared up at the ragged figure on the horse, her face barely visible between the cloth mask and the cap, then took a step backwards with a minute shake of his head, as if trying to deny to himself the evidence of his own eyes. Sophia merely returned his look, her eyes glints of light in the shadow that obscured her expression. Olivier's frown of confusion hardened into anger as she slid awkwardly from the saddle and led her horse and mine a few paces towards us.

"Why is she here?" Olivier hissed through bared teeth, turning to me with a flash of fury. "This is madness."

"There was no choice," I began, but it was clear he wasn't listening. He seemed genuinely afraid as he fixed his eyes again on Sophia.

"Olivier," Sophia whispered, stepping closer. "This is my friend Bruno. He is going to find my husband's killer and clear my name. But I had to come back to help him."

She raised her eyebrows and nodded earnestly, as if this might persuade him. Olivier pushed both hands through his hair. He puffed out his cheeks and exhaled slowly, still staring at her as if she were insane.

"Who else knows you are here?" he asked her, in English.

"We have only just this moment ridden through the city gate," I offered.

He shook his head again and glanced quickly up the lane.

"Get inside the house, then, before anyone sees you. This will kill my mother, you know," he added in French, turning his scowl on me, as if it were all my fault.

"I am sorry for any distress to your family," I said, feeling that to placate him would aid us best. "But she would not be safe anywhere else."

"She would be safe in London," he hissed back. "That was the whole point."

"Better you don't fight about it in the street," Sophia murmured, with remarkable calm, handing me the halters of both horses as she slipped past Olivier into the doorway of his house. He glared at me again.

"For one night, then. But we will speak further."

"I would be glad to, if you tell me where to find you," I said, still trying to deflect his anger with civility. I could understand how disconcerted he must feel, having thought he was free of any danger from his association with Sophia; to conceal a fugitive criminal was, as I understood the English law, itself a hanging offence. For a refugee family who had already escaped religious persecution, sought a quiet life, and risked their good name once out of kindness, being expected to repeat that same sacrifice might seem an excessive test of their faith. If I had been gratified at first to see that neither Sophia nor Olivier showed any obvious pleasure at being reunited, such sentiments were quickly supplanted by a sense of shame at my own triviality.

"Come back tomorrow morning," he muttered, darting another nervous glance over my shoulder, towards the end of the lane and the main street beyond. "My family and I will decide what to do by then."

"Tomorrow, then. And you take care of her," I added, just to let the boy know that I too had a vested interest. He took a step closer; he was taller than I, and drew himself up to emphasise this advantage.

"We all want to keep her safe, monsieur. My family and friends risked everything to get her away from this place. Now you bring her back." He brought his face closer to mine and glared from beneath lowered brows, so fiercely it seemed he hoped I would burn up from the force of his eyes. "As if we did not have enough grief here already." Then he turned and disappeared inside the house, slamming the door behind him.

I looked around carefully at the windows of the neighbouring houses in case anyone had witnessed our exchange, but there was no obvious sign of movement. Even so, I felt distinctly uneasy as I led the horses back towards the main street, as if hostile eyes were following me, marking my steps.

I STABLED THE horses at the Cheker of Hope Inn, a great sprawling place that occupied most of the corner between the High Street, as I learned the main thoroughfare was called, and Mercery Lane, a smaller street that led towards the cathedral. The inn was one of the few that still seemed to attract a healthy trade; Sophia had recommended it because of its size; it was three storeys high, and built around a wide yard that often hosted performances by companies of travelling players. Despite my accent, the landlady—a heavily rouged woman in her forties—gave me an appreciative look when I secured the room; from the way her eyes travelled over me, I gathered she was pleased with more than the sight of the coins in my purse. I deflected her questions as politely as I could, hoping that here, with more travellers coming and going, I might enjoy greater anonymity than in the smaller places we had stayed in along the road, where everyone wants to know your business.

My stomach still felt dangerously unsettled—entirely my own fault, I suspected. The heat of the room during the previous night had brought on such a thirst that in desperation I had drunk some of the water left in a pitcher on the window ledge for washing. Experience had taught me not to touch any water in England unless you have watched it come fresh from a spring or a well with your own eyes, but I had ignored good sense and now I was paying the price for it. With the horses safely stabled I was at liberty to explore the city on foot, and as I remembered noticing an apothecary's sign along the High Street when we had ridden through the town, I decided to pay the shop a visit in the hope of purchasing something to ease my digestion before I attempted to introduce myself to Harry Robinson.

Over the door a painted sign showed the serpent coiled around a staff that denoted the apothecary's trade; beside it the name Wm. Fitch. A bell chimed above the door as I entered and the front room was surprisingly cool inside, shaded from the heat of the day by the overhanging eaves, its small casements open to a vague breath of air from the street. I inhaled the sour-sweet smell that reminded me for a poignant moment of the distillery belonging to my friend Doctor Dee; a mixture of leaves and spices and bitter concoctions preserved in spirits. The apothecary was nowhere in sight so I closed the door behind me and called out a greeting as my gaze wandered over the shelves and cabinets lining the walls from floor to ceiling. Here great glass conical flasks containing potions and cordials in lurid colours vied for space beside earthenware jars of tinctures and pots stuffed with the raw ingredients for poultices and infusions, all balanced precariously alongside bunches of dried herbs, dog-eared books, and other curiosities that may or may not have belonged to the man's trade (on one shelf, a piccolo; on another, the skull of a ram). On the ware bench in front of me, a pestle and mortar containing a greenish paste had been left as if in mid-preparation. Next to it stood a little brass balance, its weights scattered round about beside a quill and inkwell. I was peering up at one jar, trying to ascertain whether it really did contain a human finger, when the door at the back of the shop opened and a small, florid-faced man with receding hair appeared in a cloud of steam, wiping his hands on his smock. He flapped his hand as if to disperse the humid air.

"Sorry about that," he said cheerfully, nodding towards the back room. "Had to check on my distillery. It's like a Roman bathhouse in there today." He paused to mop sweat from his forehead with a sleeve. "I'm a firm believer that steam purges the body of excess heat, though there are those who believe it has the opposite effect. Now, what can I do for you, sir? You have a choleric look about you—" He waved a finger to indicate my face. "Something to balance the humours, perhaps?"

"I'm just hot," I said, pushing my damp hair back from my face.

"Ah, you are not English!" he exclaimed, his eyes lighting up at the sound of my accent. "But not French either, I venture? Spanish, perhaps? Now, your Spaniards are naturally choleric, much more so than your Englishman, whose native condition tends towards the phlegmatic—"

"Italian," I cut in. "And I have an upset stomach, though I think that has less to do with my birthplace than with drinking stale water. I was hoping you might have some infusion of mint leaves?"

"My dear signor, I can do better than that," he beamed, grasping a little wooden ladder that leaned against the back shelves and moving it to the cabinet to my left. "I can offer you a most efficacious decoction of my own devising for disorders of the stomach, combining the benefits of mint leaf with hartshorn, syrup of violets, rose water, and syrup of red poppies. You will be thoroughly purged both upwards and downwards, I promise."

"It sounds tempting. But I'd prefer the mint leaves, I think."

"Really?" He paused, a bottle of something thick and dark green held aloft. When I shook my head firmly, he replaced it on the shelf with a theatrical sigh. "Ah, you disappoint me, signor," he said, descending and shuffling his ladder to the right. His hand hovered over the shelves for a moment before plucking down a small packet, which he laid on the ware bench and began to unwrap. "But you are right, it is a brave man or a desperate one who will experiment on himself with a stranger's cures. I tell you what—if you are staying in Canterbury awhile and your problems do not resolve themselves, please do me the honour of coming back and at least giving my cordial a chance. I'll do you a special price. Meanwhile you may ask around for testimony—I provide for some of the highest men in the city." He nodded enthusiastically. "Yes, including the physician to the dean and the mayor. Ask who you like—there's not a man of means in these parts who doesn't swear by Will Fitch's remedies."

I was beginning to like this Fitch, despite the fact that I had never met an apothecary who was not also a terrible fraud, and I suspected this one to be no different. If ever their remedies did work, it was entirely by lucky chance or guesswork; more often they knowingly sold wholly useless concoctions to the poor and credulous, who were too easily persuaded that the higher the price of a medicine, the more effective it would be.

"The dean's own physician?" I affected to look impressed. "No doubt aldermen and magistrates of the city too, eh?"

He puffed out his chest and patted it with the flat of his hand.

"Doctor Sykes, he's physician to them all—trained in Leibzig, you know—and he won't buy his supplies anywhere else but my shop. Mind you," he added, with another heavy sigh, "there's some things even he can't cure. Our poor magistrate was horribly murdered not a month past and they have not appointed a new one yet, nor will they in time for the assizes. Mayor Fitzwalter has his hands full trying to do the job of two men preparing for the visit of the queen's justice next week. You'll have noticed the constables on every corner." I had not, but he did not wait for me to respond, shaking his head as if in sorrow at the state of the world. "Forgive me—I have a tendency to run on, and we are all much preoccupied with our civic affairs at the moment."

"I quite understand—murder is no small matter. Though I suppose that is a hazard of being a magistrate," I said, conversationally, as I watched him measure a quantity of dried leaves in his little scales. "The family of some felon he had convicted, out for revenge, I guess."

"Ah, not in this case," Fitch said, leaning closer over the bench, his eyes bright. "It was the wife—all of Canterbury knows it. She ran away the very same day and took a good deal of his money too."

"Really? What reason would she have to kill him?"

He put his head on one side and looked at me oddly, then gave a bleat of laughter.

"From that remark, I deduce you have no wife, signor." He laughed again at his own joke, then shrugged. "They say she had a lover, but then they always like to say that. Pretty thing, she was. But she's led the law a merry dance, I can tell you—they've had the hue and cry out for her since it happened, but they can't find so much as a hair of her head. No, she's long gone—over the water, if she's any sense." He grinned, as if delighted by the audacity of the crime. "Now—do you want to take the leaves as they are or shall I make you up an infusion while you're here? If you take it here, I'll add a few fennel seeds—good against cramps of the gut. I have some spring water heating in the back room, it won't take a moment."

"Thank you, I'd be grateful," I said, thinking that the man's evident love of gossip could prove useful. He emptied the mint leaves into a small dish and disappeared through the door into the back of the shop. I wiped a trickle of sweat from my temples with the sleeve of my shirt and waited. Eventually he emerged carrying an earthenware beaker wrapped in a cloth.

"Careful, it's hot. That's sixpence for the whole—I haven't charged you for the water," he added.

I fished in my purse for the appropriate coin, which he examined closely, holding it up to the light.

"No offence," he said, seeing me watching, "but we get all sorts of foreign types passing through from the Kentish ports, and I can't trade with their coins. Not that I have anything against you lot, though many do. I like variety—keeps life interesting, doesn't it?" He tucked the coin into a moneybag at his belt. "I'd have liked to travel myself, if I'd had the means." He reached to a shelf under the bench and produced a large ledger, which he opened and thumbed through to the current page. Dipping the pen in the ink, he recorded the transaction meticulously. "May I take your name?"

"My name?"

I must have reacted more suspiciously than I intended, because he looked taken aback.

"Just for my shop records, signor. Helps me to remember what was sold and when, in case of any shortfall. I've a dreadful memory, you see." He tapped the side of his head and offered an encouraging smile.

"Oh." I hesitated. "Savolino."

Beside the amount received he dutifully inscribed "Savolino," then glanced up and smiled again, as if to prove to me that this had had no ill effect.

"Did they ever find the lover?" I asked, sipping at the steaming cup. The concoction smelled refreshing and tasted pleasant enough, though the heat made more beads of sweat stand out on my face.

"Well." He folded his arms and leaned against the bench as if settling in for the tale. "The son made a great noise, pointing his finger hither and yon, but nothing came of it. If he had a better character himself, his accusations might have stuck, but he's been in so much trouble, that one, it was only ever his father's money and position that kept him safe from the law. He's not respected in the town. You couldn't keep Master Nicholas Kingsley out of the Three Tuns long enough to notice what was going on under his own roof. Supposed to be studying the law himself, he was, up in London—well, that was a good joke. He was thrown out of his studies for drink and brawling. Ended up back here doing exactly the same at his father's expense, God rest him."

I drained the beaker. "It must have been a sore disappointment to his father."

"Well, they always were an odd family," Fitch said, squinting into the middle distance where spirals of dust eddied in the sunlight, as if trying to remember something.

"How so?"

He shook his head dismissively. "Ah, goodwives' gossip, most of it. His first wife was wealthy—she died of an ague, oh, ten years back. People whispered, as they always will, that he'd done her in, though as far as I know they had no reason to say so. But then maybe a year later he hired a maidservant, Sarah Garth, young girl from the town, and she'd not been there more than a few months when she took sick and died as well."

"Sickness is common enough everywhere, is it not?" I tried to keep my voice casual.

"Aye, of course, but folk found it strange that neither Sir Edward nor his son took ill with whatever she had. Still—in his defence, he brought in Doctor Sykes to treat the girl at his own expense. But they've taken no servants from that day to this, except their old housekeeper, Meg Turner. And there's another thing." He leaned farther across the bench and lowered his voice. "My late wife's niece, Rebecca, she helps out Mistress Blunt on her stall at the bread market."

He paused for effect; I bent towards him and nodded conspiratorially, as if I were quite familiar with the relationships of all these people.

"Not more than six months past, Rebecca was asked to run an errand, take a package of bread out to Sir Edward Kingsley's house—you know, the old priory out past the North Gate."

"I don't know it, I'm afraid."

"Oh, he leased the prior's house of St. Gregory's as was. Grand old building—the only bit of the priory left standing now, apart from the burial ground. Anyhow, she was walking through the graveyard to the door, and that's where she heard it."

"Heard what?"

"A dreadful cry." He gazed at me solemnly to let his words take effect. "She'll swear to it—freeze your blood, she says. So frightened, she was, she dropped the bread and ran all the way back to the Blunts' shop."

My chest tightened; surely it could only have been Sophia, crying out as her husband administered one of his beatings. Again I pictured it, and the stoical, dull-eyed expression on her face when she related the story. I made an effort to unclench my jaw.

"A woman screaming, was it?"

"No." He held up a forefinger as if to admonish me. "That's just it— she said it wasn't like any human sound she'd heard. When she told the story, she was fairly shaking for pity. Well, of course, the graves are still there, so you can imagine how a young girl's imagination runs wild. She said the noise came from beneath her feet, from the very graves themselves." He smiled indulgently. "Anyhow, she wouldn't set foot near the place again. Mind you, nor will any other maid in Canterbury since Master Nicholas came back from London—he'll do his best to grope any woman he can get his hands on, even in broad daylight." He frowned in disgust and I mirrored his expression in sympathy.

"Though he is a rich man now, I suppose, with his father dead. Some woman might be glad of his attentions eventually," I ventured.

"Ha! He's not got a penny till his father's last testament is sorted out," Fitch said, as if pleased by the justice of this. "Sir Edward had lately changed his bequests, but I understand nothing can be cleared up until the wife is found and tried, since she is one of the beneficiaries. Naturally, if she's proved guilty, it's all forfeit to Master Nicholas, but the law must take its course." He rolled his eyes; I smiled in solidarity. If there is one thing that can unite men from all walks of life and all countries, it is a shared contempt of lawyers.

"You are very well informed, Master Fitch, I must say." I half turned, reluctantly sensing that I could not prolong my visit much further.

"Everyone gets sick, Signor Savolino," he said sagely. "Rich or poor—everyone in this city, or their servants, has to pass through my door at some point, like it or no. So there's not much goes on that I don't get to hear about." He tapped his nose and gave me a knowing wink.

I laughed, but his words made me uneasy. Was he implying something? The apothecary may prove a rich source of gossip, but it did not take much wit to realise that, if I were to stay in Canterbury, in a very short time he would make me his business too. I wondered what more he might know and whether his stores of knowledge were for sale to the right bidder.

I was about to bid him good day when the street door was flung open to admit a broad man dressed in the long robe of a physician, tied up at the collar despite the heat. Over his mouth and nose he wore a mask with a curved protuberance like the beak of an exotic bird, like a character in the commedia. Above the mask his eyes were small and beady; they rested on me with an air of suspicion.

After staring at me for a few moments, he turned to the apothecary and pulled the mask down to reveal a heavily jowled face glistening in the light.

"Fitch, I expected you after dinner, did you not get my message? I sent a boy this morning." He gave me a brisk nod as he swept past and leaned his considerable bulk over the counter.

"Very good, Doctor Sykes," the apothecary said, unruffled, inclining his head in a gesture of deference. "We were just talking about you. Still wearing your defence against the plague, then?"

The doctor narrowed his eyes, unsure if he was being mocked. "Well, I am not dead of it yet. Aromatic herbs," he said, for my benefit, pointing to his beak. "Keeps the plague miasma at bay. William, I must speak business with you." He tapped on the ware bench, his voice impatient. "In private."

"I have not forgotten, Doctor Sykes—just let me finish up with my customer. I was telling our Italian visitor here how many prominent citizens you attend in Canterbury, and how your services are so much in demand."

Sykes turned to look me full in the face at this, peering closer as if he were shortsighted. The ring of fat between his jaw and his collar protruded as he did so, putting me in mind of a toad puffing out its throat.

"Quite so. Which is why I do not have time to stand about in idle chatter. Italian, you say? What brings you to Canterbury? Do you have friends here?"

"I stay with Doctor Harry Robinson at the cathedral. We have friends in common and I wished to see your beautiful city."

Sykes squinted, nodding. "Ah, yes, Harry. Well, you are welcome to Canterbury, sir. And now, if you would excuse us. Fitch—close the shop behind this gentleman, would you, while we go inside?" He gave me an oily smile.

Fitch hurried to obey, ushering me towards the door with an apologetic gesture.

"Come back first thing tomorrow, signor, if your stomach is not cured." He held the door for me, with another of his jerky little bows. "I will offer again my tonic and you won't regret it, I swear."

"Thank you—I may take you up on that," I said, with every intention of revisiting the talkative apothecary as soon as possible.

As I stepped back into the dust and bustle of the street I heard Sykes hissing, "Who was that?"

Chapter 6

I took a narrow road leading off the High Street in the direction of the cathedral tower, keeping my kerchief tied close around the lower half of my face in the hope of avoiding too much attention. As I walked, I glanced about me as unobtrusively as I could. Now that Fitch had mentioned the presence of the constables I felt even more conscious of how oddly I must stand out. Where the street opened into a small market square with a stone cross in its centre, I noticed a ginger-haired man in dark breeches and doublet loitering with an air of purpose, restless eyes flitting from right to left along the streets branching away from the square, hand lightly on the hilt of his sword. Was this one of the parish constables? Behind him, incongruous between two ordinary-looking houses, rose a great gatehouse with two octagonal towers four storeys high, built of pale stone intricately carved in the perpendicular style, a row of escutcheons and Tudor emblems painted in bold heraldic colours spanning the width of it above the gateway. Through the larger of the two open doors, a central arch high enough to admit horses and carts, I glimpsed for the first time the precincts of the famous cathedral.

I pulled the cloth from my mouth and stepped into the shade of the gatehouse, conscious of the man with the sword watching me from across the square with less than friendly curiosity. I met his eye briefly and looked away to find myself face-to-face with a tall, broad-set man in a rough tunic, who barred my way through the gate, crossed his thick arms over a barrel-like chest, and demanded to know my business in the cathedral.

"I am here to see the Reverend Doctor Harry Robinson," I offered, with an ingratiating smile.

"Expecting you, is he?" He didn't move.

"Yes, he is. And I carry a letter of recommendation from a mutual friend at the royal court in London."

His round face twitched with uncertainty; I guessed he was in his mid-twenties, though there were already creases at the corners of his eyes that deepened with anxiety. I brought out the paper and pointed at the imposing wax seal.

"The crest of Sir Philip Sidney, nephew to the Earl of Leicester," I added, for effect. He glanced uneasily over his shoulder, then nodded.

"Do you go armed, sir?"

I held my palms out, empty. "Only this little knife." I indicated the sheath at my belt.

"I must ask you to leave it with me. No weapons in the cathedral precincts, by order of the dean. Not after . . ." He hesitated, then appeared to think better of it and held out his hand for the knife. I noticed his left hand was wrapped in a dirty bandage with rust-coloured patches of blood on it.

"There was a murder, I understand." I unstrapped the knife from my belt and passed it over.

"Yes, sir." A guarded expression tightened his features. "The dean has taken precautions now, though. There is a watchman who patrols the precincts after dark, and the gate is always kept locked, so you need not be concerned on that account."

"A little late for the poor fellow who was struck down," I remarked lightly. "Robbers, I suppose?"

"I couldn't say." He shifted his large bulk uneasily from one foot to the other, scratching at his patchy stubble. "If you go to the right of the cathedral, past the conduit house, you will see a row of narrow lodgings before you get to the Middle Gate. Doctor Robinson's is the fourth along." He pointed through the gateway; unlike the apothecary, he showed little appetite for talk of the murder.

"Thank you. What is that handsome building opposite?" I gestured towards a large red-brick mansion visible through the archway, just to our left.

"The Archbishop's Palace."

"I heard he is never here."

"You heard right. The dean lives there mostly."

He fell silent again, squinting up at the sky and absently weighing my knife in his hands.

"Take care of that. I am very attached to it."

He frowned, as if I had insulted his competence, and stepped aside to let me pass, though I could feel him watching me as I entered the sacred precincts of what had been one of the greatest churches in Christendom.

Stepping out of the gatehouse into sunlight, I almost forgot my purpose as I took in the sight before me. I am no stranger to beauty in architecture; my travels have taken me through many of the finest cities of Europe—though not always by choice. I have taken Mass in the towering basilicas of Rome and Naples, walked the streets of Padua, Geneva, and Toulouse, attended services at the magnificent cathedral of Notre Dame de Paris in the company of the king of France. But the austere beauty of this proud monument to England's faith made my breath catch in my throat. The spires of its great towers rose perhaps two hundred feet above me, stone pale as ivory against the fierce blue of the summer sky, gilded by the afternoon sun so that it seemed lit as if by divine light. Its height, its severe perpendicular lines, its vast windows all contributed to an overwhelming grandeur that could not help but make you shrink into yourself a little. What effect must its splendour have had on the hundreds of thousands of pilgrims who first set eyes on this view after days of dragging their weary feet across the English downs? A cathedral such as this one, I thought, was intended to humble onlookers; a testament to the glory of God, perhaps, but more obviously to the might of the Church that built it. Standing at the foot of its bell tower, you could never forget your own insignificance. By the same token, might not the men who held positions of authority here also develop a distorted sense of their own power?

The precincts were empty, shadows stretching out across the dusty path that curved around the length of the cathedral. I glanced up at the sky; it must be midafternoon, not yet late enough for Evensong, but it seemed odd to see so little activity in what, to judge by the number of lodgings crowded around the inner wall of the precincts, must still be a busy community. The gatekeeper's directions led me to a row of tall, narrow houses, well-kept but plain, with small leaded windows facing the cathedral and a stretch of garden in front separating them from the walkway. At the fourth, I followed the path that led alongside the garden—which boasted two scrawny apple trees and what appeared to be a vegetable patch—and knocked firmly on the door.

After some moments it was opened by a tall man with a narrow face and thinning black hair. He was perhaps nearing forty, and looked at me down the length of his nose with an expression that suggested I had interrupted something important.

"Doctor Robinson?"

"He's not at home." He moved as if to close the door; I took a stride forward and laid a hand on it to keep him from doing so. Though he was bigger than me he flinched slightly, as if he feared I might force my way in, and immediately I regretted my action; people here must be nervous, so soon after a violent killing in what was supposed to be a place of sanctuary.

"Forgive me," I said hastily. "May I wait for him? He is expecting me."

"He's not expecting anyone." His voice was oddly nasal; it scraped at your ears like a nail on glass.

"Who is it, Samuel?" The call came from somewhere in the depths of the house. I raised an eyebrow at the man Samuel, who merely flicked his eyes over his shoulder and made an impatient noise with his tongue. Ungraciously, he opened the door a little wider and I glimpsed a figure in the shadows, shuffling towards the light. Samuel stood back to reveal a white-haired man about my own height, his loose shirt untucked from his breeches and his chin bristling with silver stubble. He leaned heavily on a stick but his green eyes took the measure of me, keen and alert as a hunting dog's.

"So. You must be the Italian. Forgive me—if I'd known you were arriving today I'd have had a shave." He spoke with an educated tone, his manner neither friendly nor hostile; merely matter-of-fact.

I gave a slight bow. "At your service."

"Are you, now? Come in, then—don't hang about on the doorstep. Samuel, fetch our guest some fresh beer."

The manservant, Samuel, held the door for me, unsmiling, a chill of dislike emanating from him as I crossed the threshold. I wondered why his immediate response had been to lie about his master's absence. Whatever his reason, he made no apology, nor did he seem at all sheepish at being exposed in a falsehood. He merely closed the door and trod silently behind me as I followed Harry Robinson into an untidy front parlour, airless and choked with the day's accumulated heat.

Harry waved me to one of the two high-backed chairs by the empty hearth. Against the far wall stood an ancient wooden buffet and under the small window a table was covered with books and papers, more books piled high on the floor to either side. Through the leaded glass, sunlight still painted the façade of the cathedral gold, though the room was all sunk in shade and I blinked as my eyes adjusted. The old man's shock of hair and bright eyes stood out against the gloom as he settled himself into the chair opposite me with difficulty, narrating the business with little grunts and huffs of discomfort as he tried to ease his stiff leg into position. When he seemed satisfied, he peered closer, reading my face, and nodded as if to seal his silent judgement.

"So Walsingham has sent you to see if I am still up to the job?"

"Not at all—that is, I . . ." I faltered and saw a smile hovering at the corners of his mouth. He had wrong-footed me with the bluntness of his question, not only because it had not occurred to me that he might regard my presence in this light but also because the servant Samuel had entered the room at the same moment and could not have avoided over-hearing. Flustered, I glanced up at him as he set a pitcher down on the buffet and poured two cups of beer, smiling to himself.

Harry Robinson barked out a dry laugh.

"Don't mind Samuel—he knows all my business, and he knows who you are," he said. "Who else would carry my correspondence to London? There's no talk hidden from him in this house. I'd trust him with my life."

Samuel shot me a fleeting glance, ripe with self-satisfaction. I felt I would not trust him to hold my coat, but I nodded politely.

"Doctor Robinson, my visit here has nothing to do with your own work, which I am certain—"

"Don't condescend to me, son. And call me Harry." He shifted his weight laboriously from one side of the chair to the other, rubbing his stiff leg. "If Her Majesty's principal secretary is sending men from London to look into the murder of a provincial magistrate, it is only because he believes there is some matter here of wider significance to the realm, and that I cannot be relied upon to discover it without help. Not so?"

"It is more that—"

"But I question where he has this intelligence," he continued, regard-less. "I had mentioned the unfortunate death of Sir Edward Kingsley in my most recent letter—I thought it of interest because he associated with those among the cathedral chapter strongly suspected of disloyalty to the English church—but that letter cannot have reached London yet, can it, Samuel?"

"No, sir," Samuel replied, handing each of us a cup with his eyes demurely lowered. He retreated as far as the window, where he stood with his hands clasped behind his back, apparently surveying the cathe-dral close. I wished he would leave the room, but he clearly felt entitled to eavesdrop on the conversation and Harry seemed content to behave as if his servant were merely a part of the furnishings.

"So whose suspicions brought you here, Doctor Giordano Bruno, I ask myself?" Harry leaned forward on his stick and fixed me with those stern eyes. I cleared my throat, glanced at Samuel's unmoving back, and pulled my chair a little closer.

"I have a personal interest, you might say." I hesitated, before lowering my voice even further. "I knew his wife."

Harry took a moment to absorb this, then he sat back and nodded. He seemed pleased by this idea.

"Well, well. So she escaped to London, did she? Canny of her—the gossipmongers here had her on a boat to France. We are not far from the Kentish ports, you see, and there is a good deal of trade with Europe. Easy for a fugitive to get out."

"And secret priests to get in, so I hear," I said.

"Very true. They apprehended a pair of them last month at Dover." He tilted his head to one side, studying me. "So you are here for the wife's sake? Gallant of you, Doctor Bruno. You are probably the only person in this entire county who cares to find out whether she is innocent. If she's caught, she'll burn, and I doubt it would spoil the crowd's enjoyment a jot if she hadn't done it. They like a crime of passion, especially where there's a spirited young woman involved. If she's gone to London, she had better stay well hidden. Of course, I never thought it was her."

"Why not?"

He rubbed his chin.

"I saw the corpse when they found him. Not the work of a woman. Apart from the gore, a woman wouldn't have the strength to wield a weapon like that. Besides, if a wife wanted to kill her husband, as plenty do, surely she'd look for an opportunity closer to home? Poison his supper or some such? That's a woman's way." He shook his head.

"Who do you think killed him, then?"

"Ah, Doctor Bruno, I have not the evidence even to hazard a guess. That is your task, is it not? I will help you as much as I can with information on our late magistrate and his associates, but you will need to tread carefully. The friends of Sir Edward Kingsley have powerful interests in this town and they may not appreciate a stranger poking too closely into their business. Foreigners are not much liked here, I'm sorry to say, for all that this city had its greatest prosperity from visitors."

I watched him for a moment as I took a drink of small beer, grateful for the sensation of liquid in my dusty throat.

"You mentioned Sir Edward was involved with papists?"

Harry laughed again, an abrupt bark.

"*Papists.* You make it all sound so black and white. Walsingham said in his letter you once professed the Roman faith yourself."

I bowed my head in acknowledgement. "I was in the Order of Saint Dominic."

"And why?" He pointed a finger at me.

"Why did I enter a monastery?" I looked at him, surprised; it was rare that anyone asked me this. "Simple—my family was not rich. It was the only way for me to study."

"Precisely." He sat back. "So you understand that what we call faith may spring from many motives, not all of them purely pious. Particularly in Canterbury." He paused to take a draught from his cup. "There are many in this city whose loyalty to the English church is only skin-deep, and not even that, sometimes—a few of them within the chapter itself. But if they are nostalgic for the old religion, it is less from love of Rome than from attachment to their own Saint Thomas and the glory he brought."

"So I understand. The queen's father tried to wipe out the saint's cult completely," I mused, remembering suddenly a Book of Hours I had seen in Oxford, the prayer to Saint Thomas, and the accompanying illumination scraped from the parchment with a stone.

"Folly," Harry pronounced, shaking his head. "They say that before the Dissolution there were more chapels, chantries, and altars in this land dedicated to Thomas Becket than any other saint in history. You can't erase that from people's minds, especially not in his home town, not even by smashing the shrine. You just drive it into the shadows."

"Not even by destroying the body?"

He regarded me shrewdly and smiled.

"You've heard the legend of Becket's bones, then?"

"Is it true?"

"Quite probably." He emptied his cup, bent awkwardly to set it on the floor, and leaned forward, one hand on his stick. "Yes, I'd say it's very likely the body they pulverised and scattered to the wind was not old Thomas. Those priory monks were no fools, and they knew the destruction was coming. But in a sense the literal truth of it doesn't matter, you see? If enough people in Canterbury believed that Saint Thomas was still among them, it might put fire in their bellies."

"And do they believe it?"

He made a noncommittal gesture with his head.

"Everyone knows the legend. I daresay many of them believe it in an abstract sense. What they really need, though, is a sign. That would rouse them."

"A miracle, you mean?"

"The cult of Thomas began with a miracle—here, in this cathedral, less than a week after he was murdered—and it could be revived by one too. Imagine the effect among so many disaffected souls. Like throwing a tinderbox into a pile of dry kindling. And Kent is a dangerous place to risk an uprising, as Walsingham knows all too well. Last time Kentish men rebelled they marched on London, captured the Tower, and beheaded the Archbishop of Canterbury and the royal treasurer."

"Really?" I stared at him, wide-eyed. "I had not heard—when was this?"

Harry laughed.

"Two hundred years ago. But Kentish men are still made of the same stuff. And the coast here is so convenient for any forces coming out of

France—it's not a place they want to risk a popular rebellion against the Crown. The queen needs to keep Canterbury loyal."

He fell silent and stared into the fireplace while my thoughts scrambled to catch up.

"Do you believe in miracles?" I asked, after a few moments.

He looked up from his reflections, his eyes bright.

"Do I believe that Our Lord can perform wonders to show His might to men, if He chooses? Yes, of course. But He chooses very rarely, in my view. If you ask, do I believe that a four-hundred-year-old shard of rotting skull can heal the sick, then I would have to say no." He shifted position again, rubbing at his leg. "When I was six years old, in 1528, there was a terrible outbreak of the sweating sickness in England. My parents and my five brothers and sisters all died; I did not even take ill. Was that a miracle?"

He fixed me with a questioning look; I made a noncommittal gesture.

"My relatives certainly thought so—they gave me up to the Church straightaway, and here I have dutifully remained, to the age of sixty-two years, because I was told so often as a child how God had spared me to serve Him. But who really knows?"

I caught the weight of sadness in his voice and wondered how often in his life as a young churchman he had stopped to wonder at the different paths he might have taken, only to be trapped by the obligation to this great miracle of his survival, God's terrible mercy. That could have been me, I thought, with a lurch of relief, if I had not taken the opportunity to flee the religious life: white-haired and slowly suffocating in the monastery of San Domenico Maggiore, rueing the life I might have lived if I had only dared to try. I wanted to reach out and touch his crooked hand, so brittle with its swollen joints, to show that I understood, but I suspected this might alarm him. The English do not like to be touched, I have learned; they seem to regard it as a prelude to assault.

"One need not be a doctor of physic to observe that some are better able to resist sickness than others," I said softly.

"True. But one might be considered impious for failing to acknowledge the hand of God in such an occurrence."

"In Paris, I once saw a man at a fair make a wooden dove fly over the heads of the crowd, and that was accounted a miracle by all who witnessed it. To those of us who knew better, it was an ingenious employment of optical illusion and mechanical expertise."

Harry raised one gnarled finger, as if to make a point.

"But there you have it, Bruno. If it looks like a miracle, most are content to believe it is so."

I was about to answer, but the closeness of the room and the weariness of days in the saddle conspired to make me suddenly dizzy and I almost fell, silver lights swimming before my eyes, clutching at the seat of the chair for fear I should faint. Harry peered at me, concerned.

"Are you unwell?"

"Forgive me." My voice sounded very far away. "Could we open a window?"

He frowned.

"Too hot? I suppose it is hot in here. Samuel never complains and I don't notice—it's a curious thing about age, one is always cold. Come—we will take a walk around the close and you can see where this monstrous deed occurred." He straightened the stick, took a deep breath, clenched his teeth, and with an almighty effort began to rouse himself to his feet. I extended a hand to him, though I still felt unsteady myself, but he brushed it away impatiently.

"Not on my deathbed yet, son. While I can stand on my own two feet, leave me to it. I call it independence. Samuel calls it stubbornness. What time is it, Samuel?"

The servant, who had remained motionless gazing out of the window and doubtless taking in every word, now turned back to the room.

"About half past three, I think, sir."

"Then we have time. I'll want a shave before Evensong, if you could have the necessaries ready when I return."

"You don't wish me to accompany you, sir?" Samuel turned dubious eyes on me, as if the prospect of allowing his master out alone with me would be a dereliction of duty.

"I'm sure you have things to attend to here," Harry said. "We shall probably manage a turn around the close. I dare say Doctor Bruno will pick me up if I fall over."

"If you'll let me," I said, and when I saw the twinkle in his eye, I knew that, despite his gruff manner, he was warming to me. Samuel looked at me with a face like storm clouds.

"My doublet, Samuel," Harry said, waving a hand. "Here, hold this, will you?" He handed me the stick and planted his legs wide to balance himself while he tucked his shirt into his breeches. "Wouldn't want to run into the dean, looking like a vagrant," he muttered, with a brief smile. "You never know who's about in this place. That reminds me—" he looked up. "Your story, while you're here. The reason for your visit— what do we tell people? They're an overly curious lot, especially the dean and chapter."

"I'm a Doctor of Divinity from the University of Padua, exiled to escape religious persecution and lately studying in Oxford, where I heard much praise for the cathedral of Canterbury and wanted to take this opportunity to see it for myself."

He considered my rehearsed biography and grunted.

"They will accept that readily enough, I should think. And how do you and I know each other?"

"A letter of introduction from our mutual friend, Sir Philip Sidney."

Harry smiled at this.

"Ah, little Philip. He was about four years old when I last saw him. Turned out well, I hear. His mother was a great beauty in her day, you know." His gaze drifted to the window, as though he was seeing faces from years long past. Samuel came in with a plain black doublet of light wool and helped his master into it. "Well, then." Harry gestured to the door. "What name do you travel under here? I had better get used to it in case I am obliged to introduce you to anyone."

"Filippo Savolino."

"Savolino. Huh." He repeated it twice more, as if to accustomise himself to the feel of it.

"It is unlikely that anyone in Canterbury would know my reputation, but—"

"We do read books here, you know. We're not entirely cut off from learned society."

"No, I didn't mean to imply—"

"There's quite a trade in books from the Continent, too, being so near the ports. Legal and otherwise. Including plenty from your country." He regarded me thoughtfully. "Padua, eh? I have never travelled beyond England, though as a young man I dreamed of doing so. I would have liked to see Italy for myself. A country of wild beauty, I am told."

"I think no man can say he has seen beauty until he has watched the sun set over the Bay of Naples, with the shadow of Mount Vesuvius in the background."

"A volcano. I can hardly imagine a volcano," he said, with simple longing.

"Perhaps you may see it one day."

He slapped his bad thigh and barked out another laugh. "With this leg? No—while you are here, you must describe it to me and I shall be able to picture it. I do not think these eyes will ever look on the Bay of Naples."

"Nor will mine again," I said, and the weight of this struck me as I spoke the words, so that I heard my voice catch at the end.

We looked at each other, the moment ripe with regret. Harry shook his head briskly, as if to rid himself of sentiment.

"Come then, Savolino, we have work to do."

AIR, REAL AIR, with the faintest hint of a breeze carrying the indignant cries of seagulls; I was so grateful that I stood still on the garden path, head spinning as I gulped down great lungfuls like a man who has narrowly escaped drowning. Harry shuffled ahead of me into the cathedral close and motioned to his right; when I had recovered and my blood felt as if it were pumping once more, I followed him. Samuel stood in the doorway watching us with an inscrutable expression in his eyes. I could not help noticing that Harry's limp became less pronounced and his pace speeded up a little once we had rounded the corner and were out of his servant's sight.

"Have you ever been married, Bruno?" he asked.

"No," I said, surprised by the question. Shielding my eyes, I looked up to our left; sideways on, the cathedral had the appearance of a vast warship, ribbed with buttresses, its high windows so many gunports.

"Nor I," he said. "When I entered the clergy, churchmen didn't marry, and once it became acceptable, I had missed the boat. Instead I have Samuel—all the fussing and nagging of a wife, with none of the benefits." He gave a deep, rasping laugh.

"He doesn't like me, I'm afraid."

"Don't mind him, he doesn't like anyone. He has a suspicious cast of mind and he's jealous as a wife, too—likes to feel that I'm dependent on him. Can't bear to share my attention. This way."

The path passed through a gate by a block of stables and continued around the east end of the cathedral. Cut timber and logs were piled against its wall behind a makeshift fence, covered by oilskin cloths. To our right, a wooded area of thick oak trees in full leaf cast long shadows over the grass beneath, stretching back as far as the precinct walls, a relic from the priory that had stood on the site before the Dissolution, I supposed. Here the heat of the day had begun to subside; I loosened my collar and breathed deeply. The leaves stirred as the breeze lifted, sending light flickering through the foliage. The place seemed so at peace with itself, it was hard to believe it could be the setting for bloody murder. Perhaps Thomas Becket had once thought the same, I reflected.

Harry paused and craned his head back to look at the sky. "What a fine day. God's bones, I should leave the house more often. I'm sure it would do wonders for my constitution."

"You are confined by your health?"

He laughed again.

"By my work. When I arrived in Canterbury six years ago, I took it upon myself to compile a history of the cathedral from its foundation in the sixth century to the Dissolution." He smiled at my expression. "I know—utter folly. My allotted span is almost up and I've only got as far as the martyrdom. Still another four hundred years to get through."

"You may yet finish it."

"Even if I had another score years left to me, that would not be enough to sort through the manuscripts in the cathedral library—hundreds of years' worth of documents and papers buried there, but they've never been archived or catalogued properly, and I doubt they ever will, unless someone comes along prepared to dedicate his entire life to the job. There could be all manner of treasures gathering cobwebs."

"Surely the librarian has some idea of what books are in his care?" I asked.

Harry gave that dry bark of laughter that I now recognised as cynicism.

"He may well. If so, it must suit him to keep them hidden from the rest of us." He resumed his shuffling as the path curved around the eastern end of the cathedral. Here he raised his stick and pointed to the semicircular tip of the building. "The corona, they call this part. Built to house the reliquary that contained the fragment of Becket's skull hacked away by his murderers. Come." He waved me forward with his stick.

On the north side of the cathedral more houses had been built amid the ruined masonry of the old priory, as if in their haste to replace the old religious house the builders had not even bothered to clear its traces away. Naked arches stood stark against the sky like the ribs of a great decayed beast. Harry led me around into the shadow of the cathedral church. Just past these houses, where a small chantry chapel jutted out from the side of the main building, he paused and pointed with his stick to a spot on the path. A dark stain, though faded, could still be seen in the dust, like the outline of a puddle.

"There."

I crouched to look at the bloodstained ground. So this was the spot where Sophia's vicious husband had lain for his last minutes, lifeblood leaking away into the dust, surprised by the blow that came out of the darkness. Had Sir Edward seen who stepped towards him, weapon held aloft? Would he have known his killer, or known why that person had come for him? I traced a line in the reddish dirt with the tip of my forefinger. It was hard to summon any pity for the man when you knew his history. Sitting back on my haunches, I peered up, trying to imagine the last sight he would have seen: the towering walls of the cathedral on one side, the houses among the priory ruins on the other. I noticed that the path continued around the side of the chantry chapel and disappeared.

"Where was he coming from?" I asked, trying to work out the dead man's last route.

"He dined with the dean in the Archbishop's Palace that night," Harry said, leaning on his stick. "I was there."

"The Archbishop's Palace is directly opposite the main gatehouse, though, at the western end of the cathedral, is it not? Why would he come around the back of the cathedral on his way home, then? Is there another way out?"

"He mentioned at table he was going to take a glass with the canon treasurer after supper. They were friends. But I was tired and went home early that night so I didn't see if he left the Archbishop's Palace alone."

"Whoever attacked him must have known he would come this way," I said. "You don't cut a man down like that by chance. And you say anyone at the dinner could have heard him mention where he was going. What else is this side of the cathedral, apart from the cloister?"

Harry considered.

"The Chapter House, but that is only used for official meetings. And the library, which is housed in a disused chapel just behind us, the other side of this chantry. Then there are more of the canons' residences." He hesitated. "The canon treasurer's house is on this side, of course." He rubbed his stubbled chin.

"Are the cathedral doors locked at night?"

He shook his head.

"God's house should be open around the clock, according to the dean. Not to just anybody, of course—the precinct gates are closed so the town can't get in. Only the crypt is locked after Evensong, by the dean himself, as some of the more valuable ornaments are stored there. He is the only one with a key. But any of the residential canons may go into the main church and pray at any time of the night. Provided they're not afraid to brave the ghosts." That rasping laugh again; he fluttered his free hand in an approximation of spectral movement.

"You have ghosts?" I glanced at him, amused.

"Oh, naturally we have ghosts. Several, I should think. The southeast end of the cathedral precincts was formerly the monks' cemetery, and beyond it the lay cemetery. The dead of centuries are piled up under our feet. Not to mention our most famous murder victim."

"Perhaps your most recent one too."

"I'm sure he has joined the queue. Do you believe in spirits, Bruno?"

I hesitated, considering how to answer this without compromising myself.

"I have seen nothing to persuade me that the spirits of the dead walk among us, if that's what you mean."

He smiled.

"Nor I. Yet there are plenty who are persuaded, and not just among the simple folk." He gestured towards the cathedral. "There are stories of candles lit at night, statues that shift shape, human figures that form themselves from the very shadows. I know good stout Protestant canons who will not walk the precincts after dark for fear of what might come out of the mist."

"A pity Sir Edward Kingsley didn't have the same qualms—he might have kept his head intact."

Harry gave an irreverent chuckle. "Do you want to take a look inside?"

I agreed eagerly, keen to see the interior of the great church, though my thoughts were distracted. I had even less idea since arriving in Canterbury of how to proceed with the business of Edward Kingsley's murder. Seeing the place where he had died had only led to more questions, just like my encounter with Fitch the apothecary.

Harry shuffled his way along as the path rounded the chantry chapel and we found ourselves in a small courtyard with the cathedral on our left and a smaller chapel on our right. Ahead of us was a well-kept cloister, a stretch of green lawn visible through the range of rounded arches that enclosed it on all four sides. I followed at Harry's frustrating pace, thinking as I watched him that his physical health must surely restrict his ability to gather information, even if his position in the cathedral chapter did give him intimate access to the dealings of the dean and the other canons. If he was confined to his house with his head buried in historical manuscripts most of the time, I wondered how much use he could be here to Walsingham.

We passed into a flagstoned passageway touched with a sharp smell of damp, where the sudden cool of the shade made my skin prickle like gooseflesh. The passage ran between the body of the cathedral church and a majestic building on our right that Harry pointed out as the Chapter House, before opening out into the cloister. He turned left along the tunnel of columns branching into delicately traced vaults overhead and we found ourselves in front of a small door into the cathedral. Harry turned the handle and we stepped through into the reverent silence of ancient stone. The metallic click of the door closing behind us echoed a hundred feet above us in the vast arches of the ceiling. I craned my head upwards, realising only belatedly that I was holding my breath.

"Right here." Harry lowered his voice; the place seemed to demand it. "This is where they killed Becket." He pointed to the floor in front of a blank wall of white stone, to the right of an elaborately carved screen into a private chapel.

Though sunlight still streamed through the high windows on the other side of the cathedral, licking the walls above our heads, this little corner was sunk in shadow. There was nothing remarkable about it;

when I had learned the story of Becket's murder as a young novice, I had pictured the saint struck down by the gang of knights before the high altar, in the heart of the church, not in some side chapel that was barely more than a vestibule. Harry moved to stand beside me and we remained in respectful silence for a moment; one sound Protestant churchman and one heretical ex-monk, both of us derisive of the superstition that attended saints' cults, yet both apparently caught by the sense that this famous death demanded acknowledgement.

I was distracted from my thoughts by the sensation that we were not alone. I glanced up and was startled by the sight of a woman standing just behind us, tall and slender, dressed in the mourning clothes of a widow, her face veiled in black. Beside her stood a thin boy with large eyes. They seemed to have been watching us. The woman lifted her veil to reveal an expression of curiosity. She was perhaps my own age, with delicate features and haughty blue eyes that roamed over my face mercilessly. Her skin was white as a marble effigy against the black of her dress.

"Mistress Gray," Harry said, with a polite bow. "Good day to you."

The woman dipped her head, her eyes still on me. Then, without a word, she reached for the boy's hand and swept past us towards the door, giving me a nod on the way out as if to suggest that we knew each other. Something in her penetrating look made me uncomfortable.

"Who is that woman?" I asked, when she had gone, still looking at the door.

Harry smiled. "That is the Widow Gray. A woman of mystery."

"Really?"

"Whether she is really a widow is the subject of much debate in the town."

"Ah."

"Some say she was a wealthy courtesan, that her son is really a bastard prince, that she is a disgraced royal cousin—you know what idle gossip is. I pay no attention, myself."

"Of course not."

"But she keeps to herself, the widow, and she is beautiful and evidently has means, so naturally people feel entitled to make up her story for her. Now—wait here." He shuffled away into the chapel to our left. I waited, wondering if it was possible I had met the Widow Gray in another place or time. She had looked at me as if she knew me, but it seemed impossible. Harry returned a few moments later with a stub of candle.

"Borrowed from the altar. They won't notice. Hold this."

I took the candle while he fumbled in the pouch at his belt for a tinderbox and struggled painfully to light it with arthritic fingers. I had to bite my lip and resist the urge to snatch the box from him and finish the job myself. Finally, he conjured a spark, a small flame blossomed from the wick, and he nodded to a rounded archway beside the site of the martyrdom, where a flight of worn steps led down to an open door and smudges of shadow concealed what lay beyond.

A faint line of light touched the darkness ahead of us as we descended. I kept close to Harry, one arm half extended in case he should need help, though not so obviously as to offend him, but he seemed to know the stairs into the bowels of the cathedral by touch alone, and it was I who almost missed my footing as we reached the bottom. The air felt denser here, cold and mineral, as if it had stood still in this unlit sanctum for centuries.

As my eyes adjusted to the gloom, I peered around and began to make out the dimensions of this vast crypt, which seemed to stretch ahead in an endless maze of columns and arches, disappearing tunnellike into the obscured distance and fanning overhead into vaults that bore traces of coloured patterns in cobalts and crimsons, untarnished by the passing of ages. Some of the columns had been carved with twisting, concentric designs, their capitals wrought with fantastical creatures: dragons and horned beasts, green men of pagan legend and gryphons seizing winged serpents in their jaws, men with tails fighting creatures with the heads of wolves and the bodies of dragons, that seemed to wink and shift shape in the dancing flame. To either side these vaulted arches branched out, repeating in parallel rows of thick pillars as broad as the trunks of oak trees, drawing the eye always forward. Some of the spaces between had been filled in with tombs, where stone effigies reclined prayerfully, their royal or episcopal features erased by time so that they wore the distorted expressions of lepers or the victims of fire.

Neither Harry nor I had spoken since entering the crypt. It was a place of silence thick as shadow, a silence ancient and brooding as the great stones. As my gaze roamed over the walls, I thought I heard a soft noise intrude into the stillness; an unexpected breath of cold air touched the back of my neck and I shivered violently. Harry, ahead of me with the candle, kept walking, noticing nothing; I turned sharply, but behind me there was only darkness. Yet as I followed the wavering light down the avenue of stone columns, I could not shake the sense that someone was watching.

At the heart of the crypt stood a small enclosed chapel amid the arches, with a plain altar at the front and tombs to either side.

"Is the crypt used for worship?" I asked.

"The French Huguenots use the chapel at this end once a week. Her Majesty gave it to the community when they first arrived so they would have somewhere to hold their services in their own tongue. They brought their own pastors and deacons. The eastern end is only used for storage now." Harry paused and held up his candle. "You know, the priory monks hid Becket's body down here in the years after his murder, for fear it would be stolen," he whispered.

I glanced around again.

"Perhaps he is still here. After all"—I gestured to the tombs that surrounded us—"where better to hide a tree than in a forest?"

Harry shrugged. "Even if we opened every tomb, how would we know? The man has been dead for four centuries. His bones will look like anyone else's."

"Except that the top of his skull is missing." I shook my head. "Someone knows."

"I have sometimes wondered—" Harry began, when a noise to our left made him break off, his face alert; he reached out and laid a hand on my arm, as if for reassurance.

By instinct my right hand flew to my belt, though even in the act of reaching for it I remembered that my little knife was in the care of the gatekeeper. Out of the shadows behind the tomb, a figure took shape as if from the darkness and approached, seeming to glide across the pavement with no sound other than the ripple of his black robe. Harry held up the candle and as the man moved closer its light revealed a bony face composed of hard angles, stern eyes that fixed on me with restrained curiosity, a close-shaved skull whose stubble glinted silver-grey. It was a severe face, not without dignity, lined by perhaps fifty winters, with a thin scar that ran from his nose to the corner of his mouth, causing his lip to curl upwards in an unfortunate sneer. I fought the impulse to step back under the force of that direct stare.

The man folded his hands together in front of him and turned to Harry, inclining his head with a polite smile.

"Doctor Robinson. It is rare to find you down here. I hope I am not disturbing a moment of private devotion?"

It was clear even to a stranger that Harry disliked this man intensely, despite returning his smile with an equally chilly civility. In nearly two years I have not yet managed to understand this about the English; in Naples, if a man despises another, he spits in his face openly or insults his family, and then a fight ensues. Here, they shake each other's hand, dine together, smile with their teeth only, and wait until the other's back is turned before striking their blow, and this agreed deception is called etiquette. Watching these two men, I had the sense that Harry would gladly knock this tall bony fellow to the ground in the blink of an eye. Instead, he returned the cursory bow.

"I was showing my visitor the historical wonders of our church, Canon Treasurer. May I present Doctor Filippo Savolino, a scholar from Italy and a friend of the Sidney family?"

The tall man turned his unhurried gaze back and arched his brow as he studied me.

"Savolino, you say? A pleasure." He reached out one hand and I took it, reluctantly; his fingers felt bloodless and dry against mine and I had for a moment the impression that he had just stepped out of one of the tombs. "John Langworth, canon treasurer. We have few visiting scholars here, Doctor Savolino. I wonder what could interest you about our little community."

"I am making a study of the history of Christendom," I replied, glancing at Harry. "Naturally I could not miss the opportunity to visit the site of one of the greatest shrines in all of Europe."

"You are about fifty years too late, my friend," he said, pressing his lips together so that the scar whitened. "Nothing of greatness remains to be seen here."

"Your magnificent church, for a start," I said, trying to sound placatory.

He made a dismissive noise.

"You may find more impressive basilicas throughout Europe. It is a long way to travel for some stone and glass."

I didn't like the note of suspicion in his voice, so I merely smiled in the English manner.

"All relics of the church's history are of interest to me, Canon Langworth."

"Well, you will find this an empty reliquary. How long do you intend to stay?"

"Until I have seen all I wish to see."

"I cannot imagine you will find much to detain you. What is your faith? I mean no offence," he added, though his tone suggested he did not care if any had been taken. "But one should never make assumptions."

Harry sucked in his breath audibly through his teeth. I merely inclined my head.

"Raised Catholic, like all my countrymen. But now that I live as a subject of Queen Elizabeth, I worship as she commands." Seeing his eyes narrow, I added, "I have more interest in what our different faiths hold in common. There is as much to bind us together as to divide us, I believe."

Langworth pursed his lips. Those cold, steady eyes did not waver from mine.

"Ah. You are an ecumenist. Some would say that is the surest way to heresy. You will not find many here would agree with you. Nor in Catholic Europe, I doubt. Still"—his face relaxed a little and he peered closer at me in the candlelight—"your views would make for an interesting discussion at the dean's supper table. You should speak to Dean Rogers, Harry—have your friend invited to dinner while he is here. We are always glad of anything to enliven our debates," he added, turning back to me. "I'm afraid we are rather starved of news from the outside world."

I glanced at Harry; he wore a pinched expression, as if Langworth's suggestion had angered him. Perhaps he resented the treasurer's interference, or perhaps he was anxious that my presence might somehow compromise his position. There was a moment's awkward silence.

"Well, I shall leave you to your historical tour," Langworth said lightly, though I could see he had also noted Harry's reluctance. "I can't imagine what you hope to see down here, mind—this part of the crypt is only used for storage. I look forward to talking with you again, Doctor . . . Savolino, was it?" He paused and waved his long fingers in the direction of the tombs. "Try not to disturb the dead while you are looking around—they are only sleeping until the last trumpet." His strange, curved smile flashed briefly before he glided away towards the steps as soundlessly as he had arrived.

Harry watched without speaking until he was sure Langworth had left. He rounded on me, anger burning in his eyes.

"Do not give that man an inch, Bruno," he hissed, barely audible. He gripped my arm for emphasis. "John Langworth is slippery as a snake and just as dangerous." He paused, glaring at the shadowy staircase where Langworth had disappeared.

"Why?"

Harry hesitated, still looking towards the stairs, as if to make sure Langworth had really gone.

"He has his position at the cathedral by royal gift, you know, though he has been suspected of popery for years. But he boasts powerful friends at court—his patron is Lord Henry Howard. It was he who pressed the queen to appoint Langworth."

"Henry Howard?" I felt the hairs on my arms prickle; even after all these months, the name still inspired a chill of fear. So this was the man Sidney had mentioned.

"You know him, I believe?" Harry raised an eyebrow.

"Our paths have crossed. But he is in the Fleet Prison now."

"This was seven years ago. Howard worked hard to regain the queen's favour after the execution of his brother, the Duke of Norfolk, for treason. She gave Langworth the prebendary when it became vacant as a goodwill gesture to Henry Howard, to show he had not lost her trust."

"He's lost it now."

"Aye, we heard the news before Christmas." Harry set his jaw. "The timing could not have been worse for Langworth. He was favoured to become the next dean of Canterbury, but the fall of his patron worked against him. When the old dean died at the beginning of this year, the College of Canons elected Doctor Richard Rogers instead. I gather the archbishop leaned heavily on a number of the canons to prevent Langworth's election."

"Because he's known to have Catholic sympathies?"

"Exactly. That was Howard's whole purpose in having him appointed here—that he should one day become head of the chapter. But Langworth lost only by a very narrow margin—it would be a mistake to underestimate his influence."

"Why did you say he was dangerous? Because of his beliefs?"

Harry glanced over his shoulder. The candle was burning lower and as its circle of light diminished, the darkness at the edges of the crypt seemed to press in on us. He waved with his stick towards the steps.

"Come—let us talk of this where we will not be overheard. I should be getting home for my shave in any case. A good shave wouldn't hurt you either, if you don't mind my saying," he added, squinting at my face. "I can ask Samuel to do you after."

"I don't want to put him to any trouble," I said, privately thinking that I would rather be arrested for vagrancy than let the servant Samuel anywhere near my throat with a razor.

"Nonsense! Least we can do. I should be offering you hospitality. I'm sure Francis would expect it."

"I shall have more independence to come and go if I stay at the inn, though I thank you for the offer."

Harry grunted and continued to shuffle towards the light. I noticed his pace was slower than before. We had reached the foot of the stairs out of the crypt; a welcome shaft of sunlight lent the air a white glow above us. As unobtrusively as I could, I paused at the first step and extended my arm. Harry hesitated a moment, then grasped my elbow to steady himself for the climb. Both of us kept our gaze fixed resolutely ahead. At the top of the stairs he dropped my arm as if it had burned his fingers, leaned forward on his stick, and nodded brusquely, once, still without looking at me, before moving stiffly towards the open door of the cathedral.

"JOHN LANGWORTH IS the one I was sent here to watch."

Harry tilted his head back as Samuel, silent and impassive as ever, tied a white linen cloth around his neck. We were seated in his small kitchen, where a crackling fire heated the already stifling air. All the windows were closed. Even Harry wiped a bead of sweat from his brow as Samuel now lifted a pan of hot water from a hook over the flames and poured some into a porcelain basin. "Walsingham was concerned by Henry Howard's involvement in Langworth's appointment. He suspected that Howard and his Catholic supporters in France and Spain wanted Langworth here for some strategic reason. As dean he would have held significant power, not only over the cathedral but over the whole city. There was a time when Walsingham feared Langworth and his supporters could have inspired an outright rebellion in Canterbury—and if that were to coincide with a Franco-Spanish invasion . . ." He left the thought unfinished, looking at me with a decisive nod.

"Such as the one that was planned last autumn," I mused.

"Exactly. But Howard scuppered his own plans by getting himself arrested just prior to the dean's election," Harry said. Samuel gently eased his master's head back again before dipping his own hands in the basin and coating them with soap.

"Henry Howard is in the Fleet Prison because of me," I said, my eyes fixed on Samuel's hands as they moved in slow circles over Harry's jaw, white lather blooming under his fingers.

"Ah. I wondered," Harry said. He sat forward and spat the soap that had got in his mouth as he spoke. "Walsingham said in his letter that you had performed a great service for the queen and the realm last autumn. I guessed it might have been connected with that conspiracy."

"Howard may have corresponded with Langworth from prison about it."

"No doubt. The Earl of Arundel came to Kent before Christmas last year, not long after his uncle was arrested, and Langworth met him. We think he was bringing messages too sensitive to trust to paper."

"Henry Howard's nephew visited Langworth in person?" My mind was racing ahead, clutching at the possible implications. Perhaps messages were not all the Earl of Arundel had brought to Kent with him.

"It's my understanding that Howard trusted Langworth with some of his affairs—that's why he's still an object of suspicion. He would certainly have known about the conspiracy last autumn. God's wounds, man, don't wave that thing so near my face when I'm trying to have a conversation!"

Samuel had opened a narrow, straight-bladed razor, which he now dipped in the hot water. "It might be easier for everyone, sir, if you were to break off your discussion just until I have finished," he suggested mildly.

Harry grunted, but settled back in his chair. I watched Samuel's deft strokes with the razor around the old man's chin, but my mind was elsewhere. So it was likely that my reputation had preceded me to Canterbury after all—and in the worst possible way, from the pen of a man who wanted me dead. If Howard had named me to Langworth as his enemy, I would need to take extra care that no one in Canterbury should discover my real name—though being Italian and a friend of the Sidneys, I may already have aroused Langworth's suspicions. And here my pulse quickened, because I could not prevent my imagination from wild leaps—if Howard trusted Langworth so implicitly, might he have entrusted the canon with the care of his most treasured possession, a book he would have wanted to spirit out of London, far away from the eyes of the searchers who came to arrest him? The book he had once allowed me to hold in my hands, only because he had believed he was going to kill me immediately afterwards? If his own nephew had travelled all the way to Kent in person to see Langworth, there must have been a good reason. Any courier could carry a message.

When Harry eventually sat up, a linen towel pressed to his pink face, he looked at me with concern.

"You appear troubled, Bruno. Worried Langworth might work out who you are?"

"We will have to be careful. It is a shock to find myself so near a close associate of the Howards. When you said Langworth was dangerous—did you mean violent?"

"Violent? No, he is too clever for that. But a man with money and powerful friends can be dangerous in other ways. Here—" Harry levered himself out of his chair and gestured to me to take his place. "Samuel, fetch some fresh water and see if you can make our guest look halfway respectable."

"Really, there's no need—"

"Don't quibble, Bruno. You have the look of a Spanish pirate at the moment. If you want to gain people's trust in Canterbury, you must tidy yourself up a little."

Samuel favoured me with one of his long, withering looks from under his brows as he set about pouring a fresh bowl of water and wiping the razor. When I was nervously seated with a cloth tied around my throat, Harry pulled up a chair.

"Langworth is not a godly man. Rumours follow him—of mistresses, an illegitimate child, misappropriation of cathedral funds—this is quite apart from his suspected loyalty to the Church of Rome. But there has never been enough evidence to deprive him of his position."

"Uh-huh." I could only look up at the ceiling as Samuel smoothed the soap on to my face with a light touch. I gripped the arms of the chair tightly nonetheless.

"A couple of years ago, one of the minor canons who worked with Langworth in the treasury thought he had discovered fraudulent accounts relating to leases of some of the local manors owned by the cathedral. He went so far as to accuse Langworth of corruption."

"And what happened to him?" I asked, through my teeth, knowing the story would not be good. Out of the corner of my eye, I caught the flash and wink of steel in the sunlight.

"Shortly after he made this accusation, one of the serving boys in the dean's kitchen accused this young canon of having improperly assaulted him. Another stable lad repeated a similar claim. Then the canon was arrested for brawling in the street outside a tavern—he insisted he was set upon by two thugs, but witnesses were found to say he had provoked a fight after losing money at dice. You see?"

I tried to nod, but Samuel's hand clamped tightly under my chin. His grip was surprisingly strong.

"Head still, if you would, sir," he murmured. I felt the kiss of the blade against my throat and flinched violently; an instinctive response, to my shame. I thought I heard Samuel snigger.

"You are skittish, Bruno," Harry observed. "Bad experience with barbers?"

"Bad experience with knives," I muttered, through clenched teeth.

The memory of a blade levelled at my throat back in Oxford still pulsed vividly when I closed my eyes.

"I had no idea philosophy was such a dangerous profession." He smiled. "In short, this young canon was deprived of his position in disgrace and his career in the church ended at a stroke. Since then no one has dared to repeat any such accusation against Langworth. For myself, I would appreciate it if your investigations here gave him a wide berth. I do not want his suspicions aroused against me—any more than they are already."

"Is he capable of murder?" The razor feathered gently across my cheek; there was no denying that Samuel had a deft touch, but still I felt painfully vulnerable, my throat exposed, his left hand gripping my chin, and all my muscles were held taut as wire.

"Sir Edward Kingsley, you mean? No, they were friends. In fact it was Langworth who found the body, and he was visibly distressed by it, as far as I could see. Besides, staving in a man's skull like that? I can't picture it. Too vulgar for a man like Langworth."

"He could have paid someone to do it, like he did with the tavern brawl. Friends can fall out, with violent consequences, if there is enough at stake. And what better way to avert suspicion than by finding the body with a show of grief? Besides, what was he doing alone in the crypt just now with no light? Surely—"

"You are allowing your imagination to run away, if I may say so." Harry heaved himself to his feet again and came to loom over me as I sat. "Perhaps you didn't hear clearly. You leave Langworth to me." He sighed. "I will do what I can to help you while you are here, but I haven't spent the last six years painstakingly watching him for you to compromise my work with rash suspicions. Is that clear?"

I lifted my head to look at him and caught the stern expression in his eyes. I was too dependent on Harry's goodwill and cooperation to make any argument; no one else in Canterbury could vouch for me or smooth my way while I tried to find Edward Kingsley's murderer. I nodded obediently, before Samuel smothered the lower half of my face with a hot cloth, but I was already intrigued by Langworth's friendship with the murdered man. And what had he meant when he told me not to disturb the dead? Was that a weak joke, or a warning?

Samuel patted my face dry and held up a small looking glass so that I could approve his work. I pushed my hair back from my face, tilted my head from one side to the other, and wondered what Sophia would make of me now. She was right; I did look younger. I thanked Samuel and received only a sarcastic smirk in return.

"Dine with me tomorrow at noon," Harry said, as he saw me to the door. "You can let me know how your enquiries progress. If they are to involve prominent men in the city, it would be best for you to consult me first—I can advise you on sensitive matters and make introductions if necessary. You will be less suspicious if it becomes known in the town that you are my guest." He leaned on his stick and reached out with his right hand to shake mine. "But remember what I said, Bruno. Leave Langworth alone. Whatever ideas you may form about him, forget them. It would do no good and might well do great harm."

I bowed in reply, but said nothing. Behind Harry's shoulder, Samuel's eyes bored into me with silent resentment.

I PAID MY landlady at the Cheker fourpence extra to have a copper of hot water brought to my room—over the odds, but I was too tired and uncomfortable to haggle over the price. Once I had washed the grime of three days' travelling from my hair and body and changed my clothes, however, I felt my spirits revive. As the cathedral bells rang out across the city for Evensong, I made my way downstairs to the taproom to take supper by myself and reflect on the few snippets of information I had gathered since our arrival.

John Langworth: I had only to picture the canon treasurer, with his angular face and grave, scrutinising gaze, for a chill to creep along my neck. I must be careful, I told myself; it would be all too easy for my enmity with Henry Howard to colour my judgement of Langworth, and I had been in danger of making such a mistake before. Was Langworth the reason Walsingham had insisted I use a false name? A known Catholic sympathiser, biding his time in Canterbury; if the French invasion which Henry Howard had been instrumental in plotting had succeeded last year, would Langworth have seized his opportunity, taken control of the cathedral, produced the corpse of Saint Thomas with a conjuror's flourish, and rallied the town in a Catholic rebellion to greet the invading forces? It was not impossible to imagine. But the plot had failed, Howard was in prison, and Langworth had been beaten to the position of Dean of Canterbury; perhaps he was no longer a serious threat. Even so, I could not help wondering if Harry was watching him closely enough. The old man had certainly seemed defensive at my arrival; perhaps that was behind his insistence that I should not stir up any trouble around Langworth. But the latter's friendship with Sir Edward Kingsley had piqued my interest. Was Langworth one of the powerful friends Sophia had mentioned, who had gathered at her late husband's home to whisper behind closed doors?

The thought of her brought another sharp pang of longing; I would miss her presence in the room that night, despite the torments it provoked. After only three days it had come to feel quite natural; the rise and fall of her breathing in the dark, our instinctive modesty as we averted our eyes or covered ourselves, self-consciously trying to avoid the accidental intimacies that come from sharing a small space at night. I imagined her lying under the rafters of the weavers' cottage and wondered if she would also miss me, but I had to close my eyes against the unbidden image of her by the light of a candle, turning the warmth of her smile on young Olivier and his pout.

Declining the entreaties of my landlady to stay and drink with her after my meal (it's not every inn would be so welcoming to foreigners, she assured me, though for herself it was a rare treat to encounter such a well-mannered and handsome gentleman), I gathered a full purse and my bone-handled knife and set out into the dusty street. The heat of the day was abating as the sun slid down towards the horizon like a melted seal of crimson wax; at the corner of the street a group of children played a game that involved jumping over a crudely made grid scratched into the dirt. They fell silent as I passed and stared up at me with wide, unblinking eyes; one of the smaller ones crept behind an older child and peeped out with an expression very like awe.

"Where will I find the Three Tuns?" I called to the older boy.

He took a step back as I stopped, putting out a protective hand towards the little one clinging behind him. Mute, he pointed to his right.

"Watling Street." His voice came out barely more than a whisper.

"Thank you." I tossed him a penny; it landed in the dust at his feet, where he looked at it suspiciously for a moment before reaching down, never taking his eyes off me.

Their reaction puzzled me; did I look so unusual to them? I followed the direction of the boy's pointing finger, and turned back at the end of the street to find them still staring, rooted to the spot. Children like novelty, I told myself, as I continued around the corner. But I couldn't quite shake the uncomfortable sense that their response had been one of fear. Perhaps, even clean-shaven, I looked like one of the murdering Spanish pirates their mothers warned them about.

From the outside, the Three Tuns gave the impression that it had lost the will to keep up appearances; plaster cracked and peeled from the walls and the thatch of the roof suffered from threadbare patches. But the taproom was crowded, busy with the din of lively chatter, snatches of song, and the occasional shout of protest as one drinker knocked another in the crush; smoke hung thickly under the low beams of the ceiling, mixing with the yeasty scent of beer and warm bread. It was clearly not one of the better inns in the town, to judge by the dress and appearance of its customers, but its roughness held a certain appeal. I guessed it was the sort of place the law would knowingly overlook, where all manner of illicit activities might go on with a blind eye turned. There was an edge to the atmosphere, as if a fight might erupt at any moment.

In the corner farthest from the door, a group of young men were gathered around a long table playing cards. A pile of coins spilled across the board between them, glistening in a puddle of beer. I pushed through the drinkers standing around the serving hatch, fending off the attentions of a couple of bawds on the way, and found a spot where I could stand and observe the game alongside the handful of other onlookers. The six players had evidently been drinking for some time. I scanned their faces, waiting for the right moment.

A skinny young man with wild red hair knocked twice on the table and his fellows laid their cards faceup. A brief pause followed for calculation, then a cry went up from one curly-haired youth, who leaned forwards and scooped up the pile of coins. His friends cursed and thumped their fists on the table in a show of resentment as the red-haired boy gathered the cards, gave them a practised shuffle, and began to deal again. I was not a great connoisseur of cards—Sidney had tried to teach me without much success—but I knew enough to see that they were playing one-and-thirty, a reasonably simple game to follow. When each player had five cards, more coins were thrown into the middle, along with more spirited cursing and threats.

"If you keep on at this rate, Nick, you'll have lost all your father's legacy before you even get your hands on it," remarked the young man with the curly hair, who had won the last hand. The boy opposite him glanced up sharply, frowning. He was unremarkable to look at, with light brown hair and a sparse beard over a solid jaw, thick eyebrows that met in the middle, and a nose that had once been broken. There was an angry cast to his features, as if he held a grievance against anyone who so much as looked at him.

"Don't worry yourself about that, Charlie," he said, slurring his words. "There's plenty there to be going on with."

"It's not in your coffers yet, though," said the red-haired boy, examining his new cards. He seemed the most sober of the lot.

"It will be as soon as they catch that bitch and burn her."

"What if they don't?"

"Jesus Christ!" The boy called Nick slammed his pot down hard on the table; beer sloshed across the cards. "I said I'm sick of talking about it. Are you going to play or sit there all night gossiping like a laundry woman?"

There was a smattering of laughter from the crowd, followed by a crash as the young man at the end of the table slumped sideways on his bench and fell to the floor.

"God's blood! There's Peter finished for the night. I've seen girl children hold their drink better than him." The red-haired boy pushed his chair back reluctantly and knelt to haul his fallen comrade into a sitting position. "Leave him there, he can sober up in his own time. Damned if I'm carrying him home again."

"Who will take his cards?" The curly-haired youth named Charlie turned expectantly to the little group standing by the table. "Anyone?"

"I've better things to do with my money than throw it to the likes of you," muttered one man, with a broad grin. The other spectators laughed.

The boy looked disappointed; he cast his eyes around the group until finally his gaze came to rest on me.

"I will play, if you like." I shrugged, unconcerned. The crowd fell silent and I felt their eyes on me, curiosity piqued by my accent. I looked only at the boy who had spoken. He raised an eyebrow, then glanced around at his friends for approval.

"All right, stranger. Join us for one game and we'll see how you go."

"You mean, if you take my money, I can stay on."

He grinned.

"See, he understands. There are men who travel from town to town making a living from cards—we want to be sure you are not one of those. Take Peter's seat. Nick, shove up, will you, make room for—what's your name, stranger?"

"Filippo."

"Where are you from?" The boy called Nick turned his belligerent glare on me as I squeezed onto the bench beside him. He smelled sharply of sweat and drink; I clenched my fists under the table as I thought of him pawing at Sophia. For this could only be Nicholas Kingsley, the son of Sophia's dead husband.

"Italy." I pulled a handful of coins from the purse at my belt and tossed them on to the pile before consulting my cards and smiling at my new companions. I may not be much of a gambler, but years of travelling had taught me that no one makes friends quicker than a man known to be a gracious loser at the card table.

And so I proved to be. I let them take money from me on the first game, laughed at my own ill fortune, was duly invited to stay for the second, bought another pitcher of beer for the table, and another—though happily my companions were so far gone in drink themselves that they failed to notice I drank off one pot to every two or three of theirs. By the end of the night my purse was considerably lighter and my head reeling from the strong ale, but I had been pronounced "a good fellow" by the red-haired boy, whose name was Robin Bates and who seemed the self-appointed leader of the group—all sons of minor gentry or gentlemen farmers, in their early twenties, with a small allowance at their disposal and no apparent inclination as yet to apply themselves to any profession.

"You should play with us again tomorrow, friend," Bates said when the night's gaming was over, chinking his winnings in his palm with a nod of satisfaction. I was about to reply when I noticed a murmuring among the group of onlookers, which died away to a pregnant silence as they parted to make way for a newcomer. The curly-haired boy elbowed Nicholas Kingsley, who sat up, blearily focusing, before his face set hard.

"Where's my money, Kingsley, you son of a whoremonger?"

I looked round and saw, with some surprise, that the speaker was the broad-shouldered gatekeeper from the cathedral. He appeared even larger in the low room, and it was clear that, despite their bravado, the man's size and the grim look on his face were causing Nicholas and his friends to shrink back in their seats. No one spoke. Eventually Nicholas rubbed his forehead and sighed.

"Not this again. I owe you no money, Tom Garth."

"Your family does." The gatekeeper stepped closer to the table, jabbing a meaty finger an inch from Nicholas's nose. His friends slid as far from him on their benches as they could manage. "Your father has owed my family reparation these past nine years, and now his debt passes to you, though you sit here gaming away money that isn't yours to lose." His voice shook with a rage he was struggling to master.

Nicholas shrugged, his eyes fixed firmly on the contents of his tankard.

"Take me to law for it, then."

This seemed to have the effect of poking an angry dog with a stick.

"As if I could!" Spittle flecked Tom Garth's lips; it was clear that he had taken a drink, though he was just drunk enough to be aggressive without losing control. "Your father *was* the law in this town—what chance did we have?" He wiped his mouth with the back of his hand. "The law has no time for the likes of us. Is it any wonder we have to take it into our own hands?"

Nicholas looked up finally, a sneer spread across his face.

"Oh, you are become a lawyer now, are you, Garth?"

This was a mistake; Tom Garth seized Nicholas by the collar of his shirt, bunching it in his fist, and dragged him forward over the table until their noses were touching.

"I know what's right and what's wrong, you little shit. Your father was a murderer and you're no better. Damned lucky for you your stepmother ran off the way she did, eh? Otherwise people might start asking what you were doing there that night." He tightened his grip; Nicholas gave a little yelp.

"Now then, Tom Garth, let's not have any trouble here." The landlord had materialised beside our table, arms folded across his ample belly, his tone a practised mixture of calming and warning.

Garth glared at Nicholas for a long moment, then shoved him forcefully onto his bench; Nicholas hit the wall with a thump and slumped back, rubbing his neck.

"You lying churl bastard!" he managed to croak. "Say that again and

I'll have you in gaol for it. Your mother's a witch and your sister was a whore, all Canterbury knows it."

Garth made as if to step forward, but the landlord laid a restraining hand on his arm.

"Probably time you all turned in for the night, boys," he added, turning to us, his tone amiable enough, though it was not a suggestion. "And you be on your way too, Tom." He clapped the larger man gently on the shoulder in a manner that made clear where his sympathies lay. "If there's any brawling in the street outside my inn, none of you'll be coming back tomorrow, or the next day, or in a month of Sundays." He looked carefully around the group to make sure we had understood.

We all nodded meekly, like chided schoolboys, and for a moment I wanted to laugh. Tom Garth ran a hand through his hair, directed a last scorching look at Nicholas, and strode to the door.

Outside in the street, no one spoke. My companions peered anxiously up and down the lane, as if afraid Tom Garth might leap at them from the shadows.

"That fellow has quite a grudge against you," I remarked.

"He's a drunk and a madman. My father should have had him locked up." Nick Kingsley untied his breeches to piss up the wall, turning over his shoulder to his friend. "I shall stay with you tonight, Robin. I'm not walking home alone with that churl waiting to knock me down."

"Again? What is the good of inheriting such a fine house if you are always too drunk to sleep in it?" Bates said, slapping his friend on the back.

"Why do you not hold the game at your own house to save you the walk?" I asked.

Nick focused his gaze sufficiently to glare at me. "Because there are no women there, of course."

I shrugged and gestured around the group. "I don't see any women here either."

"Ha! Good point, my friend. It's because he would have to provide the drink," Bates said.

"It's a good thought of the Italian's," said Charlie, leaning on Bates's other shoulder. "Better than giving all our money to that arsehole Hoskyns for the watered-down cat's piss he serves up." He jerked his thumb towards the Three Tuns. "And no one to tell us when to leave. We could keep going till dawn, if we wanted. Your father must have left some fine barrels in his cellar, Nick—someone should make use of them."

Nick rounded on him with a sudden lurch, pointing unsteadily.

"The house is not in my name yet, nor anything in it," he blurted. "The attorney says—"

"Oh, the attorney says, the attorney says!" Bates rolled his eyes. "You bleat it like a catechism. Fuck the attorney—of course it's yours! What are you, a child? Are you going to let that murdering bitch deprive you of your inheritance? Your father was hard enough on you when he was alive—the least you deserve is to enjoy his money now."

"But I can't touch it yet!" Nick wheeled about, looking from Bates to Charlie to the others until finally his wild gaze came to rest on me and I saw a dark flash of anger in his eyes, a hint of unpredictable fury.

This was a young man well capable of violence if provoked, I had no doubt, but the murder of Sir Edward, though brutal, was no hotheaded, sudden attack; the killer had planned it, waited for his opportunity, even planted evidence to condemn Sophia. I had yet to see whether this Nick was capable of such calculation.

He pointed a trembling finger at me, his eyes clouded with drink and rage.

"She will not take it from me," he said, as if this were a personal threat. "Nor will that churl Tom Garth, nor the Widow Gray, nor any of them."

I nodded in agreement, since this seemed the only possible response. Bates laughed.

"Poor Filippo has no idea what you are talking about, you arsehole," he said. "Well then, it is settled—tomorrow we shall drink the night away at your house, Nick—and you must join us, friend." He turned to me and winked. "Meet us here at seven—and be sure to bring a full purse."

I punched him heartily on the arm by way of reply, a gesture I had learned from Sidney and which he seemed to appreciate. Silently, I congratulated myself; an invitation into the Kingsley house was more than I had expected on my first day in Canterbury. It would be something encouraging to tell Sophia, in any case, when I saw her the next day; a thought I comforted myself with that night as I lay alone on my straw mattress at the Cheker, sleep held at bay by questions. What was Tom Garth's grudge against the Kingsley family? He must be a relative of the maid Fitch had mentioned, the one who had died, but what did he mean by taking the law into his own hands? What had he meant when he said Nicholas Kingsley was there that night? And what did the Widow Gray have to do with Edward Kingsley's money? I sighed, turning uncomfortably to one side and then the other. Even the release that came from imagining Sophia stretched out beside me failed to bring the sweet oblivion of sleep.

Chapter *7*

I decided to call at the apothecary's shop early the next day, as it was on the road to the weavers' houses. Though my stomach was much improved—a change I could only attribute to the ale at the Three Tuns—I calculated that the purchase of Fitch's tonic might be repaid by the garrulous apothecary's store of local gossip. Plenty of people were abroad in the High Street by the time the cathedral bells were striking the hour of eight, carrying baskets or pushing barrows of goods, and most of the shopfronts had their windows open to passersby, but when I reached Fitch's shop I found it still shuttered and the door closed fast. A plump girl in a white coif was peering anxiously in through the windows, her hands cupped around her face. A basket covered with a linen cloth sat on the doorstep.

"What time does he open?" I said, by way of conversation.

She jumped at being addressed, looking me up and down with apprehension, but then her eyes flicked nervously to the window again. "Is he expecting you?"

"He told me to come back this morning for a remedy he recommended. But I forgot to ask what time he opened."

The girl shook her head. Neat white teeth chewed at her bottom lip.

I guessed her to be in her late teens, though she had that freckled, pink-and-white English complexion that made her look younger.

"He's always open before the bells sound for eight. And he especially asked me to stop by good and early as he wanted to send me shopping before I go to work. I do what I can for him since my aunt died last year. Poor Uncle," she added, with a confidential air. "I used to help in the shop sometimes—he liked to teach me a little of his business—but Mother said it was not fit for a girl to learn, so that was an end of that. Now I have to work on the bread stall for Mistress Blunt." She made a face that left no doubt as to her opinion of her current employer.

"You must be Rebecca, then," I said, smiling. "He spoke of you when I was in the shop yesterday."

The girl blushed and giggled, but the laughter quickly faded on her lips as she turned back to the shuttered windows.

"I hope nothing's wrong. It's not like him to be late. I've tried knocking, but there's no reply and I can't see a thing inside." She bit her lip again.

I pressed my face to the nearest window, shading my face as she had done. The shutters were old and it was just possible to glimpse the inner room through chinks and splits in the wood, but the shop was so dim I could barely make out the shape of the shelves lining the walls.

"Sometimes he doesn't hear if he's in the back room with the stills all boiling and bubbling," the girl continued, just as something caught my eye inside the shop: a pale shape on the floor. I squinted harder, closing my hands around my face to shut out every slant of daylight, and realised it was a book, lying faceup, its pages spread. It was not the only item on the floor either. Though I could not make out much, it looked as if the contents of the apothecary's shelves had been scattered carelessly around the shop. Apprehension tightened in my chest.

"Is there another entrance to the shop?" I asked. The words came sharper than I meant and I saw my own anxiety reflected in her face.

"There is a yard, at the back," she faltered. "It gives on to the back room and my uncle's lodging above the shop. But why . . . ?"

"I think I should check. You wait here."

She nodded, her lips set with fear. I found a small alley running down the side of the shop next door; it led to a narrow lane behind the row of buildings on the High Street, their yards hidden by a brick wall perhaps six feet high. A small wooden gate in the wall proved locked from the inside, but it took little effort to climb and I dropped into the apothecary's yard, one hand on my knife. The door to the back room of the shop was closed, the casements to either side intact. But when I tried the door it opened easily and I saw Fitch sprawled facedown in the room he had used as a distillery, a pool of blood congealed around his head.

I took a deep breath. The room was stiflingly hot, despite the early hour, and ripe with the smell of blood and meat. Flies buzzed purposefully around the body, the sound intrusively loud in the stillness. I crossed the room slowly, absorbing the devastation. My feet crunched across broken glass; there had clearly been a struggle in the room, for the apothecary's glass bottles were smashed across the floor, sticky patches of liquid visible on the boards where their contents had spilled. Blood was spattered across the walls in places, and smeared on the floorboards, as if Fitch had not simply fallen where he lay, but careened around the room spraying blood from his wound before dropping. An iron poker lay discarded a couple of feet from the body; was this the weapon that had struck him down, or had he tried to defend himself with it?

I looked from the poker to the wide brick fireplace and understood the source of the room's infernal heat: a few embers were still smoking in the hearth. I picked my way through the mess on the floor to take a look. A blackened pot hung over the fire on an iron spit. I picked up a small bellows that lay in the hearth and squeezed it towards the ashes; a faint red glow coughed into life for a moment before fading in a cloud of grey dust. It had been some hours since this fire was stoked; if the apothecary kept it burning in this room to make his infusions, he must have been killed the night before. I wiped the sweat from my brow with my sleeve, and shook my head, suddenly overwhelmed by the enormity of what I had walked into. I had come to investigate one murder and stumbled by chance upon another; now the law would require me to testify as the first finder of the body, and there could be no pretending otherwise, since the girl was waiting outside for me. But who could have wanted to kill the cheerful apothecary? He had not given the impression yesterday that he was a man with anything to fear.

As I stood staring into the empty hearth, trying to decide how I should proceed, I noticed among the ashes a few scraps of burnt paper. Intrigued, I bent closer and realised that under the charred logs was a mass of blackened paper fragments; someone had clearly thrown a bundle of documents onto the fire not long before it was allowed to die. Most were reduced to ash, but one or two had fluttered to the back of the fireplace and escaped the worst of the flames. Pulling up my shirtsleeve, I reached in and hooked out the truant pages. They were badly burned around the edges, but in the centre some of the writing was still legible, through brown patches left by the heat and smoke. One appeared to be a page torn from the great ledger Fitch had used the day before when he recorded my purchase for his accounts. Almost none of the writing was left visible, though I could make out the line "mercury & antimony salts . . ." and beside it the name "Ezek. Syk . . ."

The second surviving page was more interesting; I held it towards the window and tried to make sense of the words I read.

"After Paracelsus," it said, at the top, "according to his *Archidoxes.*" The next few lines had been rendered obscure by the fire. But beneath, the word "laudanum" stood out clearly, followed by what looked like instructions for a remedy. "Mixed with one part rosemary oil and one part good wine and distilled will bring on the sleep of Morpheus . . ." Again the writing disappeared, but below whatever had been scorched away I read the word "Belladonna." Underneath, the author had underlined the following sentence twice, so heavily the quill had pierced the paper: "No more than eight grains diluted while under the influence, though double may be tolerated by . . . [these next two words were illegible]. *Dosis sola facit venenum.*"

The dose alone makes the poison. I knew this maxim of Paracelsus, the great Swiss alchemist and physician who had died some forty years earlier; he argued that all substances were potentially beneficial, even those we call toxic, and that the art of medicine was in judging the quantity and exposure that would heal rather than kill. But he argued a lot more besides; in his alchemical studies, Paracelsus had been a student of the philosophy of Hermes Trismegistus, the Egyptian sage whose wisdom I had studied, though in Paris it had earned me a reputation as a sorcerer. Needless to say, the writings of Paracelsus had been forbidden by my order when I was still a monk and I had risked much to track them down and study them. I recalled paying a substantial sum of money to a black-market bookseller in Naples for a copy of the *Archidoxes of Magic,* a treatise on medicine and alchemy that drew on the movements of the planets and the secrets of astrology. It was not a work I would have expected to find in the shop of a provincial apothecary, but perhaps there was more to Fitch than had been apparent in his breezy, village-gossip manner.

Nothing more could be made out; I turned the paper over but it offered no further clues. In the silence of the room I could hear the blood pounding in my ears as I struggled to make sense of the fragment. Holding it between my fingers as if it might crumble to dust at any moment, I forced my eyes back to the body on the floor.

There was no need to move Fitch to see that his skull had been staved in, though the face and neck were also badly battered, suggesting his assailant had not felled him with the first blow. His limbs had already stiffened into grotesque contortions, one arm thrown forward next to the face. Crouching beside him, I closed my eyes for a moment and laid my fingertips on the sleeve of his shirt, hard and crusted with dried blood, as a mark of respect, trying to imagine the scene that must have ensued not long after I had bid him goodbye with a promise to return in the morning for his tonic. The killing seemed the frenzied work of a madman—Fitch must have been chased around his distillery, desperately trying to fight off his attacker—but the burnt pages in the fireplace suggested something different. Who had thrown them into the flames? Fitch, to prevent someone from seeing them, or whoever had struck him down?

My thoughts were interrupted by a sharp knock at the door. I had forgotten the girl, Rebecca, waiting outside. Now I stepped carefully around the dead apothecary and through the narrow doorway into the shop. This room too was in a state of chaos, as I had seen through the shutters; books had been pulled from shelves and lay scattered about, and an earthenware jar, knocked to the ground, had broken to spill its contents—a pungent yellow powder—across the reeds that covered the stone floor. Empty spaces gaped on a number of the shelves where objects had evidently been hastily removed and not replaced.

The knock came again and I heard the girl calling, "Hello?" Crossing to the front door, I found it locked, with the key still in the keyhole. Whoever had killed Fitch must have left through the back, then. But the door had not been forced; the apothecary must have opened it to his attacker. As I turned the key, my hand froze and my breath caught in my throat as I recalled the physician Sykes in his absurd plague mask, thundering in and demanding that Fitch lock up the shop to give him private audience.

"Uncle William?" the girl asked from the other side of the door, her voice doubtful. I pulled it open just a fraction; as soon as she saw me, her lip trembled. "Where is he?"

"You must go for a constable right away," I said, keeping my voice low. A couple of goodwives with covered baskets had stopped in the street behind the girl and were watching the door with lively curiosity. "Don't stop to speak to anyone—just bring him as fast as you can. Do you know where to find one?"

"I want to see my uncle! What has happened?" She planted herself stubbornly on the threshold, her voice loud enough to attract further attention from passersby. I motioned with a finger against my lip.

"I'm afraid your uncle has met with an accident."

"Oh, God!" She pressed her hands to her cheeks and set up a wail that threatened to rouse the whole street.

"Please—you must fetch a constable." Perhaps the urgency in my voice lent it some authority; she stopped her noise abruptly, looked at me uncertainly for a moment, and nodded. "Bring him around the back," I added, giving one sharp look to the staring women before closing the shop door and locking it again. Nothing draws a crowd like a violent death, and I felt the dead man deserved better than to be made into a spectacle for gawping market-goers.

In the gloom, I bent to look at one of the books that had been thrown onto the floor. It was a volume of *A New Herbal* by William Turner, dog-eared and clearly well-used by a reader who had meticulously annotated and illustrated the margins of almost every page. Squinting, I held up the fragment of paper I had rescued from the embers against the book; the hand was the same as that of the notes scribbled on the pages, which it seemed reasonable to assume was that of Fitch himself. So the papers in the fire, with their curious reference to Paracelsus, had been written by the apothecary—but why had they been thrown into the flames? Without quite knowing why, I folded the charred paper and tucked it into the purse I carried at my belt.

The smell of dead meat by now was almost overpowering; I decided to wait for the constable outside the back door. Still I found it hard to tear my eyes from the corpse. I had looked on violent death many times in my life, especially in the past couple of years, yet it never ceased to chill me, the fragility of our bodies, the way a life can be snuffed out quicker than a candle. Presently the sound of brisk footsteps interrupted this reverie, followed by a rap at the gate in the back wall. I hurried to open the latch and found myself face-to-face with the ginger-haired man whom I had noticed in the marketplace by the cathedral gate the previous evening. He narrowed his eyes as if trying to place me, stroking his pointed beard, then waved me aside.

"Carey Edmonton, constable of this parish. An accident, the girl said?"

"I didn't want to alarm her. This was no accident—the apothecary has been murdered in his distillery."

The constable simply stared, as if he had not understood.

"Murder? How do you know?"

"Take a look."

He continued to regard me a moment longer, as if he was not certain whether to believe me, before asserting himself by brushing past and in through the open doorway, where he stopped abruptly as if slapped, gagging on the smell.

"What in God's name has happened here?" he whispered, almost to himself, his words muffled by the sleeve he pressed to his mouth. He took a step back and turned to me again, as if expecting me to make sense of the sight before him.

"He was beaten to death, but it seems he put up a brave fight before he was felled. The street door was locked from the inside, but this back door was open, though the gate from the yard to the alleyway was padlocked from the inside."

Edmonton took his hand slowly from his mouth and stepped back into the yard, frowning as if noticing me properly for the first time.

"How did you get in, then? And who the Devil are you to be poking around?"

"My name is Filippo Savolino. I came as a customer—yesterday Master Fitch had promised me a remedy. I found the girl outside, anxious because she could get no reply, so I offered to see what was wrong. When I couldn't open the gate, I climbed the wall."

He pulled at his beard again.

"I see. I have seen you before, have I not? Loitering about the Buttermarket, as I recall."

"I was not loitering—I was on my way to visit my friend the Reverend Doctor Harry Robinson at the cathedral," I said, stung by his tone. "You will see a great disturbance in the shop," I continued, trying to sound more placatory as I led him through to the front room. "It seems to me that whoever killed the apothecary was looking for something on his shelves."

"A robbery, then," the constable said, as if the business required no further consideration. He glanced at the mess on the floor, set his jaw, and nodded to himself. "Since the plague fears in London, we have more than our share of vagabonds and beggars littering the streets. Probably one of them, looking for gold or whatever he could sell. I'll have them rounded up—we'll soon find the villain that did this." He shot a brief glance back at the workshop and sniffed. "He was a good man, William Fitch, well liked by the townspeople. There'll be a great deal of anger against the incomers for this."

"And yet it seems that Master Fitch readily admitted his attacker himself without suspicion, since the shop was locked from the inside, and there is no sign of force," I said. "And see, here—it is mainly books and papers pulled from the shelves, as if the person was looking for something quite specific. I am not persuaded that this was an ordinary robbery." I hesitated for a moment, wondering if I should mention the appearance of Sykes the previous evening, but decided against it; the physician was clearly a prominent citizen of Canterbury and any suggestion that he might be implicated would only draw unwelcome attention to myself.

The constable folded his arms across his chest and his moustache twitched as his lip curled into a sneer.

"Oh, you are not *persuaded*? And who are you to offer opinions either way? Are you a parish constable? I think not. You are not even a parishioner."

I held up my hands as if to mitigate any offence.

"I beg your pardon, Constable. I was only thinking aloud."

He grunted.

"I shall want testimony from you and the girl. Where will I find you?"

"At the Cheker of Hope."

"Good. Do not leave the city, Master . . ."

"Savolino. I won't."

He nodded curtly and gestured towards the back gate.

"Now leave me to my job, if you please."

I bowed slightly and crossed to the door, with a last glance back at the workshop of the unfortunate apothecary. A more thorough search of the place would yield better evidence of the killer, I was sure, but I pulled the front door closed behind me, telling myself that it was no longer my business. I had enough to do to find one murderer, let alone another that had nothing to do with me, and it was only the merest chance that I had discovered the death of Fitch. And yet, as I emerged into the light of the High Street to see a little gaggle of interested observers gathered around the shopfront, I had to acknowledge that hiding that fragment of paper, with its mysterious reference to Paracelsus, was as good as admitting I could not let the matter go. The constable would find some hapless vagrant to blame in order to satisfy the townspeople, who would cheer for his hanging, and all would be forgotten, while the murderer congratulated himself. This was what passed for justice, more often a question of avoiding public unrest than of discovering the truth. This is not your problem, I told myself again, but the apothecary's murder troubled me, perhaps because the manner of it was so similar to the killing of Sir Edward Kingsley.

I noticed the girl Rebecca at the heart of the crowd, wailing loudly and being comforted by the two stout women who had been watching earlier. No one paid me any attention, so I took the opportunity to slip away towards the weavers' houses.

A man in his fifties answered the door of the Fleury house. He had greying hair, a full moustache and wore a beaten expression, as if hardship and exhaustion had robbed him of any vital spirit. He looked me up and down, as if I were one more burden Fate had seen fit to lay on his shoulders.

"Monsieur Fleury?"

"I know who you are. Come inside." He glanced along the lane to either side, but there was no sign of movement. "Is that blood on your stocking?" he asked as he closed the door behind me. The flatness of his tone suggested he was not especially interested either way. I glanced down; there was a streak of dark red on my ankle where I must have brushed against Fitch's body.

"I was—at the scene of an accident," I said.

Fleury shook his head.

"I have seen enough blood spilled." He took me by the sleeve and pulled me close, dropping his voice. "You must take her away. Do you understand? My son . . ." He faltered and shook his head again. "I got my family out of Paris alive while our friends and neighbours were butchered in their homes. I thought we would be safe in a Protestant country. But already we have lost one child. I will not see my son hanged as well. The girl should not be in my house. We tried to help her, but once is enough. She is dangerous."

"She is unlucky."

He set his jaw. "I say she is dangerous, monsieur. You know it and I know it. Only my son cannot see this, because he is young and she is beautiful. Perhaps you close your eyes to it as well, but I am old enough not to have this blindness." He gave a great sigh that seemed to reverberate through his bones.

He opened a door on the left of the small hallway and motioned me into a long room overlooking the river and dominated by the wooden frames of three large looms, where women sat working the treadle, the mechanism clicking rhythmically as they fed the shuttle back and forth. They gave us only the briefest glance as we passed through, their eyes fixed to the coloured yarns stretched on the frames before them. Bobbin racks and contraptions for stretching thread lined the walls. I looked out of the window at the narrow creek; a man was loading bales of cloth from a small jetty at the back of the house on to a low boat. At the far end of this workshop a narrow staircase ascended to the floor above. I glanced down at the scene of industry in the workshop below as we climbed.

"Business is good here?"

Fleury shrugged.

"Life is always precarious in a strange land. You know this, I think. But we can feed ourselves, for the moment, and for that I give thanks."

At the top of the stairs was a long landing with another staircase, even narrower, rising to the next floor. He gestured for me to climb alone.

"In the attic," he whispered, by way of explanation. "Keep your voices down."

The ceiling was low, sloping to either side under the crooked roof and I had to bend to avoid the supporting beams as I pushed open the small door at the top of the stairs. Sophia was seated at a rough-hewn table, Olivier Fleury standing by the tiny window, leaning on the sill and looking out. Both started with alarm as I slipped through the door; Sophia jumped quickly to her feet.

"Bruno!" For a moment she gave the impression that she was about to run and embrace me, but instead she flashed me a shy smile and raised her arms before letting them fall to her sides. Olivier regarded me with that same expression of sullen disdain. "Any news? Have you found him?"

I looked at Sophia. She had washed and, though she was still dressed in boy's clothes, they were now clean. Her hair hung softly, almost into her eyes, its shortness at the back emphasising her long, slender neck. I noticed the days of riding in the sun had brought out a scattering of freckles across the bridge of her nose.

"Give me a chance—I have not been here a day. But there is news— I have just come from the scene of another murder."

"What?"

Her hand flew to her mouth; she stared at me, eyes wide. But my attention was distracted by a gasp from the corner of the room; it was only then that I realised there was a third person present, a young woman dressed in black, sitting on a straw mattress tucked away under the eaves. I raised my eyebrows at Sophia; she glanced briefly at the woman on the bed.

"Hélène, Olivier's sister," she said, as if this was not of much interest. "But who has been murdered?"

"Is it a child?" the woman Hélène whispered, her voice dry as autumn leaves. She had fine fair hair and the same full lips as her brother. I looked at her in surprise.

"No—it was the apothecary from the High Street, William Fitch."

Hélène gave a sort of shudder and crumpled visibly, as if she had been struck. She buried her face in her handkerchief and though her shoulders shook violently she made no sound.

"I am sorry. Did you know him well?" I asked her gently.

"It's not that." Olivier glared at me, as if once again I had been the bringer of misfortune, and crossed the room to give his sister a cursory pat on the arm.

Sophia frowned. "Everyone knew Fitch—he was something of a busybody. I kept away from his shop—he asked too many questions." She shook her head. "But he was amiable with it. I wonder who could have wanted to kill him?"

"The manner of it was similar to your husband's murder—his skull was smashed. You don't suppose they could be connected?"

She frowned.

"I can't see how. Especially if my husband's killer wanted to be sure I was blamed. Another murder in my absence would undo that."

"Did Sir Edward know Fitch?"

"He knew everyone in Canterbury. But he didn't associate with him, if that's what you mean."

"But he knew Ezekiel Sykes the physician well, and Sykes knew Fitch," I mused, thinking again of Sykes's peremptory visit to the apothecary the previous afternoon.

Sophia made an impatient sound.

"You are overcomplicating matters, Bruno. I have told you where you would do best to look for my husband's killer. The poor apothecary was probably attacked by robbers, taking advantage of the fact that the city is without a justice of the peace at the moment."

"So the constable wants to think."

"Well, then." She folded her arms. "You see the world as full of hidden connections, Bruno. Sometimes things are no more than they appear. Didn't William of Ockham say so?" She gave me a mischievous smile, which I could not help returning.

"Something like that. May we talk in private?"

Sophia looked across at Olivier, who still kept a protective hand on his sister's shoulder. Hélène had sunk into herself, her face obscured by the handkerchief and her clasped hands. He nodded curtly at me, and extended a hand to help his sister rise.

"I hope you will find this man soon, monsieur," he said, through clenched teeth, as he passed me. "Then you can both leave us in peace."

"I will do my best," I said, with forced politeness. Hélène's gaze flickered briefly upwards to my face, then quickly back to the floor; I reached out and touched her gently on the arm and she flinched as if I had hit her.

"Pardon me," I said, in French, "but why did you ask if a child had been killed?"

Her red-rimmed eyes filled with tears; she shook her head tightly and bunched the handkerchief harder against her lips. Olivier glared at me again as he put a protective arm around her and led her to the door.

"I have said the wrong thing, somehow," I observed when they had gone. "Why is she so distressed?"

Sophia sat down at the table again and rubbed the back of her neck. She looked suddenly weary.

"That poor girl. Widowed at eighteen—her husband was killed during the massacre in Paris. She was pregnant when they fled to England and her son, Denis, was born here. Six months ago, he disappeared."

"How do you mean?"

"Just that—he went out on an errand for his grandparents and never returned. He was only eleven." She bit her lip and I noticed how she knotted her fingers together, though she kept her expression controlled, her gaze concentrated on a point on the wall. I guessed she was thinking about her own lost son and the sorrow of a mother.

"So that was what Olivier meant when he said they had enough grief already." I pulled up a stool opposite her. "They reported it, I suppose? There was a search for the boy?"

"They reported it to my husband as the local justice—that was how I first met Olivier. He refused to give up—he came to the house every day until finally Sir Edward had to threaten him with arrest for trespass.

There was a search, but since the Huguenots are not regarded by many in the town as true citizens, you may imagine how little effort was made. They told the family he had probably just run off to be a ship's boy."

"But you don't think so?"

She shrugged.

"I never met the boy. The family say he would not have done so. But Hélène has talked herself into believing the worst, because of the other child that was found."

"What other child?"

"It was last autumn, before I arrived here, a few months before her son went missing. The body of a young boy, around the same age, was found dismembered on a midden outside the city walls. He was a beggar child, they said. But Hélène has seized on it to fuel her belief that her son has been killed too."

"What do you think?"

She gave me a long look and sighed heavily.

"I think it's terrible, naturally, but . . ." She reached out and laid a hand gently over mine. "Bruno, you don't need to unravel every unsolved death in this town. Just the one you came for, remember? Have you spoken to Nicholas Kingsley yet?"

"I will be a guest at his house tonight."

She squeezed my hand, her eyes bright. "I knew you would manage this, Bruno. You will find something there to clear me, I'm certain of it."

I regarded her with a serious expression.

"You are very determined that it should be Nicholas. And he is equally determined that it was you."

"Well, obviously." She removed her hand. "As I have said, if I am convicted of killing his father, he will inherit instead."

"But if I find evidence to incriminate him, you become a wealthy widow. Am I right?"

She leaned across the table and fixed me with that look, her eyes flashing.

"And would I not deserve that, after everything I have suffered?"

"Of course. But you will inherit regardless of who the real killer turns out to be, surely, provided it can be proved? I can't produce evidence against Nicholas just because you want it to be him."

"But who else would have a motive for killing Sir Edward and ensuring I am blamed, if not him? Especially after his father's will was changed."

"Tell me about the will, then."

"Before Sir Edward married me, Nicholas was his only next of kin and stood to inherit everything. But about a month before my husband was murdered, he made a new testament. Rights to his property and all the income from his estates was made over to me to be passed to our children, whenever they should arrive." She broke off and made a face of disgust at the idea. "Nicholas was given a small allowance—barely enough for the lowest kind of food and board."

"But your husband had no affection for you. Why would he do that?"

"To humiliate his son, I suppose. He had spent so much on Nicholas's education, only for him to drink and gamble away his chances of a profession in the law. He said he had given Nicholas ample chance to change his ways, and the best way to make him grow up was to close his purse."

I nodded. "I can see that would have made Nicholas furious. But angry enough to beat his own father to death?"

Sophia rested her chin on her hand.

"I could believe it. To murder his father and have me executed for it would have been a fine revenge on both of us—with the advantage of removing any obstacle to his inheritance."

"And it rests entirely between you and Nicholas? No one else stands to benefit from Sir Edward's will?"

"Not that I know of, but then, I never read the document. I only know because Sir Edward took great pleasure in telling Nicholas and me of the changes over dinner. Perhaps he thought it would encourage me to hurry up and give him a better son."

"Then why did Nicholas mention the Widow Gray?"

"I don't know. What did he say?"

"She was one of the people he said would not take his inheritance from him, when he was in his cups last night."

Sophia looked uncomfortable.

"There is gossip about her in the town . . ." Her voice trailed off. "But who knows if there is any substance to it."

"Your husband knew her?"

She nodded.

"Could she have been his mistress?"

She shrugged, expressionless.

"Maybe. She has a son, I know that much. A boy of about twelve."

I nodded. If the boy was Sir Edward's bastard, that might explain why Nicholas Kingsley thought the widow wanted money from the estate.

"Sir Edward's friends—the ones who visited him for those secretive meetings. Might any of them have wanted him dead? Had they fallen out, perhaps?"

Sophia looked at her hands for a long moment. Eventually she raised her head.

"Bruno, those are powerful men you are talking about. If you start poking into their business, you'll draw unwelcome attention to yourself and they'll find a way to stop you."

"I thought you wanted me to ask questions?"

"Yes, but—what good will it do anyone if they have you arrested? Better that you concentrate your search—"

"On Nicholas Kingsley?" I stood up, and took a few paces, before rounding on her again, frustrated. "But what if it isn't him? What if someone killed your husband, not for his money, but for some other reason—revenge, or because he crossed them? You would not want an innocent man to die, surely, however obnoxious he may be. Think—who else might have wanted him dead? What about Tom Garth?"

"Tom Garth? Oh—from the cathedral. What has he to do with it?"

"He held a grudge against the Kingsley family. Last night I heard him talk of taking the law into his own hands. And he is gatekeeper at the cathedral—he could easily have killed Sir Edward that night."

"But Tom Garth had resented Sir Edward for years, since his sister died. Why would he suddenly take it into his head to kill him now? And why would he leave a woman's bloodied gloves where they would be found to have me blamed?" She shook her head. "I think you are wandering from the path here, Bruno."

I ran both hands through my hair.

"Look, you said you wanted me to find the truth—that's why you dragged me here. Now you are telling me what I should find!"

"Lower your voice." Her jaw was tight with anger. She took a deep breath. "Very well. His regular supper companions at home were the physician Sykes, the mayor of Canterbury, and the cathedral treasurer—"

"John Langworth."

She looked surprised.

"You know him?"

"We have met. You know that Langworth is suspected of Catholic sympathies? Did your husband share his feelings? What about Sykes?"

"I don't know!" She looked nettled. "I never heard my husband express any religious view that was other than orthodox. You have to understand, Bruno—I was concentrating on surviving."

"I know," I said, attempting to sound soothing.

We looked at each other in silence for a moment, until she dropped her gaze to the table.

"It was Langworth who brought me the news of my husband's death, and his belongings."

"And Langworth who found the body." I thought again of Harry's warning. Langworth's close connection to Henry Howard should have made me more inclined to heed the general view that to cross the treasurer was an act of wilful self-sabotage; instead it made me more determined that he should not be allowed to hide behind the reputation he had tried to create.

Sophia looked up at me, apprehensive.

"That doesn't mean—"

"I was thinking aloud." I brushed her objection aside as a thought occurred to me. "Do you think your husband knew that people heard you screaming? Visitors to the house, I mean."

"Screaming?" she said, as if the idea were absurd. A crease appeared between her eyebrows. "What are you talking about?"

"When he beat you."

"But I never screamed." Her voice became very steady and quiet. "He told me if I made a sound he would make it a thousand times worse. Then it became a matter of pride—not to cry at all, to take it all without flinching." She picked at the skin around her nails and I saw the muscles in her jaw tense.

"Perhaps you cried out without realising it," I suggested. Her scathing look told me what she thought of that idea.

"I didn't scream," she repeated firmly, closing her eyes. After a moment she opened them again and looked at me. "What makes you say that I did?"

"A girl delivering something to the house says she heard someone screaming in the grounds. Who could it be, if not you?"

Sophia shook her head. "Foxes? The house is surrounded by a burial ground grown wild—there must be dens by the dozen."

"Perhaps." I sighed. She was right; I needed to concentrate first on the obvious instead of chasing after every chance rumour I caught about Sir Edward. I recalled the girl Rebecca's noisy grief outside the apothecary's shop earlier; perhaps, as he had suggested, what she heard was no more than the effects of an overactive imagination.

"Stop pacing, Bruno, it's tiring to watch you," Sophia said gently, after a few moments. Then she pushed her stool back and crossed the room to block my path. "Have I asked the impossible?" she whispered, a sad smile hovering at her lips as she rested her hands on my arms, just below the shoulder. It was not quite an embrace, more a gentle restraint.

"I am certain he was killed by someone he knew. It shouldn't be impossible to find that person—I would wager any amount that he is still here in Canterbury."

"Don't wager too much, Bruno, you will be penniless at this rate."

"I know it." I laughed softly and placed my hands on her thin shoulders.

"I just want it to be over," she whispered. "You understand."

"I will move heaven and earth to find this man for you, Sophia, if it is in my power. I have said I will." I placed a finger under her chin and gently tilted her face upwards to me. For a moment, as she looked me directly in the eye, I thought I glimpsed her with her defences down, open and vulnerable.

She nodded without speaking, and her lips parted slightly; a pulse quickened in my throat. Almost imperceptibly, I felt her fingers tighten on my arms as the space between us seemed to grow smaller; before I had time to think of the consequences, I found myself leaning towards her, my mouth barely an inch from hers, and to my surprise she did not turn her head or pull away. For an instant I felt her breath warm on my chin, then the door opened. Olivier slipped into the room, his scornful expression for once seeming justified.

"Pardon me," he said drily, in French. "My father says you are talking too loudly. He is afraid the women downstairs will hear you." He was looking at Sophia; she lowered her eyes, and let go of my arms.

"Over the sound of the looms?" My anger at the interruption was hot in my voice. I wondered if he had been listening at the door. He merely returned my look, naked dislike in his eyes, and I saw, whatever Sophia might say about their friendship, this boy regarded me as a rival. The thought gave me a small stab of joy. I forced a smile.

"I should be leaving. I will return tomorrow, I hope with more news."

"Must you go so soon, Bruno?" Sophia raised her eyes to me, but I could not read her look.

"I have work to do, remember?" I made a playful bow in her direction and she smiled. Olivier sucked in his cheeks.

"How long do you expect us to keep her?" he hissed, as I reached the door.

"I don't know." Despite everything, I felt sorry for him. "Until I find who murdered her husband. I hope not too long."

"It was the son. It's obvious."

"If it's obvious, why haven't you told the authorities?"

He responded with a laconic shrug.

"You think they would listen to me? He's the son of a magistrate. It's easier to blame a woman, a foreigner, a refugee, anyone who doesn't have a voice to argue. It is up to you to find the evidence before they will listen. She says you have a gift for this."

"I'm doing my best," I said icily.

But his words made me uncomfortable; I recalled the constable's casual reference earlier to arresting some itinerant—as if it hardly mattered whom—for the murder of the apothecary. Olivier was right; justice here was a cursory affair, dependent upon whether you happened to be in the wrong place with the wrong face or accent. My fingers rested on the purse at my belt, where I had tucked the scrap of burnt paper with the notes from Paracelsus. Leave it, I told myself sternly. What matters is to prevent Sophia being wrongly condemned; you are not responsible for what the law does to anyone else. And yet I could not shake a sense that I ought to do something.

"Then do your best faster," Olivier replied. "My parents are terrified she will be found. Who can blame them?"

I could not find an adequate reply to this, so I nodded curtly and took one last look at Sophia before I opened the door. She met my eye only briefly and then her gaze skittered away to the window. I wondered if she regretted the fact that she had nearly kissed me, or that Olivier had seen us, or both.

Reluctantly I closed the door to the attic room but paused on the stairs for a moment, my head bent under the low rafters, hoping I might hear some of their conversation. Behind the door there was only silence.

I was distracted by a discreet cough from below; I looked down and saw Olivier's father, waiting at the foot of the stairs to show me out.

Chapter 8

Though Monsieur Fleury checked that the lane outside the weavers' cottages was empty before allowing me out, I walked into the High Street with a sense of unease; it seemed I was picking up the fear that saturated that house. Without any clear idea of what to do next, I found myself turning in the direction of the cathedral. I decided to call on Harry Robinson, to see if he had heard the news of the apothecary's murder and what he made of it. It was not yet nine. Outside the shop, a small crowd was still gathered, whispering with relish, hands clasped to scandalised mouths, the goodwives thoroughly enjoying this latest episode of town drama. I hurried past, keeping my head down, though no one paid me any attention. I noticed the girl Rebecca was no longer among them.

Who killed Sir Edward Kingsley? I half smiled to myself at the memory of Sophia quoting William of Ockham at me, as if she were the philosopher. I was fairly certain she could not share those jokes with Olivier; at least I had that on my side. If I had learned anything in the past couple of years, it was that the obvious solution was often far from the truth. She wanted me to find Nicholas Kingsley guilty of his father's murder; it would be a neat solution, certainly, and a chance for revenge on a young man with few redeeming qualities. But to assume his guilt from the beginning would make me no better than Constable Edmonton, with his talk of rounding up vagrants.

Sophia. Damn her, damn her eyes and her mouth and her throat and the curve of her hip and everything else she could not disguise. What was I doing here? I should be in London, among my books, not miles away in a strange city, regarded with suspicion and hostility and mixed up in murders that had nothing to do with me. I, who had always prided myself against the weaknesses of the heart; how often I had mocked or pitied other men who had allowed themselves to be distracted from the pursuit of knowledge by delusions of love. On the one occasion, during my stay in Toulouse, when I had grown to love a woman I could not have, I had made a decision and left for Paris one night without saying goodbye, rather than staying to waste my time and hers in useless pining. How, then, had I allowed myself to fall under the spell of Sophia? Beauty, yes, but I had seen beauty many times before and resisted it. Perhaps it was a kind of recognition; I had seen in Sophia, even from our first meeting, a searching intelligence, a refusal to accept what she was told merely because it had always been so. She and I wanted the same thing: independence, the right to choose our own path and to ask questions, and we had both been born to a station in life that kept such freedom out of reach. Perhaps that was the root of my feelings for her; she reminded me of my younger self. The thought prompted a hollow laugh; was that not the ultimate vanity? "*Sciocco,*" I told myself, under my breath, bunching my right hand into a fist until the nails dug into my palm, as if the pain would bring me back to my senses.

In the Buttermarket, crowds gathered around the stone cross and the horse trough in the centre of the cobbles, the formidable towers of Christ Church gate casting their shadow across the coloured awnings of the market stalls. There was a great deal of animation in the buzz and hum of conversation, the townspeople clearly stirred up by the excitement of another killing in their midst.

Tom Garth stood solid as a stone column in his alcove under the gatehouse arch, arms folded across his broad chest. His expression when he saw me was even more hostile than it had been the day before, yet he nodded me through, holding out his right hand.

"Your knife, sir." He did not meet my eye. "Are you here for divine service?"

I unstrapped the knife from my belt and placed it into his out-stretched palm. "What time is it?"

"Holy Communion at nine, sir. You're early."

"I will call on Doctor Robinson in the meantime." I hesitated. "You were very angry last night, it seemed."

He looked away as if he had not heard me.

"At the Three Tuns," I persisted.

"I have good cause," he said eventually, still not meeting my eye. He turned my knife between his hands.

"Young Master Kingsley's manners would try anyone's patience," I ventured.

"You seemed tight enough with him and his crowd last night, for a newcomer," he flashed back, finally glaring at me, then appeared to regret having spoken and returned his attention to the knife.

"I wished only to take his money."

Garth raised his eyes and looked at me with new curiosity.

"And did you?"

"To make money at cards, sometimes you first need to lose a little. To build the trust of your companions."

Unexpectedly, Garth smiled. It transformed his large, crude features from their habitual suspicious frown to an expression of bright amusement.

"You lost, then."

I acknowledged the truth of this with a laugh.

"I damned well did. But I'll get it back next time."

"I never heard a churchman talk like that before."

"I am not your ordinary churchman."

He nodded, as if to say that much was plain.

"Well, I wish you luck of it. Take all the blasted money you can from that whoreson, begging your pardon, sir." He glanced at the cathedral with guilty eyes, as if it might disapprove of his language, and his face grew hard again.

"If he owes you a debt, can you not go to law?"

He shook his head, his lips pressed together.

"You would not understand."

"Try me," I said gently. "I know a little of English law." A little was the truth; I lacked any knowledge to advise him, but I hoped to win his confidence.

He sighed, and glanced over his shoulder, biting the knuckle of his thumb.

"His father was the local justice, you know?" He lowered his voice, even though no one was within earshot.

"The man who was murdered here in the cathedral?"

He muttered an acknowledgement and looked down.

"What help could my family expect from the law when the man who owed us *made* the law?"

"Was it a large sum?"

He twisted his big body awkwardly and did not answer.

"The debt, I mean?"

"What that man owed my family . . ." He paused and twitched his head slightly, as if to dislodge a persistent fly. "It was a debt you can't put a price on." Another pause; this time he looked at me, as if considering whether I merited his trust. He leaned in slightly. "My sister died in his house, nine years ago."

"You think he was responsible?"

He clenched his teeth.

"There's one thing you learn quickly as the son of a poor man and that's not to accuse rich men of what you can't prove. I was only fifteen when she died. My mother near lost her wits over it. She used to stand with her hair all unbound and denounce him in the marketplace like a madwoman, till they put her in the stocks for it. Now she won't even leave the house. That's why people call her a witch. I thought I could make Sir Edward see reason, give us something for our loss. Soon learned otherwise, didn't I," he added, his voice thick with bitterness.

"What happened?"

"He said he'd have me arrested for malicious slander and extortion if I ever repeated those words or any like them. Then he had me beaten black and blue, teach me a lesson. Can't prove that either, but I know he ordered it."

"But why do you think your sister's death was his doing?"

He sniffed and fixed his eyes on a point above my head.

"Strong as a horse, our Sarah. Never seen her take ill a day all the time we was growing up. She never died of no fever, whatever he said."

"Did she see a doctor?" I asked, though I remembered that Fitch had said Sir Edward called the physician out to her at his own expense. Garth's face darkened with anger.

"He had Ezekiel Sykes out to her, didn't he, and all of Canterbury knows he meddles with what he shouldn't." He spat the words so fiercely that he had to wipe his mouth on his sleeve. I saw his hand was shaking.

"How do you mean?"

"He's one of them . . ." He frowned. "I forget the word. You know— that tries to turn iron into gold."

"An alchemist?"

"Aye, that's what they say. Witch, more like." Garth narrowed his eyes. "Why you so interested, anyway?"

I shrugged. "I took a dislike to this Nicholas Kingsley. He cheats at cards. I'd have been glad to see you teach him a lesson last night."

He nodded slowly, still wary. "I lost my temper last night. I'd had a drink. Should know by now I'll get nothing that way."

I made as if to leave, then half turned.

"Do you mind the gate here every evening, Master Garth?"

"Aye." His face closed up again; he seemed to be bracing himself for an argument.

"The night young Kingsley's father was murdered too?"

"Wasn't me killed him, if that's what you mean," he snapped, taking a step towards me, his nostrils flaring, almost before the words were out of my mouth. "It was the wife. Ask anyone. That's why she ran the next day."

I held up my hands as if to ward off misunderstanding.

"I didn't mean to suggest . . . Then you must have seen her, surely?"

He slumped, the sudden flash of anger abated, and rolled his shoulders, his face uneasy.

"I saw her come in for Evensong, that I do remember. But I don't recall seeing her leave, as I told the constable next day. First thing I know of it, Canon Langworth comes running up after supper like he's seen the Devil himself, yelling that he's found Sir Edward murdered."

"But the other gates are all locked after Evensong, are they not? So anyone leaving after that time must have to pass you here at this gate."

"Or hide themselves." He leaned in confidentially. "These precincts are full of nooks and crannies, you must have seen. The canons do the rounds and lock the gates after the service when everyone has left, but anyone with unfinished business could easily tuck themselves away unseen. The church is as good a place as any."

"But she would still have had to come out," I persisted, "to have been at home when they came to tell her the news."

"I don't recall," he repeated, more stubbornly this time, though his eyes were evasive. "Look here." He tilted his neck to one side and then the other stiffly, as if it was causing him discomfort. "I won't pretend I was sorry. It was no secret I hated him. And I can be quick with my fists sometimes, but I couldn't do what she did. Strike a man from behind, in the dark, with a crucifix?" He shook his head. "That's a coward's way. Or a woman's."

I moved back towards him, alert.

"A *crucifix*? Was that what killed him?"

"So they reckon. They found it the next day, slung into the long grass in the orchard, covered in blood and brains. Big silver cross with a heavy base, one of those they have in the church."

"So she took it from the cathedral, then?"

Garth rubbed the back of his neck.

"Must have. From the crypt, they said. It was the one used to stand on that little altar down there."

I whistled.

"To kill a man on consecrated ground, with the cross of Christ. Mother Mary! Only someone with no fear of God could think of it."

"Neither God nor the Devil," Garth muttered.

"A man with no fear of the Devil would be a fool indeed," said a new voice from behind me, smooth and polite. "Of whom do you speak, Garth?"

Garth flinched like a dog that fears a kick; I turned sharply to see John Langworth standing at the gatehouse entrance, wearing the same funereal black robe. He had appeared silently just as he had the previous day, like a bird of prey. In daylight his face seemed even sharper, the skin stretched tight over the bones so that, looking at him, I had the impression of seeing his naked skull as it would appear if his grave were opened years hence. Despite the warmth of the day, I shivered. Langworth seemed to trail the chill of the crypt around with him, as if the summer dare not venture too close to his person.

"Ah, and our Italian friend, Signor Savolino. Good day." He gave me a thin smile and offered his hand. "Back to admire the glories of our church?"

"I had rather hoped to admire the glories of your library today," I said, with forced politeness, shaking his cool hand. "Doctor Robinson has kindly offered to introduce me to the canon librarian."

"Again, I fear we have little to excite a travelling scholar," he said, inclining his head in an attitude of regret. "The great abbey of St. Augustine once boasted the finest library in England—some two thousand volumes. You may see the ruins of it outside the city wall, beyond the Burgate. A handful were saved from the flames and brought here, but nothing remarkable. Still," he said briskly, as if pulling himself back from the past, "yours is a happier task than mine today. It seems another dreadful murder has been committed in the city only this morning. I must go and see what comfort I can offer the family. I'm afraid I shall miss divine service."

I nodded and made as if to go on my way into the precincts. He swept past, his robe billowing at his heels. As he was about to pass into the market square, he turned.

"Oh—Garth! If you should happen to see any of the carpenters in the precincts, remind them of the casement in my back parlour, would you? I can never find any of the workmen when I need them. It would be convenient if they could do something this morning while I'm out."

"If I see Master Paine, I'll tell him, Canon Treasurer," Garth called back, with a nod of deference. When Langworth had disappeared out of sight, he turned to me and rolled his eyes. "Thinks his broken window should be the master carpenter's first priority," he muttered, shaking his head.

I made a vague murmur of sympathy.

"Well, I will not trespass on your time any longer," I said, smiling.

Garth squinted towards the street.

"Communion service'll be busy this morning. Always is when there's been a death. Best place for the gossips to get together." He brandished my knife at me in its sheath. "Don't worry, I shall take good care of this, sir, and see you by and by."

I nodded and passed through the archway into the cathedral precincts, where I stood for a moment, allowing my eyes to adjust to the brightness of the day after the shadows of the gatehouse and trying to decide, with racing heart, where to go next. I had thought I might take the opportunity of being inside the precincts to visit the crypt again before I called on Harry, but Langworth's departing words had given me a new idea. If the treasurer was out all morning and his house had a broken window . . .

My stomach tightened; it was almost too audacious, especially after Harry's explicit warning about Langworth. But the treasurer's friendship with Sir Edward Kingsley, together with the fact that he had found the body and raised the alarm, meant that he had to be regarded as a suspect, and if Harry was not willing to explore the possibility, despite being charged with watching Langworth, then I would not shy away from the prospect. I at least had no position in Canterbury to lose.

Sophia had mentioned that her husband kept the key to his mysterious cellar on a chain at his belt, yet Langworth had not returned any key to her along with Sir Edward's other valuables. Had Langworth taken that key? If he was one of the magistrate's close confidants, perhaps he had some idea of what was in the cellar. Was it something he needed to move, or keep hidden? Something that gave him reason to kill?

But hovering above all this was the figure of Lord Henry Howard. He trusted Langworth; did he trust him enough to make him custodian of the secret book I had seen in his house last autumn, before his arrest? That book—the lost book of the writings of the Egyptian sage Hermes Trismegistus, perhaps the only remaining copy in existence, the book Howard had believed would teach a man the secrets of immortality—was as precious to Howard as it was to me. I was certain he would not have risked leaving it among his own possessions, where the queen's searchers might find it on the occasion of his arrest. And shortly afterwards, his nephew, the Earl of Arundel, had come into Kent to meet Langworth. Arundel had also been under suspicion over the conspiracy last autumn; Howard might have told him to entrust the book to someone far from the eyes of the queen's pursuivants. If there was the slightest chance that Langworth knew the fate of that book, I was prepared to risk almost anything to find out.

I had no idea which of the houses around the edge of the precincts might be Langworth's, nor how to ask without arousing suspicion. Neither did I want to walk past Harry's house in case the sharp-eyed Samuel saw me through a window. I squinted to my left at the cathedral, pale and solid under the morning sun. Ahead of me, I noticed a man approaching from the eastern side of the precincts, pushing a barrow loaded with planks of wood; I quickened my pace and assumed an air of confidence.

"Excuse me," I said as I drew level, "but I wonder if you can help me—I have to deliver a letter to the canon treasurer's house, but I'm afraid I'm confused as to which one it is."

The man rested his barrow on the ground, wiped his hands on the front of his dirty smock, and gestured the way he had come, through the middle gate.

"All the way round the end of the corona on the other side, opposite the treasury." When he saw my blank look, he added, "The treasury is built on the side of St. Andrew's chapel. Sticks out from the north side. You can't miss the house—it's the only one of three storeys on that side."

"And will his servant be there to receive it, if he is not?"

"He keeps no servant. A woman from the town comes in to clean for him now and then, I believe. If he's not there, you'll have to come back later, or try one of the other canons."

I thanked him, relieved, and watched as he hefted his load up again and set off towards the Archbishop's Palace. Once he had rounded the corner, I glanced to my right and left; the precincts on the south side were still deserted. I could not walk around the end of the apse without passing Harry's house. The only possibility was to go through the cathedral. There was a small door at the end of the southwest transept; I hurried across, tried the handle, and found it open. As silently as I could, I closed the door behind me and stepped into the sacred hush of the cathedral church.

Just as I had the day before, I experienced a slight dizziness, the sense of being suddenly dwarfed, as I looked upwards into the multiplying geometrical vaults that fanned out more than a hundred feet above me in all directions. Almost at once, I heard the echo of footsteps on the flagstones; I froze as they drew closer, and from the direction of the choir a ruddy-faced young man appeared in the plain robe of a minor canon, a pair of tall brass candlesticks tucked under his arms. He walked in haste with his head down; I pressed myself against the wall by the door and waited until he had passed. To my left, at the far end of the nave, I saw a number of men in clerical dress milling about, presumably preparing for the divine service of communion which would begin shortly at nine. I crossed the transept briskly and slipped out of the opposite door, the one I had entered the day before with Harry, beside the site of the martyr-dom, and emerged at the corner of the cloister. Two men in black robes were approaching from the west side, but I turned purposefully to my right along the narrow passage that led alongside the Chapter House. I had learned over the years that the best way to avoid being confronted somewhere you don't belong is to give the impression at all times of hav-ing every right to be there. So I held my head up and retraced the path I had taken with Harry until I saw ahead of me a rectangular building of one storey with a gabled roof, attached to one of the cathedral's side chapels but of later construction, its windows secured with thick iron bars. I passed around this and almost opposite stood a narrow house, timbered in dark wood and three storeys high, each overhanging the one below. Beside it was a crooked row of smaller dwellings, all stand-ing in the shadows of the ruined priory buildings. The great bulk of the cathedral blocked out the morning sun from the path on this side, and the windows of the treasurer's house reflected the façade of the church, blank and impenetrable. I realised that Langworth's door was very close to the spot where Sir Edward Kingsley's body had been found. The dark stain was still visible on the path where Harry had pointed it out. Hardly surprising, then, that the treasurer on his way home had been the first to see his friend lying dead. But it was also extremely convenient.

I looked around. There was no one to be seen on this side of the cathedral, and I knew I must act quickly. Langworth had said that the broken window was in his back parlour, so I looked along the row of houses for any sign of an alley that would lead to the rear. There was a small path that disappeared around the crumbling arches of the priory infirmary; just as I made to follow it, a great peal of bells erupted from the tower above me, causing me to jump almost out of my skin. Catch-ing my breath, my heart pounding in my throat, I moved as quickly as I could past the ruins and found myself facing the backyards of the row of prebendaries' houses. These yards were no more than six feet across, separated from the path by a low wall. On the other side of the path more buildings backed onto these; I gave a quick glance to their windows, but decided I had no time to worry about who might be overlooking the treasurer's yard. If I was lucky, everyone in the precincts would now be on their way to the service.

Emboldened by the knowledge that Langworth did not have a live-in servant, I scrambled over the wall and saw immediately the window he had complained about; its latch was broken and the weight of the leading was causing it to hang open. The casement itself, to the right of the rear door, was not large; a man like Tom Garth would not have stood a chance. Even for me it was an effort, but I was able to fold my limbs sufficiently to climb through and land, with dry throat and clammy palms, inside Langworth's parlour.

The room was small, with a low wood-beamed ceiling, much like the inside of Harry's house on the other side of the precincts. Little light entered from the windows facing the yard, making it all the more dingy and ominous. Langworth's furniture was simple, austere even, like the man himself; there were no decorative touches, no ornaments. A high-backed settle of plain wood was placed near the hearth and against the right-hand wall a buffet displayed a few items of tableware, sufficient for one person; these were of silver, but unremarkable. If Langworth were siphoning funds from the cathedral treasury, he was not obviously spending them on fine living.

Where would a man like Langworth keep his most private correspondence? These old houses offered so many nooks and crannies for hiding places—loose bricks, floorboards, crevices in chimney stacks or under stairs—that I realised as I took my first step the absurdity of my ambition. The creak of the boards beneath my feet echoed through the house and I froze, listening for any telltale sign of movement. But the cathedral bells struck up another peal and after a moment I was satisfied that the house was empty.

The door of the little parlour where I had entered gave on to a narrow corridor leading to a small and basic kitchen, a staircase to the first floor, and, at the front of the house, a larger room evidently used as a library and study. Two cases of handsomely bound books stood against the wall, while a wide oak desk was placed before the windows, almost empty save for a pile of papers stacked neatly on one side with a book on top to weight them down, as well as an inkwell, penknife, and a block of sealing wax.

On my hands and knees, so that I would not be seen by anyone who happened to pass the front window, I crept over to the desk and cast my eye over the papers. Most contained columns of figures and details of expenditure on mundane items, the necessary outgoings of a cathedral community, with the occasional query in the margins. Nothing here of interest, but then I would hardly have expected him to leave any sensitive documents in plain view. There were no titles on the bookshelves to excite curiosity either; though they were fine editions, most were volumes of orthodox theology, classical literature, and approved Christian philosophy, such as you might expect to find on the shelves of any learned and pious official of the English church. Nothing contraband, nothing overtly controversial, nothing to indicate the Catholic loyalties that might tie him to Henry Howard. Here on the ground floor at least, any visitor could observe that Langworth's personal effects were unimpeachable.

Creeping as quietly as I could manage, I climbed the stairs to the floor above. The bells had ceased and an anxious silence settled over the house, in which I imagined I could hear my own blood pulsing through my veins as I held my breath. At the top of the stairs I found myself on a small landing with only one door to my right, though directly ahead was a bare wall where it looked as if a doorway should have been. I pushed open the right-hand door into what proved to be Langworth's bedchamber. The air held the faint musty smell that I associated with old men, but the bed was made and the floorboards swept clean. There was no other furniture save a wooden stand with a jug and bowl for washing. I looked around, feeling something was not right. The room was too small. This bedchamber must be directly above the study downstairs, so there ought to be another room on this floor over the back half of the house, above the parlour where I had come in. At some point, that room had been blocked off, the doorway plastered over.

On the back wall, beside the bed, hung a frayed tapestry depicting a lascivious version of the story of Susannah and the Elders. Though the colours were faded, the voluptuous curves of the nude bathing and the lustful eyes of the voyeurs were still lifelike enough to inspire less than virtuous thoughts. Quite a scene for the caustic treasurer to contemplate every night as he lay down to sleep, I thought, with a smile, amused by this indication of another side to him. But as I looked at the tapestry, I noticed not its design but its position, and on a sudden hunch I stepped forward and pulled it to one side. Concealed behind it was a door. I clenched my fist in triumph; this must lead to the back room which could not be accessed from the landing. Naturally, when I tried the latch, it was locked.

Over my years of travelling, in the course of which I had often found myself in the company of thieves, I had acquired a degree of skill in unfastening doors that people wanted to remain closed, but I had left my knife at the gatehouse and without it I could not begin any attempt at picking the lock. Then I remembered the penknife on Langworth's desk downstairs; it was at least worth a try. I bolted down two at a time, forgetting all my earlier caution about soundless steps, and returned with the knife. The lock was not straightforward and it took some careful teasing with the end of the blade to discover where the key was supposed to rotate; a business made all the more difficult by the fact that my hands had begun to sweat, both from the heat and from fear of taking too long. Eventually, I found the sensitive point that triggered the lever, releasing the latch, and a wave of sweet relief washed over me; extracting the knife, I pushed open the door gently, bracing myself for some dark secret.

The room was empty. I felt my stomach lurch with disappointment, though I told myself not to be so foolish; why go to all the trouble of disguising and locking the door if there was nothing to be found? Only one wall had a window and this was covered by thick velvet drapes, so that barely any light entered. In the gloom I could make out little beyond bare boards and an empty fireplace. Yet I had a sense of apprehension, an instinct that I had stumbled upon something important, if I only had eyes to see. Something had been, and perhaps remained, hidden in this room, something Langworth did not want anyone to come across by chance.

I crossed to the fireplace; the hearth was swept clean and it was clear that no fire had been lit here for a long while. Crouching, I felt blindly inside the chimney breast—my friend John Dee used to hide caches of letters and secret books up his chimney and I wondered if Langworth had tried the same trick—but my groping was rewarded only with a cascade of soot and dried bird droppings. There appeared to be no recess inside that I could feel. I knelt to try and brush the mess away from the tiles of the hearth to conceal evidence of my search. I dared not draw back the curtains in case anyone glancing from one of the buildings behind the house should see the movement, but by now my eyes were growing used to the gloom. As I scattered the fall of soot with my fingertips, I realised that one of the earthenware tiles that formed the floor of the fireplace was loose. At its edge was a slight indentation that allowed me to slip the tips of two fingers into the gap and lift the tile; though it was heavy, it was evidently not sealed in like the others and lifted easily, with a loud scraping. I set it to one side, wiped my sweating hands on my breeches and felt inside the cavity that had been revealed. My fingers brushed the surface of a wooden box, and with little difficulty I eased this out through the opening. It was carved with a design of serpents and vines intertwined, small enough to be held between my two hands, and it was no great surprise to find it locked. After a bit of judicious probing with the penknife, the clasp sprung open. I moved to sit beneath the window, where I lifted the drape just a fraction, enough to allow a sliver of daylight to illuminate the contents.

At the bottom of the casket I found folded papers, and I had to fight to keep my hand steady as I reached for these; their contents must be valuable, since Langworth had taken such evident pains to hide them. On top of these papers was a bunch of keys, four altogether, of varying sizes, though two were quite large and had acquired the tarnish of age. I put them to one side and turned my attention to the letters.

The first bore a broken seal in scarlet wax with a device I did not recognise and, as I unfolded it, my heart sank; the letter revealed only a series of numbers, arranged in groups of differing lengths that must correspond to words, but impenetrable to anyone not in possession of the cipher, as the writer had intended.

I sighed. I should not have been surprised; at least the coded letter told me that Langworth's secret correspondence was likely to be worth reading. Walsingham had a master cryptographer in his employ, Thomas Phelippes, a man of extraordinary abilities who could probably break this code in a matter of minutes just by looking at it. Though I had read a great deal about ciphers and seen a good many coded messages pass through the French embassy during the business there last autumn, I would not know where to begin in deciphering it and could easily waste hours in the attempt. I hesitated, holding the letter up gingerly between my thumb and forefinger. The paper was dog-eared and stained with what looked like drops of water on one side, as if it had been well-handled on its travels. I stared fruitlessly at the lines of numbers in the author's tiny, neat hand. Where had it come from? I needed to make a copy—Langworth would certainly notice if I took the original, and if it should be damaged or destroyed while in my possession, crucial evidence would vanish forever—a mistake I had made once before, to my shame and Walsingham's fury. But even supposing I had time to make a copy now, how could I get it to London? I would have to ask Harry's servant Samuel to take it, and I doubted he would be in a hurry to do me any favours.

The letter was signed not with more numbers but with a symbol, which seemed to me oddly familiar, but though I ransacked my memory trying to place it there was no jolt of recognition. Silently, I cursed my own failure; I, who was renowned in Paris as an expert on systems of memory, yet could not pull this vital information from my own brain when it most mattered. I knew that those who corresponded in code, whether to deliver secret intelligence or illicit conspiracies, often used a symbol in place of a signature to authenticate their dispatches; when I wrote to Walsingham I used the astrological symbol for the planet Jupiter as my own mark. If the sign on the letter I now held in my hands was familiar, it was most likely that I had seen it on one of the letters that had passed through the French embassy and so, logically, Langworth must be receiving letters from someone who had been involved with the invasion conspiracy of the previous autumn. Knowing of his Catholic leanings, this was hardly a surprise; the question was: Who? Henry Howard, from his prison cell, or someone outside England? And who was his courier?

The most pressing question, though, was whether I had time to copy the letter before Langworth returned. I tucked it carefully into the leather pouch I wore at my belt and hesitated, weighing the keys in my hand. What secrets did they hold, I wondered, and did I dare remove them to find out? The house remained deathly silent. In the shard of light from the window, dust drifted gently.

Outside, the cathedral bells struck up a new peal, startling me out of my thoughts. If they signalled the end of the service, people would be spilling out into the precincts and it would be harder to leave without attracting attention. I looked down at the keys in my palm, willing myself to make a decision. Was one of these the key to Sir Edward Kingsley's cellar?

It was reckless, I knew, but I was afraid I would not have another chance. I slipped the bunch of keys into my pouch too, closed the casket, and fiddled impatiently with the lock, my fingers made clumsy by haste, until I felt it click beneath the knife. At least if he found the casket locked Langworth might attribute the missing keys to some lapse of memory on his own part. I hid the box again under the tile and left the hidden room, returning to Langworth's bedchamber and closing the door as silently as possible behind me. But this time I could not make the lock turn back into place, and the persistent clamour of the bells began to seem an alarm meant to warn me that time was short. Instead of easing the knife gently, as I knew I should, I tried in my haste to force it; the blade glanced off the bolt and caught the edge of my finger. A gout of blood splashed to the floor; stifling a curse, I sucked furiously at the cut and at that moment I heard the sound of a door opening downstairs, followed by voices.

Frantic, I glanced around the room. The only possible hiding place was under Langworth's bed. I pulled the tapestry across the door, scuffed the traces of my blood away with my foot and, as quietly as I could manage, pressed myself prostrate on the floor and wriggled flat under the bed, holding my breath. The space under the bed frame was thick with dust, but the boards were warped by age and I found a gap between two of them wide enough to press one eye against. I was directly above the front room of the house, Langworth's study. Below I could see the desk where I had found the penknife I now clutched in my bleeding fingers. As I watched, a packet was flung down onto the desk and the figure of the treasurer in his black robe crossed my line of vision.

"Well, then," he said. "That is everything."

"You are certain?" I could not see the face of his interlocutor and dared not move to try and see better. I remained frozen, pressed to the floor, making my breath as shallow as I could.

"Everything I could find," Langworth replied. "It was not easy—the place was left in such disarray."

"You did not attract attention, going there?"

The other man's voice seemed disturbingly familiar. Langworth gave a cold laugh.

"The apothecary's sister-in-law stands to inherit—she is a superstitious woman and would not set foot in a place befouled by murder until it had been blessed by a man of the church."

"And now?"

"*Tacere et fidere*, my friend." Langworth's voice grew impatient. "The threads are all unravelled. We can only bide our time and wait for news. For now, the best thing we can do is to have faith, and keep our mouths shut."

"We must experiment further, if we hope for success," his companion said, lowering his voice. "There are other places to buy—"

"In time," Langworth snapped back. "There have been enough deaths lately, the town is alert. They will blame a vagrant for Fitch and hang him at the assizes in a few days. Then they will forget. Meanwhile, have you not seen the tide of refugees fleeing the plague rumours?" He folded his long fingers together and cracked his knuckles. "There will be chance enough for experiments in the days to come. God will provide. Besides," he added, moving back towards the desk and out of my sight, "nothing can be done while the Italian is here, prying. You saw him this morning, I suppose?"

"Not today. Was he here?"

The second man spoke sharply and as he stepped forward and I was able to glimpse him, my stomach constricted and I swear for a moment my heart stopped beating. It was Samuel, Harry Robinson's servant. A chill washed my whole body, as if I had been hit by a cold wave, as I realised the implications of this: *Langworth knew exactly who I was.* When he greeted me politely by my false name at the gate, he had been mocking me; if Samuel was his confidant, he must have known my identity even before I arrived. *The Italian.* My careful pretence was meaningless; I already had an enemy in the heart of the cathedral, an ally of Henry Howard's who must know my part in his patron's imprisonment. This changed everything; I could no longer imagine that I was passing unnoticed through Canterbury. Langworth must be as suspicious of me as I was of him and would be waiting for an opportunity as we danced around each other, trying not to reveal our hands.

"I saw him by the gatehouse this morning, as I was leaving," Langworth said, his voice sharp. "He said Harry was taking him to the library."

"He has not called," Samuel said. "Harry is at home. Perhaps he went by himself."

"Well, let him occupy himself there if he wishes, he can do little harm," Langworth said, dismissive. "It will serve to keep him above ground, at least. Watch him. What does Harry make of him thus far, out of interest?"

Samuel was now directly beneath me; I saw him shrug.

"Harry is wary of him."

"And rightly so."

"He fears this business with Kingsley's murder is a pretext. There are rumours from London, you know, that the queen will send forces to the Netherlands."

"Let us hope they are true. This is just the news our friends in Paris are waiting for."

"They say Walsingham plans to dissolve the richest cathedral foundations to raise money for this war. Starting with Canterbury, to set an example."

Langworth appeared again beneath my spy-hole.

"And the last thing Harry wants is for the foundation to be dissolved. Where else would he find so comfortable a situation?" His voice was cold.

"All Harry cares about is preserving things as they are. He fears the Italian is really here to find evidence of his own incompetence."

"So poor Harry finds himself caught between the Devil and the deep sea," Langworth mused, without a trace of sympathy. "The spy fears he is spied on by his own spymaster." He gave a dry laugh. "What a fitting irony."

"He has warned the Italian away from you," Samuel added.

"I doubt that will stop him," Langworth said, folding his arms and cupping his chin in his right hand. "Do not make the mistake of underestimating our friend Bruno, as my lord Howard did. He is devilishly clever and sly as a fox."

"Nevertheless, if he is determined to unearth Kingsley's murderer . . ."

"Yes. That could be awkward." Langworth paced across the room and was again lost to my narrow field of vision. Samuel turned to follow his direction, and I found myself looking down onto the shiny disk of pink skin at his crown, barely covered by the meagre strands of black hair he scraped over it. I felt an instinctive revulsion. Langworth's voice continued, from over by the window. "How much did the wife know, that is the question."

"Nothing, Kingsley always said."

"I'm not sure I believe that. She may have been sharper than Kingsley realised. After all, the damned fool didn't even have the wit to look behind him on a dark night," Langworth added, an unmistakable anger in his tone. "Walsingham would not send someone like Giordano Bruno here for the murder of a provincial magistrate, you can be sure of that. It can only be that the girl told him something significant—something she may have observed without Kingsley's knowledge. And there are others at St. Gregory's whose silence cannot be taken for granted."

"The boy, you mean?"

Langworth snorted.

"Nicholas has eyes only for whores and cards. No, I am thinking of the housekeeper. If anyone has seen what they should not, it would be that beady old bird." He fell silent for a moment, then clapped his hands together briskly, as if he had come to a sudden decision. "I had better pay another visit to St. Gregory's. Before the Italian asks too many questions. Find Sykes for me—I may have need of his skills."

"And then should I follow the Italian?"

Langworth paused, weighing up his alternatives.

"Damnation—I had forgotten that there is a meeting of the chapter today at one, and I have certain accounts that must be arranged beforehand." He shook his head impatiently. "And I dine with the mayor tonight. No—St. Gregory's will have to wait until tomorrow. Take a message to Sykes, tell him I want him here after Evensong. Watch the Italian, by all means, report his conversations with Harry. I have an idea of how to keep him out of trouble, if we need to."

"And where shall I find you?"

"In the treasury. I shall go there presently, once I have put this in a safe place." I could not see what he meant by "this," but as he crossed the room again I saw that he had picked up the packet he had been holding when he first came in. "By the cross, this heat is too much."

"We shall have a storm soon," Samuel observed.

Langworth grunted assent and I heard the sound of the latch being drawn on the front door. I tried to swallow but my throat felt as if it were filled with dust; Langworth would be coming up here at any moment and would surely notice anything awry. I wanted urgently to check that I had rearranged the tapestry over the door just as it had been, but I dared not move a muscle.

"God will reward your loyalty, Samuel," Langworth said, on the threshold.

"I hope not to wait *quite* so long," Samuel replied, and both men gave a low, knowing laugh. The door closed, and my bladder tightened as I heard the first creaking tread on the staircase.

Langworth's worn leather shoes passed directly in front of me as he crossed the room to the door behind the tapestry. I breathed out as silently as I could, watching the small bloom of dust that rose under my nostrils as I did so. I kept my lips pressed tightly together so that I should not sneeze. A bunch of keys jangled in his hand, then I heard the sound of one being fitted into the lock. One more heartbeat and Langworth would discover that his secret room had been left unlocked; one more— but before I heard the click of the key turning, there came a peremptory knock at the door from downstairs. Langworth appeared to hesitate, but the banging came again, more urgently. I heard him tut, then he threw the packet onto the bed and hurried down the stairs. It was only when I heard him lift the latch on the front door that I realised how much I was shaking.

"Dean Rogers. Good morning. To what do I owe the honour?" Langworth's voice rose from the room below; he sounded surprised and not at all pleased to see his visitor.

"John—sorry to disturb, I'm sure you're busy. It's about the chapter meeting this afternoon." The dean's tone was apologetic. "I wondered if I might have a quick look at the accounts ledgers ahead of the meeting?"

"Well—I shall be presenting the accounts myself this afternoon—I'm not sure that it would be particularly—"

"If it's not too much trouble," the dean said pleasantly, but firmly. "I'm afraid I don't have a head for figures, John, not like you, and there's always so much to take in at these meetings. I thought it would be easier for an addle-pate like me to try and understand the expenditure before we get there."

Clever old fox, I thought, smiling to myself as I recalled what Harry had said about the persistent rumours of Langworth playing fast and loose with the treasury accounts. The dean meant to put his treasurer on the spot. While Langworth began to explain at length why the ledgers might prove difficult to understand, I held my breath and slid as silently as I could so that my head was poking out from under the bed and glanced at the door behind the tapestry. Langworth had left the key in the lock, an iron ring with several others dangling from it. I eased myself out a little farther into the room, still flat on my stomach, praying that no creaking board would give me away. The heat in the room seemed to press about my face like a damp cloth; sweat dripped into my eyes.

"I do appreciate that," the dean was saying, "but it would put my mind at rest before addressing the chapter . . ."

I crawled on my belly across the floor, one hand on the keys at my own belt so that they would not scrape on the boards, until I could reach up to the lock of the door into the back room. Hoping that my knife had not damaged the mechanism, I turned the key. To my relief I heard the bolt slide into place with a dull thud.

"The account books are all in the treasury, of course," Langworth was explaining to the dean, his voice growing defensive. "I was on my way over there."

"Then I shall accompany you," the dean said, just as pleasantly. "Shall we go now?"

Langworth hesitated.

"Of course. Although I realise I have left my keys in my chamber—do go on ahead, if you wish."

"No matter," said the dean pleasantly. "I can wait a moment."

Langworth's heavy footsteps sounded again on the stairs; I scrambled back under the bed, my heart pounding in my throat, pressing a hand over my mouth as the dust scuffed up by my sudden movement itched its way into my eyes and nose. The counterpane that hung over the bed was still swaying when Langworth stormed into the room, unlocked the hidden door, threw the packet he had left on the bed into the back room, and locked the door again, muttering under his breath. I heard the flap of heavy material as he rearranged the tapestry and the metallic clink of the keys as he tossed them in his hand on his way out. Though I had fallen out of the habit of regular prayer, I offered a silent thanks to Providence for the appearance of the dean.

When I was certain that they had left the house, I crawled out from my hiding place, brushing the dust from my clothes, and crept back down to the study, again bending low so that I would not be visible to anyone passing the window. I hesitated by the desk as I replaced the penknife, first wiping the traces of my blood from its blade. There was ink in the inkwell, and paper. How long was Langworth likely to be in the treasury with the dean—long enough for me to copy the letter I had tucked into my purse? My hands were still trembling from our near-encounter. I forced myself to breathe slowly and deeply. Now that I knew Langworth and the other canons would be occupied at the chapter meeting that afternoon, I decided the lesser risk would be to take the letter away to copy and attempt to return the original later while he was out, trusting that he would not check the contents of his secret chest carefully in the meantime.

Outside, the sound of voices carried across from the cathedral. People were evidently abroad in the precincts; the service must have ended. I needed to leave Langworth's house now, while I still had time; Harry would be expecting me for dinner soon and I wanted to return to the Cheker and copy the coded letter first—though I had no idea how I could send it to London, now that I knew Samuel could not be trusted. My jaw tightened at the thought of dissembling in front of Harry's servant, as if I were ignorant of his treachery. I must find a way to speak to Harry alone, I thought, but I feared he would not believe me about Samuel, and I would lose his trust and goodwill if he knew I had defied his warning to keep away from Langworth. Worse still—and my mouth dried at the thought—I could not discount the possibility that Harry knew about Samuel. Perhaps he was even in league with Langworth, or at best turning a blind eye; it would not be the first time one of Walsingham's contacts had betrayed his trust and, though I found it hard to believe of Harry Robinson, I knew I must remain wary. The hardest part of working for Walsingham was knowing whom to trust.

I cast a last glance over the desk and as I did so, it was as if something distant echoed in my brain, an instinct that prompted me to take a second look. I picked up the first of the papers—a balance sheet, with columns of numbers, scribbled calculations beneath. Under a couple of pages of similar notes, I found another sheet itemising expenditure for the month of May 1584, an unremarkable list of outgoings for a cathedral foundation: Alms; Bread; Candles; Dean's kitchen; Eucharist (sundries) . . . I stared at the paper; something seemed odd about it. I almost laughed aloud as the realisation dawned. The list was alphabetical, and beside each item listed was a figure, set out as the number of shillings and pence paid. Could it be . . . ? Where better to hide a cipher based on the substitution of numbers for letters than among balance sheets? Holding my breath, glancing all the time at the window, I took the stolen letter from my purse and checked the numbers at the top of the page: 1271584 76201536.

Matching the numbers against the figures in the expenses column, I tried to make sense of the first set, but no matter how I divided the numbers up, there was no combination of letters that made any sense. Frustrated, I bit my lip; I had been so certain of my sudden flash of insight. I tried the next long number. Seven . . . the only item on the list beginning with 7 was "Parish priests—7s 6d." Seven and six—P. "Alms" was listed as twenty shillings, but there was no payment corresponding to fifteen, or one-and-five. I cursed under my breath and glared at the list as if to intimidate it into giving up its secrets. It seemed my imagination had overreached; this was nothing but an ordinary accounting sheet and I was being a fool. I was about to replace it when I noticed that "Incense" was set down at five shillings. Incense? Though I was not well versed in the theological disputes of the English church, I knew that the use of incense was a vexed question; some thought it too close to the orna-ments of the Church of Rome, while others argued that it had never been explicitly prohibited and was therefore acceptable in Protestant services. I had not noticed any smell of incense on either of the occasions when I was inside the cathedral, so its inclusion on the list of outgoings struck me as odd. I scanned back over the list to see if anything corresponded to the number 1, and realised that I had overlooked "Repairs (sundries)," listed at one pound. That gave us P-A-R-I . . . Heart racing, I searched the list and found what I had hardly dared hope for—the payment for "Scholars" was 3s 6d. So if I was right, and this balance sheet was indeed the cipher, the second word at the top of this letter was "Paris." What, then, was the first? I began again, cursing when every combination I matched against the balance sheet resulted in no recognisable word. I blinked slowly and tried to look at the numbers with fresh eyes, until I realised with a start that the last four numbers made sense together as a group: 1584. This first group of numbers, then, was not a word but a date—the twelfth of the seventh, 1584. A letter sent from Paris on 12 July—my instinct was right. In haste, I scrabbled on Langworth's desk for a new sheet of paper and dipped his quill in the inkwell, hoping he would not notice it had been recently used. As quickly as I could, I copied the cipher, put my copy and the letter into my pouch again, and replaced the original balance sheet in the pile of papers, feeling triumphant. It was only then that I noticed I had been careless; a smear of blood from my cut finger marked the bottom of the cipher page. There was nothing I could do about it now, though, except to hope that he would not notice until much later.

I had to trust to luck in climbing out of Langworth's back window, but fortunately no one passed along the path while I was making my escape and I emerged from behind the row of houses unobserved, as far as I could tell. The air felt thick and heavy with humidity and the blue of the sky had grown hazy with a thin gauze of cloud. Samuel was right, I thought; it seemed we would have a storm soon. I decided to take the letter I had borrowed from Langworth back to my room at the Cheker, make the copy, and decipher it as quickly as possible. I recalled Sophia mentioning that the Huguenot weavers travelled regularly to London to sell their cloth; perhaps one of them could be persuaded to take a letter to Sidney for a fee.

Chapter 9

In the privacy of my chamber at the inn, with the door firmly locked against the solicitous attentions of the landlady, I sat on the low bed, my legs crossed under me, hunched over a new sheet of paper with the letter and the cipher spread out before me, but when I applied myself to the first lines, I had another surprise. As I pressed on, it became clear that Langworth's correspondent was writing to him in Spanish. This was curious in itself, given that it was dated from Paris, but as the sense slowly emerged from the mass of numbers like a picture appearing out of fog, I felt a smile stealing across my face as I guessed at the identity of the author. More than once I had to pause, wiping lines of sweat from my brow and shaking my head in disbelief at what I read.

As for this our most blessed and holy enterprise, wrote the author of the letter from Paris, *His Catholic Majesty King Philip urges our brothers in England to remain steadfast and to regard the present difficulties as temporary.*

God has delivered into our hands the Prince of Orange, whose death is surely the blow that will topple the fragile edifice of the heretic church in Europe. With English troops committed to the war in the Netherlands,

Elizabeth's defences will be weakened. At that moment, we will pray most fervently for a miracle from Saint Thomas, by the grace of God. As a sign of his good faith King Philip entrusts to the servants of the blessed saint his holy oil in readiness.

More pious exhortations followed, to trust in God and continue to serve him with patience in this matter.

We thank you for your recent news of my lord H and pray God grant his freedom, which we expect any day.

I sat back on my heels and breathed out slowly to steady myself. "Bernadino de Mendoza," I whispered into the stifling air of my small room, as if speaking his name aloud would provide confirmation of my suspicions. For who else would be writing in his mother tongue from Paris but the gruff Spanish ambassador whom I had met the previous autumn at Salisbury Court? It was the nobleman Mendoza who had brought the promise of King Philip's support to the invasion conspiracy, giving the fantasies of Henry Howard and the Duke of Guise some prospect of becoming reality. Queen Elizabeth had expelled him from London at the beginning of this year when his part in the plot was discovered, and I knew King Philip had sent him directly to Paris, where he had joined forces with Guise and his Catholic League, as well as those exiled English Catholics who still dreamed of putting Mary Stuart on the English throne.

So Langworth was corresponding with Mendoza. Harry Robinson must be ignorant of this, or Walsingham would have mentioned it. I pursed my lips and breathed out slowly. The conspirators who had gathered at Salisbury Court the previous autumn had been routed, but it seemed those who had driven the plot were still trying to keep it alive, waiting for the right moment to revive it. Langworth had as good as said so to Samuel. Now, this letter implied, the murder of William of Orange would hasten that moment; if the queen sent English troops to support the Protestants in the Netherlands, England's own defences would be weakened against a joint attack by Spain and Guise's French army. *We will pray most fervently for a miracle from Saint Thomas,* Mendoza had underlined. A pious figure of speech, or something more concrete? And what was the "holy oil"?

Whatever the meaning, I needed to send the information to Walsingham as quickly as possible. I carefully folded the original ciphered letter together with my translation of it and the code I had copied and tucked them all back into my purse, lest anyone should find their way into my chamber. For obvious reasons, I had little faith in locks, though I turned the key anyway. In the passageway downstairs I was intercepted by the landlady, Marina, before I could reach the door. She gave a squeal of delight, as if I were a long-anticipated surprise, and scolded me playfully for my absence at breakfast.

"Why, we hardly see you, Master Savolino, you are so busy with your affairs. Quite the mystery, you are. What can keep you abroad in the city at all hours, I wonder?" She sent me a look laden with innuendo from beneath her eyelashes. I returned a patient smile. "And here you are off out again! Where to this time, may I ask?"

I was tempted to reply that she may not, but knew from experience that it is prudent to keep on the right side of your host.

"I have a sudden desire to eat an orange," I said. "I was going out to the market—unless you sell them here?" I raised my eyes in the direction of the taproom. She swatted at me in mock outrage.

"Do I look like an orange-girl to you?"

Orange-sellers, at least in London, were widely regarded as prostitutes. I glanced down at the mound of bosom straining against her corset and back up to her garishly painted mouth. With a basket of oranges under her arm she would not have looked out of place in a London theatre or pleasure-garden, save perhaps for her age, which was hard to judge under the makeup.

"Not at all. I meant no offence."

"None taken." She giggled again, then beckoned me back along the passage. "But just for you, I'm sure I can find an orange tucked away somewhere. They're expensive, mind."

"I will pay, of course."

"Oh, you can make it up to me later." She winked.

God in heaven. I smiled again, more nervously this time, and followed her along the shadowy corridor towards the kitchen, wondering what price she had in mind.

"Here," she said, pushing past the cook and kitchen maid and bending to rummage in a large basket before emerging triumphant, a small, wizened orange in her hand. "Careful eating that in your room, Master Savolino," she said, making her voice husky. "You could get *very* sticky. Let me know if there's anything else I can do for you, won't you?"

I thanked her, then hurried back to my room as fast as I could, aware that she was watching me until I reached the stairs. Marina was harmless, I was sure, but the mere fact that she had decided to take a special interest in me was a disadvantage when I had hoped to pass unobserved at the inn.

With the door to my chamber locked again, I worked quickly, squeezing the juice from the orange into the shallow dish that had held the candle by my bed. I took a quill and new sheet of paper from my bag and dipped the sharpened nib into the juice. While it was still fresh, I copied out the decoded letter, noting that it was sent to Langworth and reproducing the author's signature symbol, in the hope that Walsingham would be able to corroborate it as Mendoza's. Underneath I wrote out the cipher, so that he would have it for future reference.

I waved the paper, watching as the juice dried and the words slowly faded to nothing, leaving the sheet blank, if a little warped. It was an old trick, well known to those familiar with secret correspondence; if the letter were to fall into the hands of anyone suspicious of its contents the first thing they would do would be to hold it up to the flame of a candle to see if there was a hidden message. I could only hope that no one would suspect the weavers of carrying intelligence to London, if they agreed to take the letter.

When the paper was dry, I wiped the nib of the quill, took some real ink, and scribbled a short note to Sidney on the other side, one that would not look unusual if anyone were to glance at the letter. "I am enjoying the sights of Canterbury and have hopes that my research into ecclesiastical history will soon bear fruit," I wrote, hoping he would pick up on the mention of fruit. "I expect to be here a little longer as there is much work still to be done and it would cheer me to hear from you soon. Your messenger will find me at the Cheker of Hope, where I have much news for him." I paused, the pen hovering over the paper, wondering if I should add more. The crucial thing was that Walsingham should know the invasion conspiracy was still active in Paris; it might make the queen think twice before committing troops to the war in the Netherlands. By suggesting that Sidney send his own private messenger with any letters, I was also implying that the usual channels of communication with Canterbury were not to be trusted. I signed the letter "Filippo" and sealed it.

This time it was Olivier's sister Hélène who opened the door at the weavers' house. She ushered me in quickly, her face pinched with anxiety. From behind her I heard the rhythmic clatter of the looms and women's voices.

"Wait here. I will fetch my brother."

"I'm sorry if I upset you earlier," I said, as she turned towards the stairs. "I didn't know about your son."

She lowered her eyes, twisting her fingers together.

"How could you? No one here cares to know." She fell silent for a moment, then raised her eyes and I saw they were full of tears. "Why does God test us like this?" she burst out, her fists clenched. "When all we have ever done is try to defend His truth?"

I shook my head. "I cannot defend or explain Him, I'm afraid. That's why I gave up theology."

"Sometimes it begins to look as if He is on the side of the Catholics after all. May God forgive me," she added quickly, glancing around in case anyone had overheard.

"I often think He has turned His back on our petty squabbles altogether."

She gave me a brief, sad smile.

"My Denis. He was all I had," she whispered, the sudden passion gone out of her, seeming to shrink her again. "Why would they take him?"

"What makes you think someone took him?" I asked.

She shrugged, helpless.

"I don't know . . . Another boy was found dead not long before. On a rubbish heap. Cut in pieces."

"I had heard. But there is no reason to suppose they are connected, is there?"

"The worst is not knowing. It makes you imagine . . ." She rubbed brusquely at her cheek with the sleeve of her dress. "But it does no good to dwell on it. Let me find Olivier."

Olivier, when he arrived, seemed irritated to see me again, but he reluctantly agreed to pass on my letter to one of the weavers who would be leaving for London the following day. I handed him some coins for the man's trouble and told him the message must be carried urgently to Sir Philip Sidney at Barn Elms, assuring him that the letter was a request for more resources that would allow us to leave Canterbury all the sooner. I asked after Sophia, and he told me curtly that she was sleeping.

"You can't keep coming to this house," he said as I was leaving, his hand resting on the latch. "My father is afraid you will be noticed. Tomorrow morning I will come and find you at the Cheker and you can give me your news then."

I strongly suspected that this was a ruse to keep me away from Sophia, but for the moment, with her safety still dependent on his family's goodwill, there seemed little point in arguing. I merely nodded and asked him to find me there at breakfast.

It was almost time for me to dine with Harry, but on my way back through the town I made a detour in search of a locksmith. The keys

I had taken from Langworth's hidden chest were weighing down my pouch. I could only hope that the treasurer had been so occupied with the dean's interest in his ledgers that he had not had time to return to his secret room and notice anything was missing. If I could make copies of the keys and restore the originals to the strongbox while Langworth was out at the chapter meeting, there was a chance that my theft might go undiscovered for the moment. Without any clue as to what the keys might open, I was guessing in the dark, but the fact that they had been so carefully hidden meant they must have some significance. There was always a chance that one had been taken from Sir Edward Kingsley's belt as he lay dying. Somehow, I must contrive to find a means of trying the lock of his mysterious cellar during my visit to St. Gregory's later that night.

Tom Garth waved me through the main gate into the cathedral precincts, after I had held up my hands to show him I had no knife at my belt. This time I had thought it prudent to tuck the knife inside my boot. Now that I knew I had an enemy within the cathedral, I had no intention of making myself any more vulnerable than I already felt, working here alone, a stranger and a foreigner with Harry Robinson my only ally— Harry, whom I was not sure I could trust and who I knew did not trust me.

It was not yet noon and I had hoped for a chance to talk to Harry alone while Samuel was preparing the meal, but before I could reach his house I spotted him by the Middle Gate, leaning on his stick and deep in conversation with a tall man, almost completely bald and wearing a black clerical robe. Harry nodded a greeting and his companion turned with a flustered expression, his hands folded inside the sleeves of his gown.

"Good day to you," Harry announced with a cheerful smile as I approached. "Dean Rogers—may I introduce you to the esteemed Doctor Filippo Savolino, a scholar of Padua and Oxford and friend of the Sidney family, who is visiting me from London for a few days?" He gave a little flourish with his outstretched hand; I had the impression that he relished the chance to remind the dean of his connections at court.

I bowed to Dean Rogers, curious to see the man who had unknow-
ingly saved me from discovery in Langworth's bedchamber earlier. He
had a long, equine face, large brown eyes and a harried air about him, as
though he were constantly worried that he ought to be somewhere else.
He smiled as he shook my hand.

"It is a pleasure to welcome you to Canterbury, Doctor Savolino," he
said. "I hope we will have the honour of seeing you at divine service here
during your visit?"

"I look forward to it. I have heard glowing reports of your music."

"Mm." He looked vaguely up at the towers of the cathedral behind
me. "You will find our services conducted according to the letter of the
queen's edicts. You know, the archbishop says there has been talk of Her
Majesty visiting Canterbury as part of her summer progress next year. Perhaps a favourable report from her friends at court may help to influence
her in that direction?" His smile grew brighter, but his eyes were sharp.

I inclined my head in acknowledgement.

"It is some years since she has favoured us with a visit," he persisted,
"but I'm sure she would appreciate the many ways in which we endeavour to maintain the preeminence of our cathedral, while also fulfilling
our duties in the community—ah, education of the poor, and so on . . ."
His words trailed off into a little nervous laugh; it sounded as though he
had rehearsed this speech and used it before.

They are all afraid of losing their place, I thought. *No wonder my
presence here makes Harry nervous.*

"I'm sure she would," I said, "and I will mention as much to the Sidney family on my return." The dean smiled gratefully and I could not
resist adding, "Though she may like to postpone her visit until there are
fewer unnatural deaths here."

He blanched.

"I pray you—our recent tragedy is no matter for joking, Doctor Savolino. It was a dreadful shock to everyone that one of our most respected
citizens could be struck down on hallowed ground, but I can assure you
that such an occurrence is quite without precedent—"

"Saving Thomas Becket, of course," Harry remarked.

The dean looked irritated.

"There is no need for anyone to fear on that account—our magistrate was killed by his wife in cold blood, for profit, and she will pay the price as soon as she is found. As for the unfortunate death of the apothecary this morning, to which I suppose you refer—it is a clear case of robbery and assault, of which I'm sure you see far worse in London. I'm afraid the influx of refugees makes such things a hazard." He smiled again, as if everything were now cleared up, but the way he twisted his fingers together betrayed his agitation. "Well, I have much to do before this afternoon's chapter meeting. You must do me the honour of dining at my table soon, Doctor Savolino. We are always glad of new company."

I glanced at Harry; he sucked in his cheeks and looked away. Why was he so set against the idea of my sharing a table with the dean and the other canons, I wondered.

"You're early," Harry said, after the dean bade us good morning and strode away in the direction of the Archbishop's Palace. "Samuel is not yet back from his morning's errands. You may as well come in, though."

This was welcome news to me. When we were inside the house, Harry gestured me into the small parlour and offered me the same seat I had occupied the day before. He pulled up a chair opposite and leaned forward, hands resting on his knees.

"You heard about the apothecary's murder, then?"

"More than heard. I found him."

"You are not serious?"

I told him briefly of my visit to the apothecary earlier and my encounter with the constable. Harry's face grew grave.

"This is a bad business," he said, lowering his voice. "The whole town is talking about the murder, and you are first witness to finding the body. You could hardly have contrived to make yourself more noticeable. Soon everyone will know your name. Think yourself lucky if they don't try and pin the deed on you."

"Me?" I laughed, assuming it was one of his dry jokes, until I saw his expression. "Why should they suspect me?"

Harry rolled his eyes.

"Look at yourself. Your skin, your accent. People here like the idea of murderous foreigners. Much easier than accepting one of their neighbours might be a killer."

I nodded grimly.

"Well, I will have to rely on the truth. Can you think of any reason why someone would want to kill the apothecary?"

Harry shrugged.

"Most likely someone felt he cheated them. Maybe he sold them a remedy that didn't work, or prescribed a fatal dose. Apothecaries do nothing but guess, for all they pretend to be men of physic." He chuckled, but this time I did not join in. "In any case, what concern is it of yours?"

"A fatal dose," I repeated. *Dosis sola facit venenum.* Had Fitch poisoned someone with a fatal dose of belladonna? He had certainly been afraid of doing so, according to the notes that were burned the night he was killed. "I wondered if his death might be connected to Edward Kingsley's."

Harry frowned.

"What makes you think that?"

I hesitated; I could not tell him about the conversation I had overheard between Langworth and Samuel. I had hardly had time to gather my own thoughts about it. Langworth had been to Fitch's shop this morning to remove something; that much was clear. But was it something missed by the person who had ransacked the premises the night before, when Fitch was killed—something only Langworth knew how to find? Or was it he who had turned the shop upside down? Langworth seemed such a calculating man; I could not picture him chasing Fitch around the workshop in a frenzy, beating his skull in with a poker. "The place was left in such disarray," he had said to Samuel; was that an observation or a reproach? I wished I had paid more attention to his tone.

"He was killed in the same manner," I said. "His head beaten in."

"That proves nothing. What else?"

"Ezekiel Sykes," I said eventually. "Is he a good physician?"

"He's an expensive one, which some fools mistake for skill. Why do you ask?"

"I'm curious about him. I heard he was something of an alchemist."

"Perhaps. Don't all physicians dabble in it? Listen, Bruno." He sighed and laboriously stretched out his stiff leg, massaging it above the knee. "You seem determined to fix your attention on the most prominent men of the town. Maybe you have your reasons, but you had better make certain of your suspicions before you dare point a finger, or you will make yourself a target."

I paused for a moment to master the irritation I felt at his tone.

"I have accused no one, Harry, and I would not dream of doing so without evidence I was sure of. But if eminent men in the town have committed murder, it is all the more important that they should be brought to justice."

"You forget that it is the eminent men who dispense justice," Harry said, with a resignation that suggested such things could not be changed or resisted. I thought of Tom Garth and his fury at Nicholas Kingsley the night before—the fury of a man who knows he is impotent against powerful interests. He spoke of taking the law into his own hands—did that include murder? Sykes had a part in that story too, though there was still much I didn't know.

I watched Harry as he flexed one bony hand on his knee and studied it. I would make little progress here unless I had him as an ally, but I needed to break his unquestioning trust in Samuel.

"The dean seems anxious for the queen's approval," I remarked, looking out of the window towards the vast walls of the cathedral outside.

He grunted. "Is it any wonder? There are those on the Privy Council who would like to close us down and take the money for the queen's treasury, Walsingham chief among them." He shook his head. "Let's not pretend to be ignorant of that. But the Prince of Orange changes things. If the queen needs quick money for a war, then I think this time our future might really be in danger." His hand bunched into a fist as he spoke, then he glanced up quickly to gauge my response.

"I am not here to find reasons to dissolve the foundation," I said. "My business is only what I told you. But if this murder involves someone within the cathedral chapter, I cannot ignore it."

"You imply that I would do so?"

"Not at all," I said, trying to sound reassuring. He sucked in his cheeks for a moment, still holding my gaze.

"Are you here to report on me? You may as well be honest."

"No, Harry. I am here to find out who killed Sir Edward Kingsley so that his wife need not fear for her life. But it begins to look as if this murder is part of something greater."

He leaned forward, his expression of hostility giving way to interest.

"Tell me what you have found out, then."

I hesitated. "It's possible that Langworth—" I broke off at the sound of the door latch; Harry sat upright too.

"Only Samuel," he said. "You were saying?"

I glanced over my shoulder at the parlour door and my hand moved instinctively to the pouch at my belt, where my fingers closed around the shape of Langworth's keys.

"Nothing. Speculation. Another time, perhaps."

THE MEAL PASSED awkwardly. Harry seemed angry that I refused to speak in front of Samuel, though he did not say as much, and I presumed he was also irritated that I was still concentrating my suspicions on Langworth after his warning. He made a point of talking to Samuel about cathedral business that was of no relevance to me and I was not sure who I resented more by the time we had finished the plain stew of vegetables with thin slices of salt beef—Samuel for the dark, insinuating glances he shot from under his eyebrows when he thought I wasn't looking, or Harry for his stubbornness. I was relieved when Samuel cleared the plates away and Harry announced that he must prepare for the chapter meeting.

I told Harry I wanted to accept his offer to show me the cathedral library and he grudgingly agreed to take me on his way to the Chapter House, though his manner towards me was still prickly and I could tell he was disinclined to do me any favours. But the library was close enough to Langworth's house to give me a reasonable excuse for being in that part of the precincts while the canons were occupied with their meeting; I hoped I might be able to replace the keys and letter I had stolen before the treasurer noticed anything had been touched.

"WHAT IS IT you want to look at, exactly, Signor Savolino?" The canon librarian regarded me with caution. He wore his advanced years well, though he stooped a little and I could see the joints of his fingers were stiff and swollen as he leafed absently through a large manuscript volume on the desk in front of him. Light fell through a tall arched window behind him, illuminating his few remaining tufts of hair into brilliant white. When he looked up, his face was deeply scored with lines that branched and bisected around his features like a map of a river delta.

"I am interested in the history of Saint Thomas, above all," I said, with a pleasant smile.

"An unusual field of study for an Italian Protestant," he remarked, glancing sideways at me as he levered himself up and crossed to the cases against the wall, stacked high with a jumble of books in precarious piles. Many looked to be in poor condition, their bindings gnawed by mice, pages spotted with damp. What good was it, I thought, with a stab of irritation, to save books from the destruction of a library only to neglect them like this, thrown together carelessly like corpses in a plague grave?

I thought I detected a note of suspicion in the old man's voice, so I broadened my smile further.

"I suppose I have always believed we might avoid falling into the errors of the past by understanding them, rather than by burying them," I said. "Even if we regard them as mere superstition, there is something to be learned about human folly from the legends of our forefathers, do you not think?"

He nodded with a speculative expression.

"Well said. We may as well destroy all libraries if we do not take lessons from the chronicles of history. And now," he said, folding his hands together and making an effort to smile, "I must get along to the chapter meeting. I will leave you in the care of my assistant, who will endeavour to find you the books you want." He indicated a morose-looking young man in the robes of a minor canon who was copying something laboriously at a desk in the corner. "Geoffrey! Our guest wants chronicles of the life of Saint Thomas—see what you can find for him," he called, in a peremptory tone.

Silently, though with obvious bad grace, Geoffrey rose from his seat and made his way without haste to one of the book stacks. I privately doubted whether the young man could find anything on those shelves, but I thanked the librarian and settled at a desk set in an alcove beneath one of the windows, which must once have held a statue when this old chapel was still used for worship. The assistant Geoffrey, who communicated only in monosyllables, made a slow search of the shelves and returned with a small pile of books, which he dropped heavily in front of me before resuming his own task, though I noticed he moved his books and papers to another desk from which he could usefully keep me in his line of sight. I nodded my thanks and began shuffling the volumes with the appearance of interest, wondering how soon I could leave for Langworth's house without seeming suspicious. The only sound in the empty library was the young canon's heavy breathing through his mouth and the scratching of his pen.

The first book on the pile was a bound manuscript bearing the title *Quadrilogus,* clearly of some antiquity, which on closer inspection proved to be a collection of more or less fantastical accounts of the life of Thomas Becket produced by various English and French monks three centuries earlier. Beneath it, the *Vita* of Robert of Cricklade, a twelfth-century life of the former archbishop. I sighed, flicking idly through the pages, feigning interest and offering an insipid smile to the young assistant whenever he glanced in my direction, which was more often than was strictly necessary. I reminded myself that the surest way to look suspicious was to behave as if I feared suspicion.

The air of the library was thick with the smell of dust and old paper— usually a smell I savoured, but today I felt stifled by it. A damp heat stuck my shirt to my back and inside my boot, the handle of my knife dug into my ankle. I wiped my forehead on my sleeve and leaned my head on my left hand, my elbow propped up on the table as I skimmed the book, feeling an unreasonable irritation clenching like a fist inside my chest. What on earth was I doing here, sneaking around as if I were a thief among men who at best distrusted and at worst hated me, tangling myself in two murders that had nothing to do with me, all for the sake of a woman? Ah, but was it really all for a woman, responded another, more cynical voice in the depths of my mind. Was it not more truthfully your own absurd tenacity, this voice continued, that same dogged refusal to back down that forced you to become a fugitive in your own country and an exile through Europe, living by your wits for the past eight years, because you had to prove that you knew more than everyone else? I pushed my hair off my face and gritted my teeth. Men have committed greater acts of folly than this for a woman before, I countered; in any case, was I not permitted a little licence? Every reckless or impulsive decision I had made in my life until now had been in the pursuit of knowledge. All through the years when other young men were risking their dignity or their lives fighting over women, I had dared everything for the sake of books I was forbidden to touch, in search of answers to questions I had been told I should not ask. Surely now, at the age of thirty-six, I was allowed a little ordinary folly?

Yet, if I were completely honest, I thought, curling my lip as I watched the assistant librarian rummage absentmindedly in his ear with a forefinger and examine the result, my motives were not altogether selfless. If Sophia was cleared of murder, she stood to inherit all her late husband's property. She would have achieved her heart's greatest desire—independence. And you think she will share it with you, once she has it? cut in that same mocking voice. Marry you, so that you can stay in England, living off the profits of her first ill-fated marriage—is that what you hope for? You think she would win her independence and give it straight up again—knowing her opinion of men? Do you really imagine she sees you differently?

I clicked my tongue impatiently, causing the assistant librarian to jerk his head up with a hard stare in my direction. I had not confronted the possible end of this adventure so starkly until now, and it was a shock to acknowledge the truth of my own secret hopes. It was a life I had never dared imagine for myself, or desired, until now, because it seemed so far beyond the bounds of possibility: a wife, a home, a secure income, perhaps, in time, children. In Sophia I glimpsed the image of an entirely different future, and for the first time, I found it attracted me. Whether it would hold the same appeal for her was less certain.

Outside in the precincts the great bell swung into life, tolling the hour that signified the beginning of the chapter meeting. I flicked through another few pages, watching the young assistant Geoffrey, who had returned his attention to his work, his tongue poking out of the corner of his mouth as he frowned in concentration. I was on the point of closing the book when I glanced down and one of the illustrations caught my eye. It was a plan of the cathedral, made at the time the first shrine was built. The crypt was clearly marked, as were all the chantry chapels that stuck out like fins either side of the vast body of the cathedral, as if it were some enormous sea creature. I peered closer; the treasury was not marked—it must have been built later—but the chapel it adjoined was drawn and someone had marked in ink over the book's original plan a square shape with a dotted line, overlapping between the side chapel and the crypt. There were lines showing a staircase. Beside it, this unknown hand had written "sub-vault. Sometime prison." Was this another way into the crypt, from beneath the treasury? The map was old; I wondered how many people knew about the sub-vault.

I closed the book and pushed my chair back.

"Thank you for your help," I said to the assistant librarian, my voice sounding unnecessarily loud in the still air. "I'm afraid I must leave, but may I come back and read further tomorrow?" I indicated the pile of books; he gave a grunt that may or may not have been assent, and it was all I could do to keep myself from tearing down the stairs in my haste to get to Langworth's house.

There was no sign of anyone along the path that led around the north side of the cathedral—I guessed every canon was required to attend the meeting in the Chapter House—and I was able to approach the rear of the treasurer's house unobserved. The casement at the back still hung open on its hinges and again I squeezed myself uncomfortably through. This time it took only a matter of minutes to insert the blade of my knife into the lock of the door behind the tapestry in Langworth's chamber and turn the lock; to my great relief I could make out through the gloom the shape of the packet Langworth had tossed inside the room in his haste to answer the door to the dean earlier, meaning he had not been back since and therefore would not have discovered my theft. I left the door to the chamber open so that a thin light filtered through into the back room. As quickly and quietly as I could, I lifted the loose hearth tile, replaced the keys and the original letter from Mendoza in the engraved casket, and carefully turned its clasp again. My heart was pounding as I fitted the tile back into place, but I was flushed with a sense of triumph. Langworth would never know anyone had found his secret hiding place, even as my transcript of his letter was making its way to London. The canon treasurer was already on his guard against me, but my one advantage over him was that he didn't know that I was aware of this. For as long as he felt it was in his interest to keep playing along with me, thinking he was the one with the upper hand, I could hope to gain more time. But what had he meant when he said to Samuel that he had an idea of how to keep me out of trouble, if need be? I froze, glancing at the door, my skin prickled with gooseflesh despite the heat, but there was no sound except my own breathing. Whatever Langworth had in mind for me, I would need to keep my eyes at my back at all times.

The brown paper packet he had thrown inside the room when he was interrupted lay where it had fallen. I knelt and gingerly picked it up at the corners between the tips of my fingers so as not to leave any tell-tale marks on the wrapping. Almost as soon as he heard news of Fitch's death, it seemed, he had hastened to the apothecary's shop in search of something. What could be so important that he feared it might be found?

I untwisted the paper and laid it open on the boards. Inside were two black pills, about the size of a gold angel coin and the thickness of my little finger. I lifted one; it was solid enough not to crumble between my fingers, and as I bent to sniff it I caught an odour that was familiar but I could not quite place. I closed my eyes and tried to push from my mind every pressing thought and anxiety, focusing only on allowing my memory to dredge the silt of years in search of the source of that recognition. I sniffed the black lozenge again and there flashed into my mind an image of the infirmary at San Domenico Maggiore, a workbench strewn with chopped herbs, the brother infirmarian with his hooked nose hunched over a glass jar containing some substance with this faint, musky scent . . .

"Laudanum." I whispered it aloud as the memory clicked into place, my voice immediately swallowed by the muffled silence. Laudanum—a remedy so powerful it was once considered to have magical properties, derived from the tears of the wild poppy. It was costly, certainly, but was that why Langworth had rushed to rescue it from the destruction of Fitch's shop? There were doubtless other valuable substances there too, but he had gone specifically to bring back these two pills and hide them. I exhaled slowly, closed my eyes again, letting my memory feel its way.

I had learned a little of the uses of laudanum during my apprenticeship in the infirmary as a novice. The infirmarian had used it sparingly, because of the expense, but its effects were remarkable; given in a tincture with strong wine, it could temporarily dull pain and induce an intense sleep in which the patient appeared as good as dead. I recalled when one of the monks had fallen from a ladder while repairing a window in the monastery's great church and shattered his leg; the infirmarian had tried to set it, but infection had taken hold and to save the poor brother's life, it had been necessary to saw the leg off above the knee—an operation carried out with the man deep in the sleep of laudanum. As the infirmarian's assistant, I had been the one to hold the man steady on the table as his leg was removed; I recalled watching in disbelief as the blade bit deep into his flesh while he barely twitched in his sleep. Dangerous stuff, the infirmarian had told me brusquely, seeing my amazement. Brings as much pain as it takes away. The Portuguese traders to the east smoked it, for a deceptively brief pleasure, but it drove them mad with demonic dreams. The Arabs had used it in medicine for centuries, he had explained, and because of that the Church had banned its use, believing that any substance beloved of the infidels must be the work of the Devil. So the Inquisition had ensured that for the best part of two centuries laudanum had fallen out of use in Europe, and it was only at the beginning of our own century that physicians had rediscovered its properties, thanks to the writings of—

"*Paracelsus!*" I smiled to myself in the half-light, turning the fat pill over between my fingers. Of course—Paracelsus had brought it back from his travels in Arabia in just this form, supposedly hidden in the pommel of his sword. "Stones of Immortality," he called them, these black tablets made from laudanum, mixed with citrus juice and quintessence of gold.

I thought of the burned scrap of paper I had taken from Fitch's hearth. Paracelsus again. The apothecary's papers had been burned to conceal a reference to Paracelsus, and now here was Langworth spiriting away laudanum pills which also spoke, at least obliquely, of the alchemist's work. What was the connection?

I wrapped the black pills back in their brown paper and sat for a moment in the shadows, thinking of Paracelsus. I had felt an affinity with the maverick Swiss alchemist since I first encountered his proscribed books as a young monk. I had admired the way he refused to content himself with the ideas of the past and had set out to overturn the lazy, narrow thinking of the academies, whose learning derived from tradition, not experiment. In the process he had acquired a reputation as a troublemaker and frequently found himself hounded out of the universities, accused of necromancy by those made fearful or jealous by his hunger for knowledge and his rebellious independence. Without consciously intending to follow in his footsteps, I had found myself repeating his experience half a century later, driven by (I liked to think) the same tenacious spirit of enquiry into the nature of this vast universe we inhabit.

Like me, Paracelsus had been fascinated by the secret wisdom and natural magic of Hermes Trismegistus, the Egyptian sage who was called the father of alchemy and natural magic. It was a lost manuscript of Hermes that I had followed from Italy to France to England and finally held in my hands for a moment last autumn, before Henry Howard had snatched it away. A book believed to contain the secret of man's divinity—a secret more powerful even than the philosopher's stone, which Paracelsus was supposed to have received from an Arabian adept in Constantinople. This was the book I dared to hope Howard might have entrusted to Langworth, via his nephew, to keep it from the eyes of the government searchers he knew would ransack his own houses for evidence of treason. And now here was Langworth hiding stones of laudanum, and William Fitch—or his murderer—burning recipes that spoke explicitly of Paracelsus. I pushed my hands through my hair, gripping clumps between my fingers, as if to press my brain into making the connections, but the sense of it all eluded me, swirling through my muddied thoughts.

Angry at myself, I left the parcel on the floor where Langworth had thrown it and concentrated on securing the secret room behind me. My fingers moved more deftly with my own knife and this time I succeeded in turning the lock. I climbed through the broken casement unobserved, at least as far as I could tell (those opaque windows of the building that backed on to Langworth's house seemed to bear down on me with accusatory stares, though I told myself not to be foolish). But as I was rounding the corner of the row of houses in sight of the cathedral once more, I almost collided with a black-robed figure heading in the opposite direction. I apologised, flustered, and looked up; to my surprise, it was not a cleric, as I had thought, but a woman.

"Oh. Mistress Gray—forgive me, I didn't see you."

She appraised me in silence from beneath her veil, then glanced over my shoulder, as if to judge where I might have come from. I met that look as confidently as I could, wondering for my part where she was going; there was nothing at the end of the path except Langworth's house. We stood for a moment, looking at each other. Finally her eyes flickered briefly upwards to the sky.

"We shall have a storm, I think," she observed, her tone pleasant, as if I were an old acquaintance. I followed the direction of her gaze to see that the layer of cloud had thickened into scalloped rows, pressing the heat down like a blanket. To the east, above the rooftops, the sky had taken on an edge of steel grey. I nodded, unnerved by the way she studied my face. What was her connection to Edward Kingsley? Why had he left her money? I wanted to ask her questions but could not think how to broach the subject without causing offence.

When it seemed that she intended neither to speak nor to move, I touched my forefinger to my fringe in an awkward salute, bowed my head briefly, and walked quickly away, with the uncomfortable sensation of her eyes on my back until I had turned the corner.

Chapter 10

Robin Bates and his companions were waiting outside the Three Tuns after supper as they had promised, playfully jostling one another or leaning against the hitching posts, spitting into the dirt. The boy named Peter, whose place I had taken at the card game the night before, picked up a stone and threw it at a scrawny cat, who yelped and scurried away, belly low to the ground. Bates nodded as I approached, and I noticed two of the others lean their heads together and whisper, eyes fixed on me, knowing smirks playing about their lips in a way that made me immediately wary.

"Have you brought a full purse, my Italian friend?" Bates said.

I smiled, patting the moneybag I carried at my belt. The thought had occurred that, once outside the city limits, these boys could simply take my coins by force and leave me in a ditch, though I brushed the idea aside; they might choose to fight me for sport, but their youthful aggression was straightforward, not calculating. I was clearly there to be the target of their jokes, but I did not think they would deny themselves an evening's entertainment by robbing me before we reached the card table. Bates slapped me on the back approvingly. I smiled again and laid a hand over the purse at my belt, feeling the reassuring shape of the keys I had copied from Langworth's. I was content to play the joker for these young fools if it gave me access to Edward Kingsley's house. The old priory held some secrets, that much was certain; secrets important enough for Langworth to fear that Walsingham had sent me from London to uncover them.

We walked through the town, crossing the Buttermarket and heading along Sun Street in the direction of the North Gate. The boys talked and cursed loudly, keen to draw attention to themselves with their swaggering gait and playful fighting; I noticed all carried swords in elaborate scabbards swinging at their sides. I wondered how much skill they possessed in the use of them. My little dagger, hanging at my belt, looked inadequate by comparison, yet I suspected I was probably more efficient with it than these boys who carried their fine blades as ornaments of their wealth. People scowled and turned away from them; I kept my head down as best I could and hoped we might avoid any trouble inside the city walls. It would not help my reputation in the town to be seen in the company of notorious brawlers, as I guessed these young men were known to be.

To distract him from looking too provocatively at a group of men who stood by the gate of a tavern, eyeing the boys with dislike, I turned to Bates and nodded in the general direction we were walking.

"Are you sure your friend Nicholas will be happy to see us? I gathered last night he is still in mourning."

Bates laughed.

"Mourning? Not he. Nick hated the old devil almost as much as he hated that whore he married. Though he'd have bedded her himself, given the chance. We all would." He gave a lascivious grin and I flexed my hands quietly into fists at my side, as I smiled in complicity. "No—if Nick seemed unwilling, it is only because he is afraid he will jeopardise the legal process. His father's property is not his in law yet."

"Then whose? His widow's?"

"Well, that is just the point." He turned to me, his eyes gleaming with the excitement of a story. "Nick was cut out of his father's will and everything left to the wife. But if it was she who killed Sir Edward, then naturally her rights are forfeit and all should return to Nick. The difficulty is that she cannot be tried because she has fled."

"Is that not as good as a confession of her guilt?"

"Eventually, I suppose, if she does not return. But she cannot be tried in absentia. Meanwhile Nick has a house, lands, income, and a full cellar he has been instructed by his attorney not to touch, and we his friends grow very impatient with the business. We had thought his father's death would make him a wealthy man. In fact, I believe we have you to thank for his agreement tonight—he did not want to lose face in front of a stranger." He punctuated this sentence with a friendly punch to my upper arm, which I received with good humour, inwardly gritting my teeth.

"But you said *if* the wife killed Sir Edward. Is it not certain, then?" I prompted.

Bates darted a quick, lizard glance sideways at me.

"They found her gloves, all bloodied. The next day she was gone, with a purse of his money. Hard to see how it could be anyone else. Mind you," he added, assuming a thoughtful expression, "if she had not as good as confessed by running, there are plenty who might have pointed the finger at Tom Garth—the big fellow who tried to make trouble at the Three Tuns last night."

"I remember him," I said. "You think he could have done it?"

"He had reason. I'm not saying he did it. But he wasn't the only one glad to see Nick's father go to his grave."

"Including Nick himself?"

He turned slowly, with a knowing smile.

"He was glad all right. But Nick is all talk, he could never have done it. He's a coward at heart."

I almost pointed out that a coward may well attack a man from behind in the dark—Tom Garth had said as much—but decided it was not in my interest to keep pressing the possibility of Nicholas Kingsley's guilt while I was a guest in his house.

We crossed under the North Gate, which was no more than a small chapel built across the road, supported by wooden pillars, with room for a carriage to pass beneath. Beyond it, the streets opened up into orchards and fields, baked yellow by the heat. A wide avenue followed the line of the city wall, edged with fine houses, taller and more generously spaced than those nearer the centre of the town. As we walked, my hair was lifted from my face by intermittent gusts of a hot breeze that whipped and eddied around us, churning the heavy air. Gulls circled, calling mournfully. I squinted upwards; the sun was a malevolent eye glaring through the cloud.

At the end of a row of houses, Bates indicated to the right and I turned to see a handsome manor house, built in the style of an earlier century and set back from the road behind a low wall in spacious grounds that had been left to run wild. It was only as we drew nearer that I realised what had looked like a large rambling garden was studded with crumbling stone crosses and other burial monuments, and I recalled Fitch's story about his niece being afraid to approach the house because of the old priory cemetery. The grave mounds were all grassed over and many of the headstones worn almost smooth.

We passed through a small gate. The path to the front door of the manor ran along the edge of the graveyard.

"I'm not sure I would like to live out here, surrounded by the dead," I remarked to Bates. He laughed.

"It's the vengeance of the living you have to worry about here." He gestured to the cemetery. "This belonged to the parish, after the priory was dissolved. But twenty years ago the lessee of the manor house had the burial ground enclosed as part of his private lands. When Nick's father took the lease, the parishioners petitioned him to give the burial ground back to the town, but he refused, so they have to carry their dead farther out of town now, at more expense. Created a lot of resentment. Still, they're always complaining about something, the poor," he added airily, and any respect I might have felt for him as the best of the group instantly evaporated.

To hide my irritation, I turned to look back at the graveyard. The end farthest from us, bordered by the ivy-shrouded masonry of the original boundary wall, remained steeped in shadow, but as I shaded my eyes, I noticed a low stone mausoleum with a façade of white columns, cracked and patched with moss, and the carved figure of an angel standing on the portico, wings outstretched as if it were about to step off the roof into the air. I stopped and looked around, straining for any unusual sound. It was here that the girl Rebecca imagined she had heard someone screaming, as if the sound came from beneath her feet. From the very graves themselves, Fitch had said with that wink of his, little knowing how soon he would lie in his own. I shivered, despite the warmth of the evening, and overhead a seagull uttered a sharp lament.

"Are you joining us, Filippo?" Bates said from the threshold. He had the bell rope in his hand and behind the studded oak door its clamour echoed back through the house.

I tore my attention away and smiled enthusiastically, but my curiosity was sharpened even further.

"COME IN, THEN."

Nicholas Kingsley did not have the air of a gracious host; he seemed stiff and ill at ease, glancing furtively about him as if at any moment he expected to see his father appear in a rage. He ushered us into a well-appointed dining room, with a large oak table in the centre and a polished wooden buffet standing against the back wall, where pitchers and drinking vessels had been lined up. In one corner of this room stood an elderly woman dressed in a plain brown smock of rough cloth covered by a white apron, her grey hair bound up in a coif and her hands folded meekly in front of her. She raised her eyes briefly as we trooped in— seven young men in number, including me—and I caught her glance for a moment. She flinched and looked quickly away and I saw that she was afraid. I was gripped by an urge to reassure her; this good old woman who had helped Sophia and been the only one to show her kindness during those terrible six months of her marriage.

I craned my neck to take in the elaborately carved wooded bosses of the ceiling as the others took their places, thinking how strange it was to be seated here at this table where Sophia must have endured so many meals, forcing herself to eat and make polite conversation with her husband's dinner guests, aware of the greedy eyes of her stepson on her. Without meaning to, I found myself glaring at Nick down the length of the table; he chanced to glance up at that moment and the look he sent me in return was no less hostile. I tried quickly to rearrange my expression; I was so close, I thought, to the mystery of this house, and I must continue to play my part for this evening. To make them suspicious now risked ruining everything.

WE GATHERED AROUND the table, the boys' spirits running high, pitchers of wine passing back and forth and spilling from pewter tankards as cards were thrown down amid shouts and curses, coins rattled into a heap to be scraped up by whomever luck had favoured at the end of each hand (for I had no illusion that any of them succeeded by skill, so raucous and impulsive their gaming seemed). Bates, who appeared by general consent to have appointed himself the dealer, called for hands of bone-ace, one-and-thirty, or maw, and the others reached for their purses as the pot was emptied. I lost graciously at the first three games and on the fourth, though not by any considered effort on my part, I found myself the winner of a hand and was able to return some coins to my depleted store. By this time it seemed I had earned enough of a place in the group for this small flash of good fortune not to turn them against me; in fact my companions cheered on my behalf and those nearest clapped me on the back—all except Nick Kingsley, who continued to glower from his end of the table.

If I disliked the boy before, my contempt for him was doubled by the way he spoke to the old housekeeper, Meg, as if she were a dog, demanding she fetch more wine even while she was busy bringing dishes of food from the kitchen, which the boys all set to with their fingers. The second time he barked orders at her to bring up more bottles, I gently offered to help.

"If you just point me towards the wine cellar, I could save her the trouble—"

"For Christ's sake, man"—Nick spat half-chewed chicken across the table—"she's a servant. Let her do her job. Or don't you have servants where you're from?"

"I thought she might be tired," I said, glancing at Meg, who raised her eyes briefly and gave me a faltering smile.

"Well, if she's too tired, I can always get another servant who can manage the work," Nick said, with a malicious look at the housekeeper. She turned pale and shook her head vehemently.

"No, Master Nicholas, I have not complained. I'm going right away." She backed out of the room and I saw the fear in her eyes; she would probably not find another position at her age, and was stuck here at the mercy of this young brute.

"Got to remind them who's in charge," Nick said, to no one in particular, while Meg was still within earshot. His friends murmured assent, examining their new cards and wiping greasy fingers on their breeches. I felt revolted by the lot of them, and silently hoped they would drink themselves into a stupor as soon as possible, leaving me free to explore the house.

I drank slowly; at first, from time to time one of them would remark on it, calling on me to drink up, while the others cheered for my cup to be refilled, but as the evening wore on and their drunkenness increased, my behaviour attracted less interest. They lit clay pipes of pungent tobacco, filling the room with clouds of woody smoke that ascended to hover like a blue veil above our heads; beneath the table they passed around a piss pot and soon the sharp smell of urine mingled with the pipe smoke and roast meat in the close air. I breathed through my mouth, fighting the urge to run outside into the night.

When dusk fell, Nick bellowed for candles to be brought, and the faces of the players were lit by that strange, wavering orange glow, creating shadows in the hollows of their eyes and cheeks as they leant forward over the table. By midnight, three of them had fallen asleep where they sat, heads resting on their arms on the tabletop, snoring with their mouths hanging wetly open, and the others continued their game halfheartedly, until Nick pushed his chair back abruptly, knocking over his tankard as he did so, and mumbled that he was for bed.

"Find a bed where you will," he slurred, pointing vaguely at the rest of us, then crashed into a chair and lurched towards the door, unlacing his breeches as he went. Two of the others heaved themselves unsteadily to their feet and stumbled after him. A crashing sound came from the corridor, as of someone falling into furniture. Only Bates was left, shuffling the cards and looking around the table at his fallen companions with disdain. He seemed worryingly alert. As his eyes came to rest on me, I quickly affected a cloudy gaze and swayed a little in my chair.

"Looks like we are the last men standing, Filippo," he said, a slight slur in his voice. "God, what I wouldn't give for a woman now. If only Nick had dismissed that old crone and got himself a young housemaid, we might have had some sport with her, eh?"

By way of answer, I let out a convincing belch.

"There is a bawdy house outside the West Gate might still let us in at this hour," he said, hopefully. "Shall we try it, you and I?"

I waved a hand imprecisely, shaking my head. "I would be no use to a woman in this state," I said, slumping forward across the table. "But you go."

Bates regarded me for a moment, then sighed.

"No. It can wait." He clicked his tongue impatiently and stretched out in his chair, his hands clasped behind his head. "God's blood, I had just as well go drinking with my infant nieces for all the company these fellows have been tonight. We were supposed to keep on till dawn. You will take another cup, though, Filippo? Don't leave me up drinking by myself here. I'll wager you have some wild stories to tell from your travels." He yawned and filled his tankard again and turned to me, the pitcher held out expectantly. The flush in his cheeks from the wine made him look even younger, and I saw that, for all his swagger, he was still just a boy, afraid of the silence, of being left alone. If I had not joined the Dominican order and given my twenties to philosophy and theology, might I have ended up in this kind of company? I was glad now that I never had the choice. Reluctantly I raised my cup for more.

Bates continued to drink steadily while I concealed my desperation for him to join the others in sleep, and instead recounted the tale of a young man in Naples who makes mischief by advising his lascivious elderly neighbour on the best way to seduce a beautiful courtesan, ensuring that the old man is caught out by his wife, while the young hero becomes the girl's lover himself. Into the story I wove other characters: a miser, a conniving alchemist, and a pedantic schoolmaster, all bested by the wit of the young man, who I modestly implied was my younger self. Bates roared with laughter, poured himself more wine, and I watched in hope of seeing his eyelids droop as the story progressed. He had no idea, of course, that I was telling him the plot of *The Candlemaker*, a comedy I had written for the stage some years earlier; a ribald tale with a philosophical slant, filled with characters just like those I had observed when I first arrived in the glorious noisy, filthy, sexy chaos of the city of Naples as a youth. Bringing those streets to life made me feel how much I missed it.

It is rare that a storyteller feels delight at sending his audience to sleep, but I silently rejoiced when the wine and the late hour finally worked on Bates enough for him to stand up, sway a little on the spot, and then announce his intention of finding a place to bed down. I grunted, lay my head on my arms, and waited until the sound of his footsteps on the stairs and the boards overhead faded to silence.

My own head was more than a little fuzzy from the wine. I blinked hard to clear my vision, and when I was certain that no one was stirring, I took the two longest candles from the table and moved as noiselessly as I could towards the door, leaving my fellow gamblers snoring, spit falling in threads from their open mouths to pool on the boards beneath their sleeping heads.

I crossed the stone-flagged entrance hall and took the passageway past the stairs towards the back of the house, where I found a large, well-appointed kitchen, evidently cleaned and scrubbed scrupulously by the housekeeper before she retired for the night. I paused and looked around, the candles' flames sending shadows skittering up the walls and across the black opaque panes of the casements. From somewhere in the distance came the drawn-out, wavering cry of an owl, a sound that never failed to make the hairs stand up on my neck, and I smiled in the dark thinking of the girl Rebecca and her belief that she had heard screaming coming from the burial ground. My fears that night were more prosaic; I did not want to be caught before I had a chance to uncover anything useful.

A cellar, I concluded, if it was used for storage, would most likely have some access from the kitchen. I moved carefully, anxious not to stumble into anything—pots, pans, brushes—that I might knock to the floor, announcing my presence. At the far side of the room, opposite the vast hearth with its rows of roasting spits, was a door set in a recess that appeared to open onto a rear courtyard. Beside it, an empty lantern hung on an iron hook, and with some relief I blew out one of my candles in case I had need later, and fitted the other carefully inside the glass, saving myself the trouble of shielding its flame with my hand. Immediately its light bloomed and seemed brighter, and I held it up as I tried the latch of the back door. This was firmly locked, but to the left was an archway that led through from the kitchen into a large pantry, its shelves stacked with jars and bottles, full sacks lying against the wall on the floor.

I lowered the lantern towards the floor and saw what I had hoped to find; a wooden hatch with an iron ring set into the flagstones. I set the lantern down on the floor and knelt beside it. Before I could reach out a hand to the ring, my breath was stopped in my throat by the sound of tapping from the room behind me. I swallowed silently, barely daring to turn, and it came again, sharp and insistent, a tap followed by a kind of scraping.

Slowly, I pulled my dagger from its sheath; keeping it low by my side but with my arm tensed and ready to spring, I rose and moved back into the kitchen, one step at a time, holding the lantern aloft. The room was empty. I waited, straining to listen, until eventually the tap came again, from outside the window: tap-tap, tap-tap, scrape. I felt my legs buckle with relief as I realised it was the branch of a tree, nudged by the wind; I laughed softly, and heard the trembling in my own laughter.

I worked quickly this time, determined not to be distracted again. To my surprise, the wooden hatch in the pantry opened smoothly, revealing a narrow flight of stone steps leading into a musty darkness below. Their treads were worn smooth with age and sagged in the middle from the passage of feet; I thought with pity of the elderly housekeeper being sent to fetch and carry up and down these precarious stairs. But perhaps she knew them so well by now she could find her way easily even in the dark. I was not so confident; keeping my feet within the yellow circle of the lantern's glow, I descended carefully into a wide cellar, its ceiling supported in the centre by two thick stone pillars. Wooden barrels lined one wall, while another corner was filled with a jumble of what looked like broken furniture and a stack of crates, such as might be used to transport produce on a ship. I made a slow tour of the room with the light, examining objects, looking for traces of anything unusual on the floor or the walls, though already my heart was sinking with the weight of disappointment; I knew I was in the wrong place. The cellar had opened too easily to me; there was nothing hidden here but wine and refuse. The mysterious cellar Sophia had mentioned had to be elsewhere—yet where should I begin looking for it? It could not be more than a few hours until dawn, and I dare not be found wandering the house when the others awoke.

I gave one last turn, willing myself to see anything I might have missed, straining so hard that it must have looked as if I was trying to see through the stone walls themselves. I stopped, struck by the thought. Perhaps that was it; this storage cellar was directly under the kitchen, but there could be more underground rooms beyond it, stretching out the length of the house. I shone the light again at the tangle of broken stools in the corner, splintered legs jutting into the air on top of an old wooden chest, casting spiky shadows on the ragged blocks of stone that shored up the wall of the cellar among the foundations of the old manor. Beside them, the stack of wooden crates, about the height of a man, very neatly placed. Too neatly, perhaps; I crossed the room, set the lantern on the floor, and tried to lever the boxes away from the wall. They were heavy, but I managed to shift them enough to feel into the gap behind, where my fingers brushed over wood, not stone.

Bracing myself, my palms growing slippery, I heaved the topmost of the wooden boxes from the pile and almost dropped it, staggering back under the weight so that my foot struck the lantern, which rocked for a few moments before mercifully deciding to stay upright. I steadied the box against my chest, the muscles in my arms standing out like cords as I set it on the floor with a heavy thud and paused to see if the sound had carried, sweat running down my collar at the exertion. What had Kingsley stored in these crates to make them so heavy? I lifted one edge of the wooden lid and found to my surprise that it had been left unfastened; inside was a pile of broken masonry. I lifted out a corner piece and realised letters were engraved on it, though faded almost smooth. This must be rubble cleared from the graveyard, the debris of old headstones. There could be no good reason for him to have squirreled it away in these crates, except as a useful deterrent against opening the door that clearly lay behind them.

One by one, breathing hard and pausing only to wipe the sweat from my eyes on the shoulder of my shirt, I moved the crates away until the low door stood clear. It was made of wood with iron studs, rising to a pointed arch in the old style and not even reaching to the top of my head. Naturally, it was locked. With shaking hands, I took out the keys I had copied from Langworth and tried each of them. The third fitted, with a little tweaking, and I closed my eyes with silent gratitude as I heard the bolt slide back. Just as I was about to push the door open, I caught the sound of a footfall on the stairs behind me and whipped around, my hand reaching to my side for the dagger.

If I had been a more superstitious man, I would have cried out at the sight, because the figure on the stairs seemed at first glance to have risen from one of the graves surrounding the house; dressed in a threadbare shift with a shawl around its shoulders, unbound tendrils of grey hair standing out from its head, the sunken features lit from beneath by the candle it carried in a terrible rictus. It took me a moment to compose myself, even though my rational mind realised it was only old Meg, the housekeeper, roused from sleep, and that her dreadful expression was merely a result of her own shock at finding me here. I ran a hand over my mouth, took a breath to steady myself, then pressed a finger to my lips with an imploring look.

She appeared to consider this request for a moment, then stepped closer.

"If it's the wine you mean to steal," she whispered, "you won't find it in there. That door is locked, in any case."

I shook my head urgently and beckoned her nearer.

"I am not here to steal anything. I am only looking for answers."

I saw her face draw immediately tighter, as if she knew what I alluded to.

"Meg." I bent my head and fixed her eyes with my own in the shifting light. "I am a friend of Soph—" I checked myself just in time. "Kate. Your mistress. I am here to help her. She always said you were kind to her."

The old woman hesitated; her desire to believe me seemed to be battling with her natural wariness towards a stranger and a foreigner. After a moment, her face crumpled and her thin fingers clasped my wrist.

"She didn't kill him," she said, her voice barely escaping the dry lips.

"I know." I pressed my own hand over hers for reassurance. "But to save her I must find out who did. Sir Edward had secrets . . ." I gestured with my head towards the room behind us. Fear darted across Meg's eyes again.

"I have not been through that door, sir. Not once. Only he had the key and it has not been seen since he died."

"Someone took it from his corpse while it was still warm. But I have a copy." I pushed the door an inch farther to show her it had opened. She inhaled sharply. "Well, then," I said. "Let us see what your master wanted to hide."

Meg stepped back, shaking her head as if I had just suggested she walk through the gates of Hell itself. I turned, my hand on the latch.

"Do you know what he kept in here, Meg?"

She continued to shake her head as if her life depended on it, but the candle in her hand trembled and in its light I saw tears well up and spill over her lined cheeks. My heart swelled with pity and I squeezed her hand again. "It's all right. You need not look."

"I never saw anything, sir, I swear it on the holy martyr. But sometimes I heard it. Dreadful sounds. There was nothing I could do, though, you understand? Not a thing."

"What did you hear?"

She only pressed the back of her hand to her mouth to stifle a little sob and shook her head again. My gut tightened with a horrible apprehension.

I pushed open the door and picked up my lantern, holding it up as I stepped forward into thick darkness.

Before me there stretched out a passageway, lined with damp stone, tall enough for a man to walk along, if he stooped. It smelled as if no clean air had circulated there in recent memory, and I took shallow breaths through my mouth to avoid the lingering odour of decay. It was hard to get my bearings underground, but I had the sense that the passage was leading me away from the house, under the cemetery itself, and though I consider myself above superstitions and folktales, nonetheless I had to suppress a shudder at the thought of all those corpses pressing down overhead and to each side—an impression made stronger by the unmistakable smell of dead things that seemed to grow denser with every step.

The floor beneath my feet was of compacted earth and I stepped forward carefully, keeping the lantern as steady as I could, to stop myself from stumbling, brushing thick cobwebs from my eyes and mouth with every step. After perhaps thirty yards, as I felt the faint stirrings of cold air as if from some vent nearby. I saw that three rough steps had been cut into the floor of the passage and that it ended abruptly in a wooden door. I pushed this gently with the flat of my hand and found that it opened a little way without too much difficulty; as I did so, something brushed swiftly past my foot in the dark and I leapt back, stifling a cry, heart pounding in my throat. Rats, no doubt; a faint scuffling came from whatever lay beyond that door.

Gathering my courage, I pushed the door farther and squeezed through the gap, repeating to myself that I had nothing to fear except dropping the lantern. So I thought, until the full force of the stench hit me and I had to clutch the wall, fighting for breath as my head swam and my stomach rose, so that I was afraid I would faint and retch at the same moment. It is almost impossible to convey the horror of that smell, even now; a brutal mixture of rotting flesh as from a charnel house, with undercurrents of every other filthy human effluent: piss, vomit, ordure, and a faint note of something unfamiliar, almost sweet, herbal. It was as if I had opened the mouth of Hell and all its foul vapours had rushed out to poison the earth.

Battling against the bile that threatened to choke me, I steadied myself and held up the lantern to examine this unspeakable place I had entered. I saw that I was inside an underground tomb, cut out of the earth and walled with stone, its floor covered with ancient flagstones carved with patterns I could not decipher in the candle's thin light. On each of the four walls niches had been built with stone biers inset, two lengthways along the longer walls, the lower ones complete with reclining effigies, their features still remarkably sharp, protected down here from the ravages of wind and weather and by the cool air, which filtered in through unseen ventilation holes and raised gooseflesh on my skin. I looked up; above me, high enough to stand upright, was a vaulted ceiling, and opposite the passage where I had entered, a flight of stone steps led upwards, but the exit had been bricked up. I must be directly under the mausoleum I had seen in the churchyard earlier. I thought it curious that the tombs had not been desecrated when the priory was dissolved, as I knew many had been in other religious houses, but perhaps a few monks dead for three centuries were not enough to pique the interest of the commissioners who came to raze the buildings.

Apart from the effigies on their stone biers, the tomb was empty. I moved forward with cautious steps, shining the light into the corners, keeping my sleeve pressed over my mouth, but could see no obvious reason why this place should have been so significant that Langworth needed to steal the key from Sir Edward Kingsley's corpse. If anything had once been hidden here, Langworth must have returned to clear it out before anyone could find it. I cursed and was on the point of turning back when something drew my eye: a flash from the floor close against one of the end walls. I crossed quickly and knelt to see what object had caught the light, and almost cut my knee on a shard of glass. There were several lying in the same place, and when I picked up one of the largest I saw that it was curved on one side. I gathered some of the other fragments and realised that I was holding the broken pieces of a small glass alembic. Bringing one piece nearer to the light, I saw that there was a residue staining the interior, of what looked like a dark-greenish hue, though it was hard to tell as the candle flame flattened all colours. I put my hand down to my side to lever myself up and felt something rough beneath my fingertips; lifting the light again I saw that it was a short length of rope, frayed at one end where it looked to have been cut with a knife. A couple of feet away, tucked into the shadows, was a pile of sacking. Gingerly, I lifted one corner, pinching as little of the material as possible between my thumb and forefinger. As I did so, something stirred within and a large brown rat shot out of the filthy nest past my feet. I swore aloud in Italian and from behind me I heard a muffled cry. I whipped around to see Meg standing in the half-open doorway still holding a candle in one hand, her shawl clutched across her mouth. We stared at each other for a moment, our ragged breathing amplified unnaturally in the vault, until I burst out laughing. I could hear the hysterical note in it as Meg joined in, prompted by relief.

"Dear God—damned creature nearly gave me a seizure," I whispered, and heard my voice shaking. She nodded, but the laughter had died on her lips as her gaze travelled over the old tombs that lined the walls. I was still holding the soiled sack; it was crusted stiff with some foul substance. With great reluctance I brought it closer to my face to sniff it and dropped it almost instantly as I caught the faint iron tang of dried blood. Meg coughed violently behind me and gagged as she did so.

That unbelievable smell: as I stood up it caught again in my throat and I had to press a hand over my mouth, swallowing hard to stop my gorge rising. I sniffed the air, trying to trace the worst of it to its source, which seemed to be one tomb set into the wall beside the bricked-in staircase. I knelt and read the inscription: "Hugh de Wenchepe, Prior, 1263–1278." I glanced up at Meg, who had come to stand at my shoulder; her face seemed even whiter in the shadows, her eyes fixed on the tomb of the long-dead prior with an expression of dread. I guessed that the old housekeeper thought she knew what had been hidden here, and I was gripped by the same awful sense of anticipation. I should have realised it the moment I opened the door. I had been in old tombs and burial vaults before; the ancient dead smelled of dust and mould. Yet Prior Hugh's coffin gave off a ripe stink like an abattoir, as if he had been rotting there for only a few months. A chill ran through me and as I held the lantern over his blank-eyed marble face I noticed the marks: the tracks of human fingers in the dust at the edges of the tomb's lid, where it had been recently opened.

"Meg—hold this for me, will you?"

I handed her my lantern; though I sensed her reluctance, she took it and held it above the bier as I leaned in with both hands to try and move the stone cover. This was no easy task; Prior Hugh's tomb was neatly carved to fit its alcove in the wall and the only way to open it was to slide the heavy stone towards me, with the fear that, even supposing I managed to budge it alone, it might at any moment topple forwards, crushing my leg or, at the very least, shattering so that it could not be replaced. In vain I struggled, straining with all the strength I possessed, only to see the slab shift no more than a couple of inches. Whoever had moved it before must have had help; two men might lift it between them, but I was not willing to admit defeat, having come so far. I muttered a prayer in Italian as I grabbed the left elbow of the effigy where the prior's hands were bent in prayer, to give myself better purchase. Bracing one foot against the wall of the tomb, I pulled on the statue's arm; with a great grinding of stone, I felt the slab lurch forward a couple of feet as the smell of putrefaction gusted upwards from the gaping blackness beneath. "Santa Maria!" I cried, spinning away from the tomb into a corner where, leaning with one arm against the wall, I vomited up my supper and a quantity of sweet red wine.

Meg waited patiently by the tomb, still holding the light, snatching breaths through the fabric of her sleeve. When I had wiped my mouth I turned back. Her face was unbearably bleak.

"We should leave, sir," she whispered, her voice shaking. "Leave the dead to their rest. Else we shall both take ill of the contagion."

"Not now," I said, recovering myself a little, though my voice was barely a croak. "Whatever is in here holds the answer, I am sure of it. I need you to take the light again, Meg, if you can bear it for a while longer." She hung back, understandably, though she did not take her eyes from the lid of the tomb and the hole under it.

Expelling the drink from my body seemed to have done me good; my head felt clearer as I rolled up my shirtsleeves higher and asked Meg to hold the lantern directly over the opening beneath the stone slab, which was about two feet at its widest end. I took a deep breath and leaned in, as the candle flame threw my own shadow like a giant on the wall behind me.

I made out the shape of a corpse wrapped in a thin linen shroud that appeared grey and horribly stained. I directed Meg to bend closer with the light and lifted one corner of the cloth, then jumped back as a hand fell from the wrappings onto the body's chest. The flesh was blotched and partly blackened, but still intact, the fingernails long and curled over like claws. It was quite clear that this body did not belong to a prior dead for three centuries but had been put in Prior Hugh's tomb recently. But how recently? Despite the smell, the body did not seem to be in an advanced state of decay, almost as if it had been artificially preserved. Besides, the hand was too small to be a man's.

A thought struck me then; I clenched my teeth tightly and peeled back the shroud over the face. I flinched as the linen came free, taking pieces of discoloured skin with it. Beside me, Meg turned away with a soft gasp. To gaze on the frailty of our human frame is always appalling and this face seemed more so than any corpse I had seen. Tufts of fair hair still stuck to the blackened scalp. Its features were frozen in a terrible grimace, the lips pulled back to expose the teeth, the eyes staring, the cheeks sunken in, and although the body had begun to putrefy it looked as if an effort had been made by whoever buried it to slow the effects of decay by some amateur process of embalming. It might have lain there a month or several. Worst of all, it was clear that the body was that of a boy, not yet full-grown. I turned to Meg and saw that her eyes were brimming with tears.

"Did you know?" I asked.

She shook her head.

"I swear, sir, no. But I had wondered . . . Is it the beggar child?"

"Beggar?"

"I saw him only once, sir. Last autumn, before the lady Kate came to us. It was supposed to be my day off, but I came in because the timber merchant had to change his delivery day, and there was Master in the kitchen feeding this lad bread and milk. Terrible skinny thing he was, half starved. He never came back and Master gave me to understand it

was not to be mentioned again. But sometimes I noticed food was missing . . ." Her voice trailed off into silence.

"You think he kept the boy down here?" I glanced behind me to the
frayed rope. "Sweet Jesus. Why? What did he do to him?"

Meg only closed her eyes very slowly, as if this might erase the horror
before us. There was one obvious reason why a man might keep a young
boy prisoner, but nothing I had heard about Sir Edward suggested this was
his vice. Had he procured the boy for others, I wondered—his influential
friends, perhaps? Poor, poor child, I thought, sickened to the guts by the
thought of the boy tied up in this place of death, no doubt terrified out of
his wits. I was seized by an urge to run, out of the putrid air, away from
the horror of the place. I leaned over and took a last look at that dreadful
face, and that was when I noticed a glint of metal in the depths of the tomb.

"Bring the light closer," I whispered urgently, as I reached in, steel-
ing myself against the touch of that flesh under my fingers.

The corpse wore a silver chain around its neck; shreds of skin caught
in the links as I pulled it to the front. Hanging from the chain was a
round medallion, engraved with an image that I could not make out.
I took the light from Meg and brought it so close to the face that were
it not for the lantern glass I would have singed the creature's hair. The
medallion showed the figure of a man carrying a bishop's staff in one
hand and his own severed head under the crook of the other arm. The
head was smiling and wore a mitre. *"Dio mio,"* I whispered, handing the
lantern back to Meg.

"What is it?"

I scrabbled to unclasp the chain, causing the corpse's head to bob up
and down in my haste.

"This is no beggar boy," I said, as I finally pulled it loose and held the
medallion up. "See this? It shows the figure of Saint Denis." When she
looked uncomprehending, I continued, "The patron saint of Paris. And
the namesake of a young French boy who disappeared some six months
ago."

Her eyes widened and with her free hand she made the sign of the cross. "Then there was more than one."

"There was a beggar child found though, wasn't there? Dismembered, on a midden." I glanced back at the corner where I had seen the blood-soaked sacks. They were large enough to carry a child's severed corpse.

"They arrested a vagrant for that, though," Meg said, her eyes still riveted to the tomb. "An old man, one of the former monks." She shook her head. "May God have mercy on us all." Fresh tears spilled down her cheeks. I closed the medallion in my fist and turned to face her.

"You guessed at this, didn't you?"

"Not this"—she gestured towards the tomb—"I will swear it by everything I hold dear! If I had known . . ." She left the thought unfinished.

I recalled Langworth's brisk words to Samuel concerning her.

"Meg—there are others, your master's friends. They may believe you know more than you do. I fear you too may be in danger. Is there anywhere you can go, away from this place?"

"I have no one, sir. This has been my only home for twenty years. Where should I go?"

I could only look at her in helpless silence. What protection could I offer, alone as I was in this strange city with my money fast diminishing and no one I trusted without reservation?

She gave me a sad smile in return.

"I've seen four-and-seventy summers, sir. If this is my last, it's more than many get." She glanced behind her in the direction of the house. "It's not much of a life there now, with Master gone."

I frowned, surprised at her words.

"Was he kind to you? Sir Edward?"

"In his way. He kept me on, even when I grew too old to fetch and carry as I once did. I gave him loyal service and he trusted me."

"You mean you kept his secrets." I thought of Sophia and what she had suffered in that house, while the housekeeper, cowed by a mixture of twisted loyalty and fear, said nothing.

Meg caught the edge in my voice and met my eye with a frank expression that suggested I could not hope to understand.

"I had no choice, sir."

"But he is dead now, and there are others who may not trust you so completely. They may want to make absolutely certain you don't share those secrets. If they can do this—" I gestured towards the corpse. A phrase of Langworth's drifted back to me. "Meg," I said, stepping forward and clasping her bony wrist. "Promise me that you will take no medicine from Doctor Sykes."

At this she laughed, with gentle condescension, as if I had tried to make a joke.

"You think I've lived here so long and not learned that for myself? Don't you fret, I've seen what Sykes's remedies can do—" She broke off and shot a quick look sideways at the tomb. I followed her gaze.

"Did *Sykes* kill the boys?"

She stepped back, alarmed by the urgency in my face.

"I told you, sir, I knew nothing of any boys. I only saw the little beggar child once. I was thinking of something else." She lowered her voice and looked at the floor. "No matter. It was long ago."

"Sarah Garth, you mean?"

"What do you know of that?" Her head jerked up.

"I know only that she fell sick and died here. Her family think she was murdered."

Meg passed a hand across her forehead.

"Sarah took ill with the sickness that takes all foolish girls who are easily flattered by men."

"She was with child?" My eyes widened. "By Sir Edward?"

"Maybe. They were both at her, you see."

"Nicholas as well?"

"He was fourteen then, and his father encouraged him." She shook her head again. "Sir Edward's wife was not long dead, and that poor silly girl thought she'd make the next mistress of St. Gregory's one way or another. She soon learned better when she got the child and found neither one of them meant to marry her. So she threatened to tell all of Canterbury their business."

"And Sykes came out to tend her?"

"You know a lot for a stranger," Meg said, with a shrewd glance. "Master called him in to look at her condition, yes."

"Did Sykes try to rid her of the child?"

"That I don't know. But one way or another, Master was rid of the problem after his visit."

"God's blood," I whispered, almost to myself. So Tom Garth might be right—Edward Kingsley may well have had Sarah killed discreetly to save his family a public scandal or the expense of supporting a bastard. And who better than his friend the physician to administer a fatal remedy without suspicion? The dose makes the poison. But did any of this connect with the boys who died in this hellhole, or Fitch, or Sir Edward's murder?

Meg clutched her shawl tighter around her shoulders, her eyes flitting again to the body in the coffin.

"I have seen enough here, sir."

"And I."

I set my shoulder against the stone lid of the tomb and with considerable effort managed to push it back into place, feeling a dreadful complicity as the ruined face of the boy disappeared into darkness and Prior Hugh reclined serenely again on his bier, his marble hands frozen piously in supplication. I had almost grown used to the smell; at least it was no longer making me retch. Meg took a last look around the mausoleum as if she still doubted the evidence of her own eyes.

"But your master already had one bastard, I thought?" I asked, as I followed Meg from the room. She stiffened, and turned to face me.

"No, sir, he did not. Where did you hear that?"

I bent to lock the door behind us, lowering my voice now that we were back in the passage.

"Nicholas complained that the Widow Gray was to receive a gift in his father's will. She has a son, does she not?"

Meg sniffed.

"But her boy is near thirteen and she only came to Canterbury six years ago."

"Six years?"

"Just after Canon Langworth arrived." She fixed me with a meaningful look. I recalled what Harry had said about the rumours that followed Langworth.

"You mean he is *Langworth's* son?"

"I only know what is whispered in the town. The canon visits her often, though perhaps that is just his Christian duty."

I made to run a hand through my hair but as I brought it close to my face I realised how the smell of dead flesh clung to my fingers.

"But if the boy is Langworth's, why was Sir Edward giving her money?" I could not fathom the tangled relationships in this town and my head was beginning to ache badly from wine and lack of sleep. Meg did not answer—I had the sense she felt she had said too much, forced into too great an intimacy with me by the shock of our monstrous discovery. I paused by the door that led from the secret passage back into the storage cellar and leaned against the wall, feeling suddenly faint.

"Mistress Kate," Meg said, eventually. "She is well?"

"Who?" I was concentrating on fighting the rolling waves of light and dark behind my eyes; it took a moment before I realised she meant Sophia. "She will be better when she no longer fears for her life."

"If the murderer can be found, she would inherit St. Gregory's," Meg said. I did not miss the wistful glance that accompanied this thought; perhaps she was thinking how much easier her own life would be with Sophia rather than Nicholas running the household. Perhaps I had one ally in Canterbury, at least.

I locked the low arched doorway behind us, glad to leave the underground passageway and its terrible secret buried again in silence, though I feared the foul stench of the tomb had followed us; I could almost believe that smell would accompany me for the rest of my life. Summoning the last of my strength, I piled the boxes of rubble in front of the door until it was covered and gave Meg my arm to help her up the steep steps back to the normality of the pantry.

"Will you report what you have seen tonight, sir?" she whispered, as I closed the hatch behind me.

"Not right away. There is more I wish to discover before I say anything."

"Do not tell Mayor Fitzwalter," she said. "You will get no justice from him. Better wait until the assize judge comes to town in a few days. But, sir"—she plucked at my sleeve, looking up with anxious eyes—"you will tell them I knew nothing?"

I was about to reply when a noise from the kitchen beyond made us both start. We froze; in the next room, someone stumbled into a bucket with a great clanging of metal, accompanied by some thick curses. Meg motioned to me to crouch behind a pile of flour sacks, while, pulling her shawl tighter, she stepped through the archway into the kitchen.

"Christ's body, woman, you near scared the life out of me!" The voice was Nicholas Kingsley's. "What are you doing creeping around in the dead of night?"

"I couldn't sleep, Master Nicholas. I thought since I was awake I might as well make myself useful in here," Meg replied.

"Huh. Well, you can make yourself useful by getting me something for my head. It feels as if it's about to explode. I have a raging thirst too."

He was slurring his words. I remained still behind the sacks, only now feeling the ache in my arms and shoulders from hefting the crates and the tomb's lid.

"In my experience, Master Nicholas," Meg said, trying to keep her voice light, "the best remedy for that kind of headache is bed rest and a quantity of fresh water."

"Get me some then."

"But . . ." Meg faltered. "I have not been to draw any from the well yet, Master Nicholas. It is the middle of the night, and—"

"Well, you can draw some now." His tone was growing more irritable.

"It is only that—it is very dark out there. I could get you some small beer for now, and bring water when—"

"I said draw some water, woman! Am I not the master of this house? My father might have kept you on out of pity, you crone, but I want a servant who will do my bidding without answering back."

I could not stand to listen to any more of this. I brushed the flour from my breeches and stood in the archway that separated the pantry from the kitchen.

"You can't send her out in the middle of the night. If you need water, I will go."

Nick looked at first shocked, then outraged to see me.

"You! What in the Devil's name are you doing here?"

"Same as you—looking for something to drink."

"In there?" His face hardened and he took a step towards me as I watched an idea struggling to take shape in his fuddled mind. "Have you been stealing my father's wine?"

I held up my hands to placate him.

"I have touched nothing. I only wanted water."

"You lie." He pointed at me as he took an unsteady step closer. "Do you think me a fool? Your hair is covered all over in cobwebs—you've been in that cellar! Devil take you—I told Bates I wanted no thieving foreigners in my house, but he would have you along for the sport."

"You are drunk," I said, turning away from him in disgust. He lunged at me, aiming a punch at my jaw, but his judgement was muddied by drink; from the corner of my eye I saw his fist swing and put up my left arm to block it, then landed a blow to his stomach with my right. He staggered back, winded, against the large table in the centre of the kitchen, cursing and spluttering, but I sprang forward on the balls of my feet, fists clenched, challenging him to try again. His head was clear enough to see that he would not come out of a fight well; instead he clutched at his gut and glared at me, his thick features twisted with hatred.

"Get out of my house," he hissed. "And when my friends are up we shall make you pay for your thieving, you filthy cur."

I should have taken my leave then, but I hesitated, looking at his blunt insolent face, thinking of how he had treated Sophia, how he had spoken to old Meg, and it was as if all the pent-up anger of that night rose in me and exploded. I half turned towards the door, then, almost with an impetus of its own, my fist drew back again and before I was even conscious of having decided on the action, it flew forward and connected squarely with his face. He was caught so much off guard by the blow that he lost his footing, slipped, and fell backwards, his head glancing off the corner of the heavy oak table. He hit the floor and lay there, quite still, blood trickling from his nose.

"Oh, Jesu! What have you done?" Meg cried, hastening to kneel by the motionless figure.

"I—I didn't mean—" I stepped back, rubbing my bruised knuckles, aware only now that I was shaking violently. "Is he breathing?"

The old woman bent her head over Nick's face. My heart seemed to slow to a standstill in the silence that lasted an eternity while I waited for her answer.

"Just—thanks be to God. Help me to sit him up, or the blood in his nose will choke him."

Together we pulled him upright against the leg of the table, where he slouched sideways, head lolling, his mouth hanging open as blood dripped down his chin and onto his chest. Meg held the corner of her shawl to his nose.

"Looks worse than it is, I hope," she whispered, in a tone of reproach. "Dear God, you could have killed him. Why did you not stay hidden?"

"The way he spoke to you—" I stared at the youth's battered nose and the stream that bubbled over his swollen lip. For one moment of fury I might have been facing my own trial for murder.

She looked up with a rueful smile.

"You mean well, sir, I see that. The Lord knows I have no affection for this boy, but no one will be helped by breaking his skull." Her face grew serious. "You should go. If he recalls what happened when he wakes, the lot of them will turn on you. They are foolish youths, but they swagger about with swords for all that."

"He may think you were helping me to steal."

"Leave me to worry about him. I've known him since he was an infant. You get yourself back to the city before first light. There have been enough horrors this night."

I hesitated, but saw that she was right. On an impulse, I leaned forward and planted a kiss on the top of her head. Her white wisps of hair felt discomfitingly like cobwebs.

"Keep yourself safe, Meg," I whispered. "When your mistress is free to return here, she will take care of you, I have no doubt."

The old woman laid a bony hand over mine for a moment, and I saw the sheen of tears in her eyes before she blinked them away.

"Get you gone," she said. "And remember what I told you, sir—I knew nothing of this dreadful business. God knows I speak the truth." She glanced in the direction of the cellar.

I nodded, squeezing her hand a last time, hoping she had wit enough to avoid the belligerent anger of Nick Kingsley and the infinitely more dangerous calculations of Langworth and Sykes.

The sky was already edged with pink light in the east as I retraced my steps through the priory burial ground towards the gate, casting a last glance back at the ominous shape of the dirty white mausoleum with its stone angel about to take flight. Red streaks showed between dark banks of clouds at the horizon and a welcome breeze lifted my hair and dispelled a little the foul vapours that I imagined still clung to me from the night's encounter. I passed unremarked under the North Gate and in the yard of the Cheker, as I walked by the water pump, on impulse I stripped to the waist and stuck my head and shoulders under the flow, letting the cold water wash the cobwebs and filth from my hair and face, until I could almost believe I was clean again. When I was done, I held my bruised fist in the water to bring down the swelling, bitterly regretting that I had not shown a greater degree of self-control with Nick

Kingsley. Now I had two enemies in Canterbury and it would be all but impossible to make any further investigations at St. Gregory's, with Nick and his friends looking for the chance to give me a bloody nose or worse in return.

Shivering as I dried myself with my shirt, I realised the inn was still locked up for the night, and I would have to wait until the servants rose for their early chores—unless I wanted to get Marina out of bed, a prospect I did not greatly relish. Instead I crossed to the stables and found my horse dozing quietly in his stall. I squeezed in beside him, murmuring gentle nonsense, and lay down on a bale of hay. As I drifted towards an uneasy sleep, my fingers closed around the silver medallion of St. Denis in my purse and the decaying face of the Huguenot boy rose, livid, behind my eyelids, seeming to ask what in God's name I meant to do next.

Chapter *11*

I dreamed fitful dreams in those early hours; of skeletal hands ragged with rotten flesh reaching out of a dark tomb to clutch at my clothes. At one point I imagined one of these hands took hold of my shoulder and began shaking it roughly as the foul air of the burial chamber breathed cold into my face, until I could stand it no longer and woke with a fearful cry—to find myself staring blearily into the face of Constable Edmonton, whose morning breath smelled of stale beer and onions through his ginger moustache.

"Get up, you," he ordered.

I tried to sit, and the night's excesses caught me like a fist to the head; I leaned forward and exhaled slowly while I regained my balance.

"What are you doing in here?" Edmonton said, in the same peremptory tone.

"Sleeping," I said. "At least, I was."

"Well, you can get up now. You're under arrest."

"What?" I pushed myself upright and winced as I leaned my weight on my bruised hand. A vivid image of Nick Kingsley's bloodied face flashed in my memory. "Is it a crime to sleep in the stables?"

Edmonton allowed himself a little sarcastic laugh.

"Not compared to what you're accused of, no."

It began to dawn on me that he might be serious. I looked past him and saw Marina shifting anxiously at his shoulder.

"You didn't come back last night," she said, reproachfully. "I didn't know where to find you, otherwise—" She glanced at the constable and held out her hands in a gesture of helplessness in the face of the law.

"This is absurd," I said, remaining seated and tucking my bruised fist into my armpit. I could only assume young Kingsley had accused me of theft and assault. Just in case, I reached down with my left hand and began surreptitiously untying the leather pouch from my belt. If I were to be searched, I did not want anyone finding the copied keys or the papers I had taken from Fitch's fireplace.

"Don't make difficulties," Edmonton said, as if the prospect wearied him. Then he moved to the door, shielding his eyes against the dawn light, and uttered a barking command. In the instant that his back was turned, I pulled the pouch from my belt and stuffed it firmly down behind the straw bale I was sitting on, until it was out of sight. There was just time to tuck my hands between my knees before two tall young men carrying pikestaffs appeared in the doorway of the stable.

"Are you going to walk with us of your own accord, eh?" Edmonton jerked his head towards the guards.

I stood up and felt my legs buckle beneath me for a moment. I hoped Edmonton had not noticed.

"Can you tell me what am I arrested for?"

"Murder," he said, shortly.

A ripple of panic spread through me. Had Nick Kingsley died from his injury in the night?

"No—there is some mistake," I protested. "Whose murder?"

"The apothecary William Fitch." There was a note of satisfaction in Edmonton's voice.

"*What?*" I shook my head. "It was I who found him dead! You were there! How can anyone think—?"

"Your name was written in his ledger from the day before."

"With many others, surely—"

"Doctor Ezekiel Sykes has given testimony that he was leaving Fitch's shop when you arrived. There is no name after yours in the ledger. That makes you the last person to see him alive, and the first to see him dead."

"But that is not true!" I grasped at his sleeve in alarm. "It is the other way around—I was leaving as Sykes arrived. He asked Fitch to lock the shop door so they could talk in private."

Edmonton merely raised an eyebrow.

"You are asking me to believe that our Doctor Sykes is deliberately lying to the law? And why would he do that, do you suppose? What would he gain?"

I pressed my lips together tightly. There seemed only one possible answer to that; Sykes was sharp enough to point the finger at me before I had a chance to tell anyone that he had been Fitch's last visitor on the evening he was killed, knowing that the word of a stranger and a foreigner would not stand against that of a respected physician. Which meant—what? That Sykes had killed Fitch himself? At the very least it suggested he was implicated. I stared at the constable, knowing that to accuse the physician of lying would only make my situation worse. A legion of confused thoughts chased one another through my clouded brain. There was the half-burned page from the ledger in the fireplace showing Sykes's purchase of—what had it been? I ransacked my memory, trying to picture the torn paper. Then I realised.

"*Dio mio,*" I whispered, my eyes fixed unseeing on Edmonton's face. Mercury and antimony salts. I recalled reading somewhere that solutions of mercury and antimony were used in the East to embalm bodies— the connection had not occurred to me when I first found the page, but in the light of the previous night's discovery . . . Edmonton must have caught my expression because he gripped my wrist and pulled my face close to his.

"What did you say?"

"I only said, 'My God,' in my own tongue."

"Huh." He regarded me for a moment, then reluctantly dropped my wrist. "Praying won't help you now, and neither will blasphemy. Take him away," he added, nodding to the guards. The taller of the two stepped forward and made as if to grab hold of my arm; I shook him off, grasping at Edmonton's shirt.

"Wait—you can't arrest me, I have done nothing! Fetch Doctor Harry Robinson at the cathedral—he will vouch for me. Or Dean Rogers. They will tell you I am a friend and a respectable scholar."

"We'll see."

"I have friends at the royal court."

"And I'm the King of Cockaigne."

Edmonton brushed my hand away, wrinkling his mouth in irritation, as the guards moved in to grasp me hard by the arms. I realised there was little point in struggling; my best hope was to submit and rely on Harry's standing to protect me. He would not be pleased at the unwelcome attention I had once again drawn to him, but I was sure he would do everything possible to help me. At least, I had to hope so. Was this what Langworth had in mind when he spoke to Samuel of an idea to keep me out of trouble? I caught Marina's eye over Edmonton's shoulder.

"Doctor Robinson at the cathedral—let him know what has happened. Please?"

She wagged a finger in mock reproach, as if this whole business were a great joke.

"If you will go wandering about at night, sir. You have still not paid me for the orange."

"When I get back," I called, as the soldiers dragged me towards the gate. "But tell Harry Robinson." She winked, and I hoped she would at least carry out my request; I had no faith that Edmonton would. At that moment, I would have paid almost any price.

I was marched through the streets towards the West Gate. Grey morning light only just brushed the sky; I was fortunate that not many people were about. Even so, I kept my head down, trying to hide my face. At the foot of one of the vast drum towers, we stopped and one of the guards rapped briskly on a door set into the wall. The other deftly removed my belt with my knife and handed it to Edmonton. There came a jangling of keys and the door was opened by a squat man in a dirty smock with shoulders like an ox and his front teeth missing.

"For the love of God, Constable, I've no more room," he complained, looking me up and down and turning to Edmonton. "They've brought prisoners in from all over the county for the assizes next week. Where am I supposed to put him?"

"Put him in with the other murderers. Make sure you lock him up soundly—he's dangerous."

"I'm not," I said. "And I haven't killed anyone." The gaoler looked at me briefly and curled his lip.

"If I had sixpence for every one of you that said that. Go on up, then, we'll shove him in somewhere."

The guards pushed me in the back towards the door. Edmonton stood with his arms crossed, looking pleased with his morning's work.

"See you at the assizes," he said.

I stared at him.

"You cannot leave me in here until the assizes!"

He laughed. "Then you had better find someone to stand bail for you. Good luck with that."

"Harry Robinson will stand bail—you must send for him. And take care of that knife—I want it back!" I was dragged inside the prison door before I could finish the sentence. As it closed behind me, I caught a last glimpse of Edmonton with that infuriating smirk still painted on his face. He had no intention of sending for Harry if he could help it, I was sure. Had he not as good as told me that the appearance of justice counted for more than the truth of it in this town? The sight of a foreigner hung for Fitch's murder would please the gallows crowd, but it would please Langworth more. I had no doubt that Langworth and Sykes were behind my arrest. Perhaps Edmonton had received money. I swallowed hard as I was led up a narrow spiral staircase inside the tower, and my throat hurt. I could only hope that Harry had the power—and the inclination—to save my neck.

At the top of the staircase the gaoler unlocked a thick iron-clad door and barked something incomprehensible, his hand still on the latch; from behind it came a chorus of plaintive cries and a frenzied scuffling.

"Get in," he said to me, pushing the door open no more than a couple of feet, simultaneously kicking out at the bony hand that crept through the gap and flapped at his sleeve. "Hurry up, before these vermin try and get out."

The guards shoved me up the next step and, before I could protest, the gaoler had laid a thick hand on top of my head and was trying to force me into the room.

"I have money," I whispered, clutching at his tunic. If English gaols were anything like those in Italy, a prisoner's comfort would depend entirely on his ability to hand out bribes. The gaoler's fat face creased into a mocking smile, showing the hole where his teeth once were.

"Have a little taste of West Gate hospitality, why don't you, and we can talk again about your purse when you've had time to reflect." He winked grotesquely and pushed me hard in the chest, so that I fell through the half-open doorway onto a hard stone floor. I could not even pick myself up before the lock turned behind me.

"*Figlio di puttana!*" I shouted at the indifferent door.

Recovering my balance, I sat up and took in my surroundings. The room I had been hustled into was small and narrow. Thin arrow slits provided the only light, which fell in narrow shafts on the hunched shapes of perhaps nine or ten men, sitting in their own excrement in the drifts of filthy straw that covered the floor. Some had chains securing their hands or feet; all looked half starved. A hot, vivid stench of ordure and unwashed bodies filled the cell, together with a pervasive atmosphere of despair. These prisoners were facing the assizes in a few days' time; if they were accused of murder, the only possible end would be the hangman's rope, and you could see the knowledge of it in their dead eyes. My empty stomach heaved and I tasted bile at the back of my throat.

As my eyes grew accustomed to the dimness, I began to make out the other prisoners' faces. Opposite me sat an emaciated man with a beard like a hermit and wild, staring eyes that appeared to look beyond me, as if he spied a sight of mortal terror just over my shoulder. No one spoke. I pressed myself into a space against the wall, pulling my knees close to my chest so that I took up as little room as possible. With my forehead against my knees, I closed my eyes and tried to breathe through my mouth as I struggled to piece together everything that had happened since I arrived in Canterbury, largely to keep my thoughts away from my own prospects if Harry did not intervene. A youth spent in the shadow of the Roman Inquisition had not left me with any faith in the idea that innocence was a guarantee of justice. But I did have faith in my own ability to organise the human mind and the knowledge it accumulates—my own, at least. Hours spent devising my systems of memory had kept me from despair during many lonely days and nights on the road north through Italy and beyond. This was not the first time I had been in prison, either; in Geneva the Calvinists had learned what I was teaching in my public lectures and had me arrested as a heretic and disturber of the peace. Ironic, when I had only gone to Geneva because the Catholic Church was pursuing me as a heretic.

Someone nearby struck up a low continuous moaning that seemed to ebb and flow, echoing mournfully from the walls. I turned my thoughts inward and imagined I was making notes on a clean sheet of paper. There were four deaths that may be connected—five, if you counted Sarah Garth nine years earlier. The beggar child found dismembered on the midden last autumn—there was no proof that it was the same boy Meg had seen Edward Kingsley feeding in the kitchen of St. Gregory's, except for the bloodied sacks I had found in the underground tomb, but it was a strong possibility. Next there was the Huguenot boy Denis, who was certainly linked to Edward Kingsley and had most likely died in that dreadful burial chamber beneath the mausoleum. I did not yet know who had killed the boy or why, but the crude attempt at embalming his body—to disguise the smell of decay and prevent discovery?—must surely have something to do with Ezekiel Sykes's purchase of mercury and antimony salts. Which leads to the third death: William Fitch. Someone had ransacked the apothecary's shelves in a frantic haste to destroy incriminating papers—among them evidence of that purchase of Sykes's. And afterwards, John Langworth had been back to Fitch's shop to retrieve two stones of black laudanum. Why?

And then there was Sir Edward himself, the focus of my absurd journey. Why had he died? "Didn't have the wit to look behind him on a dark night," Langworth had said to Samuel, but his tone had been one of irritation, not triumph, as if his friend's murder were more of an inconvenience than anything else. What was Sir Edward's business with the boys? He was too eminent and too recognisable in Canterbury to have gone out scouring the streets for homeless children to lure back to the priory; he must have had someone to do that for him. Fitch? The apothecary would have had the means to drug the boys—perhaps with laudanum—to keep them quiet. I rubbed a hand across my face. None of it made any sense. Those poor boys must have been imprisoned to feed someone's appetites. Both Langworth and Sir Edward himself were known to have relationships with women; that did not necessarily exclude baser tastes, but I remained unconvinced. Was Sir Edward procuring the boys for someone else, as a favour or a debt? Sykes, perhaps, or someone more powerful? As magistrate, it was a grave risk to take; if it was not for his own benefit, it must have been for substantial reward. But I still had no answer to the question of why he had to die.

Nor could I ignore the practical details of his murder. Whoever struck him down that night had been inside the cathedral precincts, taken the crucifix from the crypt, and waited for him, knowing he would come through the cloisters in the direction of Langworth's house. Only the dean had a key to the crypt. And anyone trying to leave the precincts would have been seen by Tom Garth. I sighed. Unless, of course, it *was* Tom Garth. From what Meg had told me, he had good reason to want revenge on Sir Edward. But why now, after nine years?

I glanced up and saw that the old man with the beard was crawling towards me through the filth. Repulsed, I shrank back into the wall, but there was nowhere to go. His bony hand clawed at the sleeve of my shirt; a filthy smell came off him and the hand gripping my arm ended in long brown nails that curved over, reminding me of the dead boy's hand in the prior's tomb. White spume gathered at the corners of his mouth as it worked frantically with no sound. But though I flinched and pulled back, I noticed that one of his eyes was milky with the thick film of a cataract, and both were filled with tears. He was trying to say something. Holding my breath, I leaned closer.

"What is it, old man?"

He mumbled the same phrase again; it seemed to end in "me," but he spoke so quietly I could not recognise the words.

"Tell me again," I said, gently. His eyes opened wider and he repeated his phrase a little louder, shaking my arm as if his message was of great urgency. Wincing against his foul breath in my face, I watched the movement of his shrivelled lips and realised that he was not speaking English at all.

"*Sinite pueros venire ad me,*" he whispered again.

I stared at him.

"Suffer the little children to come unto me," I repeated. "Which children?"

"*Sinite pueros venire ad me, et nolite eos vetare talium est enim regnum Dei,*" he muttered, completing the verse from the Gospel of Luke. His face clouded with despair.

"'And do not hinder them, for the kingdom of God belongs to such as these.' Do you know more Latin?" I asked, intrigued. "Are you an educated man?"

His good eye roamed my face and his mouth twisted into something like a smile.

"*Monachus,*" he said.

"You were a monk?" I asked, in Latin. He nodded sadly. I laid a hand over his and tried to keep my voice low as I pointed to my chest.

"And I."

At first I thought he had not understood, but after a moment's consideration he shook his head.

"Impossible. You are too young. They tore down the sanctuaries and put us on the road before you were even born, son."

"Not here. In Italy. Were you a monk here in Canterbury?"

He nodded. "At Christ Church Priory." Then he pushed back the matted strands of hair that grew around the fringes of his head to show me his burned ear. I studied his weathered face; he must have been near to eighty.

"I thought all the brothers were dead."

"I am dead." He gave a far-off smile and pointed at himself. "Look here—is this not the face of a corpse? I have been dead these fifty years."

"What did you mean about the children?" I asked, still in Latin.

The old man's eyes opened wider, his face tight with fear.

"'But whoso shall offend one of these little ones which believe in me, it were better for him that a millstone were hanged about his neck, and that he were drowned in the depth of the sea,'" he quoted again, this time from the Gospel of Matthew. "This is the word of the Lord." He shook my arm, as though willing me to understand. "Better a millstone around his neck," he repeated, his unfocused gaze sliding off me and around the walls.

"Whose neck?" I persisted.

"The one who hurts the children," he hissed, snapping his attention back to me so suddenly that I flinched again, and it was as if a wick caught light in my mind. Meg said an old monk had been arrested for the murder of the dismembered child on the rubbish heap. Was that what he was trying to tell me about, in his confused way?

"Do you know him? The one who hurt the children?" I was gripping his hand harder now.

"It was not me!" he cried out, in English, as if someone had struck him. "I didn't touch him!"

"'Course you didn't, mate," said a rough voice from the shadows across the room. "None of us did." One or two of the others laughed weakly, until they lapsed back into their defeated silence.

"I know you didn't hurt him," I said softly to the old monk. "But who did?"

He fell silent and shook his head, and I thought I had lost him. I sat back, frustrated. Perhaps it was only the ramblings of a madman, after all. But he did not sound as if he had lost his wits—at least, no more than anyone would in a place like this.

"I only prayed for him," he whispered, reverting to Latin, just when I thought he would not speak again. "That poor child. He left him there, like offal. I sat by him all night and prayed for his little soul, that was all. Our Lord welcomed the children." He looked up as if imploring me to understand. Tears coursed down his cheeks. I stroked the back of his hand and nodded. I sensed that I was close to something vital here, and I did not want to ruin it by pushing the old man too hard; these memories were touching some deep grief in him.

"Where did you find him? Was it on the midden?" I prompted, cautiously.

"You saw it too?" His eyes widened, and he shook his head. He leaned closer, fixing me with his milky eye. "Cut in pieces. Such wickedness. He was a good child. Always a smile, for all he had nothing of his own. All I did was keep vigil and pray to Saint Thomas for his innocent soul. I told them that. I couldn't harm a living creature. Do you know the worst of it?" He rubbed the tears away with the back of his hand, leaving grimy streaks down his face. "They claimed I butchered him for food, driven mad by hunger. For *food!* For pity's sake—a child?" He ran a hand across his face. "God knows I have suffered hunger in my wanderings, well He knows how many times it has nearly taken me from this world. But I had rather die a bag of bones than let such a black thought enter my mind. Any Christian man would." He scrabbled at my wrist again. "You believe me, son, don't you?"

"Of course." I could guess what had happened; the old monk had been found by the boy's body and blamed for his murder. "You said 'he left him.' Who? Did you see him—the man who put the boy there?"

"The tall one." His eyes drifted away again.

"Yes, that's him." I tried not to sound too eager. "You remember him? What did he look like?"

The old monk frowned, seemingly lost in the dusty corridors of memory. I wondered if anything he dredged up would contain a grain of truth or if he was mixing up recollections of different times and places from a long life, as old men do.

"Tall, he was. Thin."

"Old or young?"

"I don't know. Everyone looks young to me." He broke into a cackle at this and I waited patiently while he recovered from the coughing fit it brought on. Finally he spat a gobbet of phlegm into the straw and looked back to me, his face serious. "He was bald, like me, but not old like me. You understand? But I didn't see him close. He brought bread one evening and gave it out to the children that beg outside the walls. He spoke to them. After he'd gone, the boy—that poor boy—shared his bread with me, because I'd not eaten for days. I never saw him again until he dropped out of a sack in pieces." He shuddered violently and clawed at my arm again.

"Was it night? Could you be sure it was the same man?"

He must have caught the urgency in my voice, because his eyes grew frightened and he seemed to shrink inside the rags that hung off his skeletal frame. He turned his face away.

"Sure . . . I am sure of nothing anymore, son, except that soon I will face judgement. And that I will not live to see Saint Thomas return to Canterbury."

I stiffened.

"He will return, then? You are sure of that?"

The old monk turned his head slowly back to me, his face lit by a sly smile, like a child hugging a great secret to himself.

"He never left us."

"It is true, then?" I whispered, though I doubted any of the prisoners around us understood Latin. "Where is he?"

A glimmer of life sparkled in the rheumy eyes. He gave a low, cracked laugh.

"Only the guardians can tell you that. And they are sworn to silence. Men have died to protect the secret of his bones."

"Which men? When?"

He leaned in, his face earnest.

"You want to know the story?"

"Yes. Yes, I do."

"It was near fifty years ago, you understand? In some houses, the monks who would not take the new religion were executed as traitors, their quarters nailed to the city gates. But Canterbury surrendered willingly. No monk here died on King Henry's orders." He left a significant pause. The emphasis had been on King Henry.

"But on someone else's orders, then?"

His fingers tightened around my wrist.

"The night they moved Becket's bones, I saw what I should not have seen. I could not sleep and had gone to pray in the chapel of Saint Andrew, near to the great shrine of Saint Thomas. I hid when I heard the door, because I should not have been out of the dormitory and did not want to give account of myself to the prior."

I nodded, half smiling, recalling the nights I had spent sneaking around the monastery, trying to avoid being caught by the abbot with my forbidden books.

"Five men came," the old man continued, his breath buzzing hot against my ear, "carrying between them what looked like a coffin. Some while later they left carrying one likewise. So I followed them at a distance. They were taking it to the crypt."

"Who were they?"

"They kept their cowls up. But one I saw by the light of the lantern he carried to guide the others—he was the assistant cellarer. A sevennight later he was dead."

"How?"

"A fall, on a staircase in the tower. But he was one who had said he would not take the oath of allegiance to the king. No one knew, then, what the consequences of that might be."

"So"—I frowned, trying to follow his reasoning—"you think the others were afraid he might be tortured and reveal the truth about Becket's body?"

He nodded.

"I think they wanted to be sure of his silence. And he was not the only one. The day the king's commissioners came and broke open the shrine, when they ground the saint's bones into dust before our eyes so nothing remained as a holy relic, no monk standing there believed it was truly Saint Thomas. But we dared not speculate aloud."

"But those who knew where the real body was hidden must all be dead by now?"

"They say there were four guardians, to match the number of Becket's murderers. Each guardian hands on the secret to one who keeps the old faith in his heart, in preparation for the day England returns to the true Church, like the prodigal son." He passed a hand over his brow. "But who the guardians are now, I cannot tell you. Ask me no more, son. They will hang me this time for certain, and I am ready. I am weary of this life. God knows I have only ever tried to serve Him faithfully, though He has seen fit to send me so much suffering at the hands of heretics."

I laid a hand over his and a silent tear trickled down his hollow cheek. His words reminded me of Hélène's, and I felt suddenly overwhelmed by the weight of their grief and bewilderment; all over our bloody continent, Catholics and Protestants alike went on dying at one another's hands, all looking up to heaven and crying out to their God, *Whose side are You on?* While their God remains deaf, saying nothing, because on both sides they have failed to understand who or what He is, as they spill more blood in His name.

Hours passed, or what felt like hours. The old monk leaned against my side and I watched with almost filial concern as his papery eyelids fell and his ragged breathing slowed. I may have dozed myself for a while; it was hard to tell, in that half-light and filth, what was real. The only means of telling that time had passed at all was the way the light fell at a different angle through the arrow slit in the wall opposite. I rested my head back against the dank stone and repeated the old man's words over to myself, trying to fit them into the puzzle.

Eventually there came the sound of a key grinding in the lock and the prisoners stirred as one from their stupor. The door opened a crack and the gaoler's face appeared.

"You. The Spaniard." He pointed his stick at me. "Get up."

"I am Italian," I said wearily.

"You're a lucky bastard, is what you are. Don't keep them waiting."

I disentangled myself from the old monk, who clutched at my shirt in alarm.

"*Frater!*" he whispered, his voice hoarse. "Don't leave me."

"I will come back," I told him, with a stab of guilt; still his hand flailed at me and I had to shake him off. As I stood, the gaoler gripped me tight around the arm and dragged me through the narrow gap to the top of the stairs. When he had locked the door behind me, he pointed his stick at my chest and motioned downwards.

"Follow me and don't try anything. You're wanted at the Guildhall."

I had no idea of what this might mean, but his mention of luck kindled a small flicker of hope in my breast. Had my message reached Harry, and had he been able to use his influence with the authorities?

Edmonton awaited us at the foot of the stairs, his face tight with anger. The same two guards stood beside him and took up their places flanking me with their pikestaffs as I stepped out of the door, squinting into the shade beneath the gate, but this time they did not hold my arms. I was escorted back up the High Street, where curious shoppers and traders paused to follow our party with their eyes, leaning in and whispering to their neighbours. I did not meet their eyes, but kept walking in a straight line, following Edmonton's stiff back. He had not said a word to me, but the contained fury of his demeanour encouraged my hopes further; he had the face of a man who is about to have a prize snatched out of his hands and can do nothing to prevent it. He strode on ahead of me and my guards, head set high, enjoying the appearance of control and the deference his position seemed to elicit from the townspeople. Let him have his little parade, I thought, as long as I walk free at the end of it. Above us the sky was still overcast, with rows of clouds bunched like dirty wool, and the heat trapped beneath it felt thick and stale, as if the air could not move. The sun was no more than a pale gleam; it was hard to tell what time of day it might be. I guessed at early afternoon.

Edmonton stopped in front of an imposing building in the old style, with crooked beams of black timber and stone pillars either side of the main door. He gestured brusquely with his head and I followed him up the steps, through a high tiled entrance hall where he paused for a brief exchange in low voices with a man in the robes of a clerk. This man glanced at me warily throughout the conversation, which I could not hear, at the end of which we were led through a small antechamber into a larger room with a high ceiling and a series of leaded windows. My gaze fell first upon two familiar faces—Dean Rogers and Samuel, who stood to the left of a broad oak desk. The dean took a half step forward as I was ushered in by the guards, his face creased with concern, but it was Samuel's eyes I met and held with my own, wanting to see what might be written there. But the look he gave me was empty of any emotion, except perhaps insolence, as if he knew I was waiting for him to betray himself and did not mean to give me the satisfaction.

"You are the prisoner Filippo Savolino?" A clear, precise voice cut across my thoughts. Reluctantly I switched my attention from Samuel to the speaker, the man seated behind the desk, and noticed for the first time that he wore a heavy gold chain of office around his neck. He was perhaps in his early fifties, with fair hair that receded from his high forehead but compensated by curling down over his collar, and a beard thickly flecked with grey. He might have been a handsome man if his eyes had not been curiously small, as if he were permanently squinting into a strong light.

"I am," I said, then, glancing at his chain, added, "Your Worship," with a deferential lowering of my head. I did not get out of Geneva without learning how to deploy a little judicious humility. So this was the mayor Meg had warned me about. Also a friend of Edward Kingsley, according to Sophia.

The mayor's face visibly softened at this recognition of his status, though I noticed he winced slightly every time he caught the stench coming off me.

"Well, Savolino. I am Humphrey Fitzwalter, Mayor of Canterbury, as you have divined. Dean Rogers tells me you are a distinguished scholar and an esteemed guest of one of his canons, with letters of introduction from one of the first families of Her Majesty's court. Yet Constable Edmonton here seems to believe you are a dangerous brigand and murderer. Naturally, I am inclined to respect the dean's judgement, but I am nonetheless curious as to how you could have given the constable reason to suspect you?"

"I fear my face and my voice are reason enough, Your Worship," I said, again lowering my eyes.

"Your Worship," Edmonton cut in, breathless, "I have sworn testimony from Doctor Sykes himself that this man was the last to enter the apothecary Fitch's shop before he was beaten to death."

"This is a lie." I folded my arms. "I was the first to find the apothecary, as the constable knows. Perhaps this testimony was meant to draw attention away from the real perpetrators." I glanced at Samuel as I said this, but he merely returned my look with that same level stare and I found myself gripped by a sudden urge to punch his inscrutable face.

The mayor looked from me to Edmonton with an expression of mild curiosity.

"Well," he said, stretching out his arms on the desktop and clasping his hands together. On the little finger of each he wore a fat gold ring. "You are fortunate in your connections, it seems, Savolino. Doctor Harry Robinson has agreed to stand bail for you and Dean Rogers himself has come in person to attest to your good character. So I am persuaded to grant you your liberty, on condition that you do not leave the city. You may answer the accusations against you at the assizes in two days' time."

"It is absurd that I should have to answer any charges at all," I said, drawing back my shoulders and looking him in the eye with as much dignity as I could muster in my present state. "This accusation is no more than malicious prejudice."

Fitzwalter blinked.

"That statement could be construed as slander. The law must take its course, and the innocent have nothing to fear from its process."

I gave a dry laugh. "In my country, the Holy Office says this to men it means to burn."

Fitzwalter's eyes narrowed until they were no more than red-rimmed slits in his pale face, and I glimpsed a hardness beneath the affable exterior.

"If I were you, Savolino, I would show a little more gratitude to the friends who bought your freedom, and a little more respect for authority while you are a visitor here, especially one whose name is not yet cleared." He shuffled some papers on his desk and nodded curtly at the dean, as if to show we were dismissed. "I would also suggest you clean yourself up. You have the smell about you of a seven-day-old corpse."

"I smell of the gaol where men are made to lie in their own filth among the rats. Your Worship," I added, emphasizing the words.

"Oh? Would you have us provide them with feather beds?" He drew himself up, needled.

"No. But clean straw might let them feel they were still regarded as fellow men. You would not stable your horse in such conditions, I am sure."

"No, sir, I would not. But then my horse has not murdered anyone. Dean Rogers, this man is released into your care. Against my better judgement, I will allow his knife to be returned to him. Now please get him and his peculiar ideas out of my office."

The dean smiled nervously and bustled me out of the room, pressing my knife in its sheath into my hands. In the entrance hall, I bowed and thanked him for his intervention as I strapped it back onto my belt. He moved as if to shake my hand, but my present condition evidently made him think better of it. Instead he looked down at me with a crease in his brow as his fingers worried at the front of his robe.

"Doctor Savolino—I hardly know how to apologise for this insult to your person and your integrity. That a friend of Her Majesty's court should have been treated so . . . But you understand there is a delicate relationship in this town between the cathedral foundation and the civic authorities. The cathedral remains powerful and"—here he gave a nervous little laugh—"for the moment, wealthy. There have been occasions when we have felt it necessary to intervene in matters of city governance, and this creates a certain, ah—*resentment*. If it were within my power to have this accusation against you withdrawn . . ." He held out his hands to indicate his helplessness.

"I thank you for your support, Dean Rogers," I reassured him. "The only way for me to answer these charges, it seems, is to find out who really killed the apothecary."

The dean looked doubtful. "But how could you begin to do that?"

"I might consider the motive of the man who wants me found guilty."

His face tensed at this.

"I am sure Doctor Sykes was only acting as he thought best."

I was poised to argue but was aware of Samuel's sharp gaze boring into me.

"Of course," I murmured.

The dean looked relieved. Why was everyone so afraid of Sykes, I wondered?

"Harry would have come for you himself, but the walk would have been a trial for him. He sent Samuel with the bail money, but asked me to accompany him to support the case for your innocence."

I glanced at Samuel. "It was good of you both to take the time."

Samuel merely offered a thin smile.

"A condition of the bail is that your whereabouts are now Harry's responsibility," the dean continued, as we stepped out into the High Street and began to walk in the direction of the cathedral, attracting curious glances along the way. "I'm afraid you will have to leave your lodgings at the Cheker and stay in his house until the assizes."

I nodded, keeping my face steady, but this news was a blow. To be trapped there, under Samuel's eye, with the prospect of his relaying my every word back to Langworth, was not how I had envisaged my return to freedom. I had to find some means to get Samuel out of the way; without his influence, there was a chance Harry might listen to me. I was already compromised on every side: Langworth knew who I really was and to the rest of Canterbury I was now a suspected murderer. I badly needed even one ally here, and I had no choice but to trust Harry. The fact that he had paid my bail out of his own pocket suggested that he had a little faith in me—or at least respect for Walsingham—which I might hope to work on, if only I could do something about the brooding, watchful presence of his servant.

I glanced over my shoulder at Samuel; at my side, the dean was earnestly explaining how helpful it would be in my current situation if, for the sake of public opinion, I were to be seen frequently at divine service in the cathedral in the company of the canons. Samuel walked a few paces after us, dressed in his customary doublet and breeches of plain black linen, his hands folded behind his back, as if he were our appointed escort. I noted with distaste how several long strands of black hair still clung stubbornly to the front of his bald scalp like the legs of spiders. Tall and bald, the old monk had said of the man who came to give bread to the beggar children. Was it Samuel, at the bidding of his powerful friends? He caught me looking at him and returned my stare with a raised eyebrow, as if daring me to state my challenge. Calmly I shifted my attention to the dean, who was still talking though I had not heard a word, recalling as I did so what Harry had said about Samuel carrying his messages to Walsingham. That was the answer. I was so pleased with the idea that I had to stop myself smiling like a half-wit. Samuel must be made to carry a letter to London; not only would that take him out of the way, but I would contrive to include an invisible message in the letter that the bearer should be detained and taken for questioning.

"And I should be honoured if you would accept," the dean said, laying a hand on my shoulder before withdrawing it in haste and surreptitiously wiping it on the side of his robe.

"The honour would be mine," I replied, smiling, though I was not sure what I had just agreed to.

"Splendid. Directly after Evensong, then—you and Harry can come together. I keep a plain table, as you will see—no untoward extravagance, as befits a servant of God and Her Majesty, I assure you"—here he gave his nervous little laugh again—"though I venture to boast that my cook has talents enough to make a feast from the simplest fare."

Ah. So I had been invited to dinner.

"I am easy to please at table, sir. So long as it is hot and filling."

This was untrue; such atrocities as the English practised upon their food I found baffling and almost impossible to stomach, though I had been obliged to accustom myself to it over the past year. But my denial seemed to please the dean.

"The best kind of guest," he beamed, as we reached the Christ Church gate. "Very well, then. I shall leave Samuel to deliver you safely to Harry and will see you at divine service this evening." His brow furrowed again as his eyes travelled over me. "I trust you have a change of clothes?"

"Do not fear, sir—I will have shed all traces of the gaol by this evening," I reassured him.

He sighed. "If only one could wash away the stain to one's reputation so easily," he murmured, before taking his leave and passing through the gate in the direction of the Archbishop's Palace.

Samuel gestured towards the cathedral with his head and I stepped through the archway. Tom Garth appeared from his cubbyhole to stare at us and even moved forward as if he would speak to me, but I walked on without a word. My thoughts now were all on the purse I had stuffed behind the hay bales in the stable of the Cheker; once I had thanked Harry and found a way to dispatch Samuel to London, my first priority must be to retrieve it. And then what? I rubbed my forehead, catching again the sickening smell of dead flesh still clinging to my fingers. Go after Sykes? Could I find a way to get into his house and find some proof to connect him to the death of Fitch before the assizes?

Samuel and I walked in silence to the door of Harry's house. Perhaps he thought, as I did, that to speak was the surest way to betray oneself. I had no idea how much he guessed I knew about him, but between us there was a wariness and suspicion so pronounced you could almost hear it crackling in the air; I sensed it as if we were two strange dogs circling each other, each waiting for the other to bare its teeth first. He paused with his hand on the latch.

"You should not expect to find him in a good humour, after your antics." He did not even give me the courtesy of looking at me while he spoke.

"My antics, as you call them, consist of no more than being falsely accused by a man who has judged me because my face and voice are unfamiliar to him."

Samuel sniffed.

"Nonetheless, you have cost my master dear. No one asked you to come here," he added, unnecessarily.

I bit my tongue and looked at the ground. Someone did ask me to Canterbury, I wanted to say, and she still has faith in me. Though I feared I was running out of time to justify it.

"I am sorry to have caused him trouble, and I will tell him so," I said. Samuel hesitated, but seemed wrongfooted by my show of humility. He could find nothing to say in response, and instead opened the door.

"By the cross, you are determined to be a thorn in my side, Bruno." Harry heaved himself up from his familiar place in the front room when

I entered. Grey afternoon light fell across his face and his bushy brows cast his eyes into shadow. "You must be parched. Samuel, fetch our guest a jug of beer and some bread."

"Thank you. I will reimburse your expenses—"

He waved a hand, as if this were unimportant.

"Of course you will. That's not my worry. Christ's body, you stink, man—where have you been?"

"I will tell you everything in due course—there is much to tell. But first, with this arrest, it is essential that I get a message to Walsingham—some intervention by his hand may be my only hope at the assizes. And the message must be taken with the utmost urgency." I looked at him expectantly. Slow realisation dawned on the old man's face as his servant came back bearing a tray.

"But—Samuel would be gone for some days." His voice rose a notch and I realised that, for all his gruff show of independence, he was alarmed at the prospect of being left alone.

"Gone where?" Samuel asked, his tone sharp, glancing from me to his master.

"I have no other means to send a message to London," I said, ignoring him and turning to Harry. "In any case, I will be staying here with you. I understand those were the terms on which I was released?"

"You?" Harry looked doubtful. I wondered again how close he was to Samuel and how much he might know of his servant's deceit, but there was no time to worry about that now; I had no choice other than to confide in Harry. There was no one else. "Can you light a stove and cook a meal? Can you lay out my clothes of a morning?"

I smiled in a manner which I hope inspired confidence.

"I can try any task, if you instruct me."

"A philosopher to make my breakfast. There's a fine thing." Harry turned again to Samuel and a look passed between them that I could not read. "Well, I suppose we have no choice. We are all Walsingham's servants, and it appears your recklessness in blundering about this town with no regard for the sensitivities of position and authority has landed you in a bind that only Master Secretary can get you out of."

I lowered my head and took his reproach without protest; there would be time enough to explain myself to Harry. For now, as I looked at my boots, I fought against a smirk of triumph at the prospect of Samuel's imminent departure.

"I thank you both." Raising my head, I shone the full beam of my most sincere smile at Samuel. "You may be sure Sir Francis will reward you for your trouble."

"Oh, I shall tell him you have promised me so on his behalf," he replied softly, his smile dripping sarcasm.

"I will return to the inn for my belongings and come back with the letter I need Samuel to take," I said. "The dean has asked me to be present at Evensong tonight, Harry, and to accompany you to his table for supper."

Harry grunted.

"Well, it won't do any harm for folks to see you showing a bit of Christian piety," he muttered. "God alone knows what they are saying about you in the town. And what they will say of me for giving you lodging."

"My name will be cleared at the assizes," I said.

"Maybe." He did not sound convinced. "But mud sticks. Come back with your things, then, and make yourself comfortable. Samuel can ready his horse."

"I hope he is a fast horse," I said, with a meaningful look at Samuel to let him know I was in earnest.

"He's the only horse we have, so you'll have to make do," Harry snapped back, and his tone warned me not to overstep the mark. I was fortunate that he was willing to part with Samuel at all.

I wolfed down the bread so quickly that I could not swallow it fast enough and it lodged like a ball in my upper chest; I had to sip at the beer to try and shift it, pain shooting into my dry throat as I doubled over.

Samuel watched me with contempt for a few moments before stalking from the room in silence.

"There is much I need to say to you," I told Harry, when I had recovered enough to speak.

"Take your time. Collect your things, and you and I shall talk," he said. "You may as well bring your horse—there is stabling here and Samuel's will be out. Save you paying at the inn." This time there was a kinder note in his voice. My earlier doubts began to recede and I dared to hope that I might yet be able to confide in Harry and find him ready with some advice. My spell in the gaol and my appearance before the mayor, when I had been so relieved to see the dean and even Samuel, had served to remind me of how alone I was in Canterbury, and how vulnerable. There was no question in my mind that Langworth and Sykes between them had contrived to have me arrested to stop me asking questions. Their plan had been thwarted by Harry's willingness to stand bail and the dean's testimony, and I imagined they would not be pleased by the fact that I was once more abroad in the city. I would have to keep my wits about me; if the process of the law did not serve their purpose in removing me, there was every chance they might decide to bypass it. After all, I had seen what they did to William Fitch, even if I did not yet know which of them had done it.

Chapter 12

A hot wind whipped up the dust in the streets as I made my way through the Buttermarket and on towards the Cheker. Pieces of straw eddied in the air and goodwives clasped their coifs to their heads. After the heavy stillness of the past days the breeze should have been welcome, but it was a sickly wind, humid and pregnant with the promise of a storm. Clouds bore down overhead as if in a basin that threatens to spill over at any moment.

I attracted glances from passersby as I walked but I kept my head down and ignored them, my thoughts once again turning to Sophia. My whole purpose in coming here had been to save her from the taint of murder and now I was faced with the same fate myself. Though I was not yet seriously afraid—I had a quick wit and powerful patrons, which was more than most of those wretches in the gaol could claim—I was nevertheless uncomfortably aware that I was a long way from the protection of Walsingham here, and that local justice was notoriously corrupt. I had no doubt that Samuel would do his best to delay or lose my message altogether, with the aim that I might be convicted before any help could come from Walsingham. My hope lay entirely in the message I had sent to Sidney with the weavers. I knew well enough from my years as a fugitive that only a fool puts his faith in the fact of his innocence, especially if he is a foreigner.

My heart was heavy as I entered the inn yard. Sophia was just a few streets away, yet it seemed impossible for me to see her until this business was all over, my innocence proved, and the real murderers brought to justice—if such a conclusion was even possible. As an accused man facing trial in a few days, my comings and goings would be noticed around the city; I could not risk visiting the weavers' houses and drawing the people's attention to them by so doing. I cursed quietly under my breath; Sophia was out of reach to me until I had found the killer—or killers— and all the while, I imagined Olivier at her side in that attic room, whispering his reassurances into her ear. Even if I were able to clear her name and my own in the assizes, would she not owe him almost as great a debt of gratitude by now?

The stable hands were busy across the yard and I was able to slip into the stall where my horse stood patiently chewing at his hay, his animal smell all the sharper in the heat, but strangely welcoming and wholesome after the foul stench of human waste I had endured in the gaol. He whickered softly at my approach and I laid my head against his neck for a moment as the full weight of my exhaustion began to seep through my body. My eyes drifted closed; I could have sunk to the floor right there and slept, but I caught the scratch of a broom on the cobbles in the yard and roused myself. I felt behind the straw bale and for an awful moment my stomach lurched as I feared the purse had been taken. But more frantic searching revealed that it had only slipped farther down; perhaps the horse had shifted the bales with its movements. I almost wept with relief as I drew it out and tucked it inside my breeches.

Before I reached the door of the inn, one of the stableboys caught sight of me and rushed inside, so that Marina was already waiting for me on the stairs as I entered. She came forward with her arms outstretched as if to embrace me, but drew back at the last minute at the smell, for which I was grateful.

"I knew they would have made a mistake," she cried, though her face was still anxious. "I was going to give it until tomorrow morning before I let your room to another."

"That was good of you," I said. "A whole day."

"This isn't an almshouse." She folded her arms and looked me up and down. "I sent a boy with your message to Doctor Robinson—was that how they let you go?"

"It must have been." I smiled then, with genuine gratitude. As I had guessed, the constable would have let me rot until the assizes without ever taking word to Harry. I wondered if he was in Langworth's pay as well. On an impulse, I took her hand between mine and kissed it extravagantly. "I don't know how to thank you."

Marina giggled like a girl and gave me a slow, lewd wink. "I daresay we'll think of something. You'll be wanting to clean up, I suppose?"

"I would like that more than anything."

She nodded. "And the rest of my guests will thank you for it, too. I'll have some hot water fetched up to your room, and fresh towels. Bring those clothes down and I'll give them to the laundress—with luck she can have them drying by this evening. We'll have a storm tonight for sure."

"Thank you. Oh, and—may I have another orange?"

She shook her head indulgently, as if at a demanding child.

"You have not paid me for the last one yet. Go on with you, I'll send it up with the rest. Anyone would think you were a great lord, the way you have me fetching and carrying."

I thanked her, forcing myself to smile patiently, and took the stairs to my room. While I waited for the water, I found a clean sheet of paper and wrote a short note to Walsingham using the cipher I was accustomed to use in my communications with him. The orange would be an extra precaution; there was no way of knowing how proficient Samuel might be with ciphers, so I kept the content of my letter to the facts of my wrongful arrest, in case he should work out how to read it along the way. A serving girl arrived with an orange and a bucket of hot water; when she had gone I squeezed a little of the juice into the candle holder as I had before, crammed the flesh into my mouth, and along the bottom of the letter, below where I had signed off with the symbol of the planet Jupiter, I wrote, using the juice, "Arrest the bearer of this letter on suspicion of murder." I had no great faith that this note would ever find its way to Walsingham, but it was worth a try. As the ink was drying, I stripped off my filthy clothes and tried as best I could to scrub the filth of the past night and day from my skin.

DRESSED IN CLEAN shirt and breeches, damp hair clinging to my face and with a full stomach, I waited in the inn yard while a stableboy saddled my horse and loaded him up with my packs. Marina had feigned great offence that I was leaving, but I soothed her by settling my account with a generous tip and assuring her that I would take my supper there the following day when I came to collect my clean clothes. The wind had risen further and I shielded my eyes against the grit blowing in gusts from the flagstones; above me gulls wheeled and shrieked in a sky that had taken on a lurid, shifting light behind the clouds, such as you find sometimes out at sea. A horse whinnied; I turned and caught sight of a figure skulking at the gate of the yard. He leaned against the gatepost and wore a cap with a peak pulled down low over his eyes; in the shadow of the stable building I could not get a clear look at his face.

My stomach clenched; since the previous night I had feared that Nick Kingsley and his friends would not let my ill-judged attack on him go unpunished. I felt the familiar quickening of the pulse, the prickling of my nerves as my hands balled into fists; would I have to stand and fight here, in the yard, and would anyone come to my aid? But as I squinted at the man, breath catching in my throat, I realised that he was alone, and that he was looking at me in a shifty manner from under his cap, as if he was waiting for my attention. He was too tall and rangy for Nick Kings-ley; curious, I took a step in his direction and he nodded sharply, as if to beckon me. I glanced over my shoulder; the boy was still occupied with my horse and paid me no attention. I took another step towards the man and he slipped into the open doorway of an empty stall close to the gate. Bending slowly, I removed my knife from its sheath and followed him.

There was little daylight inside the stall, but I heard him moving to the left of the doorway, his feet scratching on the straw.

"Who are you?" I hissed, the knife held out before me.

"Shh! *Viens ici.*" He stepped forward and I lowered the knife with relief.

"Olivier. Why are you skulking about like a thief?"

"Because I don't want to be seen with you. Listen." He leaned closer, glancing over my shoulder towards the doorway as if fearful we might be overheard. "She cannot stay with us any longer. It is too dangerous."

"It is only two more days, until the assizes. Please—"

"You don't understand. You have made it impossible." His words came sharp and urgent, as if he might impel me by the force of them. "The constable came to our house this morning. Someone told him you have been seen at our door—he asked my father a lot of questions about who you were, how we knew you."

"*Merda.* I am sorry for that. What did he say?"

Olivier made a noise of contempt. "Don't worry, my father is practised at thinking on his feet. He said you had come to pay your respects because you had known Protestant friends of ours when you lived in Paris."

"And the constable believed him?"

He shrugged.

"How do I know? It was only as he was leaving that he told us you had been arrested for murder." He curled his lip at me. "My father said he was sure there was some misunderstanding. But after the constable left—you can imagine."

I nodded, picturing the distress of those good, beleaguered people. I had no affection for Olivier, but I could not deny how much his family had risked for Sophia. Now I had unwittingly brought the constable to their door while they harboured another murder suspect in their attic.

"My mother has not stopped weeping and wringing her hands,"

Olivier said. "They fear it is only a matter of time before your arrest becomes an excuse to harass us further. And if they search our house and find her . . ." He did not need to finish the sentence. The whole family could be executed along with Sophia to make an example.

"What can we do?"

"My father says we must give her into your care. You brought her back to Canterbury, after we had got her safely away." He gave me a hard look.

· "I have only been allowed out of prison on bail, on condition that I lodge inside the cathedral precincts until the assizes." I held out my hands in a show of helplessness.

"Exactly. They will not think to look for her in the house of a cathedral canon."

I hesitated. With Samuel out of the way, it was almost conceivable, though the prospect of proposing such a plan to Harry chilled me; he had a duty to me because of our shared service to Walsingham, but Sophia was no part of that. Walsingham had no idea that I had brought her to Canterbury, and I suspected he would be furious if he knew I had compromised my own safety and Harry's for her sake.

"My father says he will have no choice but to put her out on the street if you will not take responsibility for her this time," Olivier added, sensing that I was wavering.

"And you would let him do that? You care for her, I think." I met his gaze frankly for a moment but he looked away.

"I care for my family also. My parents have lived most of their lives in the shadow of death. Here they thought to escape it. They should not have to fear it again because of me." He spoke quietly, but his voice was tight with feeling.

Because of me. What did he mean by that? Because he loved Sophia? I watched Olivier as he kept his eyes fixed on the ground, scuffing patterns in the dust with the toe of his threadbare shoes. He was not helping Sophia out of Christian charity, but because he hoped for a reward at the end of this ordeal—presumably the same reward I wanted. Which of us would win?

I pushed my hair back off my face and nodded. "Well, then. She cannot be left on the street. But how will you bring her to the cathedral without being noticed?"

"Our church holds a service this evening in the crypt, at the same time as Evensong in the cathedral. We could bring her there in disguise and hand her over to you."

I paused to consider the implications.

"Not disguised as a boy, she will be too obvious here. Dress her as an old woman, heap her with scarves and shawls. She can walk crook-backed—it would be less noticeable. But I have to eat at the dean's table tonight, I can't take her back after Evensong."

"Then when?"

"Wait, I am trying to think." My hand closed around the purse at my belt and the shape of Langworth's keys inside it. Into my mind flashed the image of the map I had found in the library, with the treasury and its sub-vault clearly marked. The crypt. I could not shake the sense that everything centred on the crypt, and tonight I would be inside the cathedral precincts with three untried keys in my possession. I recalled the old monk's story about the exchange of coffins in the last days of the priory. If Thomas Becket was anywhere, he was down there, in some unmarked grave, and Langworth almost certainly knew where. Tonight I would find him, and anything else Langworth might have hidden down there with him. I turned to Olivier with renewed purpose.

"After your service ends, find a place to hide her in the crypt. There are nooks and crannies, side chapels, alcoves and shadows. Find somewhere. Tell her after dark I will come for her."

He looked doubtful.

"The crypt is locked after dark."

"Trust me."

"I don't like it. What if she should be found before you get there?"

"A moment ago you were ready to put her out on the street." I folded my arms. "If she hides herself well, that won't happen. Tell her to wait for me, keep silent until I call her by name, and have faith."

"Faith." He spat the word out like a bitter fruit. In that moment I contemplated telling him that I had found the body of his nephew, if only to put an end to the pain of uncertainty, but the set of his jaw persuaded me against it; he was young and hotheaded and the boy's body would be vital evidence, it must not be revealed until I was sure the right person could be punished for it.

"Master? Your horse is ready." The voice of the stableboy cut through the sounds of gulls and wind, carrying across the yard outside.

"I must go. Do everything as we have said. And take care you don't get caught. All our lives depend on it."

Olivier looked at me coldly. "Do not take me for a fool," he said, retreating back into the shadows as the stableboy called again and I slipped out of the door to the yard, my heart hammering against the vault of my ribs as I tried not to contemplate the enormity of what we were to attempt that night.

THE MARKETPLACE WAS emptying as I led the horse towards the Christ Church gate. Hot gusts of wind snapped at the stallholders' canvas awnings; some cursed and struggled to tie their ropes tighter, while others—those selling fresh produce—sought to cover their goods with weighted cloths to protect them from the whorls of dust whipped up from the dry earth. A man in the motley of a jongleur crouched on the ground, packing his juggling balls and spent firebrands into a square of canvas. People moved aside for me, staring, as I passed the market cross; to either side I caught the low rumble of murmuring as neighbours turned to one another, though perhaps it was fortunate I could not hear their commentary. Defensive, I glanced around and saw the apothecary's niece, Rebecca, hovering beside a bread stall, now almost empty. She had hooked a covered basket over one arm and smiled shyly when she caught my eye, looking quickly down and back to me, then glancing over her shoulder at the broad-hipped goodwife who was untying the colourful awning from its posts.

"Do you still tarry, good-for-nothing?" The woman straightened with a scornful look at the girl. "Get you gone, or we shall have rain and those loaves will be spoiled before ever they get there."

"But Mistress Blunt, I had much rather—"

"Enough of your contrariness—I don't want to catch sight of your apron strings next time I look up. Get on that road." So saying, she went back to the dismantling of her stall. When the woman's back was turned, I mimicked her pompous expression and manner and Rebecca pressed her sleeve to her mouth to stifle a giggle. But her face quickly fell sombre and reluctantly she raised a hand in farewell before turning towards the street that led east out of the marketplace. An idea struck me; instead of continuing to the cathedral, I waited until Rebecca was out of sight around the corner before gently easing the horse in the same direction. This gesture did not pass unnoticed among the observers in the market square, though thankfully the formidable woman on the bread stall was too occupied in her business to pay me any heed.

I caught up with Rebecca a little way along the next street. Her blush and ready smile told me she was pleased by the attention, though she bit her lower lip and looked anxiously past me towards the market we had just left, as if someone would appear at any moment to chide her for talking to me.

"You seemed downcast back there, Rebecca," I said, keeping my voice light. "I wondered if there was anything I could do to help?"

"I ought not to speak to you, sir," she whispered. "All the talk in the market is of how you were arrested for the killing of my uncle. Mistress Blunt says it's no more than can be expected of foreigners who are little better than savages with no respect for God or the queen. Begging your pardon," she added in a mumble, looking down.

"Mistress Blunt is a fat fool," I said. Her hand flew to her mouth to cover a delighted gasp at the audacity of this. "You do not believe I killed your uncle, surely?"

Her eyes travelled my face for a moment as if uncertain. She shook her head.

"No. Why would you? Besides, no money was taken, so they said. You are right about Mistress Blunt, but I would not dare say so aloud. Like now, for instance." She fell into step beside me, her talk more relaxed, as if our shared view of Mistress Blunt eclipsed all previous concerns. "I am to take this basket to old Mother Garth out by the Riding-gate, though her son Tom is gatekeeper at the cathedral only spitting distance from our stall. I don't see why it can't be left with him, but no—Mistress Blunt says I must take it in person, though all Canterbury knows Mother Garth is mad as a hare and like as not to scream blue murder at you just for standing on her doorstep. I wouldn't even be surprised if she was a witch and all." She nodded a full stop, as if this were the definitive verdict.

I smiled.

"Well, then—how would it be if I were to accompany you to her door, and if she screams at you I shall shout back at her in Italian, see what she makes of that. And if she sees fit to turn me into a cat or a rat, I shall depend on you to use what you learned from your uncle and make a remedy to turn me back."

Rebecca laughed, looking up at me with all her young untried yearnings transparent on her face. I had no interest in her outside what she might know of her uncle's business, but I realised again how easy it is to flatter a giddy girl, and how easily a man with fewer scruples might use that to his advantage. I thought of the maidservant Sarah Garth and how Sir Edward must have beckoned her to his bed—and his son's bed—with a few judicious compliments. A quick stab of anger knotted my gut at the idea; if I could feel outrage at my own sex on behalf of a girl I never knew, how much fury must her own brother still carry in his breast? Perhaps a visit to Mother Garth might yield more than the chance to quiz Rebecca undisturbed.

"It is true that my uncle taught me plenty of remedies when I helped him in the shop," she was saying, and I brought my attention back to the stream of her chatter. "But my mother will not let me practice them, for fear. She says a woman who knows how to heal is judged a witch."

"Only by the ignorant. But perhaps your mother is afraid that you would have to work with dangerous ingredients. Your uncle must have kept many in his shop—poisons, even?"

"Only the dose makes the poison," she said importantly, and the hairs on my arm prickled. "Uncle William always used to say that."

"Surely not!" I affected to laugh. "A poison is a poison, is it not so? I mean, something like belladonna, for instance—what good remedy could you make from that?"

"You would be surprised," she said, her face earnest. "People think it dangerous because of the berries, but I'll wager you did not know that a tincture of belladonna is the only antidote to laudanum poisoning?"

I stopped dead in the street and stared at her. The horse snorted in protest at my sudden halt.

"Laudanum, did you say?"

She nodded, pleased to show off her store of knowledge.

"You can give a person laudanum to dull pain or help them sleep, as everyone knows, but if you give too much by mistake, the person passes into a state almost between life and death, where you cannot even tell that he breathes, and he will never wake unless he be given belladonna. Come—we must talk and walk at the same time, or I shall be in trouble."

She giggled again and I resumed my pace, fighting to keep my face steady.

"So, you are saying—if you give a man a heavy dose of laudanum, he will pass into a sleep that looks almost like death, but if he is given belladonna, he will wake again?"

"So my uncle claimed, though I never saw it done. But he said the method had been tried."

"What if you give too great a dose of belladonna by mistake?"

She shrugged.

"I don't know. I suppose the person would die then as well. I will tell you another curious fact about belladonna, though," she said, brightening. "Children can tolerate a dose of it that would kill a grown man. Is that not strange? You would think, being smaller, they would die quicker. But up to the age of twelve or thirteen it is the opposite, my uncle said."

"How did he know this?" I asked, too sharply; I saw a flicker of concern cross her face.

"I suppose he read of it somewhere. He had a great curiosity for new ideas in physic, though he would not speak of it when there were customers in the shop. People have no spirit of adventure when it comes to remedies, he used to say. They want you to give them what they have always had, no matter whether it works or not. Try something new and they will accuse you of alchemy or witchcraft, he said."

"That is sometimes said of Doctor Sykes, is it not?"

"Huh. Uncle William was a great admirer of Doctor Sykes for that." The curl of her lip as she spoke made her own feelings clear. "He said Sykes was not afraid to experiment."

"What did he mean by that, do you think?"

She gave an impatient little shake of the head, as if the subject was no longer of interest to her, holding on to her coif with her free hand against the chafing wind.

"Oh, I don't know. Uncle William was always in awe of those he thought his betters. Fawning, my aunt used to call it. He liked to say he could have been a physician if he'd been born a gentleman's son and had the leisure to study. I never liked Doctor Sykes, though perhaps that's unkind of me, on account of his looks. Puts me in mind of a great toad, with all his chins. And the way he fixes you with those cold eyes—like he's picturing cutting you open on a slab to see how your insides work."

"I would not put it past him."

I had only seen Sykes on that one fateful occasion in Fitch's shop, but she was exactly right about his cold eyes. So Sykes liked to experiment. Something nagged at the corner of my thoughts. I took a deep breath and deliberately focused my mind inward to the theatre of memory. Yes— Langworth and Samuel had talked of experiments that day I had hidden under Langworth's bed. Langworth had said they should wait, there had been too many deaths in the town; had he meant that further experiments would lead to more deaths? Was that what the dead boys had been—subjects of experimentation? Sykes and Fitch shared an interest in medicine, but what was Langworth's motive in such business?

"Is Sykes married?" I asked Rebecca. She grimaced.

"Not he. What woman would choose to marry that foul toad-face?"

"Is there any gossip in the town that he inclines another way?"

"Men, you mean?"

"Or boys."

She considered this for a moment before a decisive shake of the head.

"I have never heard it said. And Mistress Blunt knows every scrap of gossip in Canterbury, she prides herself on it. Goodwives come to her stall for the tales as much as for the bread. If there were rumours like that about Doctor Sykes, she would be the first to know of it. Why do you ask?"

"No reason." I smiled. "Only that it is sometimes said of men who are not married."

"Are you married?" she asked, with a coy sideways glance.

"I? No."

"And is it said of you?"

I laughed. "Not to my face."

She still looked a little concerned; I winked to reassure her and she blushed pleasingly. "We turn down here," she said, indicating a narrow unpaved street that ran parallel to the city wall, whose squat flint towers rose over the roofs of the cottages ahead of us.

These were poorer dwellings, few of them more than one storey and many badly needed their plaster and thatch to be restored. There was a strong smell of refuse and human waste here; the horse seemed reluctant to be led this way. I tugged gently on his bridle, whispering encouragement, and as I did a large brown rat scurried between my feet and disappeared. So this was where Tom Garth lived with his mother. Small wonder he had such a grievance about the soft lives of youths like Nicholas Kingsley.

Rebecca's pace slowed as we progressed along the street, as if dragging out the moments before she was obliged to face Mother Garth. I wondered how frightening one old woman could be.

"This one," she whispered, stopping at a run-down cottage with a crooked roof. One pane of glass in the front casement was broken and the gap was stopped by a sheet of canvas, which the wind had loosened to slap against the frame. Rebecca looked at me expectantly, so I stepped forward and knocked smartly three times on the door. The wood was not sturdy and I felt it bend even under the force of my knuckles. We waited for a few moments, Rebecca nervously twining the strings of her coif around her fingers. Eventually it seemed clear that no one was going to answer. I knocked again and leaned close to the door to listen out for some movement inside, but there was only silence and the crying of the gulls above us.

"No one is home," I said, after a few moments more. The horse was growing restless and I was also impatient to be gone. "Perhaps you could leave the basket with a neighbour—"

Rebecca shook her head.

"She is there. She never leaves the house. We will have to go in." She bit her lip at the prospect.

"I cannot leave the horse alone in a street like this," I said. "He is valuable and I have paid good money as a surety for him in London."

"I will wait and hold him," she said, eagerly holding out a hand for his bridle. "It won't take you a moment." She shone a hopeful smile at me and I rolled my eyes indulgently, reaching for the basket. It ought to prove easier to question Tom Garth's mother alone and I could not refuse the chance.

I pushed at the flimsy door and it opened easily into one small, low room with a fire in the centre and a hole above in the blackened thatch to let the smoke escape. In one corner was an ancient-looking wooden settle and beside the fire two rough stools. Over the fire stood an iron frame for hanging a cooking pot. In a far corner, a straw pallet was stacked neatly against the wall. I wondered if that was where Tom slept. The room was empty of life.

"Hello?" I called out. "Mistress Garth? I bring your bread."

There was no reply. I glanced over my shoulder to see Rebecca's anxious face peering in the crack of the front door. Nodding to her, I pushed it closed behind me. Opposite this door was another that looked as if it might lead to a back room. I crossed and opened it to find a dim chamber dominated by a large bed and smelling thickly of stale clothes and unwashed bodies. The one small casement was hung with a ragged dark cloth to keep out the daylight. I could hear a fly buzzing persistently against the glass in the stillness. To one side of the bed a wooden ladder rose up to what might have been a kind of loft or storage area built with planks over the rafters under the eaves.

"Mistress Garth?" I called again and this time thought I heard a scratch of movement from above, so slight it might have been a mouse in the thatch. I placed the bread basket on the floor and put my foot on the first step of the ladder. It creaked loudly. There was no further sound from overhead, but I continued up the rungs to the space at the top cut into the planks that had been nailed across the roof beams. Just as my head emerged through the gap, a bony hand shot out and gripped me by the collar; involuntarily I cried out and the creature holding me did the same, though with a note of triumph.

"You!" she shrieked, and I found myself staring into a face that would have terrified children. Wasted by age and hunger so that the skin was stretched across the bones, making the wild blue eyes seem larger and brighter, she bore on her cheeks the marks of childhood pox and a broad scar ran through her left brow. Most of her teeth were missing and her thin lips curled back over the bare gums as she fixed me with her strange, unfocused gaze. A mass of wiry curls stood out around her head, still dark in places though streaked through with silver like the pelt of a badger; with each movement of her head these ringlets seemed to quiver with life of their own and I thought instantly of Medusa and her hair of writhing snakes. I started back and almost lost my footing on the ladder; her grip tightened and she coughed out a hoarse laugh into my face.

"Are you come from the mayor?"

"I am come from the bread stall."

She took no notice of this.

"I told my Tom to send someone from the law. Thieves! They are taking her things. For what, I don't know. To sell? You tell me. Are you a constable?"

"No," I said, keeping my voice steady. She was touched in her wits, that much was clear, but I felt there was some sense in it, if I could only tune my ears. "I have brought you bread."

The feverish eyes raked my face again, though this time there was uncertainty in them.

"They are taking her things," she repeated, though more quietly, and her grip slackened on my collar. "Why? It is all I have left of her."

"Sarah's things?" I asked. Her eyes flashed with fury and she pulled my face closer. Her breath stank of sour milk.

"What do you know of it? You know something! Is it not enough that they took her from me, now they must come here in the dead of night like foxes and carry off her clothes?"

"What did they take?" I could not lean back for fear of toppling off the ladder; her face was as close as if she meant to kiss me.

"Her best gloves." Finally she let go of me, as if to concede defeat, and gave a dry laugh. "Her only gloves, I should say. I keep all her things in a chest up here, you see." She pointed to a rough wooden box in the corner of the loft. "I take them out and remember her. Sometimes I fancy they still smell of her, though my Tom says 'tis only mould and moths. He says I should have sold the good cloth years ago and burned the rest, but we have different ways of mourning. A mother doesn't let go, you know." I thought I saw the shine of tears in her eyes then, but it might only have been the fever of madness. She seemed to focus on me again and her face hardened. "So I keep vigil up here now, in case they come back for the rest. I won't sleep neither. That's when they'll come, won't they? In the night." She raised her chin as if daring me to contradict her.

"Who do you think stole Sarah's gloves?"

"The ones who killed her," she hissed, through her remaining stumps of teeth.

"And who are they?"

"*You* know," she said, and spat into the straw to show her contempt. "All the fucking town knows, but they will not bring him to justice. Ah, but one fine day justice will come to him, when he least expects it."

She broke into a lunatic cackle and I was moved by pity for her state, though her words were sending my thoughts spinning, so similar were they to Tom's. A missing pair of gloves. And a pair of women's gloves found bloodied at the place of Sir Edward Kingsley's murder. I needed to speak to Tom Garth again.

"You know Edward Kingsley is dead?" I said. The old woman stopped laughing abruptly and stared at me.

"Of course I know, you insolent fucking boy—I am not simple. My Tom told me. He should have been brought to public trial for what he did, but something is better than nothing. I hope the whoremongering devil suffered. I hope he suffers in Hell even now. But there are others must be punished for my Sarah."

"Which others?" I asked, but her face closed up like a shutter and she gave only a low laugh, knowing and wicked.

"They will learn when their judgement day comes," she muttered. Her eyes narrowed and she looked at me as if noticing me for the first time. "Bread, you say?"

"It is downstairs."

"I suppose you want money?"

It had not occurred to me to ask Rebecca if the bread was already paid for. But the old woman settled the question with a wave of her claw-like hand.

"I have no money here. Tell them to ask my Tom, he takes care of matters. Besides, I cannot leave Sarah's clothes unattended." With this, she scuttled on her hands and knees back across the straw to the corner where the chest stood and laid a protective hand over it. "Now get out of my house," she added, though without malice.

I bade her good day and retreated to the ground with some relief. Poor Tom, I thought, glancing at the straw pallet in the main room. To live like this, with her, might drive any man to violence. I had been so distracted by the discovery of Sir Edward's underground tomb, his tangled relationships with Langworth, Sykes, and Samuel, and the implications of his will that I had all but dismissed Tom Garth's motive for murdering his sister's former employer. Could it be that Fitch's murder and Sir Edward's were unconnected, and Sophia's husband had been killed in a simple act of revenge, an act imagined and brooded over for years in this squalid room?

Rebecca, relieved of her onerous task, seemed lighter in spirit as we made our way back towards the market, chattering freely and swinging the empty basket at her side, walking a little too close to me and touching my arm often to accompany whatever point she was making. I heard but one word in twenty, my thoughts all caught up in what I had learned this past half hour. But as we neared the street corner that led to the marketplace, I came back to myself and brought the horse to a halt while we were still out of sight, conscious of how our appearance together would look to the busy goodwives.

"You should go on ahead," I said, motioning briskly with my head. "It would not do for you to be seen with a suspected murderer."

She twisted her fingers together and giggled. I was beginning to find this girlish simpering tiresome and grew impatient for her to be gone; once again I appreciated Sophia's self-contained dignity and her disdain for such wiles as girls commonly use. The prospect of seeing her that night took on a sharper thrill as I remembered the graceful curve of her neck, the way she would turn her head and fix her silent steady gaze on me.

"You have done me a great service, sir," Rebecca murmured, looking up at me from under her lashes. "I wish I could think of some reward." This time she deliberately met my eyes and did not look away.

"Oh, I have had reward enough," I said, pretending to be innocent of her meaning, and thinking of the two new nuggets of information I had gained from this detour. "The pleasure of meeting Mistress Garth, for instance. And your fascinating discourse on remedies," I added hastily, seeing the girl's face fall.

"Perhaps I shall see you again tomorrow?" she said, a hopeful note in her voice.

"Perhaps. It is a small town." I smiled with what I hoped was polite detachment. Evidently this did not register, because she leaned forward on her tiptoes and planted a wet kiss full on my lips. Before I had time to react, she clapped a hand to her mouth as if scandalised by her own boldness, gathered up her skirts in both hands, and fled in the direction of the market. Left alone in the empty street, I wiped my mouth with the back of my hand and leaned back against the horse's shoulder, smiling.

"Never the one you want, eh? Why is that, old friend?"

He snorted and shook his mane.

"You're right. Human nature." I slapped him gently on the side of his neck and led him onwards.

Tom Garth came out to greet me at the Christ Church gate, surprise etched on his face.

"I heard you were arrested for murder," he whispered, approaching and patting the horse on the shoulder. "Is it true you must stay here with Harry until the assizes?"

"Don't worry, there is no case to answer," I said, with more confidence than I felt. "Where do I take this fellow?"

"All the way around the corona and past the guesthouses at the end, you will see the stable block." He hesitated, wiping his hands on his tunic, and there was a nervousness in his demeanour. I noticed he had not asked me to surrender my weapon this time. "Are you not afraid? Will you send for a lawyer from London?"

"I will defend myself by showing the court the real murderer. But you are right, Tom—it is a fearful thing to be accused of murder."

He looked at me for a moment without speaking, and it seemed that he blanched; he licked his lips and swallowed, as if his mouth had dried and I thought he was going to speak, but he merely nodded in agreement. I noticed his fingers plucking at the bandage he wore around his hand. I turned away; there were questions to be answered about his sister's gloves and his own movements on the night of Sir Edward's murder, but now was not the time. For now all I wanted was to get Samuel on the road and unburden myself to Harry.

The stables were built close up against the walls of the cathedral precinct behind the ruins of the old priory. Outside, a boy was waiting with a horse ready, saddled and harnessed. I explained that I was using Harry Robinson's stall and was reassured that the waiting horse was indeed Harry's and was awaiting his servant who would leave that evening. I gave the boy a groat and left my own horse in his care, but as I walked away I turned back and noticed a broad chestnut tree growing outside the precinct wall, its lower branches overhanging the roof of the stables. At the far end of the stable block, a set of wooden steps led down the outside wall from what I guessed was the entrance to the hayloft. So much for their great gatehouse tower and gatekeeper; it would be easy work for any fit man or boy to climb this tree, shimmy over the precinct wall, across the roof of the stable, and down into the yard. My spirits sank further at the thought; in that case, anyone could have entered the cathedral grounds the night Sir Edward was killed without having to pass under the nose of Tom Garth at the gate. But they would still have had to gain access to the crypt to take the crucifix he was battered with; that could not have been taken before dark or the dean would surely have noticed it missing when he checked the crypt and locked up for the night. Which led me back to the same conclusion: only someone with a means of entering the crypt at night could have killed Sir Edward, and if the sub-vault below the treasury was a secret means of access, I found it hard to see how that someone could have been anyone other than Langworth, or perhaps Samuel on Langworth's orders.

Samuel was waiting in the front parlour of Harry's house when I arrived with my baggage, a travelling cloak thrown over his arm and a face darker than the bruised sky over the cathedral bell tower.

"Looks like that promised storm might break tonight after all," I said cheerfully. "I hope you won't get too wet." He sent me a glare so murderous it was almost comical, until I reminded myself that this was very likely the man who had lured a child to his death and possibly smashed Fitch's skull too. Harry shuffled into the room and leaned on his stick, eyes flitting from one to the other of us, appraising the situation.

"Well, Samuel, you had best get on the road before Evensong—you should make some progress by dusk. Every moment counts, I suppose." He spoke grudgingly and I fought hard to keep my face sombre.

"I appreciate your efforts, Samuel, as will Sir Francis," I said, with deep sincerity, as I brought out the letter, hastily sealed at the Cheker. I had the sense he would have liked to spit on me then, but for Harry's sake he nodded and tucked it inside his doublet.

"Do not forget your licence to travel. And have you a cloak against the rain? Good. Take Doctor Bruno's letter to the usual place and tell them it must reach Walsingham with all speed." Harry pursed his lips and looked Samuel over like a grandfather fretting over a child. "Have you food for your saddlebag?"

"I have all I need for the journey, thank you, sir," Samuel said. "And I should get on the road now, before the storm comes." He shot a last glance at me and pushed past to the doorway.

"God go with you."

Harry embraced him, and I saw how the old man lingered, reluctant to let his servant leave. He shuffled out after Samuel and I waited in the parlour, cracking my knuckles as I heard them murmuring at the front door, dreading the conversation I must now have with Harry and wondering what lies Samuel was pouring in his ears on the threshold.

Eventually I heard the door close and the tap of Harry's stick on the boards as he limped back to the front room.

"I hope he travels safe," he said, with an accusing look at me. "God knows the roads are dangerous enough in these times, with a poor harvest and fear of plague . . . Samuel will do his best, but you will be lucky if he reaches Walsingham in time for an intervention before the assizes.

You will have to hope for clemency from the judge. And it will not be easy—people round here have no fear of perjuring themselves, they will say anything under oath if it means coins in their pockets. If Langworth and Sykes want you found guilty, they can make it happen."

"I would be amazed if Samuel reaches Walsingham at all, and not because of any danger on the roads," I said calmly. "Sit down, Harry. You are not going to like what I have to tell you."

As succinctly as I could, I laid out for Harry everything I had learned since arriving in Canterbury. For the most part he listened without interruption, the shrewd eyes fixed gravely on my face, with the occasional nod to demonstrate his attention.

"God's teeth, man, have you lost your mind? You *stole* his keys?" he cried, when I told him about breaking into Langworth's house.

"A key was taken from Edward Kingsley's body after he died. Langworth found the body. I had to find out if it was one of those keys, and why."

"And did you?"

"I am coming to that part."

He fell silent and pressed a hand to his mouth when I told of Samuel's conversation with the canon treasurer, so as not to betray any emotion. At one point he shook his head; I could not tell whether it was in sorrow or disbelief. Either way, he was gracious enough to hear me out until the end of my account, including my discovery of the mausoleum beneath Sir Edward's house and the conversation with the old monk in the West Gate gaol. When I had finished he sat back in his chair, one hand resting on his stick, and looked at me for a long time, but as if his gaze was focused through and beyond me on some hidden meaning. I felt a profound sense of relief at having discharged all this, though I had no way of knowing yet whether Harry's loyalty to his servant would outweigh the credibility of my story.

Finally he gave a great sigh that seemed to rack his whole body and he shook his head again.

"Samuel," he said, and left a long pause. "He has been with me these ten years, since before I came to Canterbury. It is so hard to believe. And yet . . ." He left the thought unfinished.

"I am sorry," I said, feeling the weakness of the words. "But I am speaking the truth, Harry. There is no one else in Canterbury who will believe me, if you will not."

He gave a bitter laugh.

"I imagine this is how a cuckold must feel," he said. "There is a very particular shame in having one's poor judgement exposed, is there not, Bruno? Intelligent, educated men like us—it is hard to accept that we could be so easily deceived."

I felt sorry for him—he had clearly developed an affection for his servant over the years and a betrayal of trust on that level was indeed a brutal shock.

"It would be hard to go through life suspecting everyone we know of deception," I said, gently.

"And yet we are servants of Walsingham," he said, with a sharpness that may have been directed at himself. "This is an age of deception—we should know to be vigilant. Every man has his price, I ought to have realised that. I cannot believe Samuel was moved by ardent devotion to the church of Rome. Langworth must have paid him well. Better than me. But even so—*murder*. And murder of children . . ." He shook his head again. "Do you have a theory yet that will draw all these elements together?"

I pushed my hair out of my eyes.

"My ideas are more tangled than any cat's cradle. First there is the matter of the murdered boys. Sir Edward, Langworth, and Sykes seem to have been behind this, with the help of Samuel and possibly Fitch. I guess the boys were lured away by Samuel, taken to that underground tomb at St. Gregory's, drugged with laudanum while they served the mens' uses. Then perhaps the idea was to revive them with belladonna, but in both cases the dose was misjudged and the boys died, so the bodies had to be disposed of. When Fitch was murdered, all his writings referring to the uses of belladonna were burned and the laudanum removed. Perhaps they feared he had said more than he should to someone and they would be discovered."

Harry sat in silence for a long while pondering this. I was unwilling to disturb his thoughts if he was reflecting on my hypothesis, but when it seemed he would not speak at all I began to shift in my seat. Finally I cleared my throat and he looked up, frowning.

"You have assumed that these boys were abducted and drugged because one or perhaps all of the men you have mentioned wanted to sodomise them?"

I blinked, surprised by his bluntness.

"I cannot see what other purpose they would have. A taste for boys is not one that men in prominent positions could indulge openly."

"True. And yet . . . Edward Kingsley, John Langworth, Ezekiel Sykes? I do not believe they would risk so much for that—a brief taste of forbidden fruit. We are talking of men who play for much higher stakes."

"Then what?"

By way of answer, he heaved himself from his chair and lurched across the room to a chest of books by the desk, his stiff leg dragging a trail through the dust on the boards. After a moment's rummaging he emerged with a leather-bound volume.

"That letter from Mendoza—you say it spoke of a miracle?"

I nodded. He grunted and sat heavily, flicking through the pages of the book on his lap.

"One of the early miracles attributed to Saint Thomas Becket, not long after his murder, was the resurrection of a young boy, about twelve years old, the son of a nobleman who had died of an ague. It was the miracle that caused his fame to spread even beyond England. Here—" He passed the book across, indicating the page he had found. It was another chronicle of the life and sainthood of Becket. I read the account in silence and looked up to face Harry, my eyes widening as I grasped his meaning.

"You think they meant to reproduce this miracle? As a public display?"

"Think about it. When you tell me what this girl says about the properties of laudanum and belladonna together . . . In theory, with the right dose, you could produce the appearance of death and then, with careful timing, bring the boy back to life. The Huguenot boy, the beggar child—these were practice runs, experiments. Suppose they were testing so that, when the right time comes—"

"A Catholic invasion, for instance?"

"Exactly. Then a dead child is brought back to life by the relics of Saint Thomas, his first miracle in decades, as a mark of God's favour to the people of Canterbury for keeping the true faith. Imagine the effect of it. The report would spread throughout Christendom like a wildfire, as it did the first time." He gestured to the book.

I sat back, staring at him, amazed by the audacity of it.

"It would mean they have the body of Saint Thomas somewhere," I murmured. "They must be the guardians the old monk spoke of."

"Kingsley, Langworth, Sykes. And a fourth."

"Samuel?"

Harry shook his head. "Not a servant. It will be another man of position in the city." He pressed his lips together. "We are speculating, of course, Bruno. We have yet to prove it, and they will close ranks. But why was Edward Kingsley murdered, and in so violent a fashion? Did he threaten to betray the plot? Such canny men could surely have found a more discreet way to silence him, you would think."

"Where was Samuel that night?" I asked.

"He was here with me when Kingsley was murdered. I told you—I left the dean's supper early, well before Kingsley, and Samuel was at home when I arrived. He sat talking with me right up until we heard the cries outside and went to see what had happened."

"Perhaps his death is not connected to the boys," I said, and told him of my visit to Mother Garth's cottage and the matter of Sarah's missing gloves. "Tom Garth had opportunity and good reason to kill Sir Edward, and we can prove he tried to cast suspicion on Sophia by leaving a pair of women's gloves near the place of the murder. He has a cut on his hand—he must have done that himself to wet the gloves with blood before he dropped them early the next morning."

I heard my voice grow more animated as my theory took shape, though I was aware of a corresponding unease. If Tom Garth was guilty of Edward Kingsley's murder, it was hard not to sympathise. What I had learned of the magistrate's disregard for others—his willingness to treat them as commodities to be used as required and discarded when they had served their purpose, together with his callous certainty that he was above the law because he made the law—only made me feel that his violent death had been a sort of unorthodox justice, on behalf of Sarah Garth, Sophia, and the dead boys. Did I really want to hand Tom Garth over to the assizes to be hanged for a crime he had been driven to by desperation? Could I honestly say I might not be tempted to such actions, in his shoes? I passed a hand over my mouth, realising the enormity of what I was facing. But if the true murderer was not brought to justice, the sentence of death would always hang over Sophia, and one day it would surely catch up with her. I had promised to find the man who killed her husband and I could not back away from that promise now merely because the likely answer tore at my conscience. Still, my heart was heavy at the thought of it. I must talk to Tom; perhaps I could persuade him to sign a confession and leave the town before the assizes. He would have time to make it to one of the ports.

Harry continued to watch me, his face guarded.

"And how shall we prove it, Bruno? Any of this?" His chin tilted up as he spoke, as if in challenge.

"Tom Garth may be persuaded to confess," I said, knowing the weakness of it. "Or his mother at least will testify about the missing gloves. If the constable has kept the one found at the place of the murder, she could identify it. As for the boys—the old monk in the gaol could be brought as witness. He is not so clouded in his wits as he first seems—"

I broke off; Harry was shaking his head.

"I know this old man—his name is Brother Anselm and he is a familiar figure around the town. People give him alms out of superstition or some respect for the old priory, and the watch are reluctant to arrest him for vagrancy. Every now and again he is sent on his way with a warning, yet he always finds his way back. But if he has been blamed for the murder, his testimony would never be taken seriously. As for old Mother Garth—her wits fled the day her daughter died. The mad cannot testify in court. It is hopeless."

"Then there must be another way," I said with feeling. "I will find the body of Saint Thomas."

"Ha! You think they will have left it lying around for all to see? With an epitaph, perhaps?"

"They will have distinguished it somehow." I was growing impatient with his determination to fix on every disadvantage. "There is also the body of the Huguenot boy in the mausoleum at the Kingsley house. It is not yet so badly decayed that it could not be identified." I stopped for a moment, imagining Hélène confronted with that terrible sight, and felt a stab of guilt that the family still knew nothing of Denis's fate. "No one but us and the old housekeeper knows of it. When the assize judge arrives—"

Harry raised a hand.

"We must tread with the utmost care now, Bruno. You have already seen how this business is protected by powerful interests. They have had you arrested on the flimsiest of pretexts and they could find a way to silence me as well, if they chose. And the unknown fourth guardian will also be a man with significant influence in the town."

"Someone like the mayor? Meg said I would get no justice from him." I thought of Fitzwalter with his pompous air of entitlement and his evident irritation at having to give way to the dean over my release.

"Possibly. Or even closer to home." He raised his eyes to the window. I followed his gaze and took in the towering shadow of the cathedral.

"Someone here? Other than Langworth?" I looked back to Harry in amazement. "Not Dean Rogers, surely?"

Harry held his hands out, palms upwards, to indicate helplessness.

"As you said, we cannot be sure of anyone. It would be very difficult to hide anything in the crypt without his knowledge. No one can gain access without him."

"Not necessarily." I told him of the old map I had discovered in the cathedral library showing the sub-vault beneath the treasury that appeared to open onto the crypt. "There are two keys untried on the ring I copied from Langworth. Tonight, under cover of darkness, I intend to try them. Becket is down there somewhere, I am sure of it. If we find the relics, we can expose the whole conspiracy."

"How?" Harry threw his hands up, exasperated. "We come to the same problem every time, Bruno. Even if you find a casket of bones in the crypt and they can be unequivocally proven to be Becket's—how do we tie them to Langworth and Sykes? If we accuse them without evidence, it is we who will be exposed. And who will help us? We cannot rely on Samuel to take that letter to Walsingham now."

"I have no doubt that Samuel will destroy that letter as soon as he has the chance," I said. "Fortunately, my hope lies elsewhere." I told him of the copy I had made of Mendoza's letter to Langworth and how I had sent it with the weavers to Sidney. "There is a chance, if they make good time on their journey, that Walsingham could send a fast rider to intervene by the day of the assizes. Cheer up, Harry—remember we are protected by powerful interests too. The queen herself."

Harry's face remained clouded.

"Aye. And how will she take this, I wonder—a conspiracy to revive the cult of Saint Thomas, right in the heart of the cathedral? A conspiracy that has flourished under my nose while I was buried in my books. Walsingham will strike me from his service after this. And it is all the reason Elizabeth needs to suppress the foundation and take its funds for her wars." His eyes lingered on mine for a moment with an expression more of resignation than anger. "All this to save one girl from the pyre, Bruno? A girl who is far away from this town by now and has nothing to fear from its justice. Was it worth your while?"

I caught the bitter edge in his voice and paused for a moment before I spoke, leaning my elbows on my knees and steepling my fingers together as I weighed up my words.

"I was not sent here to find reasons to shut down the foundation, Harry, whatever you may believe. I did it all for the girl. And, yes—if I save her it will have been worth it." I hesitated again and took a deep breath. "But, actually, she is not as far away as you think."

Harry raised an eyebrow and I told him how Sophia had journeyed to Canterbury with me, how the Huguenots had sheltered her but were afraid to go on doing so since my arrest, how I had promised to find her this coming night in the crypt.

"And bring her here?" He looked less outraged by the idea than I might have supposed.

"With Samuel away she would be well hidden. It is only until the assizes. Everything will be resolved then."

"I admire your optimism, Bruno. But by this you would make me an accessory to murder."

"She is not a murderer."

"You are chopping logic—she is a thief and a fugitive from justice, and that is a felony." He shifted in his chair and let out a despairing laugh. "It doesn't seem that I have any choice in the matter. I suppose I am already harbouring one suspected murderer—the more the merrier. Well then, Bruno, you had better find this evidence, or we may all end with a rope around our necks."

THE BELLS JOLTED me awake in an instant, so loud they seemed to make the walls vibrate, and I came to on the narrow bed in Harry's guest chamber, sitting up in all the disarray and confusion of interrupted sleep. I had only meant to lie down for a moment, but the bells must mean Evensong; I had no idea how long I had slept. Harry's voice floated indistinctly up the stairs, no doubt urging me to hurry. I dressed quickly, ran a comb through my hair, and hastened to join him.

The first fat drops of rain had begun to fall as we made our way at Harry's halting pace along the path to the south transept entrance. Overhead the clouds were swollen and heavy and the air was taut with heat and the salt wind, as if waiting for the one great cleansing burst that would discharge all the pent energy of the sky.

"One thing puzzles me," Harry said, holding his free hand ineffectually over his head against the rain. "Where did they mean to get another boy when the time came to stage their great miracle? Pluck one off the streets again?"

"Beggar children are easy enough to find in these times," I said.

"I'm not so sure. And how to persuade the people to take notice of this supposed death and resurrection? It pains me to say it, but the death of a street boy would hardly concern most of our good citizens. They would need someone of more significance. The boy in the legend was a noble's son."

"Perhaps the beggar boy and young Denis were just to test the dosage. My friend Doctor Dee used to keep mice in his laboratory for the same purpose. It was all the same to him whether he killed them in the course of his experiments. He used to say the pursuit of science took precedence." I felt my throat tighten at the thought of treating children in the same way.

"And they will test on more, according to what you heard Langworth say," Harry said, lowering his voice as we approached the door. "They will need to be certain of the mixture if they are not to ruin their public conjuring trick."

"All the more reason to stop them now."

We joined the line of townspeople entering the cathedral and I noted how they looked sidelong at me. Harry affected not to notice, though I knew he was sensitive about his reputation in the town. He led me to the right, up a wide flight of steps to the canons' stalls, which faced one another across the tiled floor of the quire. We shuffled into place beside the other canons, many of whom also regarded me with naked curiosity before turning to whisper to their neighbours, barely bothering to conceal the direction of their stares. I leaned forward and rested my clasped hands against the smooth wood of the seat in front as if praying. Candle flames danced inside their glass lanterns at intervals along the stalls, fugitive light scattered and duplicated by the curve of the casings, reflected back in the dark wood.

As the solemn clamour of the bells died away, a new sound echoed up to the stone vaults a hundred feet above us, a sweet and melancholy psalm sung in the fluting voices of the choirboys as they processed through the nave below us, the dean at their head carrying a silver cross on a stand. Though it was sung in English, there was such a comforting familiarity about the scene—these men in their black robes, heads bowed, the gentle light of the candles, the haunting polyphony of the boys' song—that for a moment I imagined myself back in the monastery of San Domenico Maggiore, and I was overcome by an unexpected surge of nostalgia, so that my throat constricted and I felt tears prick at the back of my eyes. Fool, I muttered to myself. I had not wanted the religious life—I had felt oppressed by it and begun to rebel against its constraints long before I was suspected of heresy—but at this moment I could not deny I missed the sense of community and of order it gave, the feeling of belonging to something greater than oneself. I pinched the bridge of my nose and blinked hard as the procession passed in front of us, reminding myself that the illusion of belonging is only ever skin-deep. This place is as riven with factions and backbiting as San Domenico and every other religious community I have known, I thought, idly watching the flushed faces of the boys as they walked solemnly onwards, lips pursed in song, obediently following the silver cross held aloft by Dean Rogers. As I watched, my eyes came to rest on a boy who seemed familiar. After a moment I realised he was the son of the Widow Gray, the boy I had seen that first day with Harry at the site of Thomas Becket's martyrdom. He was taller than his fellows and carried himself with unusual poise, head aloft as he sang, his gaze turned somehow inward as if he dwelt in some private world of his own. I jerked upright as an idea took shape and leaned across to dig Harry in the ribs, at the exact moment he turned to me and whispered, "Where is Langworth?"

THROUGH THE SILENCES of the service the rain could be heard gaining force against the high windows of the cathedral, lashing the panes so hard that the canons who ascended to the lectern to read aloud from the Scriptures had to raise their voices above it and the dean almost had to shout his address from the pulpit. The jewel colours of the glass flattened and dulled as the sky outside grew darker with the storm. Inside, the shadows lengthened and the candles seemed to glow brighter. Beside me, Harry curled and uncurled his fingers repeatedly over the carved top of his cane as he muttered the psalms and prayers by rote, never once taking his eyes off Langworth's empty seat in the stalls opposite.

I shared his foreboding about the treasurer's absence. Langworth was like a snake: less dangerous if you could keep him in view and move accordingly. The senior canons were all expected to attend divine service and my thoughts travelled downwards to the crypt below, where the French church would be celebrating their own service in their small chapel. With gritted teeth, I offered a silent prayer to whoever might be listening that Olivier had successfully smuggled Sophia into the crypt and that she would find a safe place to hide until the night. I only hoped that Langworth was not down there as well, prowling between the tombs as he had been the day I first met him, a silent guardian angel with black wings.

After the service was concluded, the dean hurried down the steps to the nave. Harry motioned to me to follow him and I held out my arm for him to balance as we descended towards the vast body of the cathedral, where the congregation were making their way to the west door, understandably in no great hurry to leave the shelter of the church for the sheeting rain outside.

Harry ushered me through the crowd in the direction of the door. I glanced up and by the entrance to a small oratory I saw the Widow Gray standing alone, elegant in her customary black gown, her hair bound up and her face veiled in black lace. I supposed she was waiting for her son. It was hard to tell under the veil where her eyes were focused, but as I continued to watch her she lifted the lace for a moment and met my look with a smile. I returned it with as much detachment as I could, though the exchange of glances did not escape Harry's sharp eyes.

"Would that the women still smiled at me that way," he murmured, with a gentle nudge to my ribs.

"Edward Kingsley made her a settlement in his will," I whispered. "Perhaps she received other payments from him. What if they had made some sort of bargain?"

Harry looked puzzled for a moment, then understanding lit up his face.

"You mean, for the boy?"

I nodded.

"He is of an age with those that were killed. Suppose he was intended for the miracle all along—they would have chosen boys of a similar age and build to ensure they had the dosage right. And the death of a gentlewoman's son would attract more attention in the town than that of a beggar boy."

Harry rubbed a hand over his chin and moved in still closer.

"You know some like to say the boy is Langworth's."

"Is it true?"

He shrugged.

"Perhaps there is a resemblance, but then once the thought has been put in your head you are primed to see it, no? But to sell your own child—" He broke off and looked past me with disgust to where the Widow Gray stood, aloof and a little fragile, silhouetted against the candles.

"Perhaps they assured her it was safe," I said. "She may not know how many other boys have died in preparation."

"May still die," Harry said ominously, a little too loudly, for we had reached the door by now and arrived within earshot of Dean Rogers, who looked up from shaking the hands of his congregation and twitched like a startled rabbit.

"Goodness—who may still die, Harry?" he said, with a tight little laugh.

"This wind," Harry said, pointing outside. Through the open door rain gusted in curtains so thick you could barely see the buildings opposite. People huddled in the porch, those who wore cloaks or jerkins drawing them up over their heads in readiness for stepping out into the downpour. "I was just saying this wind may still die down in time for us to walk home."

"Ah." The dean smiled, but it looked strained. "I hope you have not forgotten you are both dining with me tonight? If you want to make your way to the Archbishop's Palace, my steward will serve you drinks. I will join you when I have bid good night to my flock and locked up the crypt. It is but a short walk and there will be fires to dry your clothes," he added, seeing us hesitate at the prospect of a soaking.

"No sign of the canon treasurer tonight, then?" Harry said cheerfully, almost as if it was an afterthought.

"Alas, no. John received a rather distressed message earlier this evening from young Nicholas Kingsley. The son of our late magistrate," he added, turning to me.

"I have made his acquaintance," I murmured. The dean nodded.

"A wayward boy, I'm afraid. He is not coping at all well since his father's death, and as John was close to Sir Edward I think he feels an obligation to look out for the lad, offer him some guidance. So John is dining there tonight and sadly won't join us for supper. Still, I hope we will have lively company nonetheless." He beamed and I did my best to return the smile, though my skin prickled with unease. I exchanged a look with Harry. Langworth at St. Gregory's was bad news, but there was nothing we could do now if his purpose was to remove any evidence. I only hoped that old Meg was able to take care of herself.

Chapter *13*

The rain continued, unabated, long after darkness had fallen, relentless in its force, as if the heavens meant to compensate for the weeks of drought by unloading all their water at once. I lay awake on the truckle bed in Harry's spare room, listening to the torrents streaming from the eaves, pelting the roof above me like pebbles thrown in endless handfuls. Through the open casement I could smell wet earth and something metallic in the charged air. I stretched and clenched my fingers repeatedly, waiting until I could be sure all the residents of the cathedral close were sleeping; my nerves were taut, my mind as alert as if it were morning.

Supper at the dean's had been a tedious affair, despite the quality of the food and the undoubted beauty of the dining room in the Archbishop's Palace. The canons talked in wearisome detail of cathedral business and regarded me—when they bothered to acknowledge me at all—with an air of suspicion that bordered on outright contempt; apart from the dean, who interrogated me about my life in London and who else I knew of any standing at court, barely bothering to disguise the fact that his whole interest in me was in seeing what influence I might be placed to exert on his behalf in London, once the awkward business of the assizes had been dealt with. The food was excellent and I gathered that the dean and his circle of friends and colleagues dined like this as a matter of course; I could see why Walsingham might resent the resources tied up in furnishing this small group of well-educated clerics with the comfortable life of gentlemen. I was conscious that the dean was giving me an opportunity to ingratiate myself with the other canons and to counter some of the gossip they may have heard about me; I appreciated the thought, but I was too preoccupied with the coming night to be good company and I was relieved when Harry, perhaps sensing my discomfort, declared himself to be too tired to stay for port and pipes and asked me if I would accompany him home through the rain.

Now I moved to the window and looked out across the darkened close. The night was still hot, despite the storm, and the rain seemed to rise again from the ground, misting the air with moisture. The cathedral was a dense black shape solid as a fortress against the inky clouds chasing across the sky behind its towers. There was no sign of life on the ground and no light to be seen at any window. The world was silent except for the insistent drumming of the rain and the hiss of water running down stone. I doubted whether Tom Garth or the watchman would be abroad in this weather, but I would have to take my chances. Somewhere under that vast dark church, Sophia was waiting for me.

I descended as quietly as I could manage, pausing on each creaking stair and hoping I had not woken Harry. Before he retired to bed he had left a pair of new candles and a tinderbox for me on the buffet in the front parlour, and I now tucked these inside the black doublet I wore over my shirt. With black breeches, I hoped I would not be visible as I moved around the precincts; I could keep close to the cathedral wall and hope to blend into the shadows. From the corner of my eye I half glimpsed a movement and turned to see Harry in the doorway in his nightshirt, his white hair even wilder than usual.

"Sorry to startle you." He held up what looked like a black cloth. "Take my cloak. It'll keep the rain off and you'll be less recognisable if you wear the cowl up."

I breathed out, aware again of how on edge I was. Even Harry's unexpected appearance had set my pulse racing in my throat.

"Thank you." I pulled the cloak around my shoulders and drew the hood over my head. In the purse at my belt I carried the copies of Langworth's keys and my bone-handled knife was tucked into my boot.

"I don't like this at all, Bruno, but we are in so deep now that our only hope is to turn up solid evidence against Langworth and his fellow conspirators. If there is something hidden in that crypt, you had better find it. And without getting caught. If you are found breaking into the treasury it will hardly help the case for your innocence." He sighed, and clapped me on the shoulder. "Godspeed."

I thanked him and opened the door into the storm.

IT WAS IMPOSSIBLE to see more than a few feet ahead and I had to move slowly as my eyes adjusted to the darkness. Rain clouds obscured the moon, though the clouds themselves seemed lit from behind by a violet storm light. Surely, I thought, if any watchman was out on a night like this he would have to carry a lantern, which would give me warning of his presence so that I could slip into the shadow of a buttress or outbuilding; without a light myself, I was unlikely to be noticed in this weather. I stumbled as far as Harry's front gate and paused there, grateful for the hooded cloak which kept the worst of the rain out of my face. When I was sure that all was quiet, I ran as fast as I could across the open path and into the shelter of the cathedral wall. Keeping close to the wet stone, I crept forward through the gate and past the timber yard until I rounded the corona at the eastern end. Here I felt my blood quicken again; I now had to pass the row of houses that ran parallel to the north side of the cathedral, and to reach the treasury I would have to walk right by Langworth's front door. I had no way of knowing whether he had returned or stayed overnight with Nicholas Kingsley, but I was certain that if he was at home and heard any suspicious sound near the treasury he would not hesitate to investigate.

I edged around the curve of the corona until I could see the outline of the row of houses opposite. All the windows were dark; the rain continued to beat down, obscuring any sound. My steps were muted by the wet earth of the path. Just as I was almost on the north side of the apse, an almighty crack exploded overhead and for the space of a heartbeat the whole sky flared into a brilliant white light, leaving me outlined against the stone wall as starkly as if it were noon. The thunder grumbled on for a few moments longer and eventually died away, as I pressed into the corner by a buttress, chest heaving, legs trembling with shock. The rain seemed to attack even more fiercely as I tried to slow my breathing and recover my composure. If the heart of the storm was now upon us, I had to move fast; every sheet of lightning would illuminate me as if I were on a stage.

Before the next burst, I quickened my pace, trying to keep all my senses alert through the torrents of water now streaming from the cowl of Harry's cloak. I passed Langworth's house with a shudder, glancing up nervously at the dark windows, but I could see nothing except rain and shadows. I was relieved when I turned the corner around the chapel that jutted out and found myself on the path between the library and the cathedral and out of sight of any residential houses, with the treasury on my left.

Here between the buildings it was pitch-black. I felt my way along the wall to the carved stone of the shallow porch. The rain was beginning to soak through Harry's cloak and the first rivulets were trickling down my neck as I fumbled at my belt for the bunch of keys. But I could not find the latch and my fingers scrabbled frantically across the pitted wood of the door, slick with rainwater streaming down its surface, as I searched for the keyhole, cursing under my breath. It was only at the moment of another apocalyptic crack overhead, accompanied by a flash that lit the scene in its strange bluish glare, that I was able to see clearly enough to insert the first key. Prompted by some instinctive unease, I

glanced quickly over my shoulder and thought for a moment I saw a figure outlined against the archway that led through to the cloister, someone dressed like me in a hooded cloak. I froze, all my senses prickling,
straining for any sound over the dying rumble of thunder and the con-
stant battering of the rain, but no movement came. The lightning had
lasted only a fraction of a moment and I told myself it must have been my
fevered imagination, seeing shapes in shadows. The second key I tried
fitted the lock and turned smoothly, and I gave a small exclamation of
triumph as the treasury door opened to me with a portentous creak.

I dropped back the dripping hood of Harry's cloak and took out one
of the candles tucked into my doublet. Here inside the building was only
the silence and the peculiar musty smell of damp stone; in the chill I
shivered as I struggled to strike the tinder. After some efforts I had the
candle lit, and holding it up could see that I was in a stark, high-ceilinged
room, with a stone floor and walls, unadorned except for the shelves
of ledgers and scrolls neatly arranged under the windows. There were
two broad desks standing at right angles to each other in one corner
and to the left of these, a low wooden door set into the wall. I turned
slowly, shielding the flame with my hand, searching the walls and floor
for some evidence of an opening to the vault I had seen marked on the
map. If the map was right, the vault was built under the treasury and
connected with the crypt through its southern wall. So the entrance
should be somewhere along the wall of the treasury that backed onto
the cathedral, to my right. As I walked, I could hear the drip of water
from the cloak's hem and the sound of my wet boots on the flagstones; I
had to hope the trail would dry quickly or it would be immediately clear
that an intruder had entered.

The southern wall of the treasury held no bookshelves; instead there
was a wide brick-lined fireplace. I leaned in and attempted to look up
the flue, but the candle's light was too feeble to illuminate much beyond
my own height. Looking down, I saw that the hearth had been carefully swept; it was clearly some time since a fire had been lit there. The
entrance to the vaults had to be concealed somewhere inside the fire-

place; I could see no other place that would make sense. It was just a question of finding it. Crouching, I moved farther in and began to press my fingers along the brickwork. On the right-hand side, I thought I felt a seam that suggested the outline of a doorway, but in that light it was impossible to see. I continued to push at the bricks with no success and a growing anxiety. If I could not find the entrance to the vault, there was no way of reaching Sophia before the dean came to open up the crypt in the morning, and even if I did locate it, the night was short—I still had to find Sophia and get her back to Harry's before dawn crept across the sky, and that was without the task I had set myself of searching for Becket's bones.

I took a deep breath to calm my racing pulse; if I allowed my fears to overcome me now I would not be able to think clearly and everything would be forfeit. As I tried to settle my thoughts, another burst of thunder exploded like cannonfire above me, rattling around the walls, as the lightning whitewashed the room so that all was hard-edged light and shadow, and in that moment there flashed before me on the stage of my memory the image of another such brick wall, in a house I had seen in Oxfordshire. There a concealed entrance had been built on a pivot operated by pressing one of the flagstones on the floor. Hopeful again, I half stood so that I could try the same here by pushing my weight onto my heel. Nothing happened. Gathering all my determination, I tried the same with the next flagstone along and heard a distinctive click, as the wall I was leaning on shifted almost imperceptibly. I pressed against it with my shoulder and the wall swung soundlessly inwards on its hinges, more lightly and easily than I had expected; the outward layer of brick was just to disguise a wooden door panel that had been built into the fireplace. In front of me the candle illuminated a flight of spiral steps curving downwards into darkness. With great relief, and no small sense of triumph, I began my descent, pulling the doorway closed behind me.

So this was Langworth's secret vault that allowed him into the crypt unseen, I thought, as I felt my way down the narrow stairs. That first day when he had appeared to Harry and me as if from one of the tombs, he must have come through this entrance. With his house positioned almost next to the treasury, it would be easy for him to visit the crypt at night, unseen by any of the other residential canons. The door in the fireplace had opened smoothly, as if it was well-used. I guessed that Langworth must visit his hidden treasure frequently.

The staircase opened out into an underground vault that was perhaps half the size of the treasury building above, dank with the smell of mould. I reached out to the wall to guide myself and my fingertips met something cold and slimy. I recoiled in haste, and held the candle up to see dark green moss growing on the stones. At intervals iron rings were fixed into the stone, rusting and leaving an orange-brown trail that bled into the green. I recalled that the map said the place had once been used as a prison. I shuddered to think of it, and thought of the frayed rope in the underground tomb at St. Gregory's, where those poor boys must have been kept while Sykes carried out his experiments on them as if they were no more than mice. I determined that, for the sake of those children, I would find the evidence to convict Langworth and Sykes and make sure no more boys had to see the inside of that tomb.

Opposite the staircase was a low iron-clad door; locked, naturally, though as I had hoped the last untried key of Langworth's fitted and turned stiffly. The door opened inward and I slipped through into another dark space, where almost immediately I walked into a solid object so unexpectedly that I nearly dropped the candle. Fortunately I managed not to exclaim aloud, and held the flame up so that I could see a wooden panel some eight feet high fitted over the niche where the door to the vault entered the crypt to conceal the entrance. A few moments of impatient searching revealed a latch hidden on the inside of the panel; when pressed, it swung outward on its hinges, allowing me to pass into what I now realised was one of the small chantry chapels of the crypt. I pushed the panel shut behind me. In the wavering light I saw that the side facing outwards showed a handsome painting of the Nativity—and stepped forward into the dark.

In the depths of the night, the empty crypt with its forest of columns and endlessly repeating arches seemed more menacing than before, and more vast. After a few steps I paused to get my bearings, alert for any sound that would betray the presence of another person, but all I could hear was the rasp of my own breathing and the intermittent rumble of thunder from outside, sounding far distant, as if I were hearing it from underwater. As I advanced, I realised I was parallel with the small altar I had seen on my first visit, the one that lay at the heart of the crypt, flanked by stone tombs. Was Becket hidden somewhere here? I moved closer until the candlelight caught the silver crucifix in the centre of the altar cloth. I picked it up and weighed it in my right hand. Though the cross itself was no more than eighteen inches high, the base was square and solid and certainly heavy enough to crack a man's skull if brought down with sufficient force.

I tried to picture that night: Sir Edward Kingsley walking back from the Archbishop's Palace on the north side of the cathedral, towards Langworth's house. Someone waiting in the shadows as he passed the treasury building; a step forward, and a single blow to the back of the head would have been enough to fell him, but it would have been growing dark. Whoever struck him must have been very sure of his aim. And then, according to the reports, the killer had continued to bludgeon Kingsley as he lay there, until his skull was almost destroyed and his brains spilled over the ground like the cathedral's famous martyr. A murder fuelled by hatred or vengeance, not merely the need to dispatch someone because they presented an inconvenience. Or at least made to appear that way. I looked down at the crucifix, puzzled. A tall strong man like Tom Garth might wield such an object efficiently as a weapon, but how would Tom have smuggled it out of the crypt before the dean locked up for the night?

I thought I heard a noise beyond me, somewhere in the eastern end of the crypt. Replacing the crucifix, I moved as quickly as the darkness allowed towards the part that Langworth had made sure to tell us was cordoned off and used for storage. Now that I remembered that encounter, it seemed to me obvious that he was deliberately directing us away from that part of the crypt; here, then, I would begin my search.

At the eastern end the crypt appeared to open up, the ceiling vaults were higher and the broad stone columns gave way to delicate pillars, spaced more widely and made—I noticed as I drew nearer—of a glossy polished marble. The floor was piled with chests, wooden crates, and the skeletal outlines of broken furniture. There were small chapels built off to each side and they too were filled with unwanted or forgotten items. It was from one of these that I heard the sound again; a kind of scratching, like the movements of a rat. I held up the candle; its flame was burning lower now, elongating as I tilted it to avoid the hot wax dripping down my wrist.

"Sophia?"

No response; just the scratching noise again.

"Are you here? It is I." I moved closer to the source of the noise, tripping as I did so on some box I had not seen, sending it into a pile of crates with a terrifying clatter. "*Merda!*" I stooped to rub my injured toe and heard a muffled laugh from the far corner of the chapel. "Where are you, damn it?"

"Bruno? Is it really you?"

From the mass of objects heaped up by the disused altar, a shape detached itself and approached, picking its way carefully through the debris. Bundled into a bulky cloak, the figure stopped in front of me and drew back its hood.

I swear she had never looked more beautiful to me; the sweet relief on her face when she saw me, after what must have been hours of fear alone in the dark; her fragility in that moment, the tears that sprang involuntarily to her eyes as they searched my face. Was that the moment when I knew I loved her, and would do whatever it took to make her love me? Perhaps; all I know is that when she threw herself on me and clung around my neck as if she would never let go, I felt I would have willingly endured any amount of time in that filthy gaol cell for the glory of feeling how much she needed me in that moment.

"Oh God, Bruno, I thought you would never come," she murmured against my neck, and then a great sob welled up within her and erupted into my shoulder.

I felt her thin shoulders shaking as she gave vent to the tension and fear that must have been building during her hours of hiding in the darkness, not knowing who would find her first. I held her until her silent cries subsided as she pressed herself fiercely against me, and I don't remember how it happened but suddenly her open mouth found mine and I was kissing her as I had once kissed her in Oxford, but this time she did not pull away. Instead she responded, as hot and hungry as I, knotting her fingers into the hair at the back of my neck to pull me closer; I felt the wetness of the tears on her face and the wetness of her mouth, and I was still holding the candle precariously away from us in my right hand, my arm outstretched, while with my left I scrabbled at the fastening of her cloak. As it fell to the floor I pulled at the strings that held the bodice of the rough dress she wore underneath and slipped it from one shoulder; she arched backwards with a soft moan as I bent my head to take her small breast in my mouth, and at that moment I heard, unmistakably, the sound of footsteps on stone.

We froze. It was Sophia who reacted first, while I stood, helpless, dazed by desire; she blew out the candle and grabbed at her cloak, pulling me by the other hand back to her hiding place behind the altar. But I was afraid we had made enough sound to draw the attention of whoever was down here. Sophia sank to the floor, her back against the altar; I felt her trembling beside me. Trying to regain my wits and silence my ragged breath, I shuffled into a position where, by craning my neck, I could just about see through the piles of boxes into the main body of the crypt. The wavering light of a lantern crept along the floor. I slid a hand into my boot and drew out my knife.

The footsteps grew closer, then stopped, as if the person was looking around. After a few moments the light moved away a little distance. Perhaps he had not heard us after all and was searching another part of the crypt. I continued to move cautiously towards the entrance to the chapel. From here I could see that it was Langworth, his gaunt black figure outlined against the glow of the lamp, pacing slowly, turning, his right hand held out before him holding something—what? He turned again and I saw it clearly; he had a dagger too. My stomach tightened; I would wager he knew how to use it. He paused, seeming to sniff the air like a dog and I froze, expecting that at any moment he would turn in my direction with his light and see me crouching on the threshold of the chapel. But instead his behaviour was more curious. He stopped between two of the delicate marble columns and genuflected, making the sign of the cross before kneeling with his back to me and lowering his face close to the stone floor, as if he was examining it. He set the lantern on the ground beside him and pressed both hands to the stones, feeling his way along. I watched him for a moment, intrigued, before I realised this was my best chance.

Rousing myself, I leapt to my feet and ran towards him. His head jerked up at the sound but he was not quick enough and I hurled myself at his kneeling form, throwing him to the ground. He lashed out with his dagger as I did so, catching me along the length of my left forearm, but in an instant I had my own knife to his throat and I grasped his wrist with my other hand, forcing him to drop his weapon.

"What will you do, Giordano Bruno—murder me here, on hallowed ground?" he hissed, as I pressed his head against the cold stone. "You think even your puppet master Walsingham could protect you from the consequences of that?"

"Did you think twice before you murdered in a place of sanctuary?"

He let out a hollow laugh, though it emerged strangled by the angle of his head. I had him pinned facedown against the stones, one hand holding his head, the other keeping my knife point at his throat, yet I had the strange sensation that he was not afraid of me.

"I have killed no one," he said, with remarkable calm.

"What about Edward Kingsley?"

Again, that sardonic laugh, as if my ignorance amused him.

"Edward Kingsley was my friend. I am the very last person who would have had an interest in his death. In fact, it has caused me nothing but inconvenience. And sorrow, naturally," he added, as an afterthought. "The only person whose blood I should not be sorry to have on my hands is yours."

"You are very free with your threats for a man with a knife to his throat," I said, nettled.

"You will not kill me. You cannot. You must present me to Walsingham alive so that I can be questioned in the Tower, is it not so? We both know you would not be forgiven for destroying such a valuable source of information. Besides, you need someone to answer for Kingsley's murder at the assizes or his wife cannot be found innocent, and that is your whole purpose here, is it not?" The scar at the edge of his lips curved into a lascivious smirk. "I have no intention of letting you hand me to the queen's torturers, by the way. Henry Howard warned me you were slippery, but I have allies in this town and you have none."

I took a deep breath, keeping my knife steady. He was right; I could not kill him, here or anywhere, and if I hurt him it would only strengthen the case against me at the coming trial. I dug my knee harder into his back and he winced sharply, but would not give me the satisfaction of crying out.

"Where is Thomas Becket?" I hissed in his ear.

"Dead and gone," he said, but I noticed his eyes flicker towards the place he had just been examining.

"You lie."

By way of answer he laughed softly. My patience snapped; transferring my knife to my left hand, I hooked my right arm around his throat so that his Adam's apple fitted in the crook of my elbow and began to squeeze gently. The movement took him by surprise and he tried to cry out but I was already crushing the breath from him. I could feel my arm trembling as I increased the pressure; I had learned this trick in Rome, where I had also learned that if you misjudge the timing by even a heartbeat it can be fatal. In barely a moment, Langworth's eyes began to bulge and cloud over and his body went limp under me. I lowered him to the floor and tucked my knife away, heart thudding against my ribs. When I looked up, Sophia was standing beside me, her eyes wide with fear.

"Christ's blood, Bruno, have you killed him?"

"I hope not." I reached under Langworth's slumped form and pressed my hand to his chest. At first I feared my gamble had not paid off, but after a moment's groping I found the faint flutter of his heart. "No, thank God. He has passed out, but I don't know how long before he comes round. We have to work quickly. Take this." I handed her Langworth's lantern. "See if there is anything stored in that side chapel we could use as a lever."

I took the tinderbox and my spare candle from inside my doublet. When it was alight, I melted a little wax on the floor and stood the candle upright. Though the light was poor, I could make out traces on the flagstones where Langworth had been kneeling, the outline of an oblong shape where the stone felt of a different texture. He had made the sign of the cross here; his piety had given him away.

There was a narrow gap between the flagstones and I tried to prise one by inserting my fingers but it was too heavy. Impatiently, I watched Langworth's face for flickers of life as I waited for Sophia to return. After a moment she appeared, triumphant, holding a rusting shovel in one hand and the light in the other.

"Better than I had hoped," I said, taking the shovel from her. I inserted the digging edge under the flagstone, hoping it was not so fragile that it would snap with the weight. But the stone lifted easily, as if it was used to being moved. I motioned to Sophia to bring the lantern closer and my heart sank; in the cavity I could see only rubble.

"There might be something beneath that," she said.

Kneeling, she began to scrape away the loose covering of stones and earth. I leaned in to join her, one eye still on Langworth, until eventually she gave a small cry.

"I can feel a sharp corner here," she whispered. I brought the lantern in close and she brushed away the dirt with her hand; there, only a foot beneath the surface, was the edge of what looked like a marble coffin.

"We need to get up the other flagstones," I said. I worked quickly; though the stones were heavy, I barely felt the weight of them as I lifted them and Sophia helped me to brush away the rubble hiding the box beneath. When we had cleared enough to see, I sat back on my haunches and surveyed what we had uncovered. A marble coffer, but not sufficiently long or wide to contain the body of an adult man. Unmarked, unadorned in any way. Sweat prickled on the back of my neck and the palms of my hands. Somewhere overhead, thunder boomed and died away, more distant than before.

"Help me with this lid," I hissed through my teeth. I moved to one end and she grasped the other. I nodded and we both lifted together and almost fell backwards; the slab covering the coffer was not attached in any way and was much lighter than I had expected. We shifted it to one side and I knelt to examine what lay beneath.

As I looked, a strange frisson shook me the length of my body, and I felt my hands trembling. I had long ago left behind the Catholic faith and its rituals of saints and relics, but some dormant instinct prickled with awe at what I saw before me. At one end of the coffer was a raised stone square and placed carefully upon it, as if on a pillow, lay a human skull. Surrounding the skull were the remaining bones of the skeleton, arranged in three sides of a square. The body had evidently been moved to this place when the bones were all that remained. I did not dare touch them, though I could see they were very old—perhaps centuries old. But what caused the hairs on my arms and the back of my neck to stand up was the gaping hole at the back of the skull where a killing blow had broken away the crown of this man's head. I exhaled slowly, hearing the shudder in my breath, and looked up to meet Sophia's stare.

"Is it him?" she asked, her voice barely a whisper. "Is it Becket?"

"It could be. Certainly it looks as if people believe it's him, and that is all a relic ever is. For their purposes, that is all that matters."

"It is absurd to believe that old bones have any power," Sophia said, with a scornful frown. "Superstitious nonsense of old women."

"And yet, sometimes it seems to work. It's almost as if it is the belief itself that is powerful." I reached out and touched the top of the skull with my fingertips. "In Italy I once witnessed what you might call a miracle. A merchant's wife healed of a wasting sickness by a vial of the holy blood."

"So you believe in it?" She looked sceptical.

"Not in the relics, no. I think that somehow she cured herself simply by having faith that she would be healed. It is the human mind and will that have the ability to effect miracles—one day I should like to study this further. Our minds have untold power if we only knew how to harness it. But we haven't much time. Look at this—" I leaned forward; at the far end of the stone coffer, separate from the skeleton, there were more objects buried. I shone the light over bulky shapes wrapped in oil-cloth to protect them from decay and damp. Sophia took the lantern as I lifted the first item out and unwrapped it. I held up an ampulla of smoky glass, about the size of my hand, round and plain with a long neck and a handle on each side. It was full of a pale liquid; I pulled out the stopper and sniffed, but it had little odour, save for a slight stale, greasy smell. I tipped the ampulla and touched a drop to my finger; some sort of oil, certainly. The ampulla looked like the sort used by priests.

"What do you think this is? Chrism, perhaps? Do they say the Mass down here over the bones?"

Sophia tilted her head to one side and looked at the ampulla.

"There is a legend—I heard my husband speak of it once. The holy oil of Saint Thomas. In the story it was given to Thomas Becket by the Virgin, to anoint the true king of England. Then it was supposedly lost for centuries and found again hidden in a secret chest in the Tower. The legend says the last English sovereign to have been anointed with it at her coronation was Bloody Mary, Queen Elizabeth's half sister."

"The last Catholic monarch of England," I mused. "Who was married to Philip of Spain—that makes sense. 'King Philip entrusts to the servants of the blessed saint his holy oil in readiness,'" I recited, recalling the words of Mendoza's letter. "So they not only believe they have Becket himself, they also have his holy oil to give divine approval to England's next Catholic king or queen." I shook my head, half in admiration. "They have thought of everything. This might all have fallen into place if the invasion had succeeded last autumn."

A small moan came from my left; Sophia and I froze, staring at Langworth, but it appeared he had only made an involuntary noise exhaling. Nevertheless, we could not waste any more time. I wrapped the ampulla in its covering again and replaced it, then pulled out the last object hidden in the coffer and extracted it from its oilskin. As I brought it into the light, I experienced such a jolt of recognition and disbelief that I felt I had been struck by lightning; my heart and my breath seemed to stop, my brain swam, and I was forced to sit back quickly on the floor of the crypt, my prize held in my lap, for fear I would fall down in a faint.

In my hands was a carved wooden casket, its surface traced with elaborate designs of geometric patterns all inlaid with gold. I had seen this box before, in the secret chapel of Lord Henry Howard. With trembling hands, I lifted the lid, hardly daring to hope . . .

Inside the casket was a linen cloth, and inside the cloth, carefully protected, a book; small, about the size of a personal prayer book, with worn calfskin bindings. It had board covers holding together manuscript pages that were warped with age, though—as far as I could see in that light—the closely written Greek characters remained clear and bold. The book was not remarkable for its rich illustrations—it had none—nor for the sumptuous decorations of its binding. At first glance it would be of little interest to an antiquary or collector, since there was no obvious value in its shabby exterior. But I knew what this book was; I knew why Henry Howard had sent his nephew the Earl of Arundel to deliver it into Langworth's hands for safekeeping before the queen's searchers ransacked his house, and I also—together with only a handful of other men in Christendom—knew its true value. This book was the gem I had been searching for since I first learned of its existence some years before from an old Italian bookbinder in Paris. It seemed ironic, given its content, that the safest place Langworth could think of to hide it was in the coffin of the holiest relics in England.

"Are you all right, Bruno?" Sophia said, holding up the lantern. "You look as if you've seen a vision."

I put the book quickly into its casket and tucked it inside my doublet. "We have to get out before he wakes. Quick—help me with this."

We shifted the coffer's lid back into place with some effort and scraped the loose covering of rubble over it. The flagstones made an almighty crash as we dropped them back into place, but Langworth still did not stir, though it was with some relief that I caught the sound of his effortful breathing rasping beside us. I knew that I was risking my life in taking the book; Langworth could not publicly accuse me of theft without revealing the secret of Becket's bones, but after tonight he might decide it was more efficient to dispose of me without waiting for the process of the assizes.

I left the treasurer's lantern burning low beside his prostrate form; holding the last candle, I picked up Harry's cloak, grabbed Sophia's wrist, and led her as quickly as possible—stopping only to pick up the old woman's cloak she had worn as her disguise—back through the crypt to the vault below the treasury and out into the cathedral precincts.

The storm had spent the worst of its energy and was rolling away towards the sea, leaving behind a thin rain that seemed to ripple in silver sheets across the grounds. I pulled up the hood of my cloak to hide my face and Sophia did the same with hers. With no light, we felt our way around the corona and were poised to make the dash across the exposed part of the cathedral close to Harry's house.

"I think it's clear," I whispered to Sophia, peering into the misty darkness. "Take my hand—as fast as we can now."

I had run barely three steps when I felt Sophia's hand slip from my grasp; an arm hooked around my throat and jerked my head back and I was thrown face forward onto the wet ground.

Chapter *14*

The fall knocked the breath out of me for a moment and as I hit the ground I heard a sharp crack, accompanied by a pain in my side; I hoped it was the wooden casket I was carrying that had broken and not my ribs. As my face smacked into wet grass, my only confused thought was that Langworth must have recovered quicker than I could have imagined and had some other secret exit from the crypt that had allowed him to attack us on the way home. But the man now pinning me to the ground was too solid to be the treasurer, the arm that now tightened under my chin too meaty.

"Let's see who we have here then, sneaking around in the dead of night," said Tom Garth's voice.

I tried to lift my head and protest but he was holding me too tight and when I tried to speak no sound came. I was afraid he might choke me by accident, not knowing his own strength—a fitting retribution, I could not help thinking, after what I had done to Langworth—but just as I was beginning to see flashing lights before my eyes I heard Sophia say, calmly, "Let him go."

Tom released his grip on my neck and lifted his weight from my torso; I gulped air desperately and tried to twist my head to see what gave her the confidence to command such a large man with such apparent coolness. In the dark and the mist I could only make out that she was holding a hand out towards his throat.

"All right—put the knife away," he grumbled, moving off me entirely.

I sat up and almost laughed. Was Sophia brandishing the little knife I had told her was good only for peeling fruit? If so, I had to admire her spirit. Presumably Tom could only feel the edge of the blade on his skin; if the light had been better, he might have seen how ineffectual her weapon would be. Quickly I checked inside my doublet to see that the casket was still safe, then struggled to my feet, drew my own knife, and held it out, at the same time lifting back my hood.

"Tom. We will not harm you if you promise the same."

"By the cross!" He sat back on his haunches and peered through the rain at me. "Master Savolino—what in the Devil's name are you doing? And who is this?" He gestured at Sophia, who stepped away, pulling her cloak closer around her face. Fortunately there was not light enough for him to see her clearly; he jumped to his own conclusions and gave a low laugh. "A whore, is it? Well, you would not be the first of the clergy to use them, but inside the cathedral grounds? That *is* bold. I fear it is my duty as gatekeeper to report that." He paused, as if weighing up his options. "Tell you what—I might be persuaded to keep my mouth shut if she would give me a little something for my trouble . . ."

I sighed. "Tom, you and I must talk—"

But I was cut short by Sophia, who flew at him like a wildcat, spitting and scratching, forgetting in her fury that she was supposed to be here in secret.

"Call me a whore, would you? Call me it to my face then, coward!"

Taken by surprise, Tom raised his hands to shield himself from her flailing nails. I jumped up to try and pull her off him and in the struggle her hood fell back, just as a weak flash of lightning jagged through the clouds, illuminating her face for an instant like a figure in a stained-glass window. Tom gasped in disbelief.

"By Saint Thomas! Mistress Kingsley! But you were supposed to be gone . . ."

"Supposed to be?" I leaned forward, my knife closer to his face, and spoke through my teeth. "You mean you *wanted* her to escape?"

Tom looked up at me, his face twisted in fear.

"It wasn't me—" he began.

"Wasn't you? Not you who took a pair of your sister's gloves, cut your own hand to cover them in blood, and left them where they would be found the morning after you killed Sir Edward Kingsley?"

"What proof do you have?"

"Only your mother's word."

"My mother lost her wits years back. All Canterbury knows it." His voice was strained.

"Oh, I think your mother is quite clearheaded in many ways, especially when it comes to her daughter's possessions. She would recognise those gloves in an instant. And you told the constable you did not see Mistress Kingsley leave the precincts after divine service, did you not?"

"It wasn't me who killed him!" His voice lurched up in pitch and I hissed at him to keep quiet; we were not far from some of the canons' residences and it would only compound the night's misfortunes if one of them should be roused by our voices and come out to investigate. "You have to believe me." He glanced frantically from me to Sophia, the whites of his eyes gleaming in the darkness. "I can explain."

"Let us get out of the rain, then." I lowered the knife cautiously but he made no threatening move. I sensed that he was more afraid of me than I of him, which I must use to my advantage for as long as I could.

"There is a lean-to just around the corner by the timber yard," he said, more quietly. "We can talk in there."

Keeping ourselves pressed against the stone of the cathedral, we felt our way around the jutting buttresses until we reached the shelter of a small wooden hut next to the stacks of timber. A few workmen's tools hung on nails from the central roof beam and I moved preemptively to snatch up the axe, not wishing to leave anything to chance. Tom saw and gave a bitter laugh as he seated himself on a pile of planks.

"You think I would strike you down? I could not kill a man in cold blood, master, though I have often wished I could. I'll tell you this much—I envy whoever did kill that bastard. May God forgive me, but if I'd been a different man, I'd have loved to hear the sound of his skull smashing open."

"And I," Sophia said, with feeling, and in the darkness I sensed rather than saw that they looked at each other with something like under-standing.

"Why should I believe you did not? When you went to such lengths to make sure his wife would be blamed?" I kept my tone deliberately hard; though I still struggled to believe that the gatekeeper really did murder Sir Edward, I had to get at the truth with the cold detachment of an inquisitor. I could not afford to let him see that I sympathised with him. Besides, I reminded myself, he would have been willing to let Sophia burn for a murder she did not commit.

"I panicked," he said, and his voice cracked. "When they found him, I knew I would be the first suspect. I was inside the precincts that night, and everyone knew I hated him. Not without good reason," he added. "The constable asked me a lot of questions and I answered them honestly, but he has a way of needling people and I knew he was working up to accusing me. I was afraid I would condemn myself by mistake—I had to do something to point the finger elsewhere. Then I thought that I'd seen Mistress Kingsley earlier coming in for divine service and leaving alone. So in all the confusion I slipped away home and took our Sarah's gloves—may she rest in peace—and, as you say, I bloodied them and left them where the constable was sure to find them first thing when he came back to search further in daylight."

I sighed. It was hard to believe that he was not sincere.

"You didn't care that Mistress Kingsley could have been burned alive for it?"

"But it was me that told Meg, the housekeeper, that Mistress Kingsley was under suspicion," he protested. "I hoped that would give her the chance to escape, and so I thought it had. I supposed everyone's problems would have been solved."

"Forcing an innocent woman to become a fugitive with a price on her head is hardly solving her problems," I said.

"You say that. But I know what Sir Edward Kingsley was," Tom said, with quiet contempt. "Going on the run might be better than living with him."

"In a sense you are not wrong," Sophia agreed. I shot her a look to suggest she was not helping, but it was lost in the dark.

"For God's sake, do not tell the dean, sir," Tom said, turning to me and clutching blindly at my cloak. I could not see his expression but I heard the urgency in his words. "I cannot afford to lose this job. My mother—well, you have seen her, I suppose. She depends on me. And suspicion will fall on me doubly." He stopped and sucked in a ragged breath, as if he were battling a sob. "I'm handy with my fists sometimes, but I could not kill a man," he repeated quietly. "Not even him, who did so wrong by my poor sister. I no more killed him than you killed the apothecary."

I laid a hand on his arm.

"I believe you. It seems that we must become the keepers of one another's secrets, Tom. Listen—I am doing my utmost to find out who did kill Sir Edward by the time the assize judge arrives. If I succeed, you will be free of suspicion and so will Mistress Kingsley. In the meantime, then, you will say nothing to anyone of her presence here. Swear it."

"On my oath," he said solemnly. In the silence, rain dripped steadily from the eaves of the shelter.

I glanced up at Sophia, who was no more than a shadow outlined among other shadows, her eyes and teeth pale in the dark. "We should not waste time. It will be getting light soon. One last question," I said, standing stiffly and turning back to Tom.

"Yes?"

"If you needed someone to blame for the murder, why did you not accuse Nicholas Kingsley? You had a grudge against him too, and he came to the cathedral precincts that night, so you said?"

"So he did. I tried to keep him out—he was drunk, of course—but he swore blind his father had sent for him and he must be let in. In the end I thought he would only make a fool of himself, interrupting the dean's supper table. As it happened, the dean's steward would not admit him and he came back to the gatehouse barely ten minutes later, raging under his breath."

"And had his father sent for him?"

"How should I know? I doubt it. But I knew he'd have gone back to his friends at the alehouse and any number of people would see him there so it would never stick if I'd tried to say it was him. Besides"—he sucked in another great shuddering breath—"I have seen how that goes. Someone like me, up against someone like Nick Kingsley, with all his father's powerful friends. And I wouldn't even have the truth on my side this time. Whereas with a woman . . ." He left the thought unfinished.

"Lower even than a gatekeeper," Sophia said scornfully, looking down at him from under her hood.

There was a noise; a sudden crack that jolted us all from our thoughts and made us glance around, startled, nerves bristling. It was nothing to fear; Tom had leaned too hard against a pile of logs and his weight had caused them to shift, one falling slightly against another. But the sound had reminded us of the danger of our being caught. I reached for Sophia's arm in the dark.

"Let us leave. Tom—I rely on your silence, as you may rely on mine."

"You have my word, Master Savolino."

I led Sophia through the wet grass to the shelter of the wall beside the middle gate. To our right, the ink-blue of the night sky was shading to a pale violet above the rooftops in the east; the pitch-blackness of the precincts was giving way to a haze of grey shadows. We ran across the open path to Harry's front gate, hand in hand, cloaks pulled tight over our faces and I still clutching the box inside my clothes hard to my ribs, through the curtains of drizzle until I was able to fumble open the front door and we fell damply, breathing hard, into the entrance hall and the door was closed behind us against the night. We paused there, listening for any sound or movement, but there was only the creaking of the old timbers and the patter of the rain on the glass. Sophia lifted her hood back and looked at me frankly; in the dimness I saw the gleam of her eyes and moved towards her as if by instinct. She raised a hand and laid it for a moment flat to my cheek, then she leaned closer and our mouths met again. I pulled her to me and felt the sharp edge of the casket press into my chest beneath my doublet, sending a stab of pain through my bruised ribs.

"Come," I whispered, and led her upstairs to the room under the eaves as quietly as I could, though I feared every tread of the stairs would wake Harry and we would be obliged to sit with him and answer his questions. My blood was feverish with hunger for her now, quickened by the wordless encouragement of her apparent desire for me.

I shut the door of my room behind us and dropped my wet cloak to the floor. The wooden casket I placed carefully on the window ledge, to be examined later; it had suffered a crack when Tom Garth threw me to the ground, but appeared otherwise undamaged. If you had told me a month ago that I would have the lost book of Hermes Trismegistus in my hands and leave it aside for a woman, I would have laughed; but Sophia had an effect on me that no woman had had for years and there were some longings that no book could satisfy.

As the sky shaded slowly into the shimmering light of a wet dawn, I slipped the rough dress from her thin shoulders and laid her down on the narrow truckle bed, tracing circles over her damp skin with my tongue while she curled her fingers into my hair and arched her back like a cat in the sun, softly moaning as I moved lower, over the sharp bones of her hips and the softness of her belly and lower still. She wanted me: I felt it in the mounting tension of her muscles and the urgent way she gripped my head as my mouth matched the rhythm of her rocking motion, until eventually she subsided in a liquid cascade of snatched gasps and shuddering sighs. She reached down and pulled me to her, covering my face in kisses and whispering my name while I wrestled, impatient and clumsy, with the ties of my breeches. And then I was inside her, moving with her, looking into those wide tawny eyes that had haunted me since Oxford, hardly daring to believe that we were here, now, joined. She kept her eyes fixed on mine as I began to move faster, more deliberately, her gaze fierce and inscrutable, so that I could not tell whether she was looking at me with love or pity. Perhaps both. As my breathing grew more ragged, she seemed to awaken from her reverie and I felt her pushing me urgently away from her. It took me a moment to understand: her fear of getting with child again. I felt a brief pang of irrational, inexplicable rejection, but in the last instant I slid away from her and spent myself into the sheet beside her, my face buried in her shoulder to muffle any involuntary sounds.

For a long while we lay without speaking, side by side; her hand continued to caress my hair, but absently, and when I glanced at her face I knew she was elsewhere, far from me, her eyes fixed on the ceiling but her gaze turned inward to her own thoughts, and a strange melancholy stole over me, a bleak fear that what we had just done marked not a beginning but an ending. Though my arm remained across her body, my fingers lightly stroking patterns along the curve of her waist, I fell asleep feeling oddly alone as the pale dawn light crept across the bare plaster of the walls.

Chapter *15*

A persistent peal of bells from the cathedral tower woke me, though it seemed only moments since I had closed my eyes. I reached across and found the bed empty. Gulls were clamouring outside the window; when I squinted into the morning light, I saw Sophia, already dressed, leaning on the window ledge with the precious book in her hand. My throat clenched; I had to fight the urge to leap up and tear it out of her hands. But she could have no idea what she held, and I did not wish to whet her curiosity further.

"Greek," she said, without looking up. "What is it?"

"Can you read it?"

"Only a little. I had some schooling with my brother, but my Greek was never advanced and my father would not allow me to study with a tutor after my brother died. Why was this book buried with Becket? Is it forbidden?"

She raised her head and looked at me and I saw the glint in her eye. In Oxford she had pestered me to tell her the secrets of natural magic and I recalled the same light in her expression when I had told her of occult books I had read on my travels. She would have made a fine scholar, I thought; she had the necessary hunger for any knowledge she was told she must not seek.

"I think it is a book I saw once in London," I said, waving a hand as if it hardly mattered, "but I need to study it further to be sure. In the meantime we have more pressing questions. I have only one more day before the assize judge arrives to try and find some evidence against your husband's murderer."

"But you don't know who he is yet," she said, biting her lip. "That is, if you believe Tom Garth didn't do it. We only have his word for that."

"True. And perhaps I am mistaken. In any case, we have no choice but to rely on his oath—he could land you, me, and Harry in gaol with one word about your presence." I shook my head. "But in my gut I do not feel it was Garth. It *must* be Langworth and Sykes, or Samuel acting on their behalf, and it must be because of the boys. What did your husband do that made him suddenly a danger to their plot instead of an ally, that is the question?"

She looked confused.

"What plot? Which boys?"

I told her, as briefly as I could, of my night at St. Gregory's Priory, my altercation with Nicholas Kingsley, the gruesome discovery under the mausoleum, and the suspicions Harry and I had formed about the three men's intention of staging a miracle by the bones of Saint Thomas when the time was right. When I reached the part about finding the medallion of Saint Denis around the neck of the corpse in the underground tomb, she covered her mouth with her hand and tears sprung to her eyes.

"Oh, sweet Jesus," she said, when I had finished, her voice barely audible through her fingers. "To think of that happening underneath my own house."

"The beggar boy would have been before you married Sir Edward. But the Huguenot child—yes. He was kept prisoner and poisoned while you were enduring your own sufferings above ground."

"That poor family. After all they have done for me. How will Hélène bear it? She only survives the days by praying her son will be found safe and well. Dear God."

"It will be a dreadful blow, there is no doubt," I said. "But perhaps at least they can do away with uncertainty. Once the boy's body has been examined as evidence they will be able to give him a Christian burial and that might give them some comfort. Assuming the body is still there," I added, almost to myself, remembering the unease I had felt at the news that Langworth had been to dine at St. Gregory's the previous night. Nick Kingsley would surely have told him of my visit to the old priory and that I had been near the cellar. If Langworth suspected that I was close to understanding the business at Sir Edward's house, he might well have taken the opportunity to dispose of the body in the tomb. Perhaps young Denis would go the way of the beggar boy, hacked to pieces and dumped on a rubbish heap. But no—to have surprised us in the crypt in the early hours Langworth must have returned from the Kingsley house by at least midnight, and if he dined and talked with Nick that would hardly have given him time to exhume a body and move it unnoticed. Besides, he seemed to have relied on Samuel for those kind of dirty jobs and though God only knew where Harry's servant was at that moment, I doubted he was at liberty to dispose of corpses for Langworth.

"I tried to look in the cellar once and old Meg stopped me," Sophia said, turning back to the window again. "She seemed genuinely frightened— she told me my husband would kill me. She must have known all along. How could she?"

"She felt she had no choice. Perhaps she was afraid your husband would kill her too. Oh, God in heaven!" I leapt out of bed and grabbed at my underhose, scrabbling around frantically for a shirt.

"What is it?" Sophia's face mirrored my alarm.

"Meg is a witness. She saw Sir Edward with the beggar boy in the kitchen—she could testify. And Langworth was there last night. I have to find out if she's all right."

"Wait, Bruno. How will you do that? You can hardly just go and knock on the door—you said yourself, Nicholas Kingsley will kill you."

I finished tying my shirt and pulled on the breeches I had discarded in such haste last night. I had hoped to wake with Sophia in my arms and attempt to recapture that fleeting intimacy of the night before. I could not help feeling a little cheated by her early rising and apparent indifference. But I had to put such thoughts out of my mind, I told myself, and concentrate on the matter in hand.

"There is someone who is sure to know any news as soon as it happens," I said. "When I have broken my fast, I must go out to the marketplace. I will bring you some bread and small beer first, if you like. I'm afraid you will be confined to this room—and you would do better to keep away from the window."

It was only a small casement jutting out from the sloping eaves of the attic, but it faced the cathedral and there was always a chance someone passing might glance up. I did not want to bring Harry any more trouble than was necessary.

"Who will help you in the marketplace?" she asked, curious, moving away from the window to sit on the end of the bed and curling a strand of hair around her finger. The severe boy's cut was beginning to grow a little longer; it accentuated the sharp angles of her face.

"Oh, just a girl who is keen to help me any way she can," I said, with deliberate nonchalance, and was gratified to see a brief expression of pique flit across her features. "I'll take that, if I may."

Reluctantly, she handed me the book. I wrapped it in its linen cloth and returned it to the damaged casket, then put the whole into my leather travelling bag and slung it over my shoulder. From now on I did not mean to let this book out of my sight.

In the kitchen I found Harry opening cupboard doors and slamming them with a disgruntled air. He straightened up when I entered and leaned on the edge of the table, looking at me knowingly.

"There you are. We have no bread or milk, you know—Samuel would go out for them early to the market and since he is not here because of you—"

"I am going," I said, clapping him on the shoulder.

"You look rough," he observed, without sympathy. "Don't suppose you've had much sleep."

I acknowledged the truth of this with a half nod and concentrated on my purse. I could not be sure how sharp the old man's hearing was and how much he might have heard when Sophia and I returned last night, but he was no fool; he knew I was hiding her in my room and no doubt imagined the rest.

"Was your excursion useful?" he asked.

"I think so. At least, there is a body in the crypt that has every appearance of being Becket's and could certainly be presented as such. An ampulla of oil was buried with it."

"The holy oil of Saint Thomas," he murmured. "So they claim to have that too, do they? Legend says it was given to Becket by the Virgin to anoint the true sovereign of England."

"So I understand. Do the people care about such trifles?"

He considered.

"It would certainly lend weight to the coronation of a Catholic monarch, should such an event ever come to pass. It would have the appearance of being sanctioned by England's greatest saint."

"But it needs to remain where it is for the queen's justice to see when he arrives. My fear is that Langworth and Sykes between them will find a way to move the relics to another hiding place." I thought of Langworth lying half choked on the floor of the crypt. My situation would be much simpler now if I had finished him off last night. God knows that is easily done—a tavern brawl, a threat, your life or his—and I doubted I would have been the first to solve a problem that way on Walsingham's business, but Langworth was the key to the whole plot in Canterbury and the connections with the French and Spanish conspirators; it was essential that he should be taken alive for questioning. The treasurer was nothing if not shrewd; he would have realised as soon as he came to with a swollen throat on that stone floor that I had discovered his great treasure; the question was whether he would have time to move his saint to another hiding place before I made my discovery public.

"Perhaps I should make it my business to pray in the cathedral today," Harry said, rubbing his chin. "See who comes and goes. They can do nothing if they know they are being watched."

"That would be an excellent idea." I glanced uneasily at the ceiling. "But someone should stay in the house to keep an eye on your other guest."

"That sounds like a job for a young man," Harry said, a smirk playing around the corners of his mouth. "I haven't the strength to get up those stairs, let alone attend to the needs of a female. Mind you, I'd be surprised if you have, after last night." He gave me a stern look, but the ghost of a smile remained. "Now go and get me my breakfast, I'm half starved here."

THE NIGHT'S STORM had broken the pressing heat of the last few days and outside it no longer felt as if we were living inside a glass jar; the sky seemed rinsed clean, pale with a thin gauze of cloud, and a crisp breeze whipped my shirt around my chest. The bells had fallen silent and the only sound was the frenzied cries of the gulls and the crunch of my boots over the wet ground. Fighting my lack of sleep, I tried to keep alert, glancing about me as I walked towards Christ Church gate. At the conduit house I turned back and looked up at the top storey of Harry's house; I thought I saw a shadow move at the window, but I could not be sure. Tom Garth appeared in the doorway of his lodge by the gatehouse and nodded solemnly, as if to acknowledge the bond between us. I nodded in return and passed out into the Buttermarket, one hand laid protectively over the satchel hanging at my side.

The market was busy despite the early hour; by the stone cross, a pair of jongleurs had already drawn a small crowd as one casually juggled flaming torches and the other moved stiffly about on stilts, calling out to drum up an audience. His shouts could barely be heard over the cries of the market traders selling their wares and the barking of the dogs chased away from the food stalls; the air was thick with the smells of warm bread and fresh pies. I found Rebecca behind her bread stall; her face lit up when she saw me, though I did not fail to notice the disapproving glance her employer sent me from the corner of her eye while deep in conversation with a customer. I chose a couple of loaves and leaned in as I handed over the coins.

"I need your help again, Rebecca, I'm afraid. Do you know the housekeeper from St. Gregory's Priory? Does she buy her bread from you?"

"Old Meg?" She looked surprised. "Some days she comes. They used to pay to have the bread delivered when it got too far for her to walk, but since Sir Edward was"—here she made a face—"they have fallen behind with their account. Mistress Blunt said not to take any more until the debt is settled."

"Have you seen Meg this morning?"

She glanced about the marketplace and shook her head.

"Listen." I beckoned her in closer, nodding sideways at the sturdy goodwife who was quite clearly whispering to her customer about me. "You said Mistress Blunt knows all the gossip there is to know in this town. I need to find out if all is well at St. Gregory's with the old woman. I cannot explain, but it is important. Do you think you can find out somehow? But subtly. I only wish to be assured Meg is all right."

Rebecca smiled.

"If anyone can find anything out, it is Mistress Blunt. I will see what I can do. Come back in a while."

"Thank you. I will be forever in your debt." I winked and the girl blushed violently. As I turned to leave, I caught Mistress Blunt's eye and executed a deep bow, the bread clutched to my chest. She broke off her conversation with the goodwife and folded her arms across the vast ledge of her bosom.

"*You,*" she said, giving me a severe look, "are not welcome loitering about my stall."

"Do you say that to all your customers?" I indicated the loaves.

She pursed her lips.

"Don't think I'm not wise to your game. If there's one blessing to growing old, it's that you're no longer taken in by a handsome face. And you, silly chit of a girl," she said, turning to Rebecca with the same sour expression, "ought to have better sense, making eyes like a calf at the man who's supposed to have killed your own uncle."

Pink spots flared in Rebecca's cheeks.

"Well, I don't believe he did, and neither will the judge. Signor Savolino has friends at court, is it not so?" She looked up at me, her face flushed and expectant.

"I don't care if he's friends with Queen Bess herself, he's not hanging about my stall trying his luck while you're supposed to be working for me, girl."

"Alas, I cannot claim so grand a friendship, though I did see Her Majesty in person once, when I was invited to a concert at one of her royal palaces," I said, casually looking away across the marketplace. "I am no expert in fashion, but I believe I have never seen a dress like it."

"No! Did you really? In person? Was it French silk?" Mistress Blunt leaned forward, lips parted, her former severity entirely eclipsed by awe.

"The sleeves, I believe, but the bodice was cloth of gold, all embroidered with tiny seed pearls . . ."

She whistled, delighted, and I continued to embellish my description, making up details as best I could with Mistress Blunt hanging on my every word, nodding sagely, her hands clasped in delight as I elaborated on buttons, necklaces, lace collars, and anything else that came to mind, silently congratulating myself on having found a way to win her over. When there came a cry from behind me and her attention was distracted by something over my shoulder, I followed the direction of her gaze and saw that a scuffle had broken out in the little crowd around the fire juggler. A group of youths were jostling and shoving, and suddenly broke away to run down a side street. Left behind was another, younger boy, who stood white-faced, his hand clutched to his mouth. Through the bobbing heads I saw that it was the Widow Gray's son.

I rushed across and pushed through the people gathered around him.

"What happened?"

The boy looked up, visibly distressed. His lip was bleeding and he seemed taken aback by the abruptness of my manner.

"My purse," he said miserably, holding up his empty hands and nodding to where the gang of older boys had disappeared. I looked around at the rows of blank faces but saw no one stirring themselves to help the boy.

"Hold these," I said, thrusting my loaves into his arms, and tore off down the alley. The thieves, who were no more than fourteen or fifteen years old, had not run far; I caught up with them at the corner of the next street. When they saw me running towards them they attempted to flee again, but I pursued the biggest of them, who held the purse in his hand. Some of his fellows broke away into the gaps between houses, but I followed him doggedly. Though he was tall, he was a stoutish boy and could not outrun me for long; I threw myself at his legs and brought him down hard on the wet cobbles. He tried to lash out but I fetched him a swift punch to the ribs that knocked the breath out of him and he stopped struggling. I did not want to draw my knife unless it was absolutely necessary; I had acquired enough of a reputation for violence in this town without threatening children.

"You have something there that doesn't belong to you," I said, kneeling hard on the small of his back.

"What's it to you?" he puffed out through clenched teeth, his prize still clutched close beneath him.

I grabbed a handful of his hair and raised his head a little way off the ground.

"You will be glad of your teeth later in life, son—don't make me smash them out for you one by one. Give me the purse."

He hesitated, and I pulled his head back farther as if in readiness to thump it against the ground; with a cry of pain and fury he brought out the purse and smacked it into my palm.

"He's a whey-faced priest's bastard," he said belligerently, as he struggled to his feet and brushed his clothes down.

"And you are a fat coward. But we are to believe that even you are made in God's image." I held the purse up and chinked it against my hand to see that he had not had time to empty it.

I could see him weighing up whether to lunge at me, so I fixed him with my fiercest stare and allowed my right hand to wander to the knife at my belt. He eyed it warily and appeared to decide his best course was to back slowly away.

"Spanish cunt!" he shouted, when he was safely at the corner of the street and poised to run.

"Half right. Italian," I called back and made as if to pursue him again; he yelped and fled and I returned to the marketplace, smiling to myself.

The Widow Gray's son was not smiling. He stood with his thin arms wrapped around my loaves as if his life depended on protecting them, a little apart from the crowd, none of whom seemed inclined to offer him any comfort. A few spots of blood had dripped from his cut lip onto his shirt. I felt a sudden stab of anger at these stolid, gossiping people: Would they hold off from taking care of a bleeding child because of the rumours they had sown about his mother's virtue? Did they think they would find themselves somehow tainted? No wonder children could be dumped on rubbish heaps here without anyone turning a hair. The whispering intensified as I approached the boy and held out his purse. I allowed a defiant glare to roam around the onlookers; one by one, they lowered their eyes and turned away, murmuring among themselves.

"Come." I put a hand on the boy's shoulder and he flinched. "Let me take you home. Is all your money here?"

He opened the purse, scanned its contents and nodded, still without speaking.

"Which way?"

He pointed to the street that led away from the Buttermarket opposite the cathedral gate. I made to move in that direction but he held back, looking at me with the same dumb anxiety.

"Those boys will not bother you again while I am around," I said gently.

He shook his head. "It's not that. My mother will kill me."

I smiled.

"I doubt that. She will be relieved to see that you and your money are safe, will she not?"

"I am not supposed to go out on my own," he said, his voice barely a whisper. "But she was occupied and I took her purse." He hung his head, contrite. "I only wanted to see the fire-eater and eat a pie, like the other boys are allowed to."

I glanced sideways at him as we began to walk in the direction he had indicated, the low hum of the marketplace talk following at our back. He was a tall boy for his age, but slight, with prominent cheekbones and solemn grey eyes.

"What is your name?" I asked presently, as he pointed to the turning into another lane.

"Matthias."

"Well, Matthias, I am Filippo. Was the fire-eater worth the trouble?"

"Oh, yes!" He turned to me then as if seeing me for the first time, his expression alight with pleasure. "He juggles with flaming torches and he never misses once—have you seen? And after, he swallows the flames without burning his tongue—I wish I knew how he did it."

"It is an old trick and takes years of practice. Don't try it at home, eh."

He smiled, but it faded quickly.

"I dream of running away with the jongleurs, but I have no skills to offer. I cannot even catch a ball. My mother took me to see them once in the yard of the Cheker at midsummer when I was younger—it was all lit up with torches and garlands and they did such tricks, it was like belonging to a magic world." He paused, breathless, as the excitement of the memory subsided into fear. "We don't go out much anymore."

"But you go to school?"

The boy shook his head.

"I have a tutor at home. And Canon Langworth comes once a week to teach me Greek and Latin—" Here he broke off, as if afraid he might be sharing too much. "I have a weak chest, the doctor says, so it is better that I stay at home." He lowered his gaze, as if apologising for all the trouble he gave everyone, including me.

You don't look all that weak, I thought; nothing a bit of red meat and a good run about in the fresh air wouldn't cure. But if I was right, it would make sense for those intending to use him to put about the rumour that the boy was sickly, fragile; it would make his planned demise all the more plausible when the time came. He could have no inkling of the part assigned to him in the restoration of a Catholic England, poor child. I wondered if his mother knew the full story. Was she also a zealot for the old religion, willing to hand her son over as a sacrifice for God's purpose, or had Langworth and his fellow conspirators duped her in some way?

"But you sing in the choir. I have seen you."

"I have to." He sounded less than happy about it.

"You don't like it?"

"I like the music. But the other boys are cruel. They say things . . ."

"Why do you not stop, then?"

"Canon Langworth makes me, in return for my lessons. Otherwise mother could not pay for them."

He turned into another street and motioned to a handsome red-brick house of three storeys. I looked up at the diamond-leaded windows. Perhaps there would be answers here.

Matthias pulled on the bell rope and eventually a maidservant opened the large front door and ushered us into a high entrance hall tiled in black and white squares. A wide staircase swept upwards and the boy gestured to me to follow him up. The maid watched us from below, silent and unsmiling.

"The alderman and his family have the first two floors and we have the apartments on the top," Matthias explained, as we ascended another floor. On the top landing, he pushed open a door and I stepped behind him into a pleasantly furnished parlour, not large but tastefully decorated. I could see at a glance that the carpets, tapestries, and cushions were of good quality, though old and faded. He was barely inside the room when the widow appeared like a fury, her dark hair unbound and swinging loosely about her shoulders as she lifted a hand as if to strike the boy.

"Where in Christ's name have you been? What possessed you? Did you not think I would be sick with worry? And with Doctor Sykes coming out to see you this morning too! Oh, dear God, what has happened to your face?"

She seized the boy and clasped him violently to her chest, her arms wrapped around his head as if to prevent him ever leaving again, her cheeks flushed with rage and relief. It was at that moment that she looked up and saw me, still standing in the doorway.

"What have you done to my son?"

"Signora, I have only escorted him home to keep him from unwanted attention."

"Why have you brought me bread? Do you think I need charity from foreigners?"

I glanced down at the two loaves in my arms. It seemed easier not to explain.

"Everyone likes fresh bread," I said, and shrugged.

Her frown softened a little, as if she could not find an argument against this, though her eyes remained guarded. She relaxed her grip on her son, who took the opportunity to wriggle free.

"What happened to your face?" she demanded.

"Some boys knocked me down and took my purse." He hung his head. "I was watching the jongleurs in the market. I am sorry."

"My purse, you mean. And you will be sorry. What has this gentleman to do with it?"

"Filippo chased them and got the purse back. No one else would help."

His mother clicked her tongue.

"Of course they wouldn't. You know what people are in this town, Matthias. Let that be a lesson to you to stay away from them, as you have been told. Now go and draw some water and clean your face."

She turned to me, clasping her hands in front of her. She wore a simple black linen gown that accentuated her slender figure and made her skin look pale as porcelain. Though she was of my own age, perhaps a little older, her face was almost unlined and her eyes the blue of Delft china. If I had not been so caught up in Sophia, I might have looked at her with more interest; even so, I could appreciate that she was beautiful and her aloofness added to her appeal. Little wonder the goodwives liked to make her an object of malicious talk. The blue eyes flickered over my face with an appraising look. "Filippo, is it? Well, you are quite the Good Samaritan, are you not? The outcast foreigner who still finds time to help those less fortunate."

I shrugged again. "I am not one of those who would stand by and watch a child robbed, if that's what you mean."

A muscle twitched in her jaw.

"Then you are a rarity in this town." For a moment she looked as if she would like to spit on the floor. "This is why he is not allowed to go roaming about as he pleases." She glanced towards the door where the boy had gone out. "He thinks me harsh, but it is only to protect him."

"Boys his age seem to need protecting in this town," I ventured.

"What do you mean?"

"One found dead, one missing in the last year. It is the worse for them that their mothers were not able to protect them."

Her eyes narrowed.

"This has nothing to do with us."

"Of course not. And you would do anything to protect your son, I imagine. Anything necessary."

"As any good mother would."

"And any good father? Would a good father want what was best for his son?"

"My husband died when Matthias was an infant," she said quietly, through clenched teeth. "I think it is time you left my house, sir."

"Mistress Gray." I shifted the bread in my arms. "If I told you your son was in danger, would you stay to listen?"

"Why should I listen to you? A stranger? A man who has not been in the town two days when he is accused of murder?" But there was a hesitation in her voice.

I acknowledged the truth of this with a nod.

"Accused by Ezekiel Sykes. You know Doctor Sykes?"

"Of course—he is my physician, and my son's. In fact he was supposed to be coming to see my son this morning. He is late, but I expect him any moment."

"Ah, of course. The boy's weak chest. Well, then, you must trust Doctor Sykes implicitly. I will say no more." I moved towards the door and paused with my hand on the latch. If Sykes genuinely was expected I would do well to be gone before he arrived. God alone knew what else he might try to accuse me of if he was given opportunity.

"Wait."

I turned to see her closing the door to the corridor where the boy had gone out so that he should not hear. She did not invite me to sit down.

"I will hear you, but briefly. What is it that you think you know?"

"Mistress Gray," I began, and she waved a hand.

"Alys. My name is Alys."

"And mine, as you know, is Filippo."

"Is it?"

She raised a carefully plucked eyebrow and for a long moment we looked at each other as sunlight streamed through the casement behind her, lighting the dust on the floorboards and making it sparkle. The tension in the room crackled like the air before last night's storm; neither of us, it seemed, was willing to venture a confidence first, in case it was a trap. Yet I sensed that she wanted to trust me; what I had said about her son being in danger must have chimed with some intuitive misgiving on her part, or she would have thrown me out instantly.

"Why—have you heard otherwise?"

She made a slight movement with her head. "People talk, in a town like this."

"I thought they didn't talk to you. Or do you mean different people?

Your friends at the cathedral, perhaps? Canon Langworth seems to take a great interest in your son's education. Does he speak about me?"

She hesitated, glanced to the window.

"He said you were dangerous. That you live by dissembling."

"As we all do. The canon treasurer included. As you yourself do, signora, unless I am mistaken. Where is he buried, by the way?"

"Who?" She sat upright.

"Master Gray, of course. Your late husband."

"Oh. Cambridgeshire. With his people." But the hesitation had been too noticeable, and she knew it. Our eyes met and held again; which of us would drop our guard first, I wondered.

"Tell me of this danger to my son, whatever you call yourself, and then leave my house, please." She kept her voice level, but it was she who looked away first. I crossed the room to the window and stood for a moment looking out. I laid the bread on the window seat, glad to put it down.

"Sir Edward Kingsley left you some money in his will, did he not?"

Her face tightened and to give herself a distraction she gathered the length of her hair between her hands and pulled it into a twist over her shoulder so she could examine the ends.

"So Nicholas Kingsley has been shouting that to all comers as if he were the town crier, has he? Yes, his father left me a small sum and, such as it is, I cannot even claim it because the will is all up in the air until they find out who killed him. But it is not for the reason you think," she added, with a stern look.

"And what is it that I think?"

"You will assume I was his mistress."

"Oh, no, not at all. I had assumed you were John Langworth's mistress."

I waited for the sharp put-down, but it never came. Instead she lowered her eyes, and her silence was eloquent.

"So the question," I continued, "is why Edward Kingsley was giving you money. My guess is that it was for some other service rendered, or promised. Am I close?"

She raised her head and answered with a defiant stare. I had placed myself to my advantage; to look at me she had to squint into the sunlight behind me.

"Some service involving your son." When she still didn't answer, I decided to venture all. "A service not to him personally, but to the Church. A service to God. Was that how they sold it to you?"

"Why should I tell you any of my business?" she said, but the fight had gone out of her voice and I knew my guess had struck home. I took the few steps across the room to stand close to her, so that I could drop my voice easily to make sure the boy did not hear.

"Because those other boys who died, Alys—they died in preparation for this service that your son is to perform. They died because the men you are trusting with your son's life don't know what they are doing. Did they tell you what would be required of him?"

She shook her head and her fingers fluttered to the gold medallion she wore around her neck.

"Only that it would be to the glory of God and the"—she faltered—"the Church."

"By the Church they do not mean what the queen of England or the Archbishop of Canterbury mean by the same word, do they?"

"You would have to ask them that question," she flashed back, quick as blinking. "Tell me about these boys." She lowered her voice and her eyes flickered to the door she had just closed, in case her son should hear. "What happened to them? How did they die?"

"They were poisoned. One was a beggar child, the other a French boy they must have persuaded to go with them somehow. They died in the course of experimenting with a poison and its antidote. The poison would make the victim appear dead. The antidote, given some time later, was supposed to revive him. If it was successful, it would appear as if—"

"As if he had been brought back from the dead," she breathed. She looked up at me, her eyes bright with fear and wonder. "And they were of my boy's age, you say?"

"I am not an apothecary, but I understand the quantities of both substances would depend on the weight and age of the person taking them. They had to test whether their idea worked before they tried it out on a public stage, with their principal actor." My gaze wandered to the door, where I suspected Matthias would be trying to listen.

"But it didn't work."

"No. There was no miracle for those boys." I allowed a pause, while she pressed a sleeve to her mouth and cast about, as if unable to decide whether or not to sit. "Still—I'm sure they will do nothing without first practising on other children. They seem to have a knack of finding them."

"Oh, Jesus, no." She drew breath. "They talked of a miracle. By the power of Saint Thomas, to restore the true Church. They said no harm would come to him, and after, my boy's name would be written in the history books, when England was brought back to God." She pulled again at her hair. "And then he said if I did not agree, I would have no more money."

"He? You mean Langworth?"

I took the bitter expression that passed across her face as answer. She cupped her hand over her mouth for a moment, as if afraid too many words might spill out uncensored, then she clasped me by the wrist and led me to the window seat, where she pushed the bread aside and gestured to me to sit beside her. When she spoke, it was almost soundless, so that I had to lean in and watch the shape of her mouth, as the deaf do.

"You are right to say that I dissemble. This"—she plucked at her widow's clothes—"is a costume I have been obliged to wear these past twelve years, for a shred of respectability." She sighed. "I was the youngest daughter of a county gentleman in Cambridgeshire with more family pride than income, who threw me out when I got with child. I tried to support us with sewing and little jobs but in the end I was forced to go to the cathedral in Ely and beg for alms. John Langworth was a canon there. He took a liking to me. I curse the day I ever knocked on that door, but what's done is done." She shrugged, as if the rest were obvious.

"He made you his mistress?"

"He paid for the boy's education and a roof over our heads. Many are not so lucky. And he wouldn't be the first churchman to keep a woman."

"That much is certain. But he is not the boy's father?"

"No. The man who sired Matthias is long gone. But since Langworth has paid for his upbringing, I suppose he has a claim to be something like a father. He brought us here with him when he was appointed canon six years ago."

That at least explained how Langworth could feel entitled to make use of the boy without any of the compunction a father might feel about gambling with his son's life.

"I have posed as a widow since my son was born," she continued. "Gray is not even my real name, though Alys is." She gave a little sad laugh, then looked up sharply, her face suddenly serious. "What can I do? I had no idea Matthias's life was in danger, and if more children might die . . ." She bit at the skin around her fingers and I realised that beneath the cool poise I had admired from a distance lay a welter of fear and confusion, a life lived under the threat of destitution, at the mercy of someone else's demands. She knew too well what it meant to live by dissembling.

"Testify for me," I whispered. "Tell the queen's justice what you were asked to do."

"At the assizes? In a public courtroom?"

"No. A written deposition. One you will swear by."

She shook her head.

"My word against Langworth, Sykes, and Mayor Fitzwalter?" She snorted. "I would succeed only in stirring up their anger against me. And if I stand in their way, it is much easier to remove me than abandon their plans. And then what becomes of my son?"

"Is that what happened to Sir Edward Kingsley? Did he threaten to stand in their way, in the end?" So the mayor was the fourth guardian. I absorbed this news with a level expression.

"I don't know what happened to Edward Kingsley," she said, looking me right in the eye. "Though I don't mourn him."

"Testify, Alys. Back me up with the truth, against their lies. You could be free of Langworth."

"You really think they would listen to us? A foreigner and a woman, against the mayor, a canon of the cathedral, and a physician?" She shook her head with a dry laugh, as if my naïveté amused her.

I pushed my hands through my hair in frustration. This was Tom Garth's attitude too; was justice so easily bought and sold in this town that no one dared stand up and speak the truth? Would it always be the same: corrupt and self-serving men exploiting those who had no voice, because they were comfortably sure they would never be challenged? Certainly it would, if no one had the courage to at least try and face them down.

"I am not talking about justice as this town understands it," I said softly. "There are those who will listen to me."

I stood and stretched in the dusty sunlight. The widow watched me, appraising; I saw how her eyes travelled over my body. Twelve years at the mercy of Langworth, I thought. God, it is a cruel thing to be born a woman.

"Who *are* you?" she whispered.

"Someone who wants to help you. Give it some thought, at least," I said, turning to the door. "You could save yourself from Langworth. And your son from Saint Thomas."

"And who would provide for us then? Will you, Master Filippo, or whatever your real name is? I didn't think so. Sometimes you have to make sacrifices."

"Would you sacrifice your son?"

She stood too and looked at me, wrapping her arms around her chest as if hugging herself against a coming assault.

"Thank you for helping us," she said, in a tone of empty politeness. "You may see yourself out now." And she watched me all the way to the door, her face guarded once more against any show of emotion. I had done my best, I thought, as I ran down the wide stairs and past the staring servant. I had no promise that she would help me, and if she chose to tell Langworth what I had just told her, he might well see fit to try and finish me off this very night, before I had a chance to spill a word of it to the queen's justice. I felt a tightness in my chest and throat; so much was still unknown, the outcome still uncertain. By tomorrow we would see how the cards would fall. For Sophia, Harry, and me, a bad hand could mean the difference between life and death.

I walked back to the marketplace, emptying now as people made their way towards the cathedral to wait for divine service, baskets of goods hanging from their arms, jostling and chatting as they funnelled towards the gatehouse. I had just edged into the crowd when I felt a tug at my sleeve and turned to see Rebecca beside me, wide-eyed. In my brooding on my exchange with the Widow Gray, I had all but forgotten what I had asked the girl to find out for me. Her apprehensive expression gave me a terrible sense of foreboding; I beckoned her over to one side, out of the flow of people.

"What you asked me to find out? It is the most curious thing, but not a few moments after you left the stall, one of the goodwives from the North Gate parish came bustling up to tell Mistress Blunt that apparently Doctor Sykes was called out at first light to the Kingsley house to attend the old housekeeper." Her hand still rested on my sleeve and her eyes were bright with the excitement of sharing her news; now she adjusted her face to a more appropriately sombre mien. "It is the saddest thing, but it seems the old woman had a bad fall in the night. Down some steps to the cellar, so the goodwife said, though I don't know where she had that from. But Doctor Sykes said there was nothing he could do to save her by the time he arrived."

"I'm sure he did his best," I said, mechanically. I felt as if a stone had lodged in my chest. I had known Meg was in danger; I had heard Langworth as good as say that she knew too much. She had seen the beggar boy in the kitchen at St. Gregory's; she could have said so in a courtroom. Now she could say nothing. If the fall—which I had no doubt was the result of Langworth's visit last night—had not killed her outright, Sykes with his bag of potions would certainly have made sure of it, even as he pretended to try and save her. Just like Sarah Garth. But had I not tried to warn Meg, I argued with my conscience; what more could I have done, when she was as good as resigned to whatever befell her there?

"It is so curious, though," Rebecca was saying. "How did you *know?* To ask after old Meg, the very morning she died?"

"Did you say anything to Mistress Blunt about that?" I asked, lowering my voice.

"Not a word. But tell me. It is like you have the gift of seeing the future." She smiled; this, I supposed, was meant as a compliment.

Yet somehow I am always too late to save people from it, I thought. Old Meg would join the parade of accusing faces I saw sometimes in dreams, the people who had died because I had not been able to protect them, because I had not moved fast enough, or else as a direct result of my actions. "You cannot blame yourself," Walsingham had told me once, and he knew all too well what it meant to have blood on his hands for the sake of a greater cause. "You cannot be everywhere and save everyone, Bruno," he had said. "You must make your choices. Sometimes there will be casualties. This is a war, after all. We fight it with intelligence and ciphers and hidden writings delivered in the dead of night, but it is a war nonetheless, and sometimes it will exact a price."

"She had complained of feeling ill," I said to Rebecca. "I was concerned for her. Perhaps she fainted and fell, poor thing."

"Hm." I had expected her to press further as to how I had become so intimate with the old woman in only a few days, but her mind was elsewhere. "And I have more news—I am bound over to appear as a witness at your trial."

I looked at her. "You will speak the truth?"

"Of course." She looked indignant. "I mean to persuade them of your innocence. He was my uncle, after all, and if I don't think you killed him, why should they?"

I smiled, though I feared in her puppyish enthusiasm she might protest too much, which would be of no help to my case.

"They sometimes try to put words in your mouth," I said. "Watch
out for that."

She looked scornful.

"I would not fall for those tricks. Signor Savolino, do you mean to
stay in Canterbury after the assizes?" She twined a strand of hair through
her fingers as she asked this, sucking absently at the end of it like a child.

"I shall decide that once I have learned whether they mean to put a
rope around my neck."

"But your friends at court, they would not let that happen, for certain. Even Mistress Blunt thinks you are innocent," she added, as if this
were the decisive verdict. I smiled. As an eyewitness to the queen's bro-
cades, I was clearly now redeemed in Mistress Blunt's eyes. If only the
rest of Canterbury could be so easily persuaded.

"They say the queen's justice is expected this afternoon," Rebecca
said. "There is always quite a procession—everyone turns out along
the High Street to watch him arrive. He will take the best rooms at the
Cheker, they say, and all his clerks and servants too. Perhaps I may see
you among the crowds later," she added, looking up from under her
lashes and twisting her hair. "You will want to see him in all his pomp?"

"I suppose. It would be as well to see the man who holds my life
in his hands." I tried to keep my tone cheerful but I could not ignore
the tightness in my chest. To unravel this unholy mess I must not rely
on Canterbury justice, that much was clear. My fortunes, and those of
Sophia and Harry, were truly in the hands of this unknown man riding in from London. I only hoped that he was not so easily corrupted—
though my English friends' reports of the legal profession did not inspire
too much optimism on that count.

I thanked Rebecca for her help and took my leave, pressing through
the crowd towards Christ Church gate, unstrapping my knife from my
belt and hiding it in my boot before I arrived so that Tom Garth would
not confiscate it. After the previous night, I was not willing to enter the

precincts without a weapon. I was anxious to be back at Harry's. I had only a day to prepare the charges I wanted to bring against Langworth and Sykes and I needed to have them set out clearly if my story was not to sound even more improbable than it already did. Meg had been silenced, but there was still the old monk in the West Gate gaol—perhaps he could be made to testify to what he had seen. And there were the two buried bodies—the boy Denis and the one reckoned to be Thomas Becket—as evidence to my theory of the proposed miracle, even if the Widow Gray would not speak against Langworth. True, there was nothing to prove that he had killed Sir Edward Kingsley, but the fact that Kingsley had been on his way to Langworth's house and that he had been killed by a crucifix that only someone with access to the crypt could have taken made it almost impossible to believe that anyone else could be guilty. Edward Kingsley must have crossed the treasurer, or threatened the plot in some way, and Langworth had decided to get rid of him. And yet unease continued to gnaw at my mind as I passed through the gatehouse into the precincts and took the path towards Harry's house. Langworth was nothing if not subtle, and his friend Sykes was skilled in the use of poisons. If Kingsley had needed to be silenced, would the treasurer really have chosen to beat his former friend's skull in with a crucifix right outside his, Langworth's, house, in lieu of some less obvious means?

These doubts were dispelled as I passed the conduit house and saw Langworth himself standing at Harry's front door, gesticulating wildly and pointing up at the windows, the sleeves of his robe fluttering in the breeze like the ragged wings of a crow. Harry was planted staunchly before the closed door, hands crossed in front of him and leaning on his stick with an implacable expression. He looked up and met my eye with something between relief and exasperation as I slowed to a halt some yards away from them, my mouth dry.

Though I was oddly relieved to see Langworth alive and apparently not too badly affected by my assault on him the night before, it was a relief that only lasted a moment. He turned and looked at me with such intense hatred that I found myself reaching instinctively towards my boot where my knife was hidden; I half expected him to hurl himself at me right there, and I knew in that instant that he meant to see me dead one way or another. Instead he curled and uncurled his fists several times, mastering his fury, and the smirking scar at the corner of his mouth turned white as he pressed his lips together until he was sure he had regained control of himself. I noticed that inside the collar of his black canon's robe he had wrapped a white linen scarf around his neck, presumably to hide the bruising.

I swung the satchel to my back, suddenly conscious of the stolen book as if it was burning through the leather, and took a couple of measured paces towards them, trying to betray nothing with my face.

"Ah, Doctor Savolino," Harry called out in a breezy tone, though I could see from his face that he was weary of this business. "Canon Langworth has come with a most singular set of accusations against you."

"Really? Who have I murdered this time?" I smiled at Langworth; he needed a long moment of breathing through his nose and sucking in his cheeks before he was equal to replying.

"I do hope your wit doesn't desert you when you stand before a judge, sir," he said, his voice so tight it sounded almost as if he were still being choked. "We are all looking forward to the performance. It is a charge of theft, as you well know."

"What I can't make out," Harry said, with the same forced cheeriness, "is what you are supposed to have stolen. It seems the canon treasurer cannot be specific on that count, which I can't help feeling undermines the force of his accusation. With the greatest respect," he added, with a small dip of the head to Langworth.

"I believe my house has been broken into," the treasurer said, fixing me with a hard stare. "Some personal items of value have been taken, as well as money. I believe it is also possible that the security of the cathedral treasury has been breached, which is a far graver matter."

"Indeed," I said, nodding to show that I appreciated the gravity. "How much has been taken from the treasury?"

"I—I am not certain yet," he faltered. "But if money has been taken from God's house, well, that would be a capital offence."

"Yes, indeed. And it would surely cast doubt on the competence of whoever is responsible for the security of the treasury," I said pleasantly. "But why do you suppose I have anything to do with it?"

"Tom Garth says he saw you abroad in the precincts last night. Don't play games with me," Langworth hissed, through his teeth. "You are already charged with murder and will be charged with attempted murder too. Nicholas Kingsley has told me how you tried to kill him and leave him for dead when he caught you attempting to steal from his father's cellar." Satisfied with the effect of this barb, he swung his warning finger around to include Harry. "Either you let me search your house now, Robinson, or I shall come back with armed men and a warrant from the constable, and then we shall see what we find. Eh?"

His voice was so brittle as he spoke that the veins at his temples stood out like cords against his pale skin, and he looked for all the world like a man straining at his closestool, so much so that I could not stifle a laugh in time. Langworth's throat—what could be seen of it—mottled with fury and the flush spread up over his gaunt cheeks until his eyes bulged and it seemed his head might explode. He swept his robe around him with a practised gesture and turned on his heel.

"By God you will pay for that laughter. You will all pay," he said, jabbing the pointing finger at my face as he stalked away towards the cathedral like the Devil in a masque delivering his final ominous curse.

A peal of bells clanged out from the bell tower behind us, making me start. Harry watched Langworth's retreating back and slumped forward over his stick, as if the breath had been knocked out of him.

"By God, I'm paying for it already, Bruno," he muttered. "Sometimes I can't help thinking he has sent you here to test my faith."

"God?"

"Walsingham." He looked at me darkly, then glanced up at the top storey of his house. "He is serious, you know." He jerked his head in Langworth's direction. "Whatever you took from him, he wants it back and he will get his warrant and his men-at-arms and return to search the place. If she is found, we'll all be hanged." He scratched a hand across his silver stubble. "You and I must attend Holy Communion now. As must Langworth—at least we can keep an eye on him. I will lock the house soundly and when we come out we had better put her somewhere more convenient. And I am still not shaved—once again I must face the dean looking like a tramp." He turned back to me. "And where's my bloody breakfast? You are without doubt the worst servant I have ever had under my roof."

I acknowledged this with a weary grin, realising that I had left the bread at the Widow Gray's house.

"You will have your reward some day, Harry, I promise."

"Huh. In heaven, perhaps. Now, go up quickly and tell her not to stir a muscle. I wouldn't put it past that dog to have someone break in and turn the place upside down while we are at prayer." His eyes narrowed as he looked back towards the cathedral.

I pushed my hands through my hair and cast my eyes up to the bell tower. Where the Devil was I supposed to put Sophia—and the book—out of Langworth's reach for the next few hours?

I found her slumped on the truckle bed, dressed in clothes of mine that she had evidently pulled out from my travelling bag and reading my old battered copy of Copernicus, the one I had carried halfway across Europe. She sat up when she saw me and there was something wary about her smile, as if she feared she would be reprimanded. The shirt was too broad for her across the shoulders and she had laced it only loosely; as she moved it slipped down, revealing one shoulder and the curve of her collarbone. I swallowed. She had not bound her breasts either and the small pointed shape of them was visible through the thin linen. I walked across the room to the window so that she would not see how badly I wanted to push her down on the mattress and tear it from her.

"My last clean shirt," I said softly, still not looking at her.

"Sorry. I had to take off those hideous skirts Madame Fleury dressed me in last night. They belonged to Olivier's grandmother, apparently. They smell like she died in them."

I laughed and came to sit on the end of the bed, watching her. She returned my gaze steadily but I could not be sure what I read there.

"How do you like Copernicus?" I indicated the book. "I'm afraid you will find no magic spells in those pages."

The corner of her mouth twisted into a wry smile.

"I don't suppose even you would be so bold or so foolish as to carry books of magic about the country, Bruno," she said. There was a hint of sadness in her smile. "Though God knows we could do with a magic spell at the moment."

"Even more so now," I said, and told her of Langworth's intention to return with armed men to search the house. She put her face in her hands and sank back against the wall. I took it for crying and leaned closer to rest a hand on her arm, but she lowered her hands and looked at me with the blankness of exhaustion.

"Is he looking for me? Or that book you are carrying about with you as if it were a newborn infant?"

"I don't think he saw you last night. Not clearly enough to recognise you, anyway, or he would have made reference to it as a threat, I'm sure of it. But he knows I have the book and he can't tell the constable what he's really searching for. I would not put it past him to contrive that a purse of money from the treasury should be found here too—that would as good as seal my sentence. Christ!" I ran a hand through my hair and thumped my fist into the mattress. "He means to finish me off one way or another. How did I not see the danger?"

Sophia crept forward and gently laid her forehead against my shoulder, her hand on my thigh.

"I am so sorry, Bruno. I had no idea it would be so tangled. Becket, the dead boys—I knew nothing of any of it. I thought it would be a simple matter of proving that Nicholas Kingsley did it so that I could be free. I believed he did. I never imagined you would end up—"

She left the words unspoken.

"The fault is mine. I should have seen the danger."

"But then, would you still have come?"

"Probably."

She looked up at me, eyes wide.

"Why?"

"You know why, Sophia."

She said nothing, only continued to look at me expectantly with that unreadable expression. Did she need to hear me say aloud that I loved her? The words were poised on my tongue, but some unexplained instinct held them back. Instead I reached for her hand and she twined her fingers with mine, but it seemed more a gesture of sorrow. We were both under sentence of death now, unless a miracle happened, and even Thomas Becket was unlikely to deliver one of those.

Something, some phrase I had heard that morning chafed at my mind, as if I had missed a vital part of the picture, but when I closed my eyes and tried to concentrate to recall what it might have been, I was distracted by a great shuddering sob from Sophia that racked her thin body as she leant into me, a sob that seemed to contain all the frustration and rage of the past year. I held her while she vented her pain, her face pressed to my shoulder, my cheek leaning against her hair, but although she clung to me like a child with night terrors, I sensed with a growing hollowness in my chest that after the heightened excitement of the night before, I had passed back into my previous role of reassuring friend, a part I hoped I had left behind. I kissed her hair softly. Well, I could be patient. At this moment we were both in dire need of a friend.

Chapter **16**

The morning service passed, interminably slowly. All through the singing of the choir, the reading of the Gospel, and the monotone of the dean's sermon, none of which I heard, Langworth glared across the carved stalls at me and Harry with a very unchristian light in his eyes, as if he hoped to wither us beneath his stare like a basilisk. Sun slanted through the high windows and lit the columns and the floor with geometric shapes in jewel colours. When I could tear my gaze away from Langworth's I looked up to those windows, where glass undimmed by centuries of sunlight depicted the miracles of Saint Thomas, the procession of pilgrims to the shrine, their hands thrown up in simple joy as the saint's bones give them back their sight, or their legs, or their children from the grave. Had they really thought, Langworth and his friends, that they could stage a miracle? Did they imagine people would believe in it? But why should they doubt it, I thought, recalling the trade in relics in my own country, the commerce of priests offering a touch of a weeping statue of the virgin for the chink of coins in their pockets, a statue they had engineered themselves to dispense tears at the appropriate time. For nearly four hundred years people had believed in the truth of the stories told in the windows above us in the cathedral, and they would want to believe again.

When the dean eventually pronounced the final blessing, I took Harry's keys and tried to press my way out quickly ahead of him, leaving him to watch Langworth's movements. The treasurer's eyes followed me as I left, but he had been detained by the dean.

I nodded a brisk farewell to them both as I passed, and heard Dean Rogers saying, "No sign of Doctor Sykes this morning, John? I think we can forgive his absence in the light of his tireless devotion to the health of our town . . ."

I pushed through the congregation out into the precincts and rushed to the gatehouse. Tom Garth's look of dismay told me immediately that Langworth's words were true.

"You gave me your oath, Tom," I said in a low voice, forcing my way into his small lodge.

He held his hands up as if in self-defence.

"He threatened me, sir. He said he knew you had been abroad in the precincts last night and I would be expected to say I'd seen you to the constable. He said if I lied I would lose my place." He leaned in closer. "But I never said a word about Mistress Kingsley, I swear it."

"But you will, if he threatens you again?"

He shook his head vehemently.

"No, sir—that was my promise. I reasoned if he knew about you already I couldn't very well deny it without bringing myself trouble. But I won't mention a word about her. And you won't say anything about the gloves—?"

His eyes were full of fear. I sighed.

"No. But I need your help, Tom. Langworth wants to search Harry Robinson's house—I need to put her somewhere else, just for this afternoon. Is there anywhere—an outbuilding, a shed, any place he wouldn't think to look, that we can get her to easily?"

He considered for a moment and nodded.

"There's an outbuilding behind the conduit house, the one that stands between here and Doctor Robinson's house. It was used for storage, but there's nothing much there now. I have the key—I reckon she'd be safe in there for a few hours."

"Excellent. When the crowds have finished milling around, come and find me at Harry's. We have to move quickly—Langworth will not want to waste time. He's probably on his way to fetch the constable even now."

I returned to the house. Harry arrived a few minutes later, confirming that he had seen Langworth heading in the direction of one of the side gates. I bounded up the stairs to see Sophia bundled again in the clothes of Olivier's dead grandmother.

"They will find me this time for sure," she said, her voice flat.

"Come now—where is your spirit?" I said, more cheerfully than I felt. "This is only until Langworth has satisfied himself with ransacking the house."

At the foot of the stairs she came face-to-face with Harry for the first time. He gave a stiff little bow; she offered a shy smile in return. I watched her with interest; she has a way with men, I thought. All that fierce independence of spirit that I love in her—she knows how to suppress it when she senses modesty is required. She can lower her gaze and look demure with the best of them, but that expression hides a steeliness of purpose you might never guess at, unless you caught the flash of her amber eyes from under those lashes.

"I owe you a great debt, Doctor Robinson," she was saying, and Harry had taken her hand in his. "If we all get through this, I shall try to find some way of repaying your kindness, if it takes me the rest of my life."

"Well, I doubt I'll be around for much of that," Harry chuckled. "But do not talk of debts, Mistress Kingsley. There has been great wrong done here, in this holy place, and we must rely on Doctor Bruno to put it right, with God's help."

"I would trust Doctor Bruno with my life," she said, with unexpected feeling. As she spoke, she met my eye with a smile and my anxieties almost melted away.

Tom arrived, good as his word, and when we were certain that there was no one about on the path to see us, he and I bundled Sophia between us close to the boundary wall of the cathedral and along as far as the conduit house. The outbuilding was added onto the back wall; its roof was threadbare in patches and was clearly used by gulls as a roost, judging by the quantity of guano spattered over the remaining tiles and the walls. The door was not especially sturdy but was secured by a rusting iron padlock, which Tom unlocked from a key on his belt. Inside the place smelled of mould. A decayed gardening implement leaned against one wall, and the remains of some sacking lay rotting in a corner.

"Never say that I do not take you to the finest places," I murmured, as Sophia reluctantly stepped inside while Tom cast his eye over the grounds to make sure no one came. A brief smile flickered over her face, but quickly faded as she stood in the middle of the shed, wrapping her arms around herself, unsure of whether to sit.

"I have to lock you in," I whispered, apologetically. "Just in case."

"I know. Bruno?" she said, in a small voice. "Don't be too long, will you?"

"I will be back as soon as Langworth has finished poking around," I promised. "Here." I lifted the leather satchel from my shoulder and handed it to her. "He must not find the book either. Keep it safe for me."

"One day, will you tell me what is in it?"

"Perhaps. When I have worked that out for myself. For now, your only task is to keep still and silent."

"Oh, I am good at that," she said, with a sardonic flash of her eyes. "It is what women are taught to do all our lives."

"Well, now your life depends on it," I said, and closed the door on her.

Tom secured the padlock and gave me the key from his belt.

"Return it to me when you need to. And be assured, sir, my lips are sealed."

"Thank you." I hesitated. "Tom—if it comes to it, would you be willing to testify about the gloves? To say they never belonged to Mistress Kingsley?"

His large frame visibly trembled.

"I would be punished, would I not?"

"I don't know," I said honestly. "As long as the killer is brought to justice, it would be clear you only acted to protect yourself. You might hope for clemency."

Tom narrowed his eyes.

"But you can't promise the killer will be brought to justice, can you? And I might not get clemency."

"The only evidence against Mistress Kingsley is that pair of gloves. Until you tell the truth, they could still hang her."

"I will give it some thought," he grunted, and walked away towards the gatehouse.

No one in this town has any faith in the law, I thought. I am the only fool here who thinks truth has a chance. A gull landed on the roof of the outbuilding and looked at me enquiringly with its yellow eye, its head tilted to one side. I prayed it would not shit through the holes on to my book, which I had no doubt Sophia was puzzling over even now.

When I returned to the house I found Harry shuffling about the kitchen at the back, peering into cupboards, lifting the lid on pots.

"Well, Harry. If you have anything hidden away in this house that you wouldn't want Langworth to see, now would be the time to dispose of it. Letters, for instance."

"I burn all Walsingham's letters. I'm not a fool. Tell you what—they won't find anything in this godforsaken kitchen, that's for certain," he grumbled, poking an iron spoon into the cauldron suspended above the empty grate to make his point.

"Yes, I hear you, there is no food here," I snapped, exasperated. "Looking in every pot won't change that."

"And whose fault is that?" he shot back. "Who sent my servant out of town and promised to take his place? God knows I am Her Majesty's loyal servant, but this mire you have dragged me into is not the crown's business, it is all for the sake of your doxy!"

"Not the crown's business? That you have sat by while a viper's nest of traitors keeps guard over forbidden relics and plots to revive the greatest saint's cult in England, as a direct rebellion against the queen? Is that not her minister's business?"

"Keep your voice down, can't you?"

We glared at each other for a long moment, until my anger subsided first and I looked at the floor.

"I'm sorry. I have asked a lot of you, I know. But we are on the same side, Harry."

He pushed a hand through the front of his white hair and continued to look at me without speaking, his head to one side as if he were calculating the balance of my faults and my virtues.

"I have failed Walsingham here," he said eventually, deflated. "It is I who should be apologising to him. If you had not come and seen what I should have seen long ago, Langworth and Sykes might one day have achieved their aim. And most likely more children would have died along the way." He sighed and shook his head.

"The outcome is in the hands of the queen's justice now," I said.

"Let us hope he is competent," Harry said, in a tone that did not inspire hope. "So many of them can be bought. Still, I will not argue with you, Bruno, not with my stomach growling like an angry bear. Get yourself round to the Sun Inn while there's still time and bring back a dish of their beef stew, if they have it. And some pickled beetroot . . ."

I was turning to go when a brusque rapping sounded at the front door. Harry and I froze, looking at each other.

"Open up, Doctor Robinson," came Langworth's voice from outside. "I have the constable with me and two armed men. We demand the right to search your property for stolen goods."

"Watch him like a hawk," I hissed. "If he tries to pretend money was found anywhere here, we must contradict it on the spot, as eyewitnesses."

Harry raised a sceptical eyebrow.

"You think that will help?"

Another knock; louder, more impatient.

"All right, all right," Harry called. "Give an old man time to find his stick." Under his breath he said to me, "Get upstairs and make sure there's nothing of hers lying around that room."

When I returned, taking the stairs two at a time, Harry's small entrance hall was full: Langworth, Constable Edmonton, and two armed men in the mayor's livery. I recognised one of them as one of the guards that had taken me to the West Gate prison; I nodded to him and he blinked hard, surprised, before nodding back, as if we were old drinking companions.

"Well, then," Langworth said, barely troubling to conceal his pleasure at the prospect before him. "Constable, you begin upstairs. Find the Italian's room. You know what you are looking for. I, meanwhile, will make a start in here." He indicated Harry's front parlour.

"Where shall I search, sir?" one of the guards asked, hand on his sword hilt.

Langworth looked at him with faint impatience.

"You are not searching anywhere. What we are looking for requires a practised eye. Your job is to keep the peace, and make sure the householders give us no trouble." He eyed me with resentment.

"Yes—mind I don't start a brawl and knock you to the ground, son." Harry waved his stick at the guard in mock threat.

We followed Langworth into the parlour. He crossed to Harry's desk and regarded the jumble of papers and books.

"This should prove interesting." He lifted the topmost paper of one pile, gave it a cursory examination and discarded it on the floor.

"You will discover nothing there but my work, John," Harry said, rubbing a hand across his chin. "Hard as you will find this to believe, there is an order to those papers, though it is known only to me. I would be grateful if you—"

Langworth waved a hand.

"We are investigating a serious crime of theft, Doctor Robinson, you can hardly expect us to observe all the niceties." He tossed a pile of papers onto the floor and looked at Harry as if daring him to object. I watched Harry's jaw working as he battled to master his anger. When Langworth turned his attention to the desk once more, I backed slowly out of the room. If Edmonton was poking about in the upper rooms, I wanted to be there to witness whatever he claimed to find there.

But I had hardly set foot on the stairs when there was more furious hammering at the door. I looked back at the guard in the hall.

"Reinforcements?"

He shrugged. Langworth emerged from the parlour, his mouth twisted in irritation, followed by Harry.

"Yes?" Langworth flung the door open to reveal Tom Garth, breathing hard, his face flushed. "What is it, Garth? We are all occupied here."

"Masters—" Tom snatched a breath and his eyes flitted nervously from one face to the next. "There is a man at the gate just now wanting Constable Edmonton, as a matter of urgency. There's been another killing, he says."

"Another—? Good God. Call the constable down," Langworth barked over his shoulder to the guard. I pressed closer, so that I could see the vein begin to pulse in his temple. "Did he say who it was, Garth?"

"Doctor Sykes, he says. Found in the river up past St. Radigund's Street, where the two streams meet."

"*Sykes? No—*"

Langworth staggered back a step; it was barely noticeable and he composed himself almost immediately, but I was near enough to see that this news had dealt him an unexpected blow. I was reeling from it myself. Over my shoulder I looked at Harry, who only opened his eyes wide in disbelief.

"Where is this man?" Langworth demanded, his voice firm again.

"Right here, sir," Tom said, and stepped aside to reveal a young man, sweating profusely. When he saw Langworth, he ripped his cap from his head and stood twisting it between his hands.

"A woman saw the body in the creek, sir, just a few moments past," he blurted. "Well, she screamed and run for the nearest house. My father and I pulled him out, sir."

"Drowned?"

"No, sir, stabbed. Looks like he was put in the water after. He was weighted down."

"What?"

"In the water. There was a stone tied around his neck with a rope, except it wasn't really big enough for the job, he was still drifting with the current. We didn't know it was him till we got him on the bank. You could only see his black robes billowing in the water."

Edmonton came bounding down the stairs at this moment and elbowed me aside to stand at Langworth's shoulder.

"This man says Sykes is dead," Langworth muttered, and his voice grew shaky again. "We had better make haste—I cannot fathom . . ." He turned sharply to me, and if his face had been pallid before, it now seemed drained of all blood. "Where were you this morning?"

I looked at him, unblinking. "I? At the market, buying bread. Then at divine service—you saw me there yourself. Much as you would like me to hang for every crime in Canterbury, I cannot oblige you this time. Your friends are very unlucky, Canon Langworth, I must say."

Langworth's eyes flashed.

"You would joke over a man's corpse, you—?" He made a choking sound, as if he could find no ready insult that would do me justice. With bared teeth he took a step towards me; he might have lunged there and then if Edmonton had not put out a hand to restrain him.

"Let us go and see this dreadful business, sir," he said. "We can finish the search later. Come." He gestured to the guards. "This fellow who fished him out can answer some questions on the way. You—can you bring us this woman who first saw the body?"

"I should think so, sir—my mother was giving her a glass of something when I came to fetch the constable."

"Tell her to have a care for herself," I called, from the hallway. "Tell her you can be arrested for merely finding a body in this town."

"You would do well to keep your mouth shut until you open it before the judge," Langworth said through his teeth.

"Come, Canon Langworth. Touch nothing, Harry Robinson," Edmonton said in parting, holding up a warning finger. "We will return as soon as we are able."

The four of them left together with the young man, still twisting his cap as if he feared he might be blamed.

Tom Garth remained on the path outside, staring at us.

"Come in for a moment, Tom," Harry said, holding the door. "We may have no bloody food in this house, but I can put my hands on a bottle of wine. God knows we could all do with a drink, even if it's not yet dinner time."

Tom came in, apparently too stunned to speak, and the three of us settled around the kitchen table.

"Thank God that infernal heat has broken, at least," Harry said, uncorking a bottle.

"Doctor Sykes," Tom said, shaking his head, his eyes fixed on his glass. "Who would have thought."

"Langworth didn't kill him," I said, leaning my elbows on the table and pressing my fingers to my temples. I could hardly begin to see where this latest news fit into the tangle of deaths and plots. "You could see it in his face. Unless he is the most skilled actor I have ever witnessed. He looked as if he'd taken a blow to the balls when he heard the news."

"Besides," Harry said, pouring out three glasses and knocking back his own in one draught, "he was within our sights almost all morning."

"Sykes was alive this morning," I said, trying to piece it together. "He was called out to the Kingsley house to confirm the old housekeeper dead—"

"Sir Edward's housekeeper is dead?" Harry blinked. "Old Meg? That is sad news—she was a good woman."

"My sister was fond of her," Tom said, without looking up.

"It's more than sad," I said. "And it was no accident. But that is another matter. So Sykes left St. Gregory's in time for the news to have made it to the marketplace by about eight o'clock this morning. Where did he go after that?"

"Into the river," Tom said, helpfully.

"Not of his own will he didn't, not with a stone—oh, Mother of Christ!" I looked at Harry. He nodded.

"I thought as much when the fellow said it."

"'But whoso shall offend one of these little ones, it were better for him that a millstone were hanged about his neck, and that he were drowned in the depth of the sea,'" I murmured. "It was a punishment."

Tom lifted his head.

"I know that Scripture. A punishment for what?"

I looked at him for a moment, then fished in my purse.

"Tom—Doctor Robinson is near faint with hunger and likely to murder me if he doesn't eat soon. Is there any chance you could send to the inn for some dinner? Here's money—beef stew if they have any, and maybe a pie, and pickled beetroot. Oh, and bread. And get yourself a beer. I would go, but I should wait here in case Canon Langworth comes back with those apes."

Tom took the shilling I held out and turned it admiringly in the light, as if impressed that someone like me could so easily lay hands on ready money.

"I will, sir. And would you like me to check on that outbuilding on my way, explain the situation?"

I clutched my head. Poor Sophia—I had almost forgotten her in the drama of Sykes's death. Now we had no way of knowing when Langworth and Edmonton would be back to search the house, and she could not return until they had done so. At least she had something to read, I thought, and the hairs on my arms stood up to think of her trying to unlock the secrets of that book with her scant Greek.

"Thank you, Tom. Very much appreciated."

"Least I can do really," he said, with a sheepish smile, and stood up, knocking over his stool. It was difficult not to like this big, clumsy man, despite the fact that he had tried to condemn Sophia to save his own neck. I hoped I was not wrong to take him at his word.

After we heard the door slam closed behind him, Harry poured us each another glass and I continued to study the table, chin on my fist, as if the answer might be written in the coarse grain of the oak.

"It's not a coincidence. It can't be. Someone knew about the children. That's what the stone was for."

"Sure you're not reading too much into it, Bruno? If you throw a body in a river, you want to make sure it sinks."

"Then you would use a bigger stone. Someone wanted this gesture to be seen. But who in God's name was it, Harry? Who knew about the children? Only you and me, and Old Meg, but she is dead. After that, only Langworth himself. And if the Widow Gray is right, the mayor is the fourth guardian, but could the mayor of Canterbury stab a man in broad daylight and throw his body in a river in the centre of town?"

"Could anybody, for that matter?" Harry peered into his glass. "You told the Widow Gray?"

"That's where I was this morning."

"When you should have been buying my bread."

"Yes. Sorry. I wanted to test the theory of the miracle. She is the only one left who could testify to it before a judge."

"You won't get her to say a word against Langworth, no matter how often you bow and wink your big dark eyes at her, my friend," he said, tracing the rim of his glass with a forefinger.

"I don't suppose she could have . . . ?"

Harry laughed.

"Sykes was three times the size of her. Stabbed him and rolled him into the river, on her own?"

"Then who else? The millstone—it was the verse the old monk quoted to me in prison, about the boys. It *has* to be. But who else knew about the boys? Could Langworth have confided to Nick Kingsley when he was there last night?"

"Langworth wouldn't confide to Nick Kingsley where he keeps his ale."

"No. Of course, the only one still at large is Samuel." I raised my head and looked at him. He made a gesture of resignation.

"You hold no hope of him being on the road to London, then?"

"I don't think he's anywhere near London. Langworth wouldn't let him. But I don't see why he would need to kill Sykes, unless it was at Langworth's order."

"Perhaps Langworth feared Sykes would not be able to hold his counsel if he was questioned about the Becket plot. Perhaps he now thinks the only way to manage this is to do so alone."

"But Sykes was essential to the whole scheme. Besides, to silence him would be one thing. Why the millstone? It draws attention to the business with the boys."

"Only to us, who know."

I sighed. "Perhaps you are right. I cannot make sense of it, Harry. God, what I would not give to search Sykes's house. I'll wager Langworth is there even now, tidying away anything that would expose him."

"Before he comes back and throws my papers to the four winds," Harry muttered.

WE DID NOT leave the house until Evensong. Harry tried to read, though his eyes were more often fixed on the looming shape of the cathedral through the window than on the page. I paced endlessly, trying to piece together the disparate parts of my defence for the assizes the next day. By now I hardly knew whether I should be defending myself and Sophia, or bringing charges against Langworth for the murder of the two boys. The more I tried to make a coherent case, the more ensnared I felt; I could not mention the dead boys without explaining the plot to revive the shrine of Becket, and that was part of information so sensitive it properly belonged to Walsingham's ears alone. He would not thank me for airing it in a public courtroom with all the citizens of Canterbury looking on, agog. If enough of them learned that their beloved saint was still among them, they might even start a riot. But without an explanation of the boys' murders, how could I hope to incriminate Langworth for the deaths of Fitch and Edward Kingsley? And I had no firm proof that Langworth killed Kingsley, except that he knew Kingsley was on the way to his house and he was the only person who could have gained access to the crypt to get hold of the crucifix.

Langworth and the constable returned with their armed guard shortly before Evensong. The canon treasurer was ghostly pale, his face grimmer than usual. He did not seem a man to shed tears, even for a friend; Sykes's death seemed rather to have sparked in him a fiercer hostility. He carried himself now with the air of a man whose will has been thwarted, and who considers this a monstrous injustice for which someone must be made to pay. They tore the house apart with undisguised relish; I stood by with a hand on Harry's arm as he stoically watched Langworth scattering his papers, rifling through his clothes, knocking his few ornaments to the ground. The only moment's grace was when the canon attempted to poke about in the chimney breast in search of hiding places and dislodged a fall of soot on his own head. Stifling my laughter, I climbed the stairs to see what Edmonton was doing. I found him in my chamber, surrounded by scattered straw; he had slit the thin mattress open with a knife. When he heard my tread on the landing outside he started like a guilty creature and wheeled around, holding up a bag of money with a forced expression of triumph.

"As we suspected," he said, bouncing it in his palm so that the coins chinked. "There must be at least ten shillings in here. That qualifies as grand larceny in a court of law. Grand larceny is a hanging offence, as you surely know."

"Oh, please." I leaned against the doorjamb, affecting a nonchalance I did not feel. "You took that from inside your own doublet this very moment."

His ginger moustache twitched and he looked away. "Naturally you would try to deny it. Canon Langworth!" he shouted down the stairwell.

"It is laughable. I predicted this."

"Oh, really? Because you knew you were guilty."

"Not even a simpleton would be fooled by this trick. Do you take the queen's justice for a fool?"

Langworth appeared behind me on the stairs.

"It may interest you to know that there is a locksmith in the town who will swear on oath that the other day you came in and asked him to make a copy of four keys. Keys you could only have stolen from my house, one of which is to the cathedral treasury. How do you answer that, signor—I'm sorry, I forget your name. You have so many, do you not?"

"I say it is pure speculation. But if you wish me to confess publicly to having been in your house and in the treasury, or rather beneath it, that could lead to an interesting discussion before the queen's justice."

Langworth flicked a glance at Edmonton, who looked from one to the other of us, perplexed.

"Don't try to threaten me," Langworth said, lowering his voice. "You will spend the night in gaol for this. Your friends in high places cannot reach you now." His mouth curved into a slow smile, stretching his scar silver. I closed my eyes. I had thought I would have one last night with Sophia; if I were taken to the gaol, who would fetch her from the outbuilding? Who would protect her if Langworth and his thugs chose to come back unannounced and search the house again when I was out of the way?

Edmonton pushed me lightly, his finger between my shoulder blades.

"Let us go. Once again."

Langworth turned and began to descend ahead of me, still wearing his cold smile. I saw no choice but to follow.

Harry turned pale and gripped the banister when he saw my face. I nodded to the bag in Edmonton's hand. "Told you."

"We are taking your houseguest back to the West Gate, Doctor

Robinson," Langworth informed him, with impeccable politeness. "I fear that money you put up for his bail has been wasted. Never mind— perhaps you will learn to be a better judge of character in future."

Harry set his jaw and flexed his hands into fists. In spite of everything, I smiled; I could see how much he would have liked to punch Langworth in the mouth.

"I shall go to the dean right away," he said to me.

"Doctor Robinson, this man has been caught stealing from the cathedral treasury—do you think the dean will want to vouch for his character now?"

"You are a snake, John Langworth," Harry said, between his teeth.

"For shame, Doctor Robinson, is that how one canon of God's church should speak to another? I fear you have been infected by the company you keep."

At the front door, the two armed men closed in on either side of me. I looked up at the one I recognised from before.

"Hello. I begin to feel we are old friends."

He smiled, then quickly straightened his face when he caught Langworth's piercing look.

But outside in the precincts, by the Christ Church gate, our little procession was impeded by another, grander entourage coming in the opposite direction, from the gatehouse towards the cathedral. People clustered around a group of men, guarded as I was by liveried attendants with pikestaffs, but a good many more of them. Edmonton held up a hand and we slowed. Dean Rogers approached the mass of people from the direction of the Archbishop's Palace, arms held wide, his usual anxious expression replaced by one of restrained delight.

The crowd parted, the men with pikestaffs moved aside, and from among them a tall, corpulent man in a black robe emerged into the light, his arms held out towards the dean. From his shoulders hung a cloak of black silk that rippled like molten metal.

"Richard," he boomed, smiling broadly, in a voice that carried across the open ground to the cathedral and beyond. "As ever, your table and your company remain my one genuine pleasure at the end of this long road."

He embraced the dean and kissed him on both cheeks. When he stepped back his fleshy face was running with sweat; he extended a peremptory hand behind him and one of the legion of young men in clerk's robes jumped forward with a handkerchief.

"Welcome, Charles, welcome." Dean Rogers clasped his hands. "It has been too long since you graced my table with your conversation, that is certain. But I fear you find our town in the grip of terrible events. The angel of death has descended on us with scant regard for estate or person . . ." He cast his eyes down, as if he expected to be chided for this dereliction of duty.

The big man rubbed his hands together with unseemly relish. "Yes, I heard about Kingsley, poor devil. And Ezekiel Sykes, only this morning. Canterbury is grown lawless since I was last here."

As if it were not already obvious, Langworth turned to me with satisfaction and nodded towards the man in black.

"Justice Hale. There you see him. He dines tonight at the Archbishop's Palace with the dean and all the city dignitaries."

"Those that are left," I said.

The dean looked around at the people jostling to have a sight of the justice. Over their heads his eyes fell on our party and his face collapsed in dismay.

"Canon Langworth? Constable? What is this—you are arresting Doctor Savolino a second time?"

Justice Hale looked at me with interest. Then he chuckled deeply, and the flesh around his eyes crinkled.

"God's wounds, the man must be a shocking felon to need arresting twice. And hiding out in the cathedral precincts. Did he slip from your grasp the first time, Constable?"

Edmonton turned puce and began to stutter a response, but Langworth held up a restraining hand.

"This man was bailed on the wishes of the dean, Your Honour," he said with a little bow, his voice smooth as cream. "While under the care of Doctor Robinson here, he contrived to rob my house and the cathedral treasury. Constable Edmonton is returning him to the gaol where he can do no more harm until he faces Your Honour tomorrow."

Dean Rogers exchanged a look with Langworth and for the first time I saw at close quarters how much these two highest officials of the cathedral detested each other. I recalled what Harry had said about Langworth's ambition to be elected dean and how he had been narrowly beaten by Rogers and his moderate supporters; clearly the rivalry between them was undiminished, and Rogers seemed determined not to be humiliated by Langworth in front of the justice. Silently, I thanked providence that Dean Rogers still appeared well disposed to me, even if just to spite Langworth.

"Robbed the treasury, eh?" The justice looked impressed. "I see you are an audacious fellow, whatever else you may be."

He looked at me frankly and I held his gaze, my eyes steady, hoping to convey that I had no reason to fear him. He was perhaps nearing sixty, though his grey-flecked hair was thick beneath his hat and his size gave him a hearty air; he must have a strong constitution to be riding about the country several times a year to hear the assizes. Though his cheeks were webbed with crimson threads from fine wine, his eyes were sombre and flickered over my face as if with long practice; I sensed that beneath his good cheer was a steely will. I could only hope there was also wisdom and compassion.

Dean Rogers stepped close to the justice and whispered in his ear. Hale nodded, listening, and when the dean straightened up, he looked back at me with a hint of admiration in that appraising glance.

"Friend of the Sidneys, are you? Young Philip is a great favourite of the queen, of course. I knew Sir Henry a little, when we were younger. Now there was a fellow who could talk himself out of any scrape. England never had a finer diplomat. Well, tomorrow we'll see if you have the same gift, won't we?" His smile seemed genuinely amiable; we all have our parts to play in this pageant, he seemed to be saying, don't take it personally.

I bowed my head in acknowledgement. The dean leaned in and whispered further; Hale looked from me to Langworth and Edmonton and frowned.

"I understand bail has already been paid for this man, is it not so?"

"If it please Your Honour, he has breached the terms of his bail by committing another grievous crime," Edmonton said, tearing off his hat with anxious deference.

"Well, we don't know for certain that he has, do we? That is what tomorrow's process will determine, unless I very much misunderstand the law. Who has stood surety for this man?"

"I did, Your Honour." Harry stepped forward.

Hale peered at him.

"And you would be . . . ? A brother canon, I see. I'm sure we must have met."

"Doctor Harry Robinson, Your Honour. Resident canon of the cathedral. I had the pleasure of dining with Your Honour at the dean's table last year."

"Did you? Age has addled my memory, I fear," he said, smiling, then turned to Edmonton, his face abruptly serious. "I think, Constable, that if this man is bound over to appear before my court tomorrow and Doctor Robinson has already stood bail and is willing to vouch for him, there is no need to make him spend the night in gaol. I imagine it's quite crowded enough there as it is, no?"

"Your Honour—" Edmonton began, flushing scarlet again, but Langworth cut in, taking a step towards Justice Hale as if to reason with him, man to man.

"With the greatest respect, Your Honour, Dean Rogers and Doctor Robinson have had their heads turned by this man. He is a plausible talker. If you leave him at liberty tonight, I predict he will commit some new harm against our community."

"Why—do you have another one planned for me?" I shot back.

Justice Hale fixed me with a stern look, as you might give a precocious child.

"You would do better to hold your tongue for the present, sir. You shall have opportunity enough to entertain us with your plausible talk tomorrow." I thought I detected a twinkle in his eye, but perhaps that was wishful thinking. "Italian, are you, by the sound of you?"

"Yes, Your Honour."

"*E cosa la porta en Inghilterra?*" he asked.

I smiled, impressed.

"*Trovo la sua nazione piu illuminata su questioni religiose, mio signore.*"

He laughed again. "You are a Protestant, then, I deduce? Well, that's a good start. He says he finds our country more enlightened in matters of religion," he added, for the benefit of those listening.

I took the fact that he spoke Italian as a favourable sign. Clearly he was educated, and had a broader outlook than many of his countrymen, who considered all foreigners sons of the same Catholic whore. He was interrupted by a great cascade of bells that exploded from the cathedral tower like the thunder of the previous night, heralding the beginning of divine service.

"Ah, there we are—time for Evensong. Stand down your armed men, Constable, and let us go in and worship together like good Christians. Send them back to collect him tomorrow morning at seven o'clock— I'm sure Doctor Robinson will keep a close watch on him until then." He turned to the dean. "Now, tell me, Richard," he said, in a tone that declared an official change of subject, "is your choir still as celestial as I remember it? The music here is one of my chief pleasures on these visits, as you know—second only to your table, of course." He hooked a heavy arm around the dean's shoulders as they set off towards the west door and did not give us another look.

Edmonton glanced helplessly at Langworth, who turned to me, his sunken eyes lit with righteous anger.

"Do not imagine you have won."

He stalked away, his robe snapping in the chill breeze that he seemed to generate himself. Edmonton, deflated, made a gesture to the guards; bemused, they lowered their pikes and stood awkwardly, looking around at the milling congregation as if uncertain as to their next orders.

Harry gave a brusque laugh and clapped me on the shoulder.

"Come. You had better be seen at Evensong, praying for God's mercy."

WE RETRIEVED SOPHIA from the outbuilding at dusk, when the congregation had dispersed and the senior canons gone to the dean's banquet in honour of the justice, bundling her through the shadows and into Harry's hall. She looked numb and shivered inside her shapeless cloak, despite the fact that it was a warm night. I left them alone in the kitchen and went to the inn around the corner for hot food, carrying the covered dishes back myself rather than risking the serving boy coming anywhere near the house. Sophia gulped it down like a beggar, the way I had seen her eat that first day in London. I watched her, wishing for a moment that she had not found me again. I brushed the thought away.

"I may as well have been thrown into prison," she said, looking morosely into her bowl. "I spend my life being shut into small rooms as it is."

"What I don't understand, Mistress Kingsley," Harry said, wiping a piece of bread around his plate, "is why you would return to Canterbury when you had already made it safely to London? Knowing there was a price on your head?"

"Because I didn't want to live the rest of my life as a fugitive," she said, raising her head, her eyes bright. She pinched the rough cloth of the skirt she wore and held it up. "In borrowed clothes. Looking over my shoulder, fearing someone would recognise me. I wanted my name cleared, for good. I thought Bruno would be able to find the person who did it. And then I would be free." She sighed, and rested her cheek on her fist, as if the possibility of this was receding by the moment.

"And rich, I suppose," Harry said casually, still looking at his bread.

"If I were cleared of murder, I would inherit the greater part of my husband's estate, yes," she said, defensive. "And it would be small recompense for what I suffered at his hands, I assure you."

"Madame, I meant no harm," Harry said mildly. We finished the meal in silence.

Later, when I blew out the candles in the upper room, she turned away from me and climbed under the sheet still wearing her shift. It seemed pointless in the circumstances to undress myself, so I moved in beside her in my shirt and underhose.

"Bruno," she said, refusal in her voice before I had even reached for her, "I am exhausted, and afraid. I have spent all day in a shed with nowhere to piss but at my own feet, fearing every creak of the boards in the wind. Could we just . . ." She let the meaning hang in the air.

"Of course," I murmured into her hair, allowing her to settle herself against my shoulder, willing myself to a gallantry I did not feel. "Did you read the book?" I asked, mainly to distract myself from the pressure of her left breast against my rib cage.

"I tried. It was impossible to understand."

"All Greek to you."

"That is the point—it is not all Greek. My Greek is poor but I can usually make out some of the meaning. Part of this book is written in a language I have never seen."

I laughed.

"It is a cipher. The book was translated into Greek from a very ancient manuscript in Egyptian. The translator believed the knowledge it contained was so powerful that it should not be made visible except to a very few adepts."

"Magic?" She raised her head an inch and I heard the animation in her voice.

"Beyond magic. I believe this book contains the last great secret of the Egyptian sage Hermes Trismegistus—the truth of how man can become like God."

She whistled softly; I felt her breath tickle my neck.

"It must be very valuable."

"Only a handful of people could recognise its true worth." I pictured them: my friend John Dee, now living in Prague at the court of Emperor Rudolf; Lord Henry Howard, who had once almost killed Dee in pursuit of this book, and would have sent it down here to Langworth for safekeeping when he knew he was to be sent to prison and his house raided. "My patron, King Henri of France, is a great collector of occult manuscripts. I can barely imagine what he would be willing to pay for it. But I do not mean to sell it at any price," I added.

"Have you broken the cipher?"

I smiled. "You have had more leisure to read that book than I ever have. But I will."

"If anyone can, Bruno, it is you." She laid her hand on my chest and I rested my cheek on her hair. For a moment it was possible to imagine that this was real, that tomorrow I would not be on trial for my life. "What will happen to us?" she whispered, as if reading my thoughts.

"I don't know. The justice seems a sensible sort of man. He is friends with the dean, and the dean is anxious not to offend my connections at court, so perhaps it will go well for me. I still have hope that my letter will have reached my friend Sidney in time."

I did not think they would dare to execute me on the spot, which meant there was still time for an intervention. If my letter had found its destination, I thought, with a brief wave of despair; the weavers would not know the urgency. They may spend two or three days in town attending to their own business before they remembered they had a message to deliver.

"And me?" she asked, in a small voice.

"If Tom Garth will find the courage to speak, it will weaken the case against you to know that the gloves were not yours. There is no other evidence against you."

"Except that I ran, and took his money," she murmured. "And that I gain most from his will. I thought you would find the real killer easily, like you did in Oxford." There was a faint hint of accusation in her voice, and I bridled at it.

"Because you thought the answer was simple. You thought it was Nicholas. But I can only think it was Langworth, for some complex reason connected with the experiments on the boys and their plans regarding Becket. But I cannot prove it for certain. Not by tomorrow, anyway." I took a deep breath. "I am sorry if you think I have failed you."

"No." She stroked a finger along my collarbone. "Perhaps it is I who have failed. I have failed all along, all my life. I must have been born under a very bad aspect."

"You were just born to the wrong station in life," I whispered into the top of her head. "A spirit like yours would have been better suited to being a princess."

She laughed, a gentle bubbling sound against my chest. "Please, Bruno, aim higher. Queen, I think."

"And yet, you know the queen of England lives every day in fear of her life too?"

"At least she has never been forced to take a husband," she said, with feeling.

I slept; at least, I drifted in and out of sleep as the moon drifted among its violet tatters of cloud, its blue light slowly moving the shadows on the wall each time my eyes half opened. Sophia slept easily against my chest, her breathing rhythmic and soft, her face flushed and smooth as her eyelids twitched. The arm I had under her head grew numb but I kept still for fear of waking her. Hours passed. The moon was hidden, revealed, hidden again. And then, I heard it: a tread on the stair. The faintest of movements; as if a cat had approached the door. But my nerves sprang alive, the hairs on my arms prickled; in my gut I felt a sudden inkling of danger. Gingerly I retrieved my arm from under Sophia's head and pushed myself upright, trying to keep quiet; might it only be Harry, shuffling about on the floor below, fumbling for his piss-pot in the dark? But the movement had sounded too close at hand. I felt for my knife and realised I had unbuckled it and left it with my belt and breeches on a chair against the far wall.

I was easing myself upright slowly when the door was pushed open

and the shadow of a man loomed across the white wall opposite the bed.
I made to move but he was at the end of the bed before I could shake off
the sheet and in the thin light I caught the unmistakable glint of a knife.
I hardly needed the moon to reveal him; the long nose, the gleam of his
pale domed head.

"Well, well." Samuel nodded at Sophia's sleeping form. "Two birds
with one stone, you might say. And you will die with your sins on you,
which is no more than you deserve, you heretic dog."

Sophia stirred and opened her eyes at the sound of his voice; dazed,
she took a moment to comprehend the scene, but when she did she gave
a little scream, which she stifled with her hand.

"Why didn't you kill me sooner, if you meant to?" I asked, hearing
the tremor in my voice.

Samuel considered this.

"We didn't know how much you knew. But now you cannot be permitted to air your theories in a public courtroom."

"How will you explain my death?"

He shrugged. "Not for me to explain. I am on the road to London,
remember? I expect it will look as if Harry killed you in self-defence and
then died of his own wounds."

"Oh, God, no." My stomach lurched and I tasted bile. "You have not
killed Harry?"

"Not yet. But he cannot be left at liberty to repeat your suppositions
to Francis Walsingham or anyone else." His voice was remarkably calm.
But then a man who could drop a dismembered child out of a sack onto a
rubbish heap must be unusually free of emotion. "Now then." He looked
from me to Sophia with lascivious anticipation. "What would give you
the greatest suffering, Bruno—to watch me kill her first, or to die yourself knowing I mean to have some sport with her while you bleed your
life out on the floor like a slaughtered calf?"

Sophia muffled a sob and pulled her shift tight around her legs, hugging her knees to her chest. I glanced over Samuel's shoulder to where
my knife lay; any attempt to lunge past him for it and he would stick his

blade straight in me. My best hope was somehow to distract him and then to kick him in the arm holding the knife while his attention was divided. It was not the first time I had kept the threat of death at bay by talking; it was worth a try again.

"Why did you kill Sykes?" I blurted.

"What?" He sounded irritated by the question. "I did not kill Sykes, you fool."

"Then who did?"

"You tell me."

I stared at him, perplexed.

"*I*? What would I know? You killed him, surely, on Langworth's order, like you killed Fitch."

He made a small, impatient movement with his head.

"Fitch was becoming a problem. He didn't know how to keep his mouth shut. When Sykes saw him talking to you that day, knowing who you were—we had to make sure he said nothing else."

"So you killed him because of me?" I thought of the apothecary's merry laugh.

"It would have happened sooner or later."

"And Sykes?"

"I told you—I didn't touch Sykes. Do not think to delay me with this. I will do what I came here to do." He took a step closer to my side of the bed, his knife held out. I gathered my strength and kicked out at his hand, but he had anticipated the movement and circled it deftly away, the tip of the blade grazing my foot. "Save your energy for your prayers," he said through his teeth, and took another step towards me, blade poised.

He was perhaps three feet away now; one good thrust and he could strike me from there: face, chest, stomach. In the dim light I saw the shine of his eyes as they flickered over me, anticipating the best spot for the first blow. Then, a sound, unexpected; I felt Sophia tense and sit up. Samuel must have heard it too; he hesitated for the space of a heartbeat, knife half raised, and almost turned. There was a movement, a slicing and a rush of air, then a sickening crack and he seemed to crumple like a straw effigy, first to his knees and then onto his side. Behind him, in the doorway, Harry stood in his nightgown, a poker clutched in his shaking hands.

"He would have killed you," he mouthed, staring at Samuel's prone form and his own makeshift weapon in amazement.

"I thought you couldn't get up the stairs," I said, feeling my own limbs beginning to tremble in the aftershock.

"Well, I can when I need to," he said, transfixed by the scene in front of him, as if he could not quite believe it was his own doing. "I couldn't sleep. I heard the key turning in the front door—my ears are still good, if nothing else. I knew it could only be him. He would have killed you," he repeated, almost mechanically, and I realised he was justifying his actions to himself, reassuring his conscience, or his God, that he had had no choice.

Then, as suddenly as if he himself had been struck with a poker, his legs seemed to give way beneath him and he slumped against the wall, his free hand flapping in vain as if searching for his stick. Snapped out of my daze, I leapt across the bed and caught him under the arms before he fell, guiding him gently to sit on the bed. Sophia subsided into quiet sobs, her face pressed into her knees. I did not know which of them to comfort first.

"Let us thank God that we are all alive," I said, exhaling slowly. "The question is—what do we do with him?"

We all looked at Samuel, who chose that moment to let out a guttural moan as blood bubbled from his nose. Sophia jumped back with another little scream.

"Better thank God that he is still alive too," Harry muttered, but I could hear the relief in his voice. He wiped his forehead with his sleeve. He had feared the stain of murder on his soul.

"We must get him upright," I said, picking up the knife that had fallen from Samuel's hand. I shouldered him into a sitting position against the wall with a strange sense of familiarity; it seemed only moments since I had done the same for Nick Kingsley. "If they only knew—I haven't murdered the man they claim I did, but I have nearly killed three others since I've been here."

"*I* nearly killed this one, Bruno, don't take all the glory."

I looked at Harry and we both broke out laughing; after staring at us blankly for a moment, Sophia joined in and the three of us must have sounded like tavern drunks, doubled over and wiping tears from our faces in sheer relief, until Samuel groaned again, a throaty, bestial sound, and slid sideways.

"He must be kept safe somewhere until tomorrow," I said, as if sobering up.

On the floor by the bed, Sophia had dropped the voluminous dress of Olivier's grandmother; I found one of the underskirts made of a rough heavy linen and began to tear through it with Samuel's knife, until I had cut it into long strips. With Harry holding Samuel's body up, I bound the servant's wrists tightly together behind him, did the same with his ankles, and tied three thick strips around his mouth.

"Can he breathe through that?" Harry asked, peering anxiously into Samuel's unseeing face. "If his mouth is filled with blood?"

"We'll have to take our chances. Come now, both of you—we'll have to get him down the stairs and lock him in his own chamber. Keep him here until we are ready to have him fetched before the justice. And Langworth must not know Samuel was unsuccessful tonight, or he may try something else."

Between us, Sophia and I manoeuvred Samuel's limp body down the stairs to the first floor and into the small bedchamber he had used at the back of the house. It was plainly furnished, with no sign of personal belongings save a wooden chest in one corner, secured with a padlock. Sophia's strength belied her slender frame, and we hauled Samuel until he was propped against a stool by the wall. I retied his hands around one leg of the stool; it was not fixed down, but it would make it harder for him to free himself. Harry took a ring of keys from his servant's belt and clicked through them until he found the one he wanted. At the door, he paused to take a last, pitying look.

"Don't be sentimental, Harry," I warned, seeing his expression. "He meant to kill you after me."

Harry sighed. "And yet he seemed a loyal servant for so many years."

"Even while he was passing every detail of your business to Langworth for money. Come now," I said, stifling a yawn, as Harry locked Samuel securely into the room, "I doubt we shall sleep more tonight. Let me warm some wine—we would all be glad of a drink."

Downstairs, in the kitchen, when Sophia had returned to bed, Harry sat at the table swilling the dregs of his wine around the glass.

"You love that girl," he remarked, not looking at me.

"I . . ." I looked away. It seemed fruitless to finish the sentence.

"Will you marry her? You should, you know," he added, in a tone of mild reproach, when I did not reply.

"I have no means to support a wife, Harry. Besides, I don't know if she would have me." Even as I spoke, I felt I did know. Sophia did not want another husband. The point about Sophia, I wanted to tell him, was that you would never be sure you really had her. That was her appeal—beyond her beauty, it was this sense that she belonged wholly to herself, and always kept something in reserve. She was as elusive as the true meaning of that book upstairs in its wooden casket, and bred in me the same unsatisfied longing. But I was too tired to try and explain any of this.

"Even though she has married you in the sight of God?" He raised an eyebrow. Meaning, because I had taken her to my bed.

To my knowledge, Sophia had already married three men in the sight of God in that sense, and quite possibly more. For myself, I doubted God concerned Himself too far with such things; with Christendom still tearing itself apart over the true substance of a piece of bread and a glass of wine, did He really have time to count? I didn't say this either. We sat in sympathetic silence, like two bruised survivors of a skirmish, until the dawn light filtered through the small casement and Harry suggested I heat a bowl of water for a shave.

Chapter *17*

Sophia lay sleeping in a slant of sunlight, her lips parted, one hand slightly curled against the sheet beside her face like a child's. I stood in the doorway, hardly liking to wake her, torn between the need for some words of comfort, some recognition of all that I was facing on her behalf, and the desire to leave her in what might be her last untroubled moments. If I was found guilty at the assizes, there would be no more bail, no avuncular generosity from the justice unless I could find a means to speak to him in private, but it would be easy for them to deny me that. I would be taken directly to the gaol to await my punishment and then it would only be a matter of time before she was found and sentenced, and Harry with her as an accomplice.

I stole across the room and slid the wooden casket containing the book from my leather satchel, all the while keeping my eyes fixed on Sophia. At least if the house was searched they would not find this. With my knife, I levered up the nails holding one of the floorboards next to the bed, so that I could prise it up far enough to slide the box into the cavity above the rafters. After it I pushed my purse containing what remained of my money, the fragments of the letters I had taken from Fitch's hearth, Langworth's keys, and the dead boy's Saint Denis medal;

those, too, needed to be kept safe until I could put them into the right hands, and I suspected anything I owned would be taken from me before the trial. Especially a weapon, I thought, reluctantly placing my bone-handled knife in its sheath on top of the casket and fitting the board back into place, its nails loosely resting in their holes.

I lowered myself onto the bed beside her and leaned my newly shaven cheek towards her face. She stirred; the long dark lashes fluttered and those leonine eyes slowly focused on me. Briefly she smiled, then it was as if a cloud passed overhead, driven by a strong wind, and her face altered as she recalled the day.

"Wish me luck," I whispered, stroking a finger gently along the line of her collarbone. "Whatever happens, do not move from here until I come for you."

"And if you cannot?"

"Then you wait for Harry."

"Will he go to the courthouse with you?"

"I think he must. It would look odd if he stayed away, after he has paid my bail."

Her eyes flickered to the door.

"The man downstairs . . . ?"

"He is secure, don't worry." I glanced at the floor under the window. "Harry's poker is still there, just in case."

"Don't joke about it, Bruno." She placed her hand over mine. "You have risked your life for me." Tears welled silver against her lashes. "I don't know how to thank you."

"When this is over, if we survive—perhaps there is something we could talk about."

She rolled her eyes in mock resignation: of course, what else could a man want. I shook my head.

"Not that." I smiled. "Although that too. But something else."

"What?"

I hesitated. In the hour before dawn, when I had kept my silent vigil in the kitchen with Harry, I had weighed his words and almost persuaded myself it might be possible. With my pension from King Henri of France and the money I earned from Walsingham, might I not have enough to keep a wife, if we lived modestly? And if my book were presented to Queen Elizabeth, if she saw fit to patronise it, the sales might give me a steady income . . . I could live quietly, give up these misadventures I seemed to fall into as other men fall in and out of alehouses; write my books, keep an eye on the French ambassador for Walsingham, make a place I could call home. If, if, if. If Sophia would say yes.

"It will keep. Let us unravel this Gordian knot first." I kissed her on the forehead and stood. At the door I paused. "Pray for me?"

She sat up and looked at me with a sad smile. "I don't pray anymore, Bruno, and neither do you."

"Still. Today of all days, it might be worth a try."

⛫

AT SEVEN O'CLOCK, Harry stood in the hallway, fully dressed, considering his face in a small mirror that hung by the front door.

"You've not done a bad job," he said, tilting his head to one side and rubbing his chin. "If needs must, you could scrape a living as barber."

"It may yet come to that." I looked at him. "And how do I look? Like a felon, or a friend to kings and courtiers?"

"One may be both," Harry said, with a faint smile. "You still look like a handsome pirate, Bruno—I fear no barber can solve that for you. It's something about your eyes." Then his face grew serious. "I have been thinking. This business with Langworth and Becket and the dead boys—" He broke off and shook his head. "I fear it is too sensitive for the public assizes. You have not seen the way the crowds gather, as if it were for a bearbaiting. If they learn that the bones of their saint are still beneath the cathedral, there may be a riot. They could tear up the crypt in pursuit of him. And we are talking about matters of treason— the security of the realm. Matters that should reach Walsingham's ears before anyone else's."

"Walsingham is not here." I sighed. "I have done my best, Harry. Either my first letter has reached him or it has not."

"We need to tell the justice who you are and what you are doing here," Harry said.

"How am I to do that? They will hardly grant me a private audience with him."

"No, but he might admit me. If I can get near him in time."

A rap at the door, on the stroke of seven; Edmonton and his armed guards stood outside in the morning sun. The constable looked particularly pleased that he was finally allowed to do his job; he seized my sleeve and manhandled me down the step to the path. I pulled my arm free and he glared at me with distaste.

"You are a prisoner like any other today, sir," he said, wrinkling his nose as if I still smelled of the gaol. "Any trouble and you will be clapped in chains until you stand at the bar, bail or no bail. And that includes speaking with disrespect to officers of the law."

"I will walk with you to the gate," Harry said, taking up his stick and casting a last anxious glance up the stairs before closing the door behind him. "Then I shall make my way to the courthouse, see if I can be admitted."

At the gatehouse Edmonton stopped us and disappeared into Tom Garth's lodge, leaving us with the guards on either side, their pikestaffs raised as if to look official.

"One thing I find curious," I said, lowering my voice and leaning in to Harry while I had the chance. "Do you think Langworth meant for Nicholas Kingsley to be blamed for his father's murder?"

"What makes you say that?" Harry whispered back.

"Tom Garth said the boy was convinced his father had sent for him that evening, while he was dining with the dean. But Nick wasn't even admitted to the Archbishop's Palace, so his father clearly didn't. Was it Langworth who sent Nick a message in order that he would be seen in the cathedral precincts the night his father was killed?"

"Possible, I suppose. Although I don't see that it helps you now."

"If we could find the person who carried the message to Nick, he could say who sent him."

"I fear you may be too late for that now, even if Nick Kingsley were inclined to help you." He laid a hand on my arm. "God go with you, my boy. I wish I could accompany you all the way, but they will not walk at my pace."

"And I wish I did not have to leave you here with a fugitive and a would-be assassin," I whispered in his ear as I embraced him. "And you have not even had your breakfast."

He laughed. "I shall have to hope that French girl comes back. I might persuade her to fetch me some bread."

"What French girl?" I said, drawing back and looking at him.

"The one that came yesterday morning when you were out. Came to see your friend upstairs," he added, barely audible. "I didn't like to let her in, but there was no one around to see, and she was very insistent."

"Hélène?" I frowned. "Sophia didn't mention it."

"I don't know her name. I recognised her though, nice girl. The minister's daughter."

"Minister?"

"Try not to repeat everything like a simpleton when you're at the bar, won't you? The Huguenot minister. I forget his name."

I stared at him as if he had suddenly begun speaking the language of the Turks.

"But what did . . . ?" I began, but Edmonton strode over and interrupted, his hands behind his back.

"Sorry to break up your sentimental farewell, gentlemen, but this prisoner must be taken without further delay. And since the people like to know that things are done properly in this town, I'm afraid you must walk through the streets as befits one charged with capital offences." With a triumphant smile, he brought out a set of manacles from behind his back, joined with a thick chain.

I held out my hands without protest, still staring at Harry, my mind spinning so fast I barely felt the pinch and snap of metal around my wrists. It seemed to me that time had slowed to a trickle, so that I could see the earth turning moment by moment, all the pieces falling into place as if through water, one by one. A gull cried overhead and I looked up to see thin drifts of white cloud chased across a perfect blue sky. Now I understood—and I had to decide what I would do with that understanding. I turned as the guards nudged me towards the gate to see Harry leaning on his stick, his lips moving in what I supposed was silent prayer. In that moment I envied him the certainty of his faith; mine had shattered. I bowed my head and prepared to be led in chains past the jeering crowds.

THE ASSIZES WERE to be held in the Guildhall, being the only public building of sufficient size to contain the justice, his retinue of clerks and associates, the mass of accused prisoners, and the hordes of townspeople who came to watch for want of any better entertainment. The Buttermarket was already filling up with onlookers as we emerged from the shadow of the gatehouse; I had barely stepped into the sunlight when something whizzed past my ear and struck the guard on my right in the shoulder. I ducked out of instinct, turning to see him retrieve a limp cabbage and hurl it back where it came from.

"It's not personal," he said, in a matter-of-fact tone. "They just like to make a noise and throw things. You could be anyone in chains, they wouldn't care. It's part of their day out, you know."

"Thank you," I said, swivelling my head from side to side on the alert for missiles.

"You will be taken into the holding room with the other prisoners who have been brought from the gaol," Edmonton explained as we walked, evidently taking pride in airing his knowledge and quite unconcerned by the intermittent bombardment of vegetables. "The prosecutors and witnesses will be sworn in by the marshal. After this, the prisoners are called to the bar to hear the charges read. Cases of blood always take precedence," he added, with a smirk.

I could barely concentrate. Harry's last words to me had had the effect of opening a shutter and allowing a shaft of light into a dim room, so that everything that had once been only outline and shadow now stood clearly illuminated. And the result was horrifying. I caught Edmonton's last phrase and looked up.

"Cases of blood?"

"Crimes for which the punishment is death." The smirk widened into a sideways smile. "Then you make your plea, guilty or not guilty—"

"*Not,* as I have said a thousand times."

"—after which the jury will hear witnesses, the justice will direct them to a verdict, they retire to consider, then they return their verdict and the justice will pass sentence on those found guilty. He is efficient, Justice Hale. I've seen him work through as many as fifty cases in a day."

"*Fifty?* But how can they possibly weigh the evidence for each one in that time?"

Edmonton only gave an unpleasant laugh, as if my naïveté were comical.

"And I?" I asked. "When do I see my counsel?"

"Your *what?*" He turned to look at me, mouth open, as if I had made a great joke.

"A man of law who will speak for me against the charges." I heard my voice rise, panicked. Edmonton stopped still in the street, hands on his hips, his neat moustaches trembling with suppressed laughter.

"Oh dear—did you really think . . . ?" He shook his head indulgently, as if at a slow child. "I'm afraid English law does not permit counsel for those accused of capital crimes. Now, if you stood accused of stealing five shillings, you would have a man of law to speak for you. But not for murder. It is one of those funny little quirks. The idea being, I suppose, that to hang a man the evidence must be so clear that there can be no defence."

"But the evidence against me is all fabricated," I said, through my teeth. "I must be allowed to challenge it!"

"You will have the chance to answer the charges," he said, in a soothing tone, resuming his pace. "But you would be well advised not to raise your hopes."

The crowds lining the street grew denser as we approached the Guildhall. Outside the main door, a handful of men on horseback in city livery did their best to hold back the press of people, but it was almost impossible to get in the door. Men stood on each other's shoulders, straining for a glimpse in the windows, while women shrieked vague generic abuse as we passed.

"They are ripe for a hanging," Edmonton murmured as our guards used the shafts of their weapons to encourage a path through the crowd. "Too many acquittals at the last assizes, they went home disappointed. People do like to see justice done, don't they?"

"Well, they have not much hope of that here," I said.

"Your quick tongue will avail you nothing with Justice Hale," he said over his shoulder as he tried to elbow his way through to the door. He spoke as if the justice were an old drinking partner, a friend he had known for years. "He likes proper decorum in his courtroom. For pity's sake, good people, let us through or there will be no trial today at all!" he bellowed at the broad goodwives in their best caps and bonnets, dressed up as if for a carnival.

On the threshold I lifted my hands, the chains rattling, and clutched at Edmonton's sleeve.

"Constable? May I have one request?"

He turned to me with a face of incredulity and brushed my fingers away from his arm as if they might leave a stain. "What do you think you are, a nobleman in the Tower? Even now, you think you merit special treatment just because Harry Robinson was fool enough to pay your bail?" When I did not respond, he sighed. "Well, what is it?"

"I wish to speak to Dean Rogers."

"Before you are called? Impossible. Why?"

"I would like him to pray with me. I am sure he would not refuse."

Edmonton hesitated.

"If my friends at court should learn that I was refused that comfort, it will go the worse for you."

"Yes, yes. Your friends at court. Sing another song." But he looked uncomfortable. "Make way for the prisoner there!" he called out, as the guards drove back the spectators to allow us to enter the Guildhall.

The crush of people was even greater in the entrance hall, and small skirmishes were breaking out as the crowd fought with one another for access to the main hall. I was dragged through to an anteroom guarded by two solid-looking men holding pikestaffs at a slant across the doorway. A clerk of the court with a portable writing desk slung around his neck stood outside and looked up, enquiring, his pen poised.

"Filippo Sav— What is your name, Italian?" Edmonton snapped, turning to me.

"Savolino," I said to the clerk. He ran a finger down his list and nodded.

"Murder, attempted murder, and grand larceny," Edmonton added with emphasis, as if I might be confused with another Filippo Savolino there on lesser charges. The clerk made a mark in his register and nodded to the guards, who lowered their weapons and allowed us to pass.

The stench in this room hit you like a fist in the throat, the sickbed, sewer stink of the gaol; at least fifty men and women were packed together as tight as cattle in a market, staring large-eyed at the door with blank faces. Seeing them here, in stark daylight instead of the gloom of the West Gate cell, they reminded me of pictures of the damned I had seen in frescoes; gaunt with hunger, misshapen with disease, their eyes already dead. For many of them, I supposed, this was death's waiting room, the trial a mere shuffling of papers on their way to the gallows. They were curiously silent, the only sounds a muffled weeping and the slither and clink of chains whenever any of them moved. Looking at some of them, it was hard to feel death would not be a kindness.

Edmonton had his sleeve pulled across his mouth against the foul air, so that his words could barely escape.

"Get in. Now you wait here to be called. Use the time to pray for mercy, I should." Behind his arm he was smirking again.

"And Dean Rogers?"

He made some dismissive noise and turned on his heel. The door was closed after him.

I was forced to stand, pressed in on either side by the mass of prisoners. Across the room I saw the old monk, Brother Anselm, and sent him an encouraging smile, but he only stared, unfocused. I suspected his eyesight was not good enough to recognise me. Either that, or he was beyond encouragement, like most of those manacled together in here. I closed my eyes and retreated into my theatre of memory, that system of corresponding wheels and images that had made my name in Paris and brought me to the notice of King Henri, which in turn had led to his sending me to London, which had brought me here, to face trial at a provincial assizes alongside coiners and horse thieves. All for a woman and a book, as Sidney had said.

I knew now who had killed Sir Edward Kingsley and Doctor Sykes. I just had to make certain. And then I had to decide what I would do about it.

Minutes stretched out; I do not know how long I waited there. One of the older women passed out and fell, dragging down those manacled to her; someone else pissed themselves where they stood, past any care for human dignity. Hemmed in on both sides, I retreated into my thoughts, feeling that a hole had been ripped through me, as if with cannon-shot.

After a while the door opened a crack and the clerk's face appeared in the opening.

"Where is the Italian?" he said.

I shuffled forward, raising my hands. The chains were growing heavier and my shoulders ached from the weight of holding them. He beckoned me forward and stepped back as I passed him, as if to avoid contagion.

Dean Rogers stood outside, his long face tight with anxiety.

"They said you wanted to pray?"

So Edmonton was afraid of my connections after all. I nodded. "I also needed to ask you something."

"Whatever I can do." He glanced around, then leaned closer. "I have spoken to Justice Hale on your behalf. But—the evidence . . ." He trailed off uncertainly.

"I understand. I just need to know if anyone apart from you has a key to enter the crypt."

The dean frowned.

"Normally, no one but myself. Although," he added, with a dismissive wave, "some weeks ago I did give a copy to the minister of the Huguenot Church, for access to their little chapel, but in practice he does not need to use it. They hold their services during the hours when the crypt is unlocked. Why do you ask?"

"What is his name, the Huguenot minister?" My mouth had dried and the words came out cracked.

"He is a lay minister only, but he is ordained. Pastor Fleury. Jacques Fleury, the master weaver. But has this anything to do with your case?" he asked, concern in his eyes.

"I—" I looked up at him. "Will you pray with me now?"

"Of course." He laid a hand on my shoulder and embarked on some benign platitudes in his pleasant, soothing voice. I was grateful for the sentiment, but my thoughts were elsewhere. When he had finished, the clerk cleared his throat and opened the door into the anteroom.

"The prisoner ought to go back until he is called," he said, apologetically.

"Have you seen Harry? Is he here?" I whispered to the dean, as the guards ushered me towards the door.

He shook his head. "Not yet. I fear he may not be able to get through the crowds with his leg. Now I must take my seat in the courtroom. God be with you, Doctor Savolino."

I thanked him and submitted to being returned, none too gently, to my fellow prisoners. Had Harry found his way to Justice Hale in time to explain everything? I would only know the answer when I stood to face him.

I was crushed next to one prisoner whose head hung towards the floor as if he had fallen asleep standing up.

"Are you a Canterbury man?" I asked, nudging him in the ribs.

He raised his head slowly and stared at me, amazed at being spoken to. I recoiled a little at the running pustules around his mouth.

"Born and bred. And shall die here today, most like," he said, as if it no longer mattered.

"Where is St. Radigund's Street?" I asked. He blinked slowly.

"Out by the old Blackfriars. You know," he said, when I looked blank. "Crosses the river a little way past the weavers' houses."

"The weavers' houses," I repeated, nodding. The man looked at me for a moment longer, then hung his head again. He did not ask why I wanted to know. When you are facing the gallows, such things have no importance.

THE COURTROOM ITSELF was less chaotic than the entrance hall and anterooms; here, at least, benches were provided along one side of the room for citizens of status, though people were packed standing into the spaces behind and to every side. The air was smoky and smelled strongly like the apothecary's shop; in each corner, braziers stood on tall tripods burning aromatic herbs to ward off gaol fever. It must have been near to midday by the time I was led in along with nine other prisoners, including the old monk, all of us indicted for cases of blood; we were hustled into a corner behind a low wooden barrier. At the far end of the room a raised dais had been built, where Justice Hale sat at a broad table covered with piles of papers and surrounded by his retinue of earnest, black-robed clerks and juniors. Around his neck he wore a silver chain with a round pomander, which he raised frequently to his nose as protection against the pestilence. To his right, twelve grim-faced men shifted on their benches, arms folded. This, I guessed, was the jury; they did not have the look of men you would turn to for compassion. The murmur of conversation swelled as we filed in, chains clinking rhythmically like a tolling bell; I glanced up and saw that Hale was looking at me. Our eyes met and he held my eye for a moment with a grave expression, but he gave nothing away.

The prisoners were taken up one by one to the bar to face the prosecutor and hear the charges against them read. The old monk, Brother Anselm, was the first to be called; as the guards unfastened him from the chain and shoved him to his place, I glanced around the courtroom. Dean Rogers was seated among the city dignitaries, as was Langworth, his brow drawn, the scar pressed white with apprehension. I had not missed the expression that flashed across his face when I was led into the hall; if he had depended on my being found dead in my bed this morning, he allowed his displeasure to show for only for a moment. He would have some other weapon up his sleeve, I had no doubt. Among the onlookers standing I saw Tom Garth and the Widow Gray; Rebecca and Mistress Blunt; Nicholas Kingsley and his hangers-on. There was still no sign of Harry. I closed my eyes, as if that might shut out the pain in my chest. Twice the justice tried to speak over the din of conversation, but the crowd were so animated, talking and pointing (for the most part, I was conscious, at me), that the court bailiff had to shout for order and thump his staff on the floor several times before Hale could make himself heard.

A witness stepped up to say he had found the old monk beside the dismembered body of a young boy on a midden outside the city wall one morning when he was bringing his cart in for the market; Brother Anselm tried to explain to the bench what he had told me, but in his distress he became incoherent, clutching at his clothes and lapsing into Latin. When he spoke his plea of not guilty there was a chorus of loud boos and hisses from the onlookers. I watched, dismayed, as three of the jurymen turned to confer among themselves with barely disguised contempt. Another seemed more interested in the movements of a fly on the ceiling, leaning back with his hands folded behind his head, and another was quite brazenly falling asleep, his chin slumped onto his chest. Occasionally he would jerk upright and look around, as if unsure where he was, before his lids began to droop again. To sit through fifty or more of these cases unpaid would test any man's patience, I supposed, but my gut twisted with anger at the thought that any man could be so casual with another's life. Hale nodded for the old man to stand down. As he was taken from the bar, his eyes cast around wildly and landed on me, wide and pleading. "Speak for me, brother!" he cried out, as he was led back to us. "You know the truth!" I nodded, hoping to offer him some comfort, but that only caused more whispering and pointing in my direction.

Hale shuffled papers, made notes, replaced his quill carefully in its stand, sniffed his pomander, and eventually looked up from his list.

"The Italian, Filippo Savolino."

I was led out to the bar accompanied by a groundswell of murmuring that rose to such a crescendo that again the bailiff had to bang his stick for silence. I confirmed my name on oath, thinking as I did so that I had already perjured myself, so in a sense I was at liberty to say anything.

"One count of murder and robbery, of the apothecary William Fitch. One count of attempted murder and robbery, of Master Nicholas Kingsley. Two further counts of robbery—of keys from the house of Canon John Langworth and money to the value of ten shillings from the treasury of Christ Church cathedral. Quite a tally, for a man who has not been in the city a week, is it not, Master Savolino?" He raised an enquiring eyebrow, then glanced again at the paper in front of him. "Forgive me—*Doctor* Savolino."

I bowed my head in acknowledgement.

"What are you a doctor of?"

"Theology."

"Well." He laid one large hand flat on the desk. "It will please the goodmen of the jury to know that I will not test this claim by engaging you in theological debate." There was a smattering of polite laughter. He gave me a long, steady look, but his face was still unreadable. "Either you are a most heinous felon, travelling under false credentials and taking advantage of good men of this town to work your foul purposes"—here he left a little pause, enough to allow a hum of approval from the crowd— "or there are people here intent on making you appear so. We had better hear the witnesses to these charges before you give your plea." He lifted the paper in front of him and checked it. "Unfortunately, as most of you will know, the principal witness in the murder of Master Fitch, Doctor Ezekiel Sykes, is unable to testify before this court, having been himself the victim of a terrible murder only yesterday."

"Not guilty," I said, unable to resist. A ripple of laughter ran through the audience, in spite of themselves. Hale sent me a stern look, recalling Edmonton's words about the judge's dislike for sharp wits in court, though I fancied I saw the corner of his mouth twitch before he sucked it back to solemnity.

"Instead the court will hear the deposition Doctor Sykes gave to Mayor Fitzwalter the morning of Fitch's death."

Fitzwalter took the floor without looking at me, cleared his throat, and began to read. Whether the words had truly come from Sykes or been invented later by Langworth, it hardly mattered; the whole was based on the lie that Sykes had been present in the shop when I entered and had left me there alone with Fitch, rather than the other way around. Those of the jurymen that were still alert nodded sagely to one another; the spectators gasped and tutted at appropriate moments, like the audience at a play. I hardly listened; it hardly mattered. All my thoughts were bound up with what I should say when I was given the opportunity to speak.

I would have a ready audience: before the whole courtroom and the queen's justice I could announce that I knew the killer of Sir Edward Kingsley and Doctor Sykes. I could tell them that the weaver's son, Olivier Fleury, had used his father's key to take a crucifix from the crypt, lain in wait for Sir Edward, and struck him down as he walked from the Archbishop's Palace to John Langworth's house, knowing he was expected there after supper. But there was my problem. When the justice asked why Olivier would have wanted to kill the magistrate, I would have to explain that he did it for his lover, the woman Canterbury knew as Mistress Kate Kingsley, to free her from her husband and ensure that she would inherit his estate. They meant for Nicholas Kingsley to be blamed—they even sent a false message ensuring he would be seen at the cathedral at the right time—but Tom Garth had complicated their plan by planting evidence that meant Mistress Kingsley was accused instead. Fortunately—and here my voice would grow thick with the bitterness of betrayal—Mistress Kingsley found a solution; she knew a credulous fool, a man the king of France once declared cleverer than all the doctors of the Sorbonne put together, but a fool nonetheless, who would be all too willing to solve this difficulty for her.

And Doctor Sykes? the justice would ask. Why would Olivier Fleury want to kill Sykes? And I would have to say, because he learned that Sykes had killed his sister's son. He learned this yesterday morning from his sister, who learned it from Mistress Kingsley, who in turn learned it from me as I sat on the bed we shared at the house of Doctor Harry Robinson who, yes, has been harbouring a fugitive all this time. If Hale gave me the benefit of the doubt, both Olivier and Sophia would both be arrested.

I gripped the bar in front of me and stared at my hands as the knuckles turned white. A cold, hard knot lodged in the top of my chest when I thought about Sophia; her easy lies, her softness, her false affection. She brought me here to serve a purpose, to put her original plan back on track, to prove Nick Kingsley guilty of his father's murder so that she could inherit. So that—what? She could run away with Olivier? The thought caught me like a blow to the stomach; I doubled over with the force of it and heard Hale say, "Look to the prisoner there! Are you well enough to stand, my man?"

I raised my head and nodded; his face was creased with concern and unexpectedly I felt my eyes fill with tears, so that I had to look away in case he took it as a confession.

"Fetch him a drink," Hale barked, and after some fuss one of the army of black-gowned clerks came forward with a tankard of small beer. I took a sip, breathed deeply, and tried to compose myself.

More witnesses were called: the locksmith, who embellished his tale with details of how shifty I looked, how he had thought there was something suspect about a stranger wanting keys cut, how I had slipped him an extra penny not to mention it. Someone has certainly slipped you an extra penny or two, I thought, and my heart sank; if the witnesses had been bribed, why not the jury? Rebecca tried valiantly to defend me when her turn came, but as I had predicted, her breathless enthusiasm for my innocence began to sound overdone. "She has a liking for the Italian tongue, that one," someone called out from the back of the crowd, and the room dissolved in ribald laughter and catcalls. Nick Kingsley took the floor with relish to tell how I had talked my way into his house then attempted to break into his father's cellar and nearly beaten him to death when he tried to stop me. Finally Edmonton rose to give his account of finding a bag of money taken from the cathedral treasury in my room at Harry Robinson's house, a tale he spun with such lingering pleasure that Hale had to call him to order and ask him to hurry it up. By the time he had finished, the din from the spectators and the jurymen had swelled to a level that meant the bailiff had to pound his staff again and call for silence.

"Well, prisoner." Hale looked at me from under the ledge of his thick brow. "How do you answer?"

"Not guilty, Your Honour." A chorus of boos and hisses went up from the room. I waited for it to subside. "These are false charges. Every one. And the testimonies you have heard against me."

"You are suggesting that all these witnesses, including the late Doctor Sykes, have deliberately perjured themselves? What have you done, that so many in this town would falsely accuse you, knowing the consequences?"

I looked at him and then around me at the faces staring expectantly, weighing up how much I might say. Harry was right; it would cause more harm than good to denounce Langworth in front of all these people. His plans for Becket had to remain a secret. Langworth must be dealt with privately.

"I can only presume that foreigners are not much liked in this town, Your Honour. We are easy scapegoats. Anything can be blamed on our barbarous ways—it is so much easier than acknowledging one of our friends or neighbours could be a murderer. As for the witnesses—words can be bought."

Another wave of outraged roars and cries of "For shame!" from those standing. Hale tilted his head to one side.

"You seem to be suggesting that someone in this town would have paid people to speak against you under oath. Who do you suppose that person to be?" His eyes bore into me. "Bearing in mind that this would be a very serious accusation indeed."

I glanced at Langworth, whose lizard tongue flicked nervously over his lips. Hale's gaze followed mine. A deathly silence hung over the room.

"I make no such direct accusation, Your Honour."

Hale picked up his pen, examined its nib for a moment, replaced it. "Have you anything else to say?"

I hesitated. Olivier and Sophia. I could publicly accuse them both now; I owed them nothing. Olivier: my jaw clenched at the thought of his curled lip, his hauteur. Were they already lovers, or was he just another poor credulous fool like me, persuaded to risk everything for the promises held in those mesmerising amber eyes? She was clever. I had always known she was clever—was that not what drew me to her, more than her beauty? I should have seen it in her that day at Smithfield; after all, she had told me the truth with her first words. The dreamy-eyed, romantic girl I had met in Oxford was dead; life had replaced that softness with something cold and hard, a shard of ice in her heart. She had loved once; she would not make that mistake again. I did not truly believe she had room for Olivier in her imagined future any more than she had room for me. But her plan had failed. Neither of us had managed to deliver what she wanted—her husband's money, legitimately inherited. So what would she do now?

"Did you hear me, Doctor Savolino? I asked if you have anything to add."

Hale puffed his cheeks out; his patience was wearing thin.

I could deliver them both to their deaths now, if I chose, in revenge. Or I could show mercy.

"Nothing, Your Honour. Except to assure you that I am innocent."

"Very well. For myself, I am not remotely satisfied by the evidence for the murder of William Fitch. But the attack on Master Kingsley and the business of the stolen money are more difficult to dismiss, I grant. Nevertheless, I do not say these testimonies nor the evidence shown are conclusive." He drew himself upright in his great high-backed chair, resting his elbows on its ornately carved arms, and turned the full severity of his stare on the jury. "Goodmen of the inquest. You have heard what these witnesses say against the prisoner. You have also heard what he says for himself. Bear in mind that he is an educated man, with connections at Her Majesty's court, his reputation defended by the dean of the cathedral and one of the canons, who stood bail for him. Have an eye to your oath and to your duty. If you stand in any doubt as to the prisoner's guilt, an acquittal is the appropriate verdict. Discharge your consciences well on this matter." He began to shuffle his next batch of papers. "Let the prisoner stand down. Call the next."

As I was hurried away from the bar, he looked up and met my eye and gave me the briefest nod.

I was bundled back into the holding pen while the other prisoners' cases were heard: larceny, coining, theft of livestock. They were dealt with briskly, as if speed were all that mattered. Sunlight striped the walls of the hall; its bulging plaster, its peeling whitewash. All around me, the other prisoners scratched at the lice in their ragged clothes. It was a sordid, dispiriting business; little wonder, I thought, that the justice felt the need to surround the occasion with such pomp and feasting.

I kept my eyes to the ground, wondering what that nod was supposed to signify.

When the charges against all ten prisoners had been heard, the jury-men were given a note of each man's name and his crime and retired to consider their verdict.

"Do not give them food or drink while they are out," Hale directed the bailiff. "I want this over quickly. Tell them no more than twenty minutes or we shall be sitting all night."

It took them little over ten, by my count, though the spectators had already grown restless and noisy by the time they returned. The bailiff stamped; Hale looked up, unhurried, from his paperwork and steepled his fingers together expectantly. The foreman of the jury rose to pronounce the verdict.

"The monk known as Brother Anselm—guilty." Whoops from the crowd. "John Mace of Canterbury—guilty." The man accused of horse theft slumped like a marionette with its strings cut; the people cheered again. "The Italian, Filippo Savolino—" He had trouble reading it from the sheet. He paused for effect and looked up, enjoying his moment of playing to the crowd. "Guilty, of all charges."

The spectators screamed in triumph; hats were thrown in the air, and a chant of "Hang the papist!" went up from those standing, who began to stamp their feet like the beat of a victory drum. It's not personal, the guard had said, but as my gaze raked across those rows of faces, I saw raw hatred there; lips snarled back, teeth bared, fists pounding the air, eyes blazing bloodlust. I was the jewel of this assizes, the star attraction, and they felt this verdict as a triumph for—for what, exactly? A triumph of theirs over everything they wanted me to represent: murdering papists, foreigners who took bread from the mouths of good Englishmen, those who believed their connections put them above the law. I was all these things to them, and I realised in the din that they would not have accepted any other verdict. Langworth folded his arms and smiled, a death's-head grin. I stared up at Justice Hale, questioning. He gave a minute shake of his head, barely perceptible.

The remaining verdicts were read. All ten prisoners were declared guilty; the spectators seemed ready to carry us on their shoulders to the gallows that very instant if they were given the chance. Justice Hale stood; the bailiff banged for silence.

"The court has heard the verdict." Hale surveyed the court and adjusted his black cap. "It remains for me to pass sentence of death by hanging on those prisoners found guilty . . ." The spectators crowed again; beside me, Brother Anselm gave a low moan and one of the other prisoners cried out to Jesus for mercy. I laid a hand on the old monk's bony shoulder, but my chest was tight and I struggled to catch my breath.

"Except," Hale continued, and the cheers turned to noises of protest. "*Except*," he repeated, raising his formidable voice to a shout, so that even the rowdiest onlookers subsided, "those for whom I see special reason for leniency. In the case of the former monk Anselm and the Italian Savolino, I will allow benefit of clergy."

I slumped back against the wooden partition, afraid my legs would no longer support me. Brother Anselm fell to his knees with a hiccupping sob of relief. Benefit of clergy, as far as I understood, was an ancient loophole in English law that allowed clemency to those who could read; in place of execution they might hope for a fine or a prison term.

"But Your Honour—murder is not a clergyable offence!" Langworth cried, stepping forward.

"I preside over this court, Canon Langworth, not you," Hale said, with steel in his voice. "Perhaps I could refer this case back to Westminster instead. Would that be better, do you think—that Doctor Savolino should make his defence in the Star Chamber, before the Privy Council?"

Langworth turned white; his Adam's apple bounced in his throat as he tried to swallow his rage and I knew then that Harry must have reached the justice and told him what he knew. But the crowd were not to be deprived of their prize. A low roar began to swell among them, like the rumble of a great wave, until it seemed their force could not be contained; as the outcry reached a crescendo, some among those standing surged forward, knocking the dignitaries on their benches, jostling the clerks at their tables, and they were joined by others, swarming in from the entrance hall towards the pen where the prisoners were held. The guards did their best to hold the mob back, but they were outnumbered and they seemed reluctant to use their weapons for anything more than ineffectual buffeting. The bailiff climbed on a table and pounded with his staff, calling in vain for order, until he was pulled down by the spectators into the crush. More people seemed to be pressing in from outside the courtroom and a great cry went up from the street; I heard women screaming as I felt hands close over my arms, dragging me through the other prisoners into the tumult. Faces blurred in front of my eyes and I felt a fist strike me on the jaw as the mob bayed for the hangman; fear pulsed in my throat as I was pulled out into the courtroom, into the hands of the crowd. Did they mean to hang me themselves, to dispense the justice they felt Hale had denied them? I could not see the justice now, though I thought his was among the voices bellowing from above me.

The courtroom had all but collapsed into a riot. My head began to swim and I fought for breath in the crush as I was pulled down; for a moment I feared I would black out, but quite suddenly through the confusion and noise sounded one clear note of a herald's trumpet. The sound seemed to startle the mob; the press of bodies and hands clawing at me began to subside, and I was hauled to my feet by the collar to find myself staring into the face of a bearded young man wearing a soldier's helmet. The shouting died down to a simmering murmur and a strange calm descended on the hall. When I was able to focus I realised that one of the onlookers who had dragged me out was lying prone on the floor and the crowd were drawing back, staring at his unmoving body with fear; another soldier stood over him, sword held aloft, looking around with menace as if to ask who else dared try their luck. There were six or more of these armed men in the hall, and they were not wearing the livery of the guards who had fetched me that morning but different colours. The man who had helped me up nodded and stepped back and it was only then that I realised the badge on his coat was the arms of Queen Elizabeth.

There was a jostling among the crowd towards the door and as I watched they parted to admit a tall figure in a sweat-soaked shirt and riding breeches, hair sticking up in spikes, face haggard and dust-smeared from the road, holding out a piece of paper. The soldiers moved to keep the people away from him at sword point; most obediently shuffled back. I almost wept to see who it was; my legs buckled again and the young soldier caught me as I fell against his chest.

Justice Hale straightened his cap, regained his composure, and addressed the newcomer with an attempt at dignity.

"Sir Philip. You have a constituency of barbarians, it seems."

For once, Sidney did not smile.

"Justice Hale, I have seen tavern brawls conducted with more dignity than your courtroom." He turned to me, colour rising in his cheeks. "What in God's name is going on here? Get that man out of chains now. I have ridden through the night," he added, pointing at me, though he made it sound like an accusation. "I have ridden through the night," he said again, louder, in a voice that encompassed the whole courtroom, "with a warrant signed by Her Majesty for the arrest of Canon John Langworth on charges of high treason."

The gasp that echoed through the hall could not have been better performed if it had been played on a stage. People swivelled their heads around, looking for the object of this exciting new development.

"Where is Canon Langworth?" Hale demanded, still on his feet, his voice sonorous with authority once more. "Constable?"

Edmonton looked around, helpless. "I cannot see him here, Your Honour."

"He must have slipped out some back way in the tumult," I said to Sidney. My voice sounded hoarse. "You must get your men after him. If he is not in his own house, try the crypt."

"This court is adjourned," Hale announced, and the bailiff struck his staff three times. "I will pass sentence when we are again in session. Have the prisoners taken back to the gaol. Not the Italian or the monk,

Constable—I want them brought to my lodgings at the Cheker. You—blow your trumpet," he said irritably to the herald in an aside. "Clear the courtroom!" he shouted, when the note had sounded. "I will retire to my lodgings to speak with Sir Philip. Mayor Fitzwalter, you will accompany me. Have your men clear the way. Where is Dean Rogers?"

The dean rose from his seat, pale and shaken. Hale gave him a hard look.

"You had better get yourself back to your cathedral, Richard. Sir Philip Sidney may need your assistance there."

The trumpet sounded; Fitzwalter called his guards to make way for the justice. Perhaps emboldened by the example of the queen's soldiers, they shoved more brusquely with their pikestaffs this time and the spectators, chastened, moved back for Hale and his retinue to pass, following Sidney and his men. I watched them leave, hardly daring to believe that Sidney was here at all, let alone with a retinue of royal soldiers. Edmonton approached with a face like a bull mastiff, holding out a key.

"Sorry to disappoint you," I said, as he took the manacles from my wrists and then from Brother Anselm's. The old monk's hands were bleeding where the iron had torn his papery skin. He touched his wounds in wonder.

"Am I pardoned?" he asked, blinking up at me and then at Edmonton. "Am I not to hang after all?"

"Not today," the constable said, sucking in his cheeks.

"You are safe, brother," I said, taking Anselm's arm to steady him. His milky eyes filled with tears.

"I thought those people would tear us apart where we stood," he whispered. "But blessed Saint Thomas heard our prayers."

"Well. He has a lot to answer for," I said.

"Filippo?" A woman's voice at my shoulder; I turned, my pulse quickening, to find the Widow Gray twisting her hands together, her eyes anxious. I raised my eyebrows: yes? "I want to come with you to the justice. I think it is time I made my deposition."

‡

"Your Honour, could I—before we—I must go back to Doctor Robinson's house in the cathedral precincts. He may have need of me."

"Don't worry about Harry," Hale said, his eyes still skimming his papers. Four o'clock in the afternoon; the light soft and golden where it fell in scattered shapes on the panelled walls. With his entourage he had taken over an entire floor of the Cheker, its grandest rooms; the one we now sat in was furnished with silk cushions and embroidered curtains. Brother Anselm had been led away by one of Hale's clerks to be fed, washed, and rested before he gave his deposition, in the hope that it might be more coherent. The Widow Gray was waiting outside the door for her turn. Mayor Fitzwalter had been arrested by the justice's men as he stepped through the door of the Cheker, to avoid further public unrest. Now Hale sat behind a desk, his back to the open window, radiating calm, a glass of wine in his hand. Beside him, another clerk scribbled a note of every word that was spoken. Whenever a serving boy came in with food, the room fell silent, recognising that these were matters not to be overheard.

"I sent two of my assistants to Harry's house after he came to me this morning," Hale continued. "Nearly killed himself trying to get here before I left for the hearing. He told me everything."

"Everything?" Did he mean Sophia?

"Langworth's plot. Becket. The dead boys. Monstrous! And the attempt on your own lives last night. The servant Samuel will be removed to more appropriate conditions until he is well enough to be questioned."

"Will he live?"

"Let us hope so. We will need his testimony." He paused to sip his wine. "It is a great blessing that Sir Philip is here with the queen's pursuivants—I understand that was your doing. You are a brave man, Giordano Bruno. Reckless, perhaps, but undoubtedly useful."

"Still—I must go back to see Harry Robinson, as a matter of urgency—"

Hale glanced up; his brow seemed to bristle at the presumption.

"I sent Harry home to rest. This will not wait, Doctor Bruno—my assize is only adjourned. I have at least twenty more criminal cases to hear today, not to mention all the minor petitions. We shall be sitting until midnight as it is. Take a drink and let us begin on your deposition." He paused at the sound of the door. "Ah, Sir Philip."

The door was closed behind Sidney, who strode over and squeezed my shoulder. He looked as exhausted as I felt.

"Langworth is taken," he said, throwing himself into a chair and clicking his fingers at one of the clerks for a glass of wine. "Found him in his house trying to light a bonfire of his letters. Thankfully he had not progressed very far—should be enough to make interesting reading. But the bad news is that Becket is gone."

"Under the floor," I said, "at the eastern end, between two marble columns. I can show you the place."

"No need." He twisted his mouth in distaste, though I could not tell if it was at the wine or the outcome. "We found the place. The coffin is empty. Not so much as a holy toenail to be seen."

"Langworth has moved him, then. He will tell you where."

Sidney gave a grim laugh.

"Let us hope. When he is in the Tower he will be encouraged to tell us all manner of things."

I winced. "Langworth must have told someone. There are no more guardians left—Kingsley and Sykes are dead, Fitzwalter is arrested."

"Unless Fitzwalter was not the fourth guardian," Hale said. "He swears he knows nothing of any relics. Admits to taking bribes from Langworth and Kingsley to smooth their financial interests, but nothing more. Of course, Fitzwalter is a coward," he added, pursing his lips in disapproval. "He will say anything to spare himself hard questioning. We may yet learn something of use."

"So there could be another guardian," I mused. "If Langworth will not talk, we may never know where Becket is buried."

"Oh, he will talk eventually," Sidney said, as if there could be no dispute. He threw back the last of his wine and stood. "The pursuivants are all over Langworth's house—I should go and see what more they have found. Then, Bruno, you and I deserve the finest supper this town can provide. We have much to talk about." He gave me a meaningful look, stretched his arms above his head and cracked his neck from side to side, then swept out of the door again.

"I'll tell you another thing—it's a damned shame the physician Sykes was killed before he could be questioned," Hale remarked, reading over his notes. "Now *that* is a curious business. Was it Langworth's doing, do you think, Bruno? Stop him talking? Seems bizarre, if it was. You'd have thought Sykes was essential to the whole miracle plot."

I hesitated. No one had yet mentioned Sophia. That meant only one of two things; either she was still hidden at Harry's, or she had taken her chance to escape while the whole town was gathered at the assizes.

"Sykes's housekeeper kept his appointment book, apparently," Hale continued, in a tone of mild curiosity. "He made a note of all his patients so that he wouldn't miss a fee. He was supposed to see the Widow Gray the morning he died but he never got there. The housekeeper says someone came to the door crying that there was an emergency, begged him to go with her there and then. She says Sykes didn't even stop to write down the name of the patient or pick up his jacket, just went out like that in his shirtsleeves, with his bag of remedies."

"It was a woman? At the door?"

"The housekeeper didn't see, but she says it sounded like a woman's voice. Curious. Well," he put the paper aside and looked up, his jowls creasing into a weary smile. "I cannot worry about that now. Let us hear your story, Doctor Bruno, as quick as you can make it, so I can get back to my adulterers and coiners. Justice will not wait." He rolled his eyes. "You," he barked at the clerk to his right. "Sharpen your quill for this man's words."

☩

SO I GAVE my deposition from the beginning; how I had come to Canterbury at Sophia's request; how Walsingham had asked me to keep an eye on Langworth; how Sir Edward Kingsley had led me to the murdered boys and the plot to revive the cult of Becket. I did not mention at any point that Sophia had travelled to Canterbury with me. Hale interrupted only once.

"Where is she now? This woman—Kingsley's wife?"

I paused, weighing up my answer. Was this a test? Had Harry already told them she was at his house? Would the men who came to take Samuel have found her? Lying to the justice would not serve me well; I had lied for Sophia once before and Walsingham had given me strong words for it.

"I don't know," I answered, truthfully.

His eyes rested for a moment on my face with a practised scrutiny, then he nodded for me to continue. ·

When I had told my story—as much of it as I felt necessary for a deposition—he folded his hands together and pushed his chair back.

"An audacious scheme," he murmured, shaking his head. "You almost have to admire them for it. To revive the shrine of Saint Thomas with a miracle of resurrection—extraordinary presumption. Ha!" A sudden laugh erupted as if from deep in his chest, and his clerks echoed it with polite titters. "That a man should think to mock the powers of God Almighty. Beggars belief."

"Your Honour, the Catholic Church has been doing this for years. Red powder you shake up to make the blood of Christ. Statues of the Virgin with mechanisms that make them weep on Good Friday. Man is ingenious when it comes to aping miracles."

"And others are more than apt to believe in them. By God, Doctor Bruno—the longer I do this job, the more I feel nothing could surprise me when it comes to the baseness of human nature. It's a wonder Our Lord bothers with us at all." He stretched out his legs under the desk and leaned back. "I wish some miracle would relieve me of this day's business. I will have two armed men escort you to Harry Robinson's, in case the mob are still restless."

☩

THE STREETS WERE lively with people; the town seemed to have given itself a day's holiday in honour of the assizes. If the crowds had been disappointed at being deprived of a spectacle at the gallows, they seemed mollified by the drama of the queen's own soldiers coming to town to arrest their canon treasurer. This time there were no flying vegetables as I passed along the High Street in the company of my guards, but I felt the stares as I passed, the muted whispering, as if I were somehow more dangerous now that they did not know what to make of me.

Harry opened the door and his face gave me the answer I needed. The guards took their place unquestioningly outside and I stepped into the hall.

"She was gone when I came back from seeing the justice this morning," he said, leaning heavily on his stick.

I nodded, summoning all my remaining strength to keep my jaw tight, my face steady.

"I have not had a chance to thank you for that," I said. "You must have almost killed yourself getting there in time."

"I knew he would not leave his lodgings until the last minute. His assistants did not want to admit me but I told them the safety of the realm was at stake. I may have mentioned the Privy Council." He shifted position and sucked in a sharp breath, his face pinched with pain.

"You should get some sleep, Harry," I said. "You look exhausted."

"My leg is bad today. I have not walked so fast nor up so many stairs for months, and I can't remember the last time I nearly killed a man in the middle of the night." He tried to laugh but it ended with another wince. "Did you know she would be gone?"

"I guessed."

"But you don't know where?"

I shook my head and leaned against the wall, the exhaustion of the day and the previous night settling on my shoulders like a lead cloak. She must have realised that there was little hope of her being able to claim her inheritance as Kingsley's widow if no one could be found guilty of his murder; perhaps she suspected that I would eventually piece together the truth. But the killing of Sykes had not been part of her plan. Had Olivier decided on that course alone after Sophia had related to Hélène what I had told her about finding Denis's body? I pressed my palm to my forehead. Like Tom Garth, Olivier had believed there was no justice for people like him under the law. He had dispensed his own hot-blooded justice to Edward Kingsley and to Sykes, and part of me understood how a man might be driven to that. I could tell Hale, have the hue and cry sent after them, but what would it achieve, in the end, if they were caught and hanged for the murder of two men whose actions—some might argue—had deserved a sentence of death? I sighed. In Oxford, I had stopped Sophia from running away because I thought I was saving her life. This time, I would let her go. There was a kind of justice in that, I thought.

"This might give you some idea," Harry said. I looked up to see that he was holding out a letter, folded in quarters, unsealed. "I have not read it," he said, quickly. "It was left on your mattress."

"Thank you." I took the letter and turned it between my fingers. "I—I think I will read it in my room. You should lie down. You look terrible."

"Sleep won't cure that," he said, with an attempt at a grin, and shuffled away to the parlour, his breath rasping in his chest with every step.

The room was as she had left it, the bedsheet crumpled so that I almost fancied I could see the imprint of her body in it. I sat down and opened the letter.

Dear Bruno

By the time you read this your trial will be over. I cannot help but believe it will go your way; you can talk your way out of anything. Besides, you have a knack for survival, as I do. I had hoped you could talk me out of a murder charge and into my inheritance, but I see now that this was too much to ask. My best hope is to begin again, with a new name. I am growing so practised at this that I hardly know who I am anymore; I invent myself from day to day. You understand this, I think. You have understood me better than anyone, so you will understand, I hope, that just as I no longer have faith in God, neither can I trust in any man. Please do not think I am oblivious to everything you have done for me, and why. I do not think I can love again. The part of me that knew how to love was destroyed when my son was taken from me. You will say that I betrayed you; I still say you betrayed me in Oxford. You will find this hard to believe after what I have done, but I will miss you.

Perhaps we will meet again—I would like to think so. I cannot help but feel our destinies are tangled together somehow. Though if we do, I imagine you will want to murder me.

Yours

S.

I let the letter fall to my lap. To kill her? No. Perhaps. I placed one hand on the sheet beside me, as it might still contain some trace of her, and wondered where she would have run to with no money, no possessions . . . Then I closed my eyes. A cold realisation crept over me; I crumpled the letter in my fist and hurled myself across the bed to the corner where I had prised up the floorboard. The nails lay loosely scattered. I dug my fingers in and pulled the board away, tearing my fingernails in my haste. The wooden casket was gone. So was my purse, though it was a small consolation to see that she had left my little knife. I drew it out, weighed it in my hands for a moment. With a raw moan of rage I took the stairs two at a time; it was not too late to find them. I would go to Sidney, get him to order out the hue and cry; with men on every road out of Canterbury it would take no time to run them to ground like foxes, leave them cowering in a corner, begging for mercy. If she thought she could betray me twice, she would learn that I was not another of her doe-eyed boys, to be used and thrown away as it suited her. She would learn . . .

I stopped at the front door. If the hue and cry caught them, they would die for certain. In my anger I might wish Sophia to pay for deceiving me, but with her life? To exchange two young lives for a book; could I live with myself? I leaned my forehead against the wall, pushed my hands through my hair, called down all the curses I knew in every language I had ever learned until they all merged into incoherent, racking sobs. I did not lift my face away from the wall even when I heard that familiar shuffle-and-drag and felt a hand rest on my shoulder.

Harry did not speak until I had exhausted myself into silence.

"You will mend, son," he said, looking past me to the window. "I did. Safer, in the end, to travel alone."

Chapter 18

Morning light in jewel-coloured patches on golden stone; the cool hush of the cathedral before Holy Communion. I stared at a bare patch of floor; the wavering shadows on an empty wall, and tried to picture Thomas Becket standing where I now stood, when he was just a man like any other, but perhaps more stubborn, before England turned him into a conjuring show encrusted with gold. When he looked towards that door on his left to see the knights thundering towards him, swords drawn, he could never have imagined how his death would ripple out through four hundred years of history.

"*Pax vobiscum,* Thomas," I whispered. "Wherever you are."

Sidney appeared at my shoulder.

"Praying to saints, Bruno? Do I need to call the pursuivants? We could make room for you in the cart beside Langworth if you're slipping back into popery."

I forced a smile and craned my neck up to the vaulted arches a hundred feet above, their tracery fanning out like some great stone forest in a legend.

"Do you think he's still here somewhere?"

"Becket?" Sidney sniffed. "If he is, Langworth will tell us where. If not, the queen will speak directly to the archbishop, tell him to get down here and have some care for his See. They'll have every last tomb in this place torn up, if that's what it takes. She won't want Becket lurking like a snake under a stone ready to jump up and bite her at any moment. Listen, Bruno." He turned, suddenly serious. "The girl. If Walsingham should ask . . ."

After supper the night before, when the two of us had sat up late in Sidney's room at the Cheker, I had told him about Sophia, Olivier, the book, Kingsley, Sykes. I had asked his advice.

"Let them go," he had said, when he had heard me out. "No one should die for a book, Bruno—though I'll wager you would, if it came to it. What will she do with it? She can't read it, can she?"

"She will sell it," I had replied. "And then there is no knowing whose hands it might fall into. It's my own fault—I should not have told her it was valuable."

"You should not have done a lot of things where she's concerned," he had said. "But it is done now. What matters is protecting you from Walsingham's wrath. Her crime was not political, but he is scrupulous on points of law. He won't like to think you let a murderer go free because your softer feelings mastered you."

"Say only that she has gone her way," I said now, looking back to the floor where Becket's brains had once been scattered.

"I have been thinking," he said, lowering his voice. "The servant Samuel will be in no state to contradict anything that is put to him. A confession will be eased from him as soon as he is fit to sign his own name. I don't see why he can't be made to confess to the murders of Kingsley and Sykes on Langworth's orders as well as the apothecary. It would leave things tidy."

"Falsify a confession?"

"He's going to die anyway, Bruno, either at the end of a rope or from that crack in his skull Harry fetched him. Come on. It's not as if we'd be condemning an innocent man."

Seeing me hesitate, he clicked his tongue impatiently. "If you lose

Walsingham's trust, you lose any hope of a place at the English court. I cannot do it for you."

I nodded. "I understand."

"Good. That is settled, then. Take my advice now, Bruno, for what it is worth." He took me by the shoulders and bent his knees to look me straight in the eye. "You have risked your life for her twice, and twice she has deceived you. Wherever she has gone, whoever she is with—forget her."

I looked away.

"You think it is that simple?"

"No," he said, suddenly vehement. "No, I don't. Of course I don't." He let his hands fall abruptly and stalked off towards the door. After a few paces he turned back, his face full of an emotion I had not seen in him before. "Penelope Devereux," he said, in a quieter voice.

"Who?"

"The one I can't forget."

I looked at him for a moment, the agitation in his face. I had read enough of Sidney's poetry to know that the braggadocio covered finer feelings, but he had never spoken to me directly of any unrequited love.

"And where is she now?"

"Married to someone else. I can't change that. Do what I did, Bruno. Write her a fucking poem and learn to live with it."

"Will it help?"

"No." He grinned, but there was still pain in his eyes. "But it fills up the time. Come, the horses are ready at the gatehouse. Let us shake the dust of this place off our heels. There have been no certified cases of plague in London, you know. Another two weeks and the court will return."

"There is one thing I need to do before we leave," I said. "Lend me one of your armed men, will you?"

☩

THE DOOR OF the weavers' house was opened by Olivier's father, who flinched when he saw me as surely as if I had struck him. I saw his eyes flit fearfully over my shoulder to where my companion stood at a discreet distance with his pikestaff.

"*Non, monsieur,*" he faltered, shrinking, and made as if to close the door in my face, but I stuck my foot in the gap and leaned in.

"Listen, Pastor Fleury," I said, in French, "I know enough to put your whole family in front of the justice if I choose. He is still at the Cheker. You know the assize is not officially closed until he leaves town?"

"What do you want?" he asked, looking at my foot as if he would like to spit on it.

"I want to speak to Hélène." I nodded over my shoulder to the guard. "He will stay out there."

"For all the neighbours to see." Fleury closed the door behind and heaved a great sigh. A lifetime of fear was written into the lines on his face; I was sorry to contribute further.

"I wish you no harm," I said.

He looked at me with infinite pity.

"Monsieur, you are the kind who brings harm without meaning it. You and that girl. I will take you up to my daughter now, but please do not trouble us for long."

He led me to a small parlour on the first floor, where Hélène sat with her mother, dressed in mourning black. Madame Fleury rose when she saw me, her expression appalled, but she exchanged a glance with her husband and left the room. Hélène did not seem surprised to see me.

"I am glad you came." Her voice was flat, her eyes calm. "I wanted to thank you. You found him."

I bowed my head.

"I am so sorry, Hélène. If I could have spared you that—"

"No." She cut me off with a wave of her hand. "Better to know. Now we can mourn him, and bury him. And I have this."

She reached inside her collar and showed me the Saint Denis medal-lion on its chain. "You will think it strange that a Protestant should care about saint's medals, I suppose?"

"If I am honest, it has not been the question uppermost in my mind."

She smiled. "My best friend in Paris was a Catholic. She sent me this when Denis was born. I kept it for her sake. Now I wear it for him. My beautiful boy." Her eyes filled with tears and she swiped them away with the back of her hand, as if she were tired of their interruption.

I looked at the medal glinting between her fingers.

"Did your brother give you that?"

She nodded.

"Before he left?"

Another nod.

"Where have they gone?"

"I don't know." Her eyes slid to the window.

"Hélène, please." I knelt in front of her. "I need to know. They have taken something of mine . . . Sophia has taken something."

She looked down at me, her liquid eyes full of sympathy.

"Your heart," she said solemnly. "Ours too. My father can hardly bear it. My son dead, his own son gone." She bit her lip and looked back to the window.

"At least Olivier gave you justice, of sorts. He could not have stayed, after what he did."

Her face froze, shocked. "Do you—"

"Do I know? Yes. But no one else does. They will think Doctor Sykes was killed on John Langworth's orders." I paused, nodding to the window. "That little jetty at the back of your property must have been useful."

She pressed her lips together. "Why would you keep our secret, monsieur? What do you gain?"

"Because . . ." I ran a hand through my hair. "Because I find that in my heart—what is left of it—I cannot condemn your brother for wanting justice."

"Then I will tell you something else, monsieur," she said, leaning down close enough that I could feel her breath on my face. "My brother put him in the boat, but he did not hold the knife." She looked me straight in the eye when she said this, her face inches from mine, fire flashing in her look. No man should underestimate the ferocity of a mother, I thought. I imagined that fiery glare was the last thing Sykes saw as the light faded for him. Well, I could not pity him.

"And the stone? Whose idea was that, to reference the Scripture?"

She frowned.

"What Scripture?"

"The millstone."

She looked blank. "It was not a millstone. It was just—a stone. To weight him down."

I gave a wan smile. Sophia was right; sometimes things are no more than they appear. I stood, bowing my head in farewell.

"Goodbye, Hélène."

"God will pardon me," she said, defiantly. "It is the least He owes us."

As I reached the door, she called me back.

"Monsieur? Olivier always used to say he would not be afraid to live in Paris. He was only a boy when the massacre happened, he thinks it would be different there now."

I watched her as she twisted the medal between her fingers.

"Thank you."

At the front door, Jacques Fleury leaned in and kissed me once on each cheek in the French manner.

"Do not think me discourteous, monsieur," he said. He spoke as if every word required a supreme effort, as if it had to be dragged up from the depths of his being like a stone. "You gave us back our boy. For that I thank you. But please, monsieur, I ask you one favour."

"What?"

"Do not come back to Canterbury."

I smiled. "Have no fear on that score, Pastor Fleury. I will not look back."

"*Dieu vous garde, monsieur.*"

"*Et vous.*"

From a room somewhere above, I heard the sound of a woman crying.

Epilogue

*V*iens."
Michel de Castelnau, ambassador of France to the court of Queen Elizabeth, adjusted his silk doublet, arranged his short cape over his shoulder, and rolled his shoulders back, drawing himself up to his full height. He touched me lightly on the elbow and ushered me forward. I took a deep breath, pausing to tuck the book under my arm so that I could wipe my sweating palms on my doublet. My eyes remained lowered as protocol demanded, so that as the ambassador and I walked the length of the hall all I saw was the synchronised step of our leather boots across the flagstones, but I felt the many eyes trained on us, felt the hairs on my neck prickle at the sense of exposure, as if I were standing naked before the sceptical gaze of the highest nobles in England. All the while I reminded myself to breathe, slow and steady, and to concentrate only on not tripping or dropping the book. One of the court musicians picked

out a tune quietly on a lute and from all around came the murmur of conversation and the whisper of rustling silks, but all I heard was the pounding of the blood in my own ears.

The queen kept the twelve days of Christmas at her palace of Hampton Court some miles to the west of London, on the banks of the river. Here the Great Hall was wreathed in garlands of holly, ivy, pine, and yew, and smelled of cloves, logs, and good beeswax; outside, in the damp air, the scent of spiced wine drifted into the courtyard from the kitchens and the light from the blaze of candles warmed the early dark. All across London there had been an edge of manic relief to the festive celebrations; plague had not, after all, come to London in the summer, the queen was still alive and well and England's shores mercifully free from foreign invasion. None of the year's dire forecasts had come to pass, and the city was determined to fete its own survival.

The queen's own Christmas festivities were organized by the Earl of Leicester, Sidney's uncle, and for her noblemen and ambassadors, attendance at Hampton Court during the season was not a matter of choice but of duty. The tradition of New Year gifts was more than a formality; for her courtiers, it presented an opportunity to make or mar their fortunes for the coming year, depending on whether or not their gift impressed her. Sidney was pleased with himself; over the past months, at various ambassadorial receptions and diplomatic meetings, he had managed to insinuate to Castelnau that the queen was curious to read my new book, until the ambassador had become convinced that presenting it to her was his own idea. Still eager to regain her favour, he had paid from his own pocket for the handsome black Morocco binding, with gilt edges and Elizabeth's own coat of arms embossed on the cover in gold leaf, and had rubbed his hands with delight at the prospect of presenting me—and the book—at the New Year celebrations.

"She imagines herself a great champion of knowledge, the English queen," he had said, tracing his fingers lovingly over the leather binding before we had set out that morning, "but she fills her court with peacocks in crimson silks. Now she shall see the calibre of philosophers

France maintains." I doubted he had actually read the book, but he was certainly pleased with its cover.

I felt his fingertips rest lightly on my back, guiding me as we neared the dais where the queen sat on a vast carved throne with her most favoured courtiers to either side and her maids seated at her feet on velvet cushions. From somewhere to my left, a stifled growl rumbled through the crowds, causing the few ladies present to squeal and the boy choristers of the Chapel Royal to gasp in excitement. Some foreign dignitary had seen fit to bring the queen a leopard for her exotic menagerie at the Tower and the poor beast now strained at its leash in a corner, its jaws bound tight with leather straps. The queen had declared herself delighted, but her eyes held a certain weariness; perhaps after twenty-five years on the throne, one has seen enough leopards. It had seemed dazed during its five minutes of royal favour; I guessed it had been given some kind of sedative which was now wearing off. Above all I pitied Master Byrd, the queen's master of music, obliged to keep a choir of young boys focused on performing his new Christmas compositions while competing for their attention with a leopard.

Beside me, Castelnau's steps halted. I followed his lead and we knelt, eyes still fixed to the ground. Ahead I could see the wooden scaffolding that supported the raised platform where she sat, appraising us.

"Rise," she commanded, at length.

I stood slowly, knowing not to look up until I was addressed directly. I took in the vast skirt of plum-coloured velvet immediately in front of me, so dark it was almost black, with a central panel of intricate gold thread sewn with cherry-red garnets, tiny seed pearls, and lozenges of onyx that glittered blackly in the candlelight. I raised my head enough that my eyes were level with the white hands folded in her lap, heavy with gold rings and holding a fan of ostrich plumes, the handle decorated with the same stones in the same arrangement as those on her gown.

"Well, Monseigneur de Castelnau," the queen said, raising her voice so the whole court could hear the amusement in her tone, "your counterpart from Bohemia brings me a leopard. Can you better that?"

"I hope so, Your Majesty," Castelnau said, in the special ingratiating tone he reserved for diplomacy. "A leopard is a wonder of nature, it is true, but I bring you the wonders of the heavens."

"An extravagant claim. And is this he?" The ostrich feathers waved in my direction. A ripple of laughter spread through the audience. I felt myself blush. Castelnau seemed unruffled.

"This, Your Majesty, is Doctor Giordano Bruno, author of the most original and provocative book to be published in Europe since the Pole Copernicus printed *On the Revolutions of the Celestial Spheres.*"

"He sounds more dangerous than a leopard. Come, Doctor Bruno—let me look at you."

I swallowed hard, raised my head, and looked her in the eye for the first time.

She was fifty-one years old, but her face in its white mask of ceruse with pencilled brows and scarlet painted lips seemed ageless, like the face of a statue or a character in a classical play. It was a long face, stern and imperious, perched above its wide lace ruff, entirely fixed in its self-possession. Only the dark eyes betrayed the vivacity she was apparently famed for in her youth. They raked my face now as you might scan a page of text and returned to hold my gaze, steady and unblinking. According to Walsingham, it was she who had expressed a wish to see me in person after hearing about the events in Canterbury, and he, through Sidney, who had contrived this means of presentation without compromising my place in the ambassador's household.

"I have heard of you. You are King Henri's tame philosopher, are you not? The one who upsets the Catholic Leaguers and the learned doctors of the Sorbonne every time you open your mouth."

"This is true, Your Majesty. In Paris, King Henri had to keep me muzzled like your leopard, lest I offend."

She laughed.

"Perhaps I should try that with some of my courtiers. And is your book as radical as Copernicus?"

"More so, Your Majesty," I said, stepping forward in my eagerness.

"Copernicus did not follow his argument to its logical conclusion. If the Earth and the other planets revolve about the Sun, we may also posit that the fixed stars are not fixed. That is to say, there may be no limit to the universe. And who is to say there might not be other suns out there, with other worlds?"

From behind me, I heard disapproving intakes of breath. Queen Elizabeth only nodded, her jewels catching the light, and I thought suddenly of Mistress Blunt and Rebecca, and how much they would give to be standing in my place.

"Would they be identical to ours, do you suppose, these other worlds? What do you think, Robin?" She turned to her right, where the Earl of Leicester sat beside her on a carved chair several inches lower than her own. Another man might have been made awkward by this deliberate reminder of status, but Leicester, still impeccably handsome in his fifties, with his close-cropped grey hair and angular jaw, merely arranged himself across the chair, stretched out his long legs to the edge of the dais and smiled. "Would I still be queen?"

"Your Majesty—it is impossible to imagine a world in which you were not queen," Castelnau cut in, with a sweeping bow.

"Really?" The queen arched one thin brow. "There are plenty of your countrymen in Paris, Michel, who, together with my cousin Mary, find it all too easy to imagine such a world." Sycophantic laughter bubbled around us and died away. "Here, let me look. Robin, hold this." She passed the ostrich fan to Leicester, who folded it in his lap. I caught his eye and he gave me the briefest of nods. I wondered if he was remembering, as I was, the last time he and I had met in a royal palace, when one of the queen's young maids of honour had been found murdered. The queen held her hands out for the book and I placed it into them, bowing as I did so. She laid her hands flat on the cover without opening it.

"But if the universe is infinite, sir—if we are but one world among many," she said, in a softer voice, no longer performing for the crowd, "how do we understand our place in God's design? What is our worth, if we are no longer the masterpiece of Creation?"

I hesitated; my answers to these questions were complex and, perhaps even to this intellectually curious woman, potentially heretical. I weighed my words carefully before responding.

"Does it not rather increase our worth when we consider the enormity of Creation with new eyes? To realise that we are no longer prisoners of a fixed order, but citizens of infinity?" I could have gone further, but there was a warning light in her eyes.

"The cosmos demands order, sir, just as society demands it. If people were no longer certain of their place in the grand design . . ." She left the thought unfinished, but I understood. If the Earth can be so easily deposed from the centre of the cosmos, if Man can lose the sovereignty over creation that the Holy Scriptures tell us he has by God's gift, people might lose their respect for the divine order, and a real sovereign could be toppled with the same apparent insouciance.

"Nevertheless, I shall read your book with great interest, Doctor Bruno, and perhaps we shall have the opportunity to discuss it further. I should like that. Of course," she added, her eyes glinting in the frozen white of her face, "you know Copernicus had the good sense to wait until he was dead before committing his theory to print."

"He did not have the good fortune to live in Your Majesty's more enlightened realm," I countered, permitting myself a smile that was almost flirtatious. I had noticed the same tendency in Castelnau. Despite her age and the absence of beauty, she had a curious ability to inspire among her male courtiers the same desire to impress that beauty commands.

Instead of acknowledging this as the flattery it was meant to be, she tilted her head to one side, considering the truth of it.

"Enlightened. Perhaps. Even so, there are limits." She ran her fingertips over the embossed design on the cover. "Still, it is a brave man who will cling to his ideas in the face of all opposition. We should never have seen the New World were it not for men like that."

"Your Majesty, my aim is to chart the unknown universe just as your explorers and cartographers have mapped this terrestrial globe," I said, perhaps too boldly. Behind me, the whispering gradually fell silent.

"I see you are ambitious, whatever else you are," she said, with a twitch of her brow. "Very well, then, Doctor Bruno—we shall look forward to your dispatches from these unknown territories. What think you, Lord Burghley?" She turned to her left, the strings of pearls around her neck tinkling gently against her jewelled gown with the movement. "Should you like to have infinity mapped for you?"

Beside her, the lord high treasurer smoothed his white hair and looked at me, his round face creased in consternation. I wondered if he were also remembering the murders last year, when we had first met.

"I confess the very thought of infinity makes me a little dizzy," he said, running a hand over his velvet skullcap. "I have not the mind to comprehend it."

"Only a fearless mind would attempt it," the queen said. She was watching me with an expression that was difficult to read, though I fancied the ghost of a smile was hovering around the painted lips. "But remember—there is a fine line between courage and recklessness. Perhaps only time allows us to distinguish the one from the other." She held up the book and fixed me with a significant look. "England is grateful to you, Doctor Bruno."

I held her gaze for a moment, understanding that this was the closest she was likely to come to acknowledging the service I had rendered her. Walsingham's foot soldiers, his army of informers scurrying back and forth across the country carrying their nuggets of intelligence like ants, were supposed to be invisible to her. But I was no longer anonymous; she had seen me, she held my book in her hands. Perhaps my dream of finding a permanent home, and a patron who would understand the scale of my ideas, had moved a step closer. Without quite intending it, I found myself smiling broadly, and the painted line of her mouth curved slightly in response, a maze of tiny filigree cracks appearing in the white veneer like the glaze of antique porcelain.

I felt Castelnau's fingers lightly on my sleeve; together we knelt again, then backed away into the crowd as the leopard gave another strangled growl and the next dignitary was called forward.

☧

"SHE ADMIRES YOU," Walsingham said, some days later at Barn Elms, when Twelfth Night had passed and her courtiers were allowed to return to their own homes and families.

"She said so?" I looked up from the restless dance of the fire. There were pinecones burning among the logs and the room was filled with a warm scent of resin.

"Not in so many words. But she sent this." He crossed the room and placed into my lap a small wooden chest that chinked as he set it down. Surprised by the weight of it, I lifted the lid cautiously. Inside was a heap of gold sovereigns. I stared at Walsingham.

"Close your mouth, Bruno, you look like a codfish. Thirty pounds. In recognition of services rendered."

"Not a reward for the book, then?"

He smiled. "Perhaps your reward for that is yet to come. She is reading it, you know. She likes to dabble in controversy. But only in the shallows, mind," he added, catching my eye. "You have a certain reputation, Bruno. If she would not give John Dee a formal position at court in all the years he served her faithfully, for fear of the rumours of magic that followed him, you should not raise your hopes too high. Not for the present, anyway. Besides," he said, gathering up a sheaf of papers and crossing to the door, "we need you inside Salisbury Court now more than ever. My sources in France say Mary of Scotland's agents there are busy recruiting new couriers among the exiled English Catholics, and Mendoza and the Duke of Guise are inseparable. I need to know the contents of every letter that passes through the embassy from now on, understood?"

I nodded. He rested his hand on the latch and a shadow of great weariness passed over his face. "It never ends, Bruno." He looked drawn and the creases around his eyes seemed deeper. "We must not relax our guard, not even for a moment. For every John Langworth we bring in, a hundred more are waiting out there." He nodded towards the window, as if he expected hordes of Catholic assassins to breach the garden wall at any moment. He pointed a finger, the dark eyes boring into me. Then he nodded briskly and swept out of the room.

"He has not mentioned Sophia once," I said to Sidney, when the door had clicked shut behind Walsingham.

"He is exercising diplomatic restraint." Sidney leaned against the mantelpiece and peered into his wineglass as he swirled its contents.

"Does he even know she was in Canterbury with me?"

"Oh, I should think so. He knows everything. I told him you had decided to go your separate ways. He didn't press me any further, but I'm sure he has worked it out."

"That she was behind the murder of her husband?"

"That too. But he won't bring it up unless you give him reason."

"He is angry with me," I said, downcast.

"If anything, I think he is relieved," Sidney said, draining his glass and examining the dregs. "I think he was afraid you would want to marry and settle down and he would lose you. You have become valuable to him, though he never quite says it."

I smiled, not meeting his eye. "That is some consolation, I suppose."

"Will you go after her?"

I made a wry face. "I don't see how I can go back to Paris unless King Henri recalls me. If Paris is even where she is." Every day was like this now, a battle of will against desire. A thousand times an hour I vowed not to think about Sophia's betrayal, and from the moment I woke until I reluctantly submitted to sleep, it was all I thought about. I smacked my fist into the palm of my hand. "But I have to get the book back, Philip. Just that. I have to make her understand she can't just . . ." The threat trailed away to nothing.

Sidney sighed. "The book and the girl—they've become the same obsession in your mind, Bruno. Something you can't quite possess, but you won't rest until you do. You've grown thinner," he added, tracing a circle around the rim of his glass with a forefinger, before looking up, his face serious. "Unless you let them both go you will end by losing your mind. And as Her Majesty pointed out, your mind is unique. It must be preserved for the nation."

I smiled, shifting position in my chair. "And you? Are you still determined to go to war?"

He shrugged, and pursed his lips. He had grown a beard since the summer and it made him seem more adult, more careworn. "The queen is still havering over whether to intervene in the Netherlands. The Canterbury business made her think twice about the wisdom of depleting her armies here. Meanwhile, I must stay at Barn Elms and see if I can get myself an heir before the year is out. Walsingham will not hear of my going anywhere until that is achieved." He pushed a hand through his hair. "Sometimes I think I shall have to disregard them all and simply run away."

"You don't mean that."

"How do you know?" He looked at me, eyes flashing dangerously. "You could come with me." For a moment, something of his old spark seemed to light him up.

"I have been running away for eight years."

"Sorry, Bruno. I didn't think."

For a few moments the only sound was the rhythmic crackle of the flames and the occasional pop and hiss of a log subsiding.

"You know they never found Becket?" Sidney said, at length.

"Langworth couldn't be persuaded to tell them?"

He shook his head.

"Not a word, despite Walsingham's best efforts."

I shuddered; we both knew what those efforts would have involved.

"He went to his execution still clutching his secrets. He was a ruthless man, but at least he had the courage of his convictions. You have to admire that."

I looked up at him. "I don't have to admire anything about a man like Langworth."

Sidney shrugged: suit yourself. "Mayor Fitzwalter, on the other hand, pissed himself and blurted out everything he knew before he even got a look at the rack." The disgust in his voice suggested that, for Sidney, cowardice was more despicable in a man than murdering children.

"Was any of it worth hearing?"

"He confessed to being the fourth guardian, said he had been black-mailed into it, recanted any connection with the Catholic Church, all the usual stuff. But he swore blind he knew nothing about what Langworth had done with Becket's bones. Walsingham believed him. He had spilled all he knew."

"So Thomas Becket is still out there somewhere, waiting."

"We must suppose so. At least the legend will live on. But the English are always waiting for some past hero to come back from the dead and restore a golden age," he added, with disdain. "Thomas Becket, King Arthur . . ."

"Christ Himself."

"Careful, Bruno." He looked at me from under his brows. "One day your irreverence will land you in real trouble."

I had been told this before, more than once, but I had never been good at heeding advice. Sidney went on talking—about the war in the Netherlands, the necessity of English intervention—but his words began to wash over me as I continued to stare into the restless flames. I would go after the book. Despite Sidney's warning, I could not let it end like this. If Sophia had taken the book to Paris with the intention of selling it, I must find a means to hunt it down. Hunt *her* down. We had unfinished business, and I knew I could have no peace of mind until I had done everything in my power to resolve it. Call it stubbornness, call it pride; I preferred to think of it as tenacity. Whether Queen Elizabeth saw fit to patronise my book or not, I knew that nothing I wrote would ever truly live until I had unravelled the secrets of that book, and I also knew that I was the only one who could do it. I would not rest until I had it in my hands again—and until I had made Sophia understand that she was wrong.